She wielded the long needle like a veteran knife fighter, holding it with the dime-sized disk at its end, braced against the heel of her palm, the rest of the spike emerging from the top of her closed hand.

She'd committed to her first stroke and missed. Jack was beside her, his open hand slapping down and grabbing the wrist of the hand holding the needle. It was like taking hold of a snake, strong, sinewy, and wriggling. She twisted trying to get loose but couldn't break his grip.

Her free hand shot across, stabbing at him with fingers spread to spear and claw at his eyes. He bobbed his head out of her reach, still clutching her wrist.

She kneed him, but he was ready for that, too. He'd turned his body so that her knee slammed into his thigh instead of ramming home into his crotch as she'd intended. The side of his leg went numb from the force of the blow, but he maintained his balance.

She switched tactics, stomping her heel into the top of the nerve endings on his foot.

The pain took his breath away and he could feel his grip weakening.

24 DECLASSIFIED Books
From Harper

DEATH ANGEL
HEAD SHOT
TRINITY
COLLATERAL DAMAGE
STORM FORCE
CHAOS THEORY
VANISHING POINT
CAT'S CLAW
TROJAN HORSE
VETO POWER
OPERATION HELL GATE

™

DECLASSIFIED

DEATH ANGEL

David Jacobs

Based on the hit FOX series created by Joel Surnow & Robert Cochran

HARPER

An Imprint of HarperCollins*Publishers*

HARPER

An Imprint of HarperCollins*Publishers*
10 East 53rd Street
New York, New York 10022-5299

Copyright © 2010 by Twentieth Century Fox Film Corporation
ISBN 978-0-06-177153-8

First Harper paperback printing: May 2010

Printed in the United States of America

Visit Harper paperbacks on the World Wide Web at
www.harpercollins.com

10 9 8 7 6 5 4 3 2 1

1 2 3 4 5 6 7 8 9
10 11 12 13 14 15 16 17
18 19 20 21 22 23 24

11:04 A.M., MDT
Trail's End Motel, Los Alamos, New Mexico

Jack Bauer was getting ready to leave for his meeting with Peter Rhee when somebody knocked on the door of his motel room, room number eight.

The sound was almost drowned out by the shuddering wheeze of the air conditioner. The unit produced more noise than cool comfort. It wasn't much of an air conditioner, but then the Trail's End wasn't much of a motel, either. It was a grade-C lodging whose clientele consisted mainly of business travelers and tourists on a tight budget.

The room was a tight, boxy, low-ceilinged space. There was a single bed and a long cabinet with two sets of drawers. A round-topped table and an armless straight-backed chair were crowded into a rear corner. The furniture was made of synthetic composite material covered with dark brown simulated wood-grain plastic surfacing. A cable TV was bolted to the cabinet top, and the remote was secured to the night table. The bathroom was the size of a walk-in closet.

Anonymous, impersonal, the site fitted its occupant's purposes. There were no front desk managers, night clerks, or doormen to monitor his comings and goings. The motel was conveniently located midway between Los Alamos city proper and the massive lab complex on the South Mesa.

Jack's seeming isolation and vulnerability here were designed to entice the opposition out of hiding into making a try for him. He'd made himself a target—human bait in a trap that could work two ways.

Jack Bauer was in his mid-thirties, trim, athletic, clean-shaven, with short sandy hair and sharp blue eyes. He wore a lightweight brown denim vest, gray T-shirt, khaki pants, and ankle-high hiking boots. He looked like a nice, decent fellow, a caring and compassionate human being. Which he was—except when he was on a mission.

He was on a mission now.

He'd been detached from his post as Special Agent in Charge of the Los Angeles Counter Terrorist Unit, SAC CTU/L.A., for temporary duty as a field operative in Los Alamos, New Mexico.

Los Alamos, the self-styled Atomic City where the A-bomb was born and extensive research and development of cutting-edge nuclear and other weaponry continued to be its stock-in-trade.

Ironwood National Laboratory, a key component of the Los Alamos complex, had over the last six months been struck by a murder wave. Five important staffers had died under violent and mysterious circumstances. The victims

included scientists and security personnel. The fir.
had been made to look like accidents or natural caus

In the last few weeks the pace had picked up, with n
tense of the last two deaths being anything than what
were: out-and-out kills. The assassin—or assassins— gr
bolder with each fatality.

The FBI has jurisdiction in all domestic espionage cases.
There is one exception: the CIA is empowered to investigate cases of spying at all nuclear research facilities.

Created in the aftermath of the first World Trade Center
attack in 1993, CTU was established as a division of the
CIA to combat terrorist activities at home in the United
States and abroad.

Whatever else they were, the Ironwood kills went far
beyond the parameters of conventional espionage. The murder
of persons associated with a facility responsible for the research and development of America's high-technology weaponry was reason enough for CTU involvement in the case.

But it took something more than that to have Jack Bauer
detached from his post as head of the unit's Los Angeles
branch.

The inciting element was a name from the past that had
suddenly surfaced in the Ironwood affair:

Annihilax.

In feudal Japan, the shogunate's dismissal from its service
of the military samurai caste had loosed a flood of suddenly
indigent warriors and swordsmen on the land.

These masterless men, known as ronin, no longer bound
by their oath of loyalty to the emperor, made their living the
only way they knew how, by selling their blades and skills
to those who could pay, be they warlords, ambitious provincial tyrants, feuding clans, or the gambling syndicates of
tattooed men known as yakuza.

...ult was a generation-long epoch of anarchy, law-
, and ultraviolence that afflicted nobles and com-
. alike.

...nilarly, the end of the Cold War superpower rivalry
...ween the United States and the Soviet Union had set
. stage for today's era of global intrigue. Thousands of
...ntelligence professionals on both sides of the gap found
themselves without a job. Their numbers included career
professionals and contract agents of the now-downsized spy
services. Among them were spymasters, analysts, technicians, specialists in the black arts of sabotage and murder,
paramilitary types, and mercenary soldiers.

Like the ronin of Old Nippon, legions of clandestine operators now sold their skills around the world to the highest bidders. The less scrupulous among them found new
employers in the form of moneyed terrorist organizations,
ruthless industrial cartels, drug lords, and organized crime
syndicates.

In this lethal new environment, a handful of names stood
out in the subterranean milieu of the world-class elite of
professional killers for hire.

At the top of the list: Annihilax.

Who or what was Annihilax? Was it a lone individual or
a league of assassins?

The answer was unknown even among those who contracted for the services of this murder machine. What was
known was that Annihilax was stateless, rootless, owing al-
legiance to no country, creed, or ideology except that of the
highest bidder. And even that loyalty was good only until
the assignment had been successfully carried out. Once
completed, the former employer was vulnerable to targeting
by any rival who cared to meet Annihilax's price.

The exterminating agent took on only the most expensive and challenging contracts. An intricate network of
ever-shifting contacts and go-betweens handled the initial

groundwork between Annihilax and the would-be client. When the contract was finalized, exorbitant fees were deposited in escrow in secret numbered Swiss and offshore bank accounts.

Annihilax's iron-clad guarantee promised a full refund to the client—minus retainer and expenses incurred in the course of the preliminaries—in the event of failure to fulfill the contract and make the hit. The inside line among those who knew, namely rival members of the killer elite, was that no such refund had ever been made.

Targets included heads of state, big business magnates, crime bosses, spy chiefs, generals, mercenary leaders, political dissidents, cooperative witnesses in high-profile investigations, those who knew too much, and those who stood between rich and powerful clients and something they wanted.

Five years ago, fate had conspired that the paths of Jack Bauer and Annihilax should cross.

The prime mover was NATO's opening the bidding on the contract to develop a new light armored vehicle resistant to improvised explosive devices, IEDs, such as car and truck bombs so well beloved by terrorists the world over. The contract to equip all NATO fighting forces with this new LAV meant billions of euros in profits to the successful bidder.

While generally not discussed with outsiders, it is a well-known fact among professional arms dealers that the letting of a new, lucrative contract in their line is often accompanied by an epidemic of violent deaths in the ranks of competing munitions makers. Destabilizing the competition by decimating its top executives, vendors, and weapons designers can only increase the likelihood of its determined rival winning the prize.

The NATO LAV contract offering was no exception. Key personnel of various United States and West European arms dealers in the running for the winning bid began being systematically wiped off the board: thrown out of windows, pushed under buses, slain in seemingly random street muggings. This clandestine killing ground was located in Brussels, Belgium, site of NATO's administrative headquarters.

The Pentagon's Defense Intelligence Agency's operatives learned that an East European arms cartel, on behalf of a weapons developer, had contracted with Annihilax to winnow out its rivals to be assured of claiming the contract.

Knowing of Jack Bauer's outstanding record as a former Delta Force member and top counterterrorist field operative, DIA requested that Jack head the operation to seek and destroy Annihilax.

The story of that epic duel remains classified and cannot be told here. It can be said that after a ruthless covert war involving extensive casualties on both sides, Jack Bauer ultimately succeeding in neutralizing the cadre of killers assembled by Annihilax for the Brussels contract.

Jack's relentless, no-holds-barred investigation convinced him that Annihilax was not a group but a single person. He'd worked his way up to the penultimate conspirator, the last link but one in the chain leading to the master assassin. That person, Boris Zemba, was killed by Annihilax to prevent his revealing the identity of his master.

The Brussels killings stopped and Annihilax vanished without a trace.

Whether through intimidation, fear, bribery, or a combination of all three, and despite the vehement protests of its unsuccessful rivals, the East European cartel was awarded the NATO contract. Annihilax had fulfilled his bargain and earned his fee.

No refund required, leaving his winning record unbroken.

The resulting LAV was a boondoggle that proved dangerous only to its occupants and had to be replaced at another staggering expense to the taxpayers.

A year later, U.S. intelligence services reported that Annihilax had been killed in the course of backing the wrong horse in a bloody insurrection in the Congo. Jack Bauer remained skeptical. Without a body or even a name to identify the master assassin, he believed that the killer was still at large.

The years passed without so much as a whisper or sighting of an Annihilax operation. Those who should know best, top-ranked performers in the killer elite, believed that the prolonged silence proved their hated competitor was retired or dead.

In the interim they'd all picked up murder contracts that would otherwise have gone to Annihilax.

Now, a cryptic fragment intercepted by the National Security Agency had broken that silence. A scrap of communication encoded in a cipher unique to Annihilax had been recently intercepted by the NSA while it was being uploaded to an orbiting communications satellite.

NSA code breakers had never been able to decrypt the code. The fragment now in their possession proved equally immune to their efforts, but its identity as Annihilax's signature cipher was unquestionable.

The communiqué had been transmitted from somewhere in Los Alamos, New Mexico. That was enough to bring Jack Bauer to the Atomic City.

Now Jack crossed to the front of the room, lifting a fold of the curtain covering the plate-glass window so he could look outside and see who was knocking on his door.

A sad-faced older woman outfitted in the uniform worn by the motel's room maids stood on the other side of the door, facing it. She was bracketed by a utility cart and a four-wheeled canvas hopper mounted on a tubular frame. The multitray cart was laden with fresh towels, bedding, and the like; the hopper was filled with similar used items of linen collected for cleaning.

Jack studied the newcomer for a long pause. She was a stranger to him. He'd been staying at the motel for the past ten days and hadn't noticed her among the staffers. And he was a man who noticed things. That was part of his business. The business of staying alive.

She gazed fixedly at the door, hands primly folded in front of her, seemingly unaware of his scrutiny.

Jack let the curtain fall back into place. He reached under a front flap of his denim vest, his hand brushing the butt end of the pistol he wore in a shoulder rig under his left arm. He unfastened the safety strap at the top of the holster and jiggled the gun slightly to free it up to speed his draw if he needed to bring it into action fast. Gun and harness were concealed beneath the vest from casual observers who didn't know what to look for.

He wore no protective Kevlar vest under his garments. Frankly it was just too damned hot to undergo the discomfort without a compelling and immediate reason.

Maybe that reason was now at hand; he didn't know. But it was too late to don the vest now.

Jack took a deep breath, letting it out and willing himself to stay loose and relaxed. Tension slows reaction time. He set his face in a masklike expression of bland neutrality. Standing to one side of the door, he unlocked and opened it.

It was like opening the door of a baker's oven operating at full blast. A wave of hot, dry air burst into the room, the arid heat of a high desert sun nearing its midday zenith on a late August Saturday.

Jack met it without flinching but it took an effort. He could feel the heat sucking the moisture out of him.

The motel was a two-story structure consisting of a long main building with two stubby wings jutting from it at right angles. It fronted south, making an inverted U-shape facing a strip of east-west running roadway. A paved lot stood between it and the roadside.

The ribbon of road was bordered on both sides by gas stations, fast-food joints, a car wash, mini-malls, cheap jack electronics stores, discount clothing outlets, and the like.

Jack's room on the ground floor of the motel's west wing fronted east. A white concrete apron about ten feet wide extended along the building's base. Its far end was lined by a row of the lodgers' parked cars, SUVs, and pickup trucks, sunlight glaring off their brightly reflective surfaces. Shimmering heat waves rose off the pavement.

Somewhere out there a couple of FBI agents were watching Jack Bauer.

He was partnered on the investigation by FBI Special Agent Vince Sabito and a couple of underlings he'd brought with him from the Bureau's Santa Fe resident agency.

Relations between the FBI and the CIA were notoriously bad, and CTU was part of the CIA.

Working conditions between the two had improved for a time, but that time was long gone and the relationship had since deteriorated more or less to its former tone of mutual suspicion, hostility, distrust, and jealously guarded territoriality.

Sabito and his agents were supposed to be on Jack's side, but still he'd have to figure out some way to shake them before meeting with Rhee.

But first—the woman.

She stood on the other side of the open doorway in the scanty shade of the second-floor balcony. She looked like a desert dweller herself, spare and scrawny, sun-baked down to an irreducible minimum of hair, skin, and bones.

She was tall, only a few inches shorter than Jack's full six feet, even in the sensible low-heeled shoes she was wearing. Her age could have been anywhere from forty to sixty years old. A straight-backed posture argued for the former while a seamed, weathered face indicated the latter. Iron-gray hair was pulled back and tied in a businesslike bun at the top of her head.

Her pale yellow uniform was trimmed with white piping, its hem reaching a few inches below the knees. The same standard uniform worn by other room maids Jack had observed while staying at the motel.

No, not quite the same. The other outfits had all been short-sleeved. This one was long-sleeved, with wide, white unbuttoned cuffs.

The utility cart was on her right and the canvas hopper on her left. Both nestled against the side of the building, leaving the way open and unblocked for any passersby on the concrete apron. For now there was none.

"Okay if I make the room up now, mister?" the woman asked, her voice sharp with the nasal twang of a native Southwesterner.

"No Norma today?" Jack asked. "She usually cleans the room."

"She's off today."

"I don't think I've seen you around before," he said.

"I only work here on weekends." She sighed. "I've got a lot of rooms to do so I'd like to get started if it's okay with you, mister."

"Sure, come on in." Jack stepped back so she could enter.

She crossed the threshold, closing the door behind her. "Don't want to let the heat in while I'm stripping the bed."

Jack nodded, turning his back to her and going deeper into the room. Earlier he'd turned the TV set on its counter-top stand so it faced the front of the room. It was switched off, and its dead glass eye served as a mirror so he could see what was happening behind him.

The maid's right hand reached into the loose cuff of her left sleeve and pulled out a long stiletto-like weapon. She lunged forward, thrusting it at Jack's broad, unprotected back.

Only he wasn't there when she made what should have been a killing stroke. He'd sidestepped, and the weapon stabbed empty air. Jack kept moving, pivoting, and facing her sideways to present the smallest target.

She was in a half crouch, legs bent at the knees, striking arm extended to its full length, her fist closed around the shaft of something long, slim, sharp, and glittering. Her weapon was a knitting needle about ten inches long. The spike was lethal enough by itself but it had something extra. The point was covered by a gray plastic protective cap not unlike the sort found on the tip of an ordinary ink pen.

She wielded the long needle like a veteran knife fighter, holding it with the dime-sized disk at its end braced against the heel of her palm, the rest of the spike emerging from the top of her closed hand.

She'd committed to her first stroke and missed. Jack was beside her, his open hand slapping down on and grabbing the wrist of the hand holding the needle. It was like taking hold of a snake, strong, sinewy, and wriggling. She twisted trying to get loose but couldn't break his grip.

Her free hand shot across her, stabbing at him with fingers spread to spear and claw at his eyes. He bobbed his head out of her reach, still clutching her wrist.

She kneed him but he was ready for that, too. He'd turned his body so that the knee slammed into his thigh instead of ramming home into his crotch as she'd intended. The side of his leg went numb from the force of the blow but he maintained his balance.

She switched tactics, stomping her heel into the top of his foot.

The pain took his breath away and he could feel his grip weakening. She felt it, too, and redoubled her efforts to break free, but before she could do so he got his other hand on her forearm.

In one swift move that was a blur of motion he violently

bent her arm backward and thrust the needle deep into her neck. At the moment of impact the plastic protective cap split open, coming apart, leaving the dark-stained needle point nakedly exposed for an instant before it rammed home. There was a crunching sound as the steel tip penetrated flesh, cartilage, and bone.

A fatal blow but not necessarily such as to bring on sudden death. In the natural order of things she might have lived a moment or two before expiring. But for the dark substance staining the needle point, whatever toxin the plastic protective cap had been covering.

In the span of a few heartbeats the would-be killer went into spasms, shaking from head to toe in one massive total body shudder. She went rigid, catatonic. Her eyes bulged like they were trying to pop free from the sockets. They were staring, not seeing. Her mouth fell open—to gasp for breath, to cry out? The light went out of her eyes and the life left her body as the poisoned needle sent her rocketing into eternity.

He let go of her and she fell to the floor with a thump. She lay on her back faceup, the needle sticking out of her neck like a handle. A line of blood so dark it looked black clung from a corner of her mouth to her chin.

Jack stood staring down at her for a timeless interval. After a while he shook his head as if to clear it and said, "Huh!"

His voice sounded funny in his ears. He was breathing hard. "Damn," he muttered.

He'd wanted to take her alive but things had moved too fast. There hadn't been time to draw his gun before she was on him. If he'd tried she would have had him. As it was, it had been close, too close.

He was drenched with sweat, and he could feel it cooling on him. The laboring air conditioner continued its uninterrupted juddering and wheezing.

She'd been smart, stomping his foot while trying to wrestle free. The bones at the top of the foot were thin and breakable. He wriggled his toes inside the boot. They all wriggled. Nothing felt broken. He could walk on it, and that's all that counted.

His hiking boots had steel toes and reinforced tops of the kind worn by construction workers to protect against heavy weights falling on their feet and crushing them. Luck had nothing to do with it. He had selected the boots deliberately because they were good for street fighting, and on this case trouble was liable to come at him from any and every unexpected direction, and everything he had working on his side to give him an edge upped his chances for survival.

Jack was now reminded somehow of the classic mode of hunting tigers. The hunter stakes a goat to a tree as bait and then hides himself in a covert blind. When the tiger goes for the goat, the hunter shoots the tiger. Trouble was, he was goat and hunter both.

The gray plastic protective cap covering the poisoned needle point had split into several large fragments. A couple of them lay on the carpet near the corpse.

Jack held his hands and forearms in front of him, turning them around, inspecting them for any gray plastic shards that might be clinging to them. Some of that toxin might have rubbed off on the inside of the cap, and he wanted to make sure he was clear of them.

They looked clean. He eyed the front of his vest and shirt and pants, and they came up clean, too.

He circled the body and went to the front of the room, moving with a limp, favoring his left leg, the one she'd been working on. He lifted the curtain and looked outside.

There was a commotion nearby but it was of the everyday variety. A woman was trying to ride herd on a half-dozen noisy, hyperactive kids while her husband loaded some suitcases into the trunk of their car.

The oldest kid was a boy of about ten and the others were in various descending age ranges, including a babe in arms held by the mother as she halfheartedly tried to maintain some order among her brood. The whole clan couldn't have been more obliviously unaware of the mortal struggle that had just taken place in room eight.

His quick visual scan of the scene detected no sign of hostile or suspicious elements. No sign of Sabito's G-men, either, though they couldn't be far away. Jack let the curtain fall, locked the door.

He glanced back at the body sprawled on the floor. *This'll put me in solid with Vince*, he said to himself, grinning wryly.

He went into the bathroom, switched on the light. He felt like he'd jump out of his skin if anyone so much as said boo to him.

He examined himself more carefully now for flecks of the poison needle's shattered plastic protective cap. He looked into the mirror mounted over the sink, turning his head this way and that, scanning his face and neck for any gray plastic flecks that might be clinging to his skin. He found none.

He ran his fingers through his hair, tousling it to dislodge any specks that might be caught in it so that they'd fall into the sink. There weren't any.

He let out a breath he didn't know he'd been holding.

He shook out his clothes, then crouched down to peer at the tiled floor in search of any gray shards, finding none.

He washed his hands in the sink with soap and water, scrubbing his forearms up to the elbow before rinsing them. He ran the cold water and held a washcloth under it. He mopped his face and the back of his neck with the cool, wet cloth.

He caught sight of his reflection in the mirror. He looked like hell, hollow-eyed and sunken-cheeked. Pencil-thick veins stood out on both sides of his forehead. His skin had blanched under its deep tan, giving his skin a sallow cast. Wide black pupils swam in his bright blue eyes.

He thought of the corpse in the main room. Compared to her, he hadn't come off too badly. "You should see the other guy," he said aloud.

"Gal," he corrected, after a pause.

He combed his hair with his fingers, pushing it back into shape. He grinned at himself in the mirror, baring his teeth.

He went into the main room and hunkered down beside the body. He rolled up the killer's left sleeve, baring the arm below the elbow. Her flesh was disconcertingly warm. Strapped to the inside of her forearm was a red leather sheath that had held the poisoned needle.

He gave the corpse a quick frisk pat-down that came up empty. Her pockets yielded nothing but a ring with a set of passkeys to open the room doors. No ID, no personal documents.

He hadn't expected to find any. She was a pro and she'd come in clean, with nothing to identify her or her employer.

Jack straightened up, wincing as sharp pains shot through his left leg and foot. Now that the floodtide of adrenaline was ebbing, the pain from her strikes was making itself felt. His thigh ached deep in the muscle where she'd kneed him. Reinforced boots or not, it had hurt when she'd stomped his foot. That was when he'd gone into full survival mode and turned her own weapon against her.

He eyed his assailant. His post as SAC CTU/L.A. had familiarized him with the faces and dossiers of hundreds of professional killers foreign and domestic. This one had been a stranger to him at first glance, and now that he took a closer look at her that status remained unchanged.

Local talent possibly, recruited for the hit. That would fit the pattern.

The Annihilax pattern.

That was how the master assassin had operated in Brussels, assembling a team of cutthroats, most of whom came from Belgium, the Netherlands, and Germany.

Jack checked his watch. The time was 11:11. Hard to believe that only seven minutes had passed since that first knock on his door.

He got out his cell phone and called Peter Rhee, the Ironwood counterintelligence officer who'd urgently requested a private noontime meeting with him. Rhee failed to pick up. Jack didn't like that so well. He left a message on Rhee's voice mail.

"Somebody made a try for me. She was disguised as a room maid. She's dead. I'm running behind schedule. I'll be about ten, fifteen minutes late. Call me as soon as you can," Jack said.

"And watch yourself," he added.

His cell phone and Rhee's were both secure and scrambled but Jack didn't want to be more specific than that.

Next he called Vince Sabito. Sabito picked up on the third ring. "Sabito here," he said. Sabito's cell was secure and scrambled, too.

"This is Jack Bauer."

"What do you want?" Sabito wasn't the type to extend himself with a pretense of friendliness or even collegiality.

"I've got something you want," Jack said.

"Yeah? What?"

"An assassin. She's dead."

"She—?! A woman, huh? What happened?"

"She wound up on the wrong end of her own poison needle."

"You're at the motel." That was a statement, not a question. Sabito knew where Jack was. His men were staked out watching him.

"I'll be right there. You stay put," Sabito said, breaking the connection.

11:17 A.M. MDT
Trail's End Motel, Los Alamos

Jack Bauer stood in the shade of the second-floor balcony, leaning with his back against his closed room door. He was waiting for the FBI to arrive.

His wait was not a long one. Sabito had a couple of watchdogs posted across the street in a diner's parking lot. The diner was doing a brisk lunchtime business and the lot was pretty well filled with vehicles.

The FBI car was salted in with all the others and Jack didn't spot it at first. Then it got into motion, and when it did there was no mistaking it because it was in a big hurry.

A late model dark sedan suddenly came barreling out of the lot. After hanging up on Jack, Sabito must have phoned the agents and told them to step on it to secure the site and prevent Jack from leaving. The sedan was a little too hasty trying to exit the lot and had to slam on the brakes and stop short to avoid plowing into oncoming traffic.

A delivery truck driver who'd narrowly missed being tagged by it held down his horn in an angrily protesting note for a long time as he rolled east on the roadway.

When the street was clear in both directions the sedan swung around in a wide looping U-turn, crossing the east-bound and westbound lanes and darting into the Trail's End lot. Slowing to avoid pedestrians, it arrowed toward the mo-tel's west wing, nosing into a parking space near where Jack was standing. Up close he could see that the sedan was blue, so dark a blue it was almost black.

Two men got out of the car and started toward him. FBI special agents Hickman and Coates—he'd met them before.

Coates had been driving. He was big and bearish, like an ex-football lineman. He was carrying a lot of weight and he looked like the heat didn't agree with him. His face and neck were lobster-red and sweat-slick. Perched on top of his round head was a narrow-brimmed straw hat that looked a size or two too small. His navy-blue blazer, open-neck sport shirt, and slacks all looked rumpled.

He dropped the car keys into his right-hand jacket pocket. Jack took note of that; it would make things easier for him.

Hickman, the higher-ranking of the two, was neat, trim, and compact. He wore a summer-weight suit, a tie, and shiny black shoes. If the heat bothered him he showed no sign of it. His short, dark hair was parted as precisely on one side as if it had been laid out with a ruler. He looked like an accountant—one who specialized in foreclosures.

Jack nodded to the two men. Indicating his room, he said, "In there."

He went inside, the others following. Coates brought up the rear and quickly closed the door behind him to prevent any civilians outside from seeing the corpse. There was none nearby but he did so anyway.

Jack took several paces into the room and stopped short, causing the FBI men to stop in their tracks to avoid bumping into him. They milled around impatiently behind him, craning for a better look at the body.

"Watch your step," Jack cautioned.

"Yeah, we know. We've been to a few crime scenes before," Coates said, his tone sarcastic.

"Not like this one. That's a poison needle. The point was covered with a gray plastic cap to protect her from accidentally scratching herself and getting a dose of the toxin. The cap shattered when it went into her. You can see some of those gray pieces on the carpet. You don't want to get any stuck to the bottoms of your shoes."

"How do you know the needle was poisoned?" Hickman asked.

"When the stuff hit her she went out like that," Jack said, snapping his fingers.

Hickman nodded, thoughtful. "Duly noted," he said. He and Coates fanned out around Jack, moving deeper into the room to examine the corpse, stepping carefully around it.

Jack stumbled against Coates, bumping into him. He put a hand on the big man's shoulder as if to steady himself. "Why don't you watch where you're going?" Coates barked.

"Sorry," Jack said.

Hickman asked, "What exactly happened here, Bauer? How did it go down?"

"She came in to change the sheets and towels—she said. Then she made her move when she thought I wasn't looking."

"And . . . ?"

"I was looking," Jack deadpanned.

Coates hooked his thumbs in the corners of his front pants pockets, rocking back and forth on his heels. "Maybe she thought you were going to beat it without leaving her a tip."

Jack moved to one side, out of the way. He stood leaning against the cabinet with his hands folded behind him. The others had eyes only for the corpse. Jack reached behind himself and carefully deposited an object behind a plastic ice bucket, which hid it from view. Nobody saw what he'd done.

Hickman studied the cadaver intently, like an auditor searching ledger entries for a decimal point in the wrong place. He glanced at Jack. "Can you ID her?"

Jack shook his head. "I was hoping you could."

"I can't place her." Hickman turned to Coates. "What about you, Red?"

"I'm blank. She looks like somebody's maiden aunt."

"Except for the knitting needle stuck in her throat," he added.

"What tipped you to her, Bauer?" Hickman asked. "How'd you know she was a phony?"

Jack spoke directly to Hickman. "I've been here long

enough to know most of the service personnel and I've never seen her before. Not much by itself, but it got me wondering. Then she was wearing a uniform with long sleeves. All the other maids had short-sleeved uniforms. Long sleeves in this heat? It didn't ring true."

Coates was sour-faced, skeptical. "Maybe her other outfits were in the laundry. Or she had ugly arms and didn't like to show 'em."

"I thought of that, too. So I tried her out with another test. I asked her why the regular maid, Norma, wasn't cleaning my room like usual. She said it was Norma's day off."

"So?"

"Norma was just a name I made up. The maid who cleans the room is Carmen," Jack said.

Hickman nodded with a barely perceptible tilt of the head, as if acknowledging that the other had scored a point.

"You're a regular Sherlock Junior." Coates took off his hat and fanned his face with it. Thinning strands of pale orange hair were slicked back over a shiny freckled scalp.

Hickman squatted down and began turning out the woman's pockets. "She's clean," Jack said. "I already gave her a onceover."

"I bet," Coates said nastily. "You wouldn't be holding anything out on us, would you, Bauer?"

"She was a pro on a hit job. She wouldn't be carrying anything that might indicate her true identity."

Hickman stood up, reflexively straightening out the creases in his pants. "We'll see what the lab crew can turn up. Her technique might furnish some solid leads, too. Pretty exotic . . . We don't get too many poison needle kills in this neck of the woods."

"Are you sure?" Jack asked.

Coates bristled. "What's that supposed to mean?"

"Dr. Yan started off the chain of Ironwood deaths. A heart attack, they said."

"It happens. He was over fifty and he'd just finished playing a couple of sets of tennis in the hot sun."

"He had a clean bill of health on his most recent physical and had no history of heart trouble."

"An autopsy wouldn't have missed something as obvious as a needle puncture wound, Bauer."

"That toxin is so potent that I'm betting that even a scratch or a pinprick of it brings on instant death. And the symptoms could pass for a heart attack or stroke."

"Under the circumstances, I suppose we'll have to order an exhumation," Hickman said. "We might learn something new, provided the toxin is one that doesn't break down a short while after being introduced into the body."

"You might also want to circulate photos of her around the tennis club," Jack suggested, indicating the corpse. "Somebody might have noticed her on the premises about the time that Yan dropped dead."

As if inspired by the thought, he took out his cell phone and used its camera function to photograph the cadaver from several different angles. He stepped back to capture a full body image, then moved in closer to click off a series of head shots, including full frontal views and profiles.

Coates's unhappiness deepened. "What're you doing?"

"Taking some souvenir snapshots for the folks back home," Jack said. He returned the cell to its belt holder. He started toward the front of the room.

"Where're you going?" Coates demanded.

"I'm going to upload the photos on the CTU net to see if our files can get a make on the killer. I'll use the digital comm system in my SUV," Jack said. "Any objections?"

"You're damned right—"

"Don't wander too far, Bauer," Hickman said, cutting off his partner. "Sabito wants to debrief you when he gets here."

"I don't work for Vince. I've got my own bosses to answer

to and they'll want this information as soon as possible."
Jack opened the door partway. "I'll be right outside."

Hickman shrugged, as if the matter were of no importance. Jack went out. Hickman began, "Red—"

Coates was already starting toward the door. "Stuffy in
here. Think I'll take the air myself."

"Don't crowd him. But don't lose him, either."

"Fat chance of that!"

Jack's vehicle was parked near room eight. It was a tan Ford
Expedition, a CTU vehicle with all the trimmings.

CTU had branches in most major cities in the United
States, but its presence in Los Alamos was virtually nil. Its
nearest divisional headquarters was in El Paso, Texas.

An agent from CTU/ELP had driven to Los Alamos to
deliver the Expedition to Jack to use during his assignment
and taken a plane back to home base.

The machine was basically the same model with the
same options and special modifications as those used by
CTU/L.A. With one notable exception. The Los Angeles
vehicles had black exteriors. The Southwestern variety was
tan to better resist the desert sun.

Jack reached into his right front pants pocket and took
out a handheld electronic keying module. The SUV was
equipped with motion-detecting anti-interference sensors
capable of triggering a silent vibrating alarm in the electronic key component if anyone had been meddling with it.

The alarm was untripped; the Expedition had not been
tampered with. Jack wouldn't have put Sabito past planting
a homing device or bug on the vehicle so he could track
Jack's movements.

Jack pressed the button on the keying device to unlock
the SUV. It was parked head-out for a quicker getaway.
Glancing back over his shoulder, he saw Coates loitering
beside the blue-black sedan, watching him.

Jack opened the driver's side door and took a step back. The sealed SUV had been baking under the sun for hours. The heat inside was slightly terrific. He took a deep breath and climbed in, leaving the door open to let some of the heat out.

He switched on the ignition, the finely tuned engine coming alive with a surge of power. Working the push-button controls, he rolled down the windows and turned on the air conditioner. It would take a moment or two before its powerful blowers began pumping cool air into the compartment.

He glanced at Coates nearby standing beside the sedan. Coates glared back at him, scowling. No doubt he suspected Jack of planning to make a break. He couldn't be dead sure, though, because Jack would have had to turn on the engine to run the air-conditioning and also to power up its digital media station.

The Expedition was equipped with a complex array of digitized communication and information processing systems. It was also equipped with a gun locker containing a formidable arsenal of weaponry.

Jack Bauer had not lied; he had only shaded the truth. He fully intended to upload the photographs on the CTU net where the agency's extensive reserve of data banks and supercomputers could go to work to identify the assailant. He would do so.

Later.

For now he had bigger fish to fry.

He put the machine in gear and drove away. Behind him he heard Coates's choked cry of outrage: "Hey!"

The SUV exited the lot, turned right, and headed west on the roadway. It cruised along at a moderate pace appropriate to the tempo of the street traffic.

By now Coates had already jumped into the sedan to give chase. He wasn't going anywhere, not without his car keys.

Jack had lifted them earlier, back in the motel room, when he'd stumbled into the FBI agent. Crookery 101: misdirect the mark by jostling him or some other such ploy, while making the dip and picking his pocket.

Jack Bauer in the past had many times worked undercover posing as a criminal type to infiltrate a gang or syndicate operation. Along the way he'd picked up more than a few tricks of the trade. Picking pockets was one of the larcenous skills he'd mastered to bolster his cover, and for a clandestine operator such as himself it could be mighty useful at times.

He made a right turn at the second intersection he came to and began a series of evasive maneuvers to make it that much more difficult for others to pick up his trail. Maybe Hickman had a spare set of keys, but even if he did, Jack would be long gone before the sedan was fired up and in pursuit.

Jack hadn't left the G-men totally marooned at the motel. After lifting Coates's keys he'd hidden them behind the plastic ice bucket on the counter. Once he was sure he'd given them the slip, he'd phone and tell them where to find the keys.

Hickman and Coates would be sore as hell at Jack for working that gag on them. He had to admit it was a dirty trick but—

Too bad.

He was a long way from home base and operating alone deep in unknown territory here. For all he knew either Hickman or Coates—or for that matter, Sabito—could have fingered him to the assassin.

For now he'd play a lone hand, keep his own counsel, and strike off by himself whenever such action seemed called for.

That was the only way to stay alive for those up against Annihilax.

Take it another step further; tighten the screws of paranoia another notch. Jack could be riding into an ambush right now.

Peter Rhee was as much an unknown quantity as anyone else involved in the manhunt. He might be using their upcoming meeting as a setup to lure Jack into a death trap. One more tightly constructed and inescapable than the one Jack had just thwarted.

Or—Rhee might be only a pawn, an unwitting victim of a master ploy to maneuver Jack into the kill zone. The only way to find out the truth was to go the meeting place.

The motel's name was Trail's End but for Jack Bauer it was only the beginning.

1 2 3 4 5 6 7 8 9
10 11 12 13 14 15 16 17
18 19 20 21 22 23 24

....

THE FOLLOWING TAKES PLACE
BETWEEN THE HOURS OF
12 P.M. AND 1 P.M.
MOUNTAIN DAYLIGHT TIME

....

12:10 P.M. MDT
Alkali Flats, Los Alamos County

The meeting place was the Alkali Flats roadside rest area.
One didn't have to drive far in any direction in Los Alamos
County to leave civilization behind and enter a desert waste-
land of mountains, canyons, and plains.

The rest area was located on Old Sipapu Road, an obscure
strip of two-lane blacktop connecting the rugged backcountry with the main roads into town and the lab complexes. It
ran through land that was good neither for farming nor for
ranching. A road that even the local folks used only to cross
a patch of badlands on their way to someplace better.

The Expedition's GPS system had no trouble in pinpoint-
ing the site. Jack was good with directions and had gotten
a general sense of the layout of the Los Alamos terrain but

it was reassuring to have the computerized location finder for backup.

Once he'd gotten on Old Sipapu Road Jack had seen few other vehicles, and most of them were going in the opposite direction, driving northbound toward town. Jack drove south toward the meeting place.

The rest area was on the opposite side of the road. A lone vehicle was there, one he recognized as Peter Rhee's car. Rhee was nowhere in sight and neither was anyone else.

Rhee had picked the site and in theory it seemed like a good one. It was remote, isolated, and out in the open in the middle of nowhere. Seemingly immune to surveillance or ambush.

Playing it safe, Jack avoided pulling directly into the site but instead continued southbound for an eighth of a mile or so before slowing to a halt to survey the terrain.

The landscape was utterly empty of all signs of human habitation. No other vehicle could be seen on the road in either direction, and on this sprawling expanse of terrain with its clear desert air, one could see a long way.

Jack used his cell to call Rhee yet again. As before, there was no reply. Rhee had been out of communication since his last call to Jack, which had been made at 10:30 this morning. That was when he said he'd developed an important lead in the case and had to talk to Jack alone in person.

Jack offered to come out and meet him at Ironwood but that option had been flatly rejected. Rhee said that Ironwood "wasn't secure" for what he had to tell him and had instead offered the Alkali Flats rest area on Old Sipapu Road as the site for the rendezvous. It wasn't too far out of town but it offered privacy and seclusion.

Jack had all but begged Rhee to at least give him some hints about what he'd found. Rhee refused to discuss it, even on a secure phone line. Jack agreed to the terms. He couldn't blame Rhee for what others might have taken for an excess of caution bordering on paranoia. Ironwood had become a nexus of violence and sudden death. What would seem like paranoia under normal circumstances had come to be seen as nothing more or less than good common sense.

That was the last conversation Jack had had with Rhee. Since then: silence.

Rhee's car was at the rendezvous but where was its driver? His continued failure to answer his cell was foreboding, ominous. Despite the wide open spaces and sunny blue skies, the empty landscape took on an aura of menace.

Jack resolved to grab the hot iron and retake the initiative. He swung the SUV around in a U-turn and headed north toward the meeting place.

The rest area was on the east side of the road. A gravel lot featured a whitewashed concrete blockhouse restroom with a pay telephone stand nearby. Off to one side on the north was a stand of scraggly timber with a couple of picnic tables beneath it.

Behind the rest stop, the land sloped off to the east, dipping into a low, wide, dusty basin dotted with gnarled, stunted trees, boulders, and clumps of cactus. The landscape was bone-dry, not a pond, puddle, or trickle of a stream in sight. The ground was reddish-brown like the sands of Mars. These were the Alkali Flats.

Way off in the distance on the far side of the flats, a line of brown mountains ran north-south. Rhee's car was to the left of the restroom blockhouse. It was parked head-in facing the flats and at right angles to the road.

Slowing to enter the rest area, Jack decided against pulling up alongside Rhee's car. Gravel crunched under his wheels as he rolled to a halt behind the back of Rhee's car. That put the SUV at right angles to the car and parallel to the roadway.

Jack drew his weapon and got out of the machine. He left

the engine running in case he had to make a quick getaway. He dropped into a crouch, sheltering behind the SUV.

It wasn't bulletproof, but at least it provided some cover. Not only from any ambusher who might be lurking in or around Rhee's car, but also from any lurkers in the restroom facility.

Jack's outfit included a long-billed baseball cap and sunglasses. Long experience in desert conditions at home and abroad had taught him not to go out under the naked sun bareheaded or without eye protection. The sunglasses, a wraparound polarized pair, were particularly essential. The pitiless desert sun, especially at these high altitudes, could easily affect the eyes of unacclimated outsiders, quickly inducing vision problems and even sun blindness.

The air was perfectly still, without a breath of wind. The heat was broiling. The temperature must have been crowding the hundred-degree mark, a relatively moderate temperature for the area at this time of the day and season.

Jack circled around the front of the SUV, gun leveled, approaching in a low crouch Rhee's car from the driver's side. He kept the car between himself and the restroom blockhouse. Nearing it he saw that the interior and windows were sprayed red.

He went down on one knee beside the car, keeping his head below the cover of the top of the door line. He peeked under the vehicle, making sure that no one was hiding beneath or in front of it.

He popped up, gun pointing through the open driver's side at the interior. Its sole occupant was the corpse that lay crumpled in the front seat.

Jack kept moving, circling the car to rush the concrete blockhouse of the restroom facility. A door in the north wall was marked "Ladies." He flattened his back against the wall to the left of the door.

Crouching low to present a minimal target, he ducked

around the northeast corner, ready to put the blast on any hostiles who might be lurking behind the back of the building. The area came up empty.

He padded soft-footed to the southeast corner and ducked around it to come up on the building's east side where the men's room was located. No one on that side, either.

Next came the nerve-racking task of clearing the inside of the facility. He probed the men's room first, not neglecting to check the stall. It was clean, stark, and functional, smelling of disinfectant and flinty dust. Unoccupied, save for himself.

The ladies' room came up clear, too, and he went back outside. A blur of motion approached from the south driving north. It was the first vehicle to pass either way in the last ten minutes. It was moving along at a nice clip, about sixty miles an hour. A light blue pickup truck.

As it neared, Jack realized he was standing there with his gun in hand. He lowered it to his side and turned so that his body shielded it from the oncoming vehicle's occupants.

The pickup truck drove by without slowing. Jack caught a glimpse of a man in a cowboy hat behind the wheel and a woman seated beside him. A couple of young men in work shirts and jeans sat in the hopper behind the cab, talking and laughing.

One of them waved to Jack and he raised a hand back in friendly greeting.

A rancher and his wife and some hands going into town on a Saturday afternoon, Jack guessed. A vignette of everyday normality that made the murder scene seem even more macabre by comparison.

The pickup dwindled to a dot in the northbound lane and winked out of sight.

Jack glanced at the picnic tables under a handful of thin, threadbare trees whose leaves were filmed with dust. No place for anyone to hide there. He couldn't imagine anyone choosing to picnic at this forlorn locale; it would be like picnicking on Mars.

Jack holstered his weapon and went to the driver's side of the car. He walked carefully, watching his step. The unpaved rest area consisted of dirt and gravel. There was a chance that the loose-packed dirt might contain the killer's footprints or the tire tracks of his vehicle.

Or her vehicle. Why should the killer be a man? The assassin who'd tried for Jack was a woman. To assume that the killer was male was to disarm one's suspicions by half and allow for a possibly fatal mistake. Had Peter Rhee made such a fatal assumption?

In any case, the ground might hold valuable clues that could be picked up by forensics experts. Jack wanted to leave as minimal a footprint as possible while still surveying the scene.

Nearing the car, Jack noticed something so significant that it brought him to a sudden halt. The ground around the car had been smoothed out to destroy any telltale marks. Sanitized by the killer to erase all traces of evidence.

Regular swirl patterns disturbed the gravel-strewn, reddish-brown dirt, indicating that it had been raked or smoothed over. Not just the immediate area surrounding the car but an extensive patch to the left of it.

Car-sized? Could that be where the killer had parked his vehicle? It, too, had been smoothed over, obliterating not only any footprints but also any telltale tire tread marks as well.

Jack walked in a straight line to Rhee's car and peered through the open driver's side window. The interior resembled a slaughterhouse. Blood splattered the roof, windows, windshields, dashboard, and seats.

Peter Rhee didn't have much of a face left. Not much of a head left, either.

He lay sprawled across the front seat of his parked car.

He must have been sitting behind the wheel when the blast got him, and the impact had blown him out of the driver's seat, leaving him contorted in the throes of sudden, violent death.

His upper body lay on its side on the passenger seat. His legs were together and bent at the knees and his feet were on the floor on the driver's side. His head and shoulders were wedged against the passenger side door. His right arm hung down off the edge of the seat cushion, his hand dangling a few inches above the passenger side floor mat.

Jack Bauer's estimate that the delays at the motel would cause him to be about ten minutes late for his noontime meeting with Peter Rhee had been just about right.

Once he'd gotten off the highway trip and onto the open road he'd made good time getting to the rendezvous. But a killer had gotten there before him.

Peter Rhee had been shot in the face at point-blank range. And not with any mere handgun, either, not even a big-caliber job like a .357 or .44 Magnum. From the looks of the devastation he must have been on the receiving end of a shotgun blast.

No question that the dead man was Peter Rhee, though. The Korean-American counterintelligence officer had had a distinctively shaped hairline and ears that Jack had taken note of during earlier meetings.

Jack tried to put himself in the killer's head. Why a shotgun? Even a sawed-off job had a certain unwieldiness compared to a handgun. It was pointless to destroy the victim's face to conceal his identity because that could be determined by a simple fingerprint check.

Terror? That was a possibility. A shotgun was an intimidating weapon that made a real mess. Maybe the kill had been handled that way to terrorize, to throw some fear into anyone foolish enough to get mixed up in the action. Bauer had seen the tactic before from professional killers like Annihilax.

Another question: How had a shotgun-wielding killer gotten the drop on a veteran operative like Peter Rhee?

Jack stuck his head through the open window. Not so pleasant but he found out a few things. Rhee was armed. The bulge of his shoulder-holstered gun was visible beneath his jacket. Why hadn't he used it?

There were no car keys in the ignition. Rhee's jacket and pants pockets were turned out, indicating they'd been searched. The glove compartment was open—also searched?

Jack stepped back, taking a few deep breaths. The super-heated air rasped in his lungs. Absently glancing down, he noticed something: a circular hole had been punched into the ground near the undercarriage between the driver's side door and rear door.

He hunkered down for a closer look. A layer of loose dirt and sand covered the parking area. It took impressions easily. The hole was slightly wider in diameter than a twenty-five-cent piece and was about two inches deep. He couldn't figure out what had made it.

It was close enough to the car's underside that the killer might have missed it while he was smoothing over the ground to erase his tracks. Maybe the blinding glare of the desert sun had caused him to overlook it. Jack made a mental note of it.

He circled around to the rear of the car. There he found the missing ring of car keys, hanging from a lock in the trunk where a key had been inserted. Presumably the killer had unlocked the trunk to search it.

Jack resisted the impulse to unlock and open the trunk and take a look for himself. It could be booby-trapped.

The dirt on the passenger side of the car had been

smoothed over, too. The killer had been thorough—but maybe not thorough enough.

Jack was looking for it this time, and sure enough he found it: another of those curious round holes poked in the ground. This one lay in the shadow of the wheel well behind the right front tire. Like its twin on the other side of the car, this hole, too, was the width of a twenty-five-cent piece and two inches deep. Curious . . .

He prowled around the car to see if there was anything else he could turn up in the way of clues. A bumper line of telephone pole–sized logs bordered the edge of the rest area to keep parked vehicles from going off the edge right before the ground started sloping downward.

On the far side of the makeshift guardrail was a tangle of scrub brush. Amid the foliage a patch of whiteness where there shouldn't have been any caught Jack's eye. It marked where a branch had been freshly broken off a bush.

He guessed that the leafy bough had been broken off by the killer and used to sweep up the ground to sanitize the scene.

Jack reckoned he had seen all there was to see. He got back in the SUV and used the digital media station to upload the cell phone camera photo images of the maid-assassin to the CTU net.

Satellite communication gear allowed him to transmit directly to home base at CTU/L.A., to the bullpen where board operating analysts would enter it into the system of networked supercomputers accessing not only CTU and CIA data banks but also linked to military, law enforcement, and national security assets. He also sent a brief verbal report on the murder of Peter Rhee.

After that there was nothing left to do but face the music. He phoned Vince Sabito and told him where he could be found.

12:37 P.M. MDT
Alkali Flats Rest Area, Los Alamos County

Coates came at Jack Bauer. Hickman tried to restrain his partner but it was no good, like a greyhound trying to hold back a bear. Coates shook him off and kept charging.

Jack waited until Coates was almost on him, and then at the last second he ducked and sidestepped, avoiding Coates's lunge.

Momentum kept Coates moving and he staggered forward a few paces before stumbling to a halt. His hat fell off and rolled around in a half circle in the dust. He turned, gathering himself for another try.

"One free pass is all you get," Jack said matter-of-factly

Coates's florid face seemed to swell even more. He lowered his head like a charging bull.

"Coates! Knock it off," Vince Sabito said. He was the head man of the FBI squad that had been sent out by the Santa Fe resident agency.

Of medium height, Sabito was built like a fireplug, with broad oversized shoulders, powerful upper body development, a short thick waist, and bandy legs. Shiny hair as black as India ink was slicked back from his forehead. His eyebrows were thick black horizontal lines that almost but not quite met over the top of a broad, flat nose. He was swarthy with narrow gray eyes, strong jaws, and a lot of chin.

Holstered under an arm was a .357 Magnum; the gun was like the man: short, squat, and packing a lot of firepower.

Coates stood there, head down, glaring up from his eye sockets at Jack, hands balled into fists. Breathing hard. He called Jack a dirty name. But that meant that the action phase was over.

Sabito said, "Cut the crap."

"You heard the man, Coates. Cut the crap," Ferney chimed in. His title was Executive Assistant. He was

Sabito's stooge and yes-man. Slim, compact, he wore narrow-lensed glasses that banded his eyes like a visor.

"Let's try and pretend that we're all professionals," Sabito said.

"You call that professional, what Bauer did, lifting my car keys?" Coates was aggrieved and working it like a man worrying a sore tooth. "Professional crook, maybe!"

"I told you where the keys were," Jack pointed out.

"Sure, once it was too late for us to follow you!"

Hickman sighed. "Which was the point of the exercise," he said with the weariness of a man explaining the obvious.

The federal men had come in two cars, the one assigned to Hickman and Coates and another that had conveyed Sabito and Ferney to the site. The cars were parked on the shoulder on the east side of the road to avoid further contaminating the crime scene. The cars were virtually identical late model sedans, the only difference between them being that the watchdogs' car was blue-black while their boss's was black.

Jack wondered idly if that was some subtle Bureau indicator of rank or status.

Hickman picked up Coates's hat, brushed the dust off it, and handed it to Coates. Coates muttered some thanks and jammed it back on his head.

Coates wasn't letting it go so easily. "If you ask me the whole setup stinks," he said. More red color came into his face and neck. "This guy pulls a sneak to take off on his own and an hour later we find him wrapped up in the middle of another murder!"

"You didn't find me, I told you where to come," Jack pointed out. "And the first one wasn't murder, it was self-defense."

Sabito moved to the foreground, placing himself between the two men. "No matter how you slice it, Bauer, you've had a busy morning," he said.

"That's what we want, isn't it?"

"I don't know as I like the sound of that. Explain."

"You'd better!" Ferney said, indignant. He stood behind Sabito, practically hanging over his shoulder.

"Something's gone sour at Ironwood. In the last six months there's been five suspicious deaths of people connected to the facility. Then in one day—today—they try to kill me and Rhee is murdered," Jack said.

"He might be alive if you hadn't played it cagey and tried to lone wolf it."

Jack took it without flinching. "That's a cheap shot. Rhee wanted a meet and said I had to come alone. He set up the conditions, not me."

"So you say."

"The point is that suddenly things are moving. The mastermind behind the Ironwood kills is getting worried. Up to now he was content to move at his own pace, framing the deaths so they looked like natural causes, accidents, random street violence—anything but what they really were: part of a wholesale murder conspiracy.

"Now he's getting rattled, throwing caution to the winds. He sends out two assassins on open hit jobs, and damn the stealth. Somewhere he's left a loose end and he's afraid it'll be found. Whatever the answer is, I think Rhee found it."

Sabito shrugged, his massive upper body making it look like a titanic shoulder twitch. "Who knows?"

"Somebody thought he had something or they wouldn't have blown his head off," Jack said.

"Maybe the same somebody who thinks you're on to something and tried to have you killed, eh, Bauer?"

"Could be."

Sabito's manner had been deceptively easygoing but he was sore and now made a point of showing it. He got up close in Jack's face. "What are you holding out, Bauer? What makes you a target? What do you know that you're not telling? If you've got something you'd better spill it before you wind up like Rhee and take your knowledge to the grave."

"Talk, Bauer!" Ferney echoed.

That was the hell of it. Jack *was* holding out on Sabito, withholding the key factor in the case: Annihilax. The world's intelligence services, and that most definitely included the FBI, believed that Annihilax was dead. Only a tight handful of operatives in CTU, CIA, and the DIA knew otherwise.

The fact that NSA had intercepted a fragment of the master assassin's crypto-code was top secret. Even the fact that they were able to do so was top secret. Annihilax's resurrection was ultraclassified on a need-to-know basis, and the higher-ups had decided that the Bureau as yet had no need to know. As far as the Bureau knew, CTU was injecting a phony terror angle into the case so it could horn in on what should have been a strictly FBI investigation.

Jack Bauer was prohibited from divulging that information. He chafed under the restriction. But until he was authorized to do so, he couldn't level with Sabito and reveal the real nature of the opposition they were combating.

"If I had something I'd tell you," Jack said, lying with equanimity.

Sabito wasn't buying. "Like you did about your meeting with Rhee?"

Jack took the offensive. "Maybe he didn't trust your outfit to handle it properly. That's how he wanted it and that's how I played it. You guys denied there even was a pattern until the last kill when Morrow got liquidated."

A flicker of unease showed on Sabito's face, indicating that Jack's last remark had struck a nerve. He backed off, literally, taking a few steps back. Ferney had to step lively to avoid a collision with his boss.

That was a relief. Sabito's face had been thrust so close that Jack had felt his hot breath on his flesh.

"I had my suspicions long before Morrow. But the top brass felt otherwise and I had to follow orders. When Morrow got killed everything changed and I was able to take a more proactive stance," Sabito said.

"After today it's a whole new ball game. There'll be no more doubt about the what, only the who," Jack said.

"Just remember we're supposed to be partners in this investigation."

"I'm cooperating."

"You've got a funny way of showing it, Bauer."

Jack gave Sabito a refresher course on the facts of life. "There's two ways to play an assignment like this: as Mr. Inside or Mr. Outside. The first way is to work undercover and insinuate yourself into the opposition's organization. Burrowing from within as the inside man. That's not an option here because we don't know who to infiltrate.

"That leaves us with option two: the outside man. Forget about going undercover and the stealth stuff and do it the opposite way. Come in with a high profile and a big noise. Show yourself and keep pushing hard in hopes of stirring up the enemy. They don't know what you know or if you even know anything at all, but if you come on strong enough you might spook them into breaking cover and making a try for you. Make a target of yourself and hope they take the bait. If they do and you survive it you've got a lead.

"That's how I'm playing it: Mr. Outside," he concluded.

Sabito was a tough sell. "Yeah, and look how well that's working out. We've got one dead assassin and one dead counterintelligence officer."

"At least we've got the other side worried," Jack said.

"Watch out that you don't wind up playing it as Mr. Dead."

"Why Vince, I never know you cared."

"I don't. I just don't want to have to fill out the paperwork."

Jack could well believe it. "To demonstrate our newfound spirit of cooperation, let me point out a couple of things I noticed about Rhee's killing."

"I can hardly wait," Sabito said.

He and Jack crossed toward the death car, Ferney following several paces behind Sabito. After a pause, Hickman and Coates drifted along in their wake.

A few paces from the rear of the car, Sabito glanced over his shoulder at the others and came to a halt. "Let's all trample the crime scene to make sure we get rid of any clues," he said, his voice dripping sarcasm.

Everyone else froze in place.

"The killer already took care of that," Jack said easily. "See how the ground is smoothed over with those swirling patterns? The killer broke a branch off a bush and used it to sweep the ground clean."

Sabito cut a quick sidelong glance at Jack, his expression dubious. "How do you know that?"

"The smoothed-over ground is self-evident." Jack pointed at the greenery beyond the log ground rail. "There's a fresh spot on that bush where a branch was broken off. A leafy branch makes a nice broom to sweep clean."

Coates muttered under his breath. "Sherlock Junior."

"What about that set of footprints going around the car on both sides?" Hickman asked.

"I made those," Jack said. Sabito gave him a long hard stare. "I had to see if Rhee was dead or alive," Jack explained. He changed the subject. "Notice the keys in the car trunk. The killer searched the car, looking for what?—incriminating evidence, if any. Assuming Rhee had some."

"I suppose you took a look inside the trunk?" Sabito asked.

Jack shook his head. "Not me. It could be booby-trapped to take out snoopers. You know, turn the key and lift the trunk lid and set off a bomb."

"Sounds pretty far-fetched."

"Like using a disguised maid who's a poison needle artist?"

Coates pushed his way forward. "You're not buying this line of malarkey, Vince?"

Sabito fixed him with his cold gray-eyed gaze. "You going to open the trunk, Red?"

"Yeah, I'll open it—"

"Wait a minute so the rest of us can get out of range in case it is rigged to explode."

That cooled Coates off. "Well . . ." After a pause, he came to a decision. "Let the demolitions boys handle it. That's what they get paid for," he said.

Sabito nodded. "Uh-huh. I think we can all let it be for now." He turned toward Jack. "What else have you got?"

"The brush marks extend way over to the left of the car," Jack pointed out. "My guess is that that's where the killer drove in and parked beside Rhee. Rhee was sitting in his car waiting for me to show up. The other windows were rolled up so he was probably idling with the air-conditioning on. The killer got out of his car, approaching him on the driver's side. Rhee rolled down his window, probably to talk to the killer. The killer took him by surprise and shot him point-blank in the face. Looks like a shotgun blast from the extent of the damage."

"I took a look at him before. I'd go along with a shotgun. Sawed-off probably, since it's easier to get into action," Sabito said.

"Here's the big question: What was Rhee thinking?" Jack asked.

"You're telling it."

"His gun is in the shoulder holster untouched. Yet he was concerned enough about his safety to arrange a secret meeting at this out-of-the-way spot. A remote locale out in the open where he could see anybody coming from a long way off.

"His window was rolled down. Why? So he could speak to the newcomer approaching him on that side. He's already on the alert for a killer—or killers—targeting Ironwood personnel. If the newcomer had been a stranger, Rhee wouldn't have been caught napping. He'd have been ready for trouble. He would have had his gun in hand ready for action. But he didn't."

"Your point being . . . ?"

"That the killer wasn't a stranger. That it was someone he knew, someone he trusted. A colleague or a friend. Someone he didn't suspect until right before his head was blown off," Jack concluded.

"It's possible," Sabito said.

"Got a better theory?"

"An alternative."

"I'm all ears, Vince."

"Suppose the killer was a stranger, only someone so innocent-looking that Rhee never got suspicious? A type that not even a suspicious guy would ever figure as a killer. A schoolgirl in pigtails, say, or a uniformed Boy Scout. A nun or a priest, an old lady or a freckle-faced kid or whatever."

"Why not a dwarf masking as a toddler with a lollipop?"

"Why not? Hell, they tried for you with a phony room maid. That shows they're steeped in the tricks of subterfuge, camouflage, and deception. Somebody in a perfect disguise approaches Rhee, pretending to ask for directions. Being a nice friendly fellow, he rolls down the window to reply and gets a faceful of buckshot."

"Not bad. It could have been worked that way," Jack conceded. "One more thing I want to show you."

He directed Sabito's attention to the hole punched in the ground near the undercarriage on the driver's side of Rhee's car. "See that? Look like anything to you?"

"Yeah, a hole in the ground."

"I don't know what it is, either, but there's another one just like it on the other side of the car. I'll show it to you in a minute. It might have been left by the killer."

Sabito squatted down to examine it, peering at it squinty-eyed from different angles. "Beats me. The only thing I can think of is that maybe the killer accidentally pressed the shotgun muzzle down into the dirt while he was cleaning up. If it was a single-barreled job and not a double. The width would be about right."

"I thought of that, too," Jack said. "But can you picture a pro killer who knows guns do something stupid like that? It's a good way to block the barrel with several inches of hard-packed dirt and take the shooter's head off the next time he fired it if he forgot to clean and unplug the barrel."

"Hell, he'd already used it. He could always unplug it later."

"Sloppy—very sloppy for a killer who was so methodical about erasing his traces from the scene. And the funny thing is there's another just like it on the other side of the car."

Jack took Sabito around to the passenger side and showed him the identical hole poked in the ground behind the front tire.

"That is odd. Damned odd," Sabito said. "Could be a break. I'll have the lab crew make plaster casts of the impressions. Might help us identify the make and model of the shotgun—if that's what made the marks."

"And if it didn't, what did?" Jack wondered out loud.

Sabito took Jack off to one side, out of hearing of the others. "I don't like to ask for favors from anybody but you've got me on the spot, Bauer."

"How so?"

Sabito looked sheepish. "I'd appreciate it if you'd keep quiet about how you gave my men the slip—lifting Coates's car keys and all. Just so I don't look like a complete jackass in front of my superiors back at headquarters."

"My lips are sealed, Vince," Jack said solemnly.

• •

**THE FOLLOWING TAKES PLACE
BETWEEN THE HOURS OF
1 P.M. AND 2 P.M.
MOUNTAIN DAYLIGHT TIME**

• •

1:24 P.M. MDT
Route 302, Los Alamos County

The tan SUV was pulled over to the side of the road so Jack Bauer could take a cell phone call from CTU/L.A.

He was en route to South Mesa and Ironwood National Laboratory when the call came in. He pulled over to the shoulder and stopped so he could concentrate on his communication and in case he had to process any downloads on his satcom-equipped digital media station.

He'd left Sabito and his men behind at the Alkali Flats rest area where they were waiting for a special FBI forensics team to make the drive down from the resident agency in Santa Fe. Sabito had roped in the Los Alamos County Sheriff and his deputies to help secure the crime scene while at the same time keeping the county lawmen in the dark about everything except that a murder had been committed and the Bureau would appreciate it if they could keep gawkers, rubberneckers, and the curious away from the site.

Route 302 connected Old Sipapu Road with the main highway to South Mesa.

This stretch of road was so lonely and little-used that Jack could have parked in the middle of it to take the call and not blocked any traffic. There wasn't another vehicle in sight.

He liked that. It meant he wasn't being tailed.

The call was from Nina Myers, his chief of staff back at the Los Angeles home base and Acting Special Agent in Charge of the installation in his absence.

He and Nina had a long history, both professional and personal. They had been colleagues, friends, and lovers. Some months ago their longtime platonic relationship had erupted into a passionate affair. It had happened during a rough patch in Jack's marriage to his wife, Teri.

Jack prided himself on a near-photographic memory, but for the life of him he couldn't remember who had made the first move, he or Nina. Somehow they suddenly came together in a feverish embrace, and once begun there was no stopping it. Their coupling ripened into an affair, a compulsion at once both savage and tender, all-consuming.

For a while it had become an obsession, prodding Jack into separating from Teri and moving out of the home he shared with her and their daughter, Kim. Jack had been torn between the two women, but in the end his marriage and family proved too important to him to give up on without a final try.

When he told Nina his decision, that he was going to try to reconcile with his wife, she was perhaps not unduly surprised. Unhappy, disappointed, sorrowful, and angry, yes; but not surprised. She was a being of keen perceptions and had sensed from countless reactions and tics of behavior her lover being inextricably pulled back home. That didn't make her like it any better.

They parted "like adults" and agreed to comport themselves as the same in their professional lives, where they continued to work closely as a team day in and day out.

Nina continued to exhibit the same seemingly unchanged loyalty and dedication in her post as Jack's chief of staff after the breakup as she had before it, and Jack did his best to relate to her on the job with a similarly warm yet businesslike demeanor. Now they were friends, colleagues, and ex-lovers.

Still—their recent intimacy did make for some awkward moments that they both worked hard to gloss over.

Lovely Nina, fiercely competent in all the arts of sex and spy tradecraft. He could see her now, with short brown hair, a high-cheekboned, well-sculpted face with a challengingly appraising gaze that missed nothing. Coolly self-contained and elegant, yet capable of unleashing a firestorm of naked passion and raw, uninhibited sensuousness. . .

Jack put the thought out of his mind. The memories. Suppressed them reflexively, like slamming shut a door in his head.

That was over. It never should have happened. *But it did happen*, an inner voice reminded him.

"That was quick work," Jack said, returning to the immediacy of the moment.

"What was?" Nina Myers asked, her voice expressing puzzlement as it came through the other end of the cell phone connection.

Now it was Jack's turn for an instant's confusion. "The poison needle artist. Don't you have an ID on her?"

"Not yet."

"Oh. I thought that's why you called."

"No such luck, Jack." Her chuckle was rich and throaty. She shifted smoothly and swiftly back to business. "I only wish it was something as simple as identifying an assassin. This is something really dangerous: politics."

"Uh-oh."

"I hate to bother you with nonsense like this anytime, but especially now when you're out of the office on special assignment. I'd handle it myself if I could, but this one I've got to drop in your lap."

"Fire away, Nina." Jack's tone was guarded.

"There's been some more comeback on the Maulana Mosque case," she said.

Jack caught himself in time to stifle a groan. He kept his voice level neutral. "That case has been nothing but comebacks. But that's the benefit of being out here on temporary duty. I'm out of it. You're acting head of the branch, Nina. It's your headache now."

"Well, not exactly," she said. "George Mason's been after me about if for the last two days, giving it a full-court press."

George Mason was Assistant Administrative Director of CTU/L.A. Jack considered him more of a pettifogging bureaucrat than an intelligence officer. Mason was an ambitious underling, an office politician who had his sights aimed at higher posts. He was so hungry for Jack's job that you could practically feel the need coming off him like a miasma.

The Maulana Mosque case was an ongoing irritant, a recurring problem that wouldn't go away. A prime example of the maxim about too many cooks spoiling the broth. The mosque was in the Los Angeles area, a target of a longtime CTU undercover investigation. Maulana Shaheed Zubayir was a religious leader associated with the mosque, an outwardly pious and scholarly elder respected for his encyclopedic knowledge of Sharia, Muslim religious law. Maulana was his title in the ecclesiastical hierarchy.

An extensive CTU probe involving the use of informants, undercover agents, and electronic eavesdropping had proved conclusively that Zubayir was a recruiter for al-Qaeda who had sent a number of fanatical would-be mujahideen down a pipeline whose other end was in terrorist training camps in the no-man's-land frontier between Pakistan and Afghanistan.

Once inculcated with the jihadist philosophy and schooled in the black arts of sabotage, bomb making, and murder, they'd been returned to the United States to set up their underground cells in preparation for future terrorist acts. CTU/L.A. had rolled up the operation, arresting in a massive predawn sweep the Maulana, his accomplices, and the newly returned jihadis.

What should have been the conclusion of a successful investigation proved to be only the start of a ride on the merry-go-round. The usual suspects were heard from, the "civil libertarians" protesting government intrusion into a place of worship, even though that place of worship had served as a recruiting ground, preliminary indoctrination center, and terror cell nexus.

The Maulana's flock delivered a big bloc of voters who voted en masse according to their leader's dictates, provoking anguished howls from city, county, and state politicians who benefitted from their support.

Worse, a Los Angeles Police Department political intelligence unit working on its own had recruited the Maulana as a confidential informant/source for their own counterterror operations. Zubayir had played them like a virtuoso, feeding them tips about rival sectarians in other mosques while keeping his own operations a secret from the police handlers who thought they were running him.

It had all gone public, of course, and a war of charges and countercharges was currently being fought out nonstop on the 24/7 news cycle.

* * *

"George Mason I can handle," Nina Myers said. "I've been handling. But he went over my head to Alberta Green and now she's putting on the pressure in her own inimitable way."

That added a complicating factor. Alberta Green worked for Jack's boss, CTU Regional Division Director Ryan Chappelle. George Mason was a pint-sized version of Chappelle, a man of vaunting ambition and Machiavellian duplicity who aimed at nothing less than a top post at CIA headquarters in Langley, Virginia.

Alberta Green's official title was Assistant Regional Division Director; in reality, it meant that she was Chappelle's enforcer, using her mastery of legalistic tactics to carry out the dirty work that Chappelle wanted to avoid being directly associated with.

Jack swore softly under his breath.

"What was that, Jack? I didn't catch that last part you said."

"It was nothing. What does Mason want?"

"He wants Tony Almeida to be debriefed on his role in the Maulana case."

"That's ridiculous! Tony was already extensively debriefed on that matter. His testimony is all on record. There's enough there for even Mason not to screw up."

"He thinks that the court case would be sewn up solid if Tony could testify during the trial."

This time Jack did swear out loud. "Tell Mason to get his head out of his ass. What an idiot. Tony worked that case undercover. He can't testify without blowing his cover and ending his usefulness as a clandestine operator."

"Alberta Green thinks otherwise. She says that he could testify on a closed-circuit TV link to the courtroom, in the judge's chambers with the prosecutor and defense attorney there. He could be sworn in live over the hookup and answer questions. His image and voice would be digitally masked so he couldn't be identified."

"Any defense attorney worth his salt could figure out the part Tony played by asking the right questions."

"I'm not arguing, Jack. I'm telling you what Alberta Green says."

"Never mind about that. The important thing is what does Chappelle say?"

"Nothing. Not a thing. And don't think I haven't asked him. Alberta comes on like she's carrying out Chappelle's directive but when I discussed the problem with him personally he made it clear he's carefully neutral on the whole situation. He tossed the ball back into your court, saying it's your decision and he wouldn't dream of interfering."

Of course he wouldn't, Jack thought. Chappelle was playing both ends against the middle as usual. He was covered no matter what way it went down. If the case was blown and the Maulana acquitted, it was Jack Bauer's fault for not making a key witness available. If the case ended in a conviction, Chappelle would posture that he'd gone to bat for his SAC CTU/L.A. by letting him exercise his own judgment without undue pressure or interference from his boss.

Smart.

". . . Jack?"

"Even if Almeida was available to testify on a closed-circuit hookup I wouldn't allow it. It risks compromising him, our informants in the mosque, and the unit's tradecraft and methods. Such knowledge would give the next terrorists a tremendous edge in knowing what to avoid.

"But luckily the question is academic. Because Tony Almeida is currently on an undercover assignment that makes it impossible for him to make himself available now and for the foreseeable future."

"No one knows that better than I, Jack."

Yes, Nina Myers knew. She and Tony Almeida were an

item. A couple. Nina had hooked up with Tony on the rebound after the breakup with Jack. He couldn't blame her. Almeida was a good man and a top operative. After the breakup, Jack had Teri and Kim to go home to. Nina Myers had her lonely apartment.

Despite the rules, office romances were only natural in this line of work. The agency turned a blind eye to it as long as it was discreet and didn't interfere with operations and unit morale.

Hard if not impossible for an operative to maintain an ongoing relationship with an outsider, a civilian.

So now Nina Myers and Tony Almeida were a couple, a clandestine couple. They were discreet about it, just as Jack and Nina had been discreet in the office when they were together. But Jack could detect all the signs between the two; after all, he'd been there himself. A mutual gaze held a beat too long, a friendly squeeze on the arm that meant something more, a certain reserve when he came across Nina and Tony having what had been a private conversation at the water cooler or at a shared table in the office cafeteria.

"I picked Tony Almeida because he was the best man for the job," Jack said.

Nina Myers did not know what that job was and was too professional to ask a question that Jack could only refuse to answer. Two people knew Tony Almeida's current assignment: Jack Bauer and Ryan Chappelle. Now that Tony was deep into it, neither of them knew the exact particulars.

"Who said otherwise? No need to get defensive, Jack."

"Who's defensive?" he said defensively.

"Nobody's suggesting that you picked him because you wanted him to be away from the office for personal reasons—to break up a romance that you thought was unacceptable, say."

"I think you know me better than that, Nina."

"Sometimes I wonder how well anyone knows anyone

else. All we see are the actions and not what's in the heart."

"I only want what's best for you, Nina."

"I know, Jack. You made that abundantly clear."

"Nina—"

"Forget it. That was unfair of me," she said. Her tone changed, became all business. "So—what do I tell George Mason and Alberta Green?"

"I know what I'd like to tell them but we'll skip that. Tell them that Tony Almeida is on a confidential assignment and unavailable until further notice. Tell them to take it to Chappelle if it's so damned important. He's the one who hands out the assignments.

"I can honestly say that at this moment I don't know where Tony is and couldn't get in touch with him right now even if I wanted to. He's out in the field now and on his own," Jack said.

"Aren't we all?" Nina's tone was coolly ironic. "Take care, Jack, and if by any chance you should happen to be in touch with Tony—"

"I'm not."

"Of course. But if you were, I'd ask you to tell him the same thing: Take care."

"Tony can take care of himself, Nina. Anything else?"

"That's all for now. I'll keep you posted on any developments on your current assignment as soon as they come in."

"Thanks."

"Goodbye, Jack."

· ·

THE FOLLOWING TAKES PLACE
BETWEEN THE HOURS OF
2 P.M. AND 3 P.M.
MOUNTAIN DAYLIGHT TIME

· ·

2:17 P.M. MDT
VAP #8, Corona Drive,
Los Alamos National Laboratory

Los Alamos County, 110 square miles of high desert country seven thousand feet above sea level, is bounded on the west by the Jemez Mountains and the east by the Rio Grande river valley. It consists mainly of a group of mesas, flat-topped archipelagos in the sky that are separated by canyons.

The city of Los Alamos sits on a mesa known locally as "the Hill." Its population of some eighteen thousand numbers more Ph.D.'s than any other locale on the face of the earth. South of the Hill lies South Mesa.

Below that lies South Mesa, site of the massive nuclear weapons research complex of Los Alamos National Laboratory.

Jack Bauer halted at Vehicle Access Portal number eight, an outpost of LANL's security perimeter. It stood at the west end of Corona Drive, the main east-west thoroughfare across the mesa.

South Mesa was not entirely barred to unauthorized personnel. Several roads that ran through it outside LANL's perimeter fences were open to the general public. But Corona Drive was restricted to lab personnel and others with the necessary security clearances.

VAP #8 was one of a number of gated guardhouse checkpoints controlling entrances and exits to the complex. Prominently displayed along the approach were signs proclaiming BADGE HOLDERS ONLY.

Jack's Expedition halted at the entryway. A blue-uniformed guard with a hip-holstered sidearm came out of the gatehouse to examine the newcomer's credentials.

LANL's unusual security profile is a product of its unique historical origins. Despite its vital importance to the nation's defense posture, it is not under the control of the military or federal government. Since World War II it has been owned and operated by the University of California, part of a multistate research and development contracting authority that also includes the Lawrence Livermore Lab. And yet paradoxically all of LANL's nuclear-related discoveries are legally the property of the Department of Energy.

Just as LANL is under civilian supervision, its security is provided by a private contractor, the SECTRO Corporation. The blue-uniformed guards patrolling and securing the site are known as the SECTRO Force.

The security protocol makes use of a two-phase identification system: a photo ID badge that must be prominently displayed at all times, and a matching smart card ID that is processed by badge reader access scanners at entrances to all restricted areas.

To carry out his assignment Jack Bauer had been temporarily issued the coveted blue badge and smart card denoting the Q-level, the highest security clearance rating and one that allowed him virtually unlimited on-site access.

A special dispensation permitted him to carry weapons and wireless devices throughout the facility, items that were generally prohibited to all but a privileged few. Considering the double killings of the last few hours, Jack felt a certain reassurance in having his gun near at hand.

Jack wore his photo ID badge on a lanyard around his neck. He took his smart card from his wallet and handed it to the guard.

The guard scrutinized the thumbnail portrait photo in the corner of the card, ensuring that it was in possession of its rightful owner. He swiped the card through a slot in the gatehouse scanner; it came up clean.

He returned the card to Jack. He gave the go-sign to his partner in the gatehouse, the other throwing the switch that raised a yellow-and-black striped pole gate to admit the tan SUV.

"You may proceed, sir," he said, waving Jack through.

"Thanks," Jack said.

He drove through the open gateway and went east along Corona Drive. The road was a straight line stretching across flat tableland whose bright blue sky was bare of clouds. The SUV's wheels churned up a thin white line of dust as they rolled across the pavement.

The surroundings took on some aspects of a sprawling, ultramodern industrial park. Both sides of the road were lined with extensive fenced-in tracts that enclosed assemblages of cubes and rectangles that were labs, office buildings, and power plants interlaced by a webwork of transmission grids.

As always when he came on-site, Jack was not a little awed by the world-historical importance of what its denizens referred to as "the Laboratory."

It had come into being during World War II as home to the Manhattan Project, the top secret crash program to develop an atomic bomb. The high desert was an ideal locale for the venture, combining seclusion, sparse population, and vast wastelands for testing purposes. The scientists who sought to harness the earthshaking power generated by splitting the atom into a bomb delivery system were tinkering with the basic stuff of Creation itself.

On July 16, 1945, at the nearby test site of Trinity, the first nuclear bomb was successfully detonated. New Mexico—"Land of Enchantment" according to its state motto—had become the crucible of the Atomic Age.

The great work continued with no less urgency today. Behind the facades of outwardly innocuous buildings, some of the keenest minds on the planet probed the outer limits of matter, energy, and space-time, ceaselessly laboring to keep America's high-tech arsenal ahead of the competition. Implements of destruction and deterrence whose greatest triumph would lie in their never having to be used for the purpose for which they were designed.

All part of an endless race where second place could so easily become last place. Or no place at all.

A mile and a half farther down the road brought Jack Bauer to Ironwood National Laboratory. INL: epicenter of the murder plague stalking Los Alamos.

The facility was on the north side of Corona Drive, set back a hundred yards or so from the roadside. A chain-link fence ten feet high and topped with several rolls of razor-sharp concertina wire marked the perimeter. There was plenty of room between Ironwood and its immediate neighbors to the right and left, as if it craved elbow room.

Jack turned left onto a two-lane road connecting with the main entrance. The entryway was anchored by a guarded gatehouse not unlike VAP #8. It, too, was manned by armed SECTRO Force guards.

Once more Jack had to stop and be identified. Again the blue-badged Q-clearance worked its magic. Presently he was passed through and drove onto the grounds.

A cluster of buildings sat on a low rise. The administrative building fronted south, a multistory cube with vertical white concrete ribbing and glazed yellow bricks. Behind and to the right of it stood a flat-roofed oblong structure that roughly resembled in size and shape a college gymnasium. It was virtually windowless except for some narrow slitlike windows set high up near the tops of its sides that might almost be mistaken for horizontal decorative bands. It housed the Laser Research Facility.

A parking lot containing about a hundred vehicles stood at the foot of the knoll. The area closest to the knoll was marked RESERVED. Some of the spaces were empty but Jack ignored them. Not even a Q-clearance could protect from the summary towing of any vehicle without the required VIP sticker that had the audacity to intrude on this privileged section.

He found a parking space in a distant corner of the lot. Dismounting from the Expedition, he pressed a button on the handheld remote that activated the SUV's protective electromagnetic sensory field.

It was a long, hot walk across broiling blacktop to the knoll. Jack detoured to the right to take a look at the reserved parking section. Rectangular plaques on metal stands identified which slot belonged to whom.

He noted with interest that the spaces reserved for Professor Nordquist, Dr. Carlson, Dr. Tennant, and Dr. Delgado were all occupied.

Four brilliant scientists who were linchpins of the Perseus Project.

All were of interest to Jack Bauer.

A wide stone staircase with low risers and wide treads slanted upward to the top of the knoll. Jack climbed it to the admin building. Automatic glass doors slid open at his approach, allowing entry into a marble-floored lobby. The doors closed behind him.

The transition from desert heat to the coolly air-conditioned interior was almost too abrupt. He could feel the sweat cooling on his flesh.

His footsteps on the marble floor echoed hollowly through the vaulting lobby space as he crossed to a SECTRO guard station to once more present his bona fides and be duly processed through.

Beyond the barrier in the great hall there was light pedestrian traffic, mostly staffers crossing from one room to another. Ironwood personnel generally wore comfortable, casual clothes. This reflected the lab's civilian origins with so many staff members coming from a university background. They found their comfort level in a campuslike environment.

The dress code was relaxed, informal—but badge display was rigorously enforced.

Jack's attire was more casual than most but not inappropriate. He, too, was wearing his working clothes; the gun under his arm was the hallmark of his calling.

He went into the Office of Counterintelligence security annex.

2:35 P.M. MDT
SCIF, Ironwood Administrative Building

The double kills had prodded Gabe McCoy into holding an emergency conference in the SCIF.

The Secure Compartmented Information Facility was

embedded in a basement level beneath the OCI annex. It looked like an undersized conference room in a modestly budgeted office.

The shoebox-shaped space was dominated by a rectangular table with some executive-type swivel chairs grouped around it. It had pale yellow walls and a green-and-black marble-patterned linoleum floor. The sole exception to the banal decor was the door. It was a vault door, armored and electronically secured.

The room was a vault. An extensive array of unseen hardware ensured that the spy-proofed SCIF was debugged and certifiably free of all electronic eavesdropping equipment. Ventilator grilles discharged a constant current of fresh, cool air into the hermetically sealed chamber.

Attending the meeting were Jack Bauer, Gabe McCoy, Debra Derr, and Orne Lewis. They sat around the table. "Everybody here knows everybody else so let's get down to business," Gabe McCoy said.

He was Acting Director of Ironwood's Office of Counterintelligence. He had a thin, foxy face and too-wise eyes. He looked distinctly unhappy. Jack wondered how much of that unhappiness was due to worry that recent events might adversely impact McCoy's chances of changing the "acting" part of his title to "permanent."

Debra Derr was McCoy's deputy. She was lean, leggy, and plain-faced, with shoulder-length brown hair parted in the middle.

Orne Lewis could be considered a colleague of Jack's, of a sort. He could be—but Jack was as yet unsure just what he considered him. Only time would tell.

Lewis was a CIA counterintelligence agent who served as a permanent liaison to LANL. His office was in a building in another part of the mesa; the ongoing crisis caused him to spend much of his working time at Ironwood. He was six-four, long-limbed, gangly, storklike. A patch of life-less iron-gray hair that looked fake but wasn't sat on his head. The nattiest one in the group, he wore a seersucker suit, bow tie, and tassel loafers.

Jack quickly brought the others up to speed on the poison needle incident and the murder of Peter Rhee. He made no mention of Annihilax. He was unauthorized to disseminate that intelligence to anyone else in the room and would con-tinue to withhold it until directed to do so by his superior officers at CTU.

Ironwood's OCI was a civilian operation that was part of SECTRO. Lewis was CIA but he had not been cleared for the information, either. Maybe he already knew it. He might even know more about it than Jack. It was possible . . . it was possible. Jack was CTU, CTU was part of CIA, and Lewis was CIA.

That's where compartmentalization came in. Nobody knew another's classified intelligence until there was a compelling reason to know. The system was clumsy but ef-ficient, like watertight compartments on a ship. If the ship takes on water, the compartments can prevent it from sink-ing to the bottom.

Jack reached the end of his summary. "The fat's in the fire now," Orne Lewis said.

"All OCI offices are secured, but we put a special guard on Rhee's when we learned about his death," McCoy said. "We're examining his files, appointment book, and com-puter entries to see if anything links to his murder."

"Find anything?" Jack asked.

"Too much. There's so much material there it's hard to know where to start. Raw data, yes. Interviews, profiles, facts, figures, a mountain of data. But no smoking gun. Nothing that says this is it, this is why he was killed."

Debra Derr looked Jack in the face, her eyes narrowed. "Why did Peter Rhee want to meet with you? I mean, why you and not any of the rest of us?"

Orne Lewis chuckled without mirth. "There's a question."

Jack shrugged. "He said that he had something important to tell me and he wanted to do it in private. Something about the case, but he wouldn't say what."

"Why Alkali Flats?" Derr pressed.

"He thought it was safe, I guess."

"Obviously he was mistaken," Lewis said.

McCoy harrumphed. "We're not going to get anywhere unless we all put our cards on the table, Bauer."

"I showed my hand."

"What about the card up your sleeve?" Lewis chimed in.

Jack ignored him, speaking directly to McCoy. "Rhee set the time and the place. I never even heard of Alkali Flats before this morning."

Lewis turned to the OCI chief. "Face the facts. Rhee was off the reservation. Whatever lead he was following, he didn't want to share it with any of us. Except Bauer."

"But why you, Jack? Why you?"

"Vince Sabito asked me the same question and I'll tell you what I told him: I don't know."

"You were the target of an assassination attempt today—again, why?"

"Same answer."

Gabe McCoy rolled his eyes. "You've been here less than two weeks and suddenly in one day we've got a murder and an attempted murder."

"And five suspicious deaths connected with this facility in the last six months," Jack countered. "There may be more to come."

That gave McCoy a start. "Eh? How's that?"

"Peter Rhee would have been here now if he hadn't been

killed. Anyone here could be marked for death. One of us or all of us."

"That's utterly fantastic—"

"I advise everyone to be extremely cautious of their safety from now on. Watch your back. Avoid dark, lonely places. Exercise extreme precautions."

"Shun secret meetings?" Orne Lewis suggested dryly.

"It couldn't hurt," Jack said.

Debra Derr put her hands palms-down on the table. "What about Harvey Kling?" she asked Jack.

Jack was caught off-guard. "What about him?"

"He's gone missing, too."

"I don't have him."

McCoy made a disgusted face. "Don't confuse the issue, Debra. You know Harvey. He comes in late on Saturdays when he comes in at all. Too busy sleeping off Friday night's session with the bottle."

"I know you're not a fan of his but the man is part of the office."

"Don't blame me—I had nothing to do with his hiring. That was Rhodes Morrow's doing. It was a pity hire. He felt sorry for the guy. Kling was one step short of being homeless, living in his car."

Jack leaned forward, interested. "Kling used to work for the Department of Energy, didn't he?" he asked McCoy. "He was a big man there."

"He was—DOE's top investigator. Until he botched the Sayeed case, and then they bounced him out of there like a bad check."

"Dr. Sayeed, Ironwood's own atom spy," Jack mused, thoughtful.

"That didn't happen on my watch. That was a long time ago," McCoy said quickly.

"Not so long. Four years back," Jack pointed out. "Just four."

McCoy looked defensive. "Seaton Hotchkiss was OCI chief then and Morrow was his deputy. Morrow had more sense in those days. He warned Hotchkiss that Kling's obsession about convicting Sayeed for spying was putting the case in jeopardy and Hotchkiss's job, too. He was right. The case collapsed and took down Hotchkiss and Kling both."

"Morrow must have changed his mind about him since. He hired Kling when no one else would," Lewis said.

McCoy gestured as though physically trying to brush the matter aside. "Morrow felt sorry for him. Put him to work doing routine background and security checks. Donkey work that even a dipsomaniacal gumshoe like Harvey couldn't screw up. It freed the rest of staff for more important stuff."

"If he's so bad, why don't you get rid of him?" Lewis challenged.

"Please. Do you know how hard it is to get a grossly incompetent employee fired, even in a department as sensitive as this? Damned near impossible. Everybody's got lawyers nowadays and the contracting authority is terrified of a lawsuit or some bad press."

Derr cleared her throat. "Don't give me that look, Debra. You know it's true," McCoy said. "Why do you think I've been keeping Kling frozen out of this investigation? He's not going to take me down like he did Hotchkiss."

Derr flashed a quick, embarrassed smile at Jack and Orne Lewis. "Pardon us for airing our dirty laundry in public."

"No apologies necessary. I'm quite enjoying it," Lewis said.

McCoy raised his hand palm-up, as if to signal that the subject was closed. "It's ancient history. Climb out of the time machine and come back to now." He made a chopping motion with the hand.

A long, awkward silence followed. Jack broke it. "Might

be a good idea to check up on Kling, make sure he's okay," he said.

"He's fine. You know the old saying about the Lord looking after drunks and fools? Kling's doubly blessed." McCoy's upper lip curled in a half sneer. "Take it from me—the only thing Harvey Kling is fit to investigate is a whiskey bottle. Curled up in the bottom of one is where you'll find him."

Jack kept looking at the other man.

"Still—I suppose it wouldn't hurt to follow up on him. All right, I'll have inquiries made when the meeting's over," McCoy said at last. "You're so concerned, Debra, you do the follow-up."

"I will."

"Fine. Now let's get back to business, the real business at hand. Where do we stand?"

"Sabito's got an FBI forensics team coming down from Santa Fe. The County Sheriff and his deputies are helping to secure the crime scene," Jack said.

McCoy groaned. "Oh god. Nothing Buck Bender likes better than seeing his name in the papers and his face on TV. This'll get splashed big and the mud'll spatter all over Ironwood." He squeezed the lower half of his face as if trying to massage some feeling into it.

Lewis made a placating gesture. "Sabito will keep this in check and keep the lid on it if anyone can. He knows how to ride herd on ol' Buck. Lord knows how he does it but he does, somehow."

"He's probably got something on him. That G-man's got files on everybody."

"Including you?"

"And you, Lewis!" McCoy fired back. "Mark my words, Bauer. You've only been here a short time but Sabito's probably already opened a file on you, too."

"I'm sure he has—I opened one on him. I don't pretend to be an expert on him but I can tell you this: He's not dumb. He knows how to get things done. We can use the Bureau's resources and depth of backfield. We're waiting on an ID of the killer maid at the motel, an analysis of the toxin on the needle, and the forensics report from the Rhee murder scene.

"The woman's photos are up on the CTU net and available for downloading. If you ID her let me know. For now I'd like to go to the lab and talk to Nordquist, Carlson, and a few of the others."

"Good luck," McCoy said.

"Is there a problem?" Jack asked.

"Those scientists are all prima donnas. Carlson talks only to Nordquist and Nordquist talks only to God, except maybe when he condescends to take a call from Livermore or the top brass at Kirtland."

"I'd like to talk to them anyway."

"Why?"

"To see if Rhee had recent contact with any of them."

"I suppose it can be arranged," McCoy said without enthusiasm.

"I'd also like an update on Kling, as soon as you have something."

"Debra will keep you posted. Anything else, Bauer?"

"If I need anything else I'll let you know."

"Any other items on the agenda? No? Lewis?"

The CIA man shook his head.

"This meeting is adjourned," McCoy said.

When the vault door cycled open Jack was the first out of the room.

. . . .

THE FOLLOWING TAKES PLACE
BETWEEN THE HOURS OF
3 P.M. AND 4 P.M.
MOUNTAIN DAYLIGHT TIME

. . . .

3:00 P.M. MDT
Laser Research Facility,
Ironwood National Laboratory

A long enclosed walkway connected the admin building with the Laser Research Facility. Jack Bauer and Orne Lewis followed it to the LRF.

Located off the northwest corner of admin, the lab occupied a separate structure of its own. It was the matrix where the Perseus Project was being born. Perseus was the legendary hero of Greek myth who slew the snake-haired Medusa, the monster whose gaze turned living beings into stone.

The lab had its own Medusa, one with a single ruby-red eye no less lethal than that of its fabulous counterpart. A laser cannon.

"You don't have to come along if you don't want to," Jack told Lewis.

"No, no, Jack. You can't get rid of me that easily. Now that you're around, things are happening. You're what they call a catalyst. An outside agent that speeds up the rate of chemical reactions."

Jack cut him a dubious side glance. "You've been hanging around the scientific crowd for too long, Lewis."

"I'll stick to you for a while then."

"Careful—it could be hazardous to your health."

Lewis wasn't buying. "You're doing fine so far. Two dead today and you're still vertical."

"I said your health, not mine."

"I'll take my chances, Jack. Besides, this is probably the safest place to be right now. All the killing's taking place out in the world, not on-site."

"Except Freda Romberg," Jack pointed out.

"I forgot about that one. I must have blanked it out of my mind." The corners of Lewis's eyes and mouth turned down.

"That was a ghastly thing. The poor woman looked like she'd been hit by a wrecking ball. Which in a sense she had. That robotic arm weighs a ton if it's an ounce.

"No need for an ambulance to take her away. Just a sanitation crew. What was left of her after the apparatus crushed her could have been scooped up with a shovel," Lewis said, his dark eyes glittering.

"Sentimental, aren't you." Jack's tone implied the opposite.

Lewis shrugged, unconcerned. "You know how you get in this business."

They halted at the far end of the walkway. A set of gray metal double doors barred further access to the LRF. A triangular yellow metal plaque was attached point-down to the center of the wall above the doors. It was blazoned with a bold graphic of a black starburst—the scientific world's universal symbol for laser.

A boxy console was attached at waist-height to the wall on the right of the doors.

Lewis swiped his Q-cleared blue badge smart card through a slot in the top of the console.

After a pause a pinging tone chimed. The doors slid open.

Jack could have followed Lewis through the portal but so-called piggybacking on another's badge to enter a restricted area was a security violation at LANL.

Jack was a great believer in proper procedures.

He swiped his badge through the slot, triggering a second *ping*.

He and Lewis entered a reception area, the auto-doors sliding shut behind them. "These badge access reader scanners will tell us if any of the Perseus cadre went off-site today," Lewis said.

Jack nodded. "We'll use that to verify their oral statements."

Similar scanners, hardened to a greater or lesser degree, were liberally salted throughout Ironwood. They controlled and documented all coming and going to restricted areas. Some merely required a swipe of the badge. Others required the input of a PIN number via a numerical keypad; the most tightly secured areas required a badge swipe, PIN, and biometric reading of the user's fingerprints.

"Personally I doubt whether any key personnel went off-site. Nordquist would strip the bark off any of his people who dared absent themselves during a test firing day. But I'll check it anyway."

"While you're at it you might check Peter Rhee's movements for this week," Jack said. It was a command couched in the form of a suggestion. "See if he visited the LRF anytime and if so, when. I'm interested in knowing what recent contacts he might have had with any of the top cadre, if any."

"Roger that."

"Check McCoy's and Derr's movements during the same time period. Especially today."

Lewis halted, raised an eyebrow. "What are you trying to say? Surely you don't suspect either of them of anything."

Jack's response was a thin, meaningless smile.

"Oh, so that's how it is. Everyone is suspect. I suppose you'll want a report on my movements, too," Lewis said.

"Don't bother."

"That's a relief—"

"I'll get it from McCoy. He'll be more objective."

Jack resumed walking and Lewis fell into step beside him. They crossed to the reception desk. The receptionist was an attractive brunette in a sleeveless yellow dress. Lewis nodded to her. "Hello, Betty."

"Good afternoon, Mr. Lewis." She had a big smile for both of them. It brightened noticeably when she turned it on Jack. She didn't know him yet, but her smile said she'd like to know him better.

"Did they do the test firing in the LRF yet?" Lewis asked.

Betty checked the time. "No, they're still running the pre-ignition countdown sequence right now." She picked up a phone. "I'll notify Dr. Nordquist of your arrival."

"That won't be necessary. I'm sure he's very busy. We don't want to trouble him."

Betty looked flustered. "But the doctor insists on all visitors being escorted—"

Lewis flashed his badge. "We're not just any visitors. And we've got the clearances to prove it."

Betty's evident distress deepened.

"Don't worry about the good doctor, I'll take full responsibility," he added.

"You know how he is."

"We all do, but we love him anyway."

Fretting, she sighed. "Okay, Mr. Lewis, I'm sure you know what you're doing."

"I don't know about that, but I'll tell Nordquist you did your best to protect the sanctity of his domain."

Behind and to the left of Betty's workstation was a closed door with a scanner box beside it. Lewis swiped his badge, triggering an electronic buzzing from somewhere in the door panel. A relay clicked, thudding into place, releasing a locking mechanism.

Lewis turned the doorknob, pushed the door open, and went through the doorway. The buzzing continued while the door was open. Jack swiped his badge and crossed the threshold. The door was weighted so it swung shut when Lewis released his hold on it.

A relay clicked, bolting the door and sealing it shut. The buzzing stopped.

Lewis grinned. "What'll you bet she's on the phone to Nordquist right now?"

"No bet," Jack said.

"Security regs are one thing but stroking Nordquist's hyper-developed territorial imperative is quite another." Lewis frowned, his grin dissolving.

A dozen paces along a blank corridor brought them to a set of swinging double doors. No scanning was required to pass them, only a stiff-armed push.

Beyond lay a short passageway; a left turn around the corner put them in a long, empty hallway. Centered in the long wall on the right-hand side was a pair of elevators.

Opposite them was a fire door.

"Let's take the stairs, it's quicker," Lewis said.

The door opened into a stairwell. Stairways slanted up and down the shaft.

Jack and Lewis went down four flights of stairs, exiting through another door into the vast, cavernous space of the LRF.

They emerged onto a mezzanine jutting from a long, high wall. The ceiling was sixty feet above; the floor thirty feet below. The interior echoed to a clangor of machine sounds, heavy pumps, engines, and power plants. It smelled of stone and steel, dust, fuel oil, and industrial chemicals, laced with a stimulating scent of ozone.

Rows of narrow slatted windows of treated glass set high in the walls shed a weak, milky, blurred glow. A skeletal metal framework hung suspended from the ceiling, supporting banks of floodlights and spotlights that fitfully lit the gloomy interior.

Jack crossed to the end of the mezzanine where a waist-high balustrade was topped by a tubular metal guardrail. Resting his hands on the top rail, he surveyed the scene.

Lewis stood beside him. "Welcome to the Snake Pit," he said. "Some researcher tagged it with the nickname and it stuck. But don't let Nordquist hear you call it that. The LRF is his baby and he's got no sense of humor about it, none at all."

They were in the building that looked like a college gym when seen from the parking lot. A gym big enough to hold an Olympic-sized swimming pool. Where the pool would have been was a second structure, a kind of building within a building: a flat-roofed concrete blockhouse forty feet high.

It bristled with spiky bunches of antennae and was hung with multilevel metal frame scaffolding, catwalks, and flights of stairs. Roof and walls were draped with various colored pipes and tubes that came together in tangled knots before branching off in different directions, only to rejoin later at other junctions.

Jack had had enough of the view. He and Lewis went to the right-hand end of the mezzanine and descended several flights of steeply slanted metal stairs to the main floor.

A figure approached, coming from the blockhouse. "It's Stannard," Jack said. "Let's keep quiet about Rhee's death for now. The scientists have enough on their minds. They'll hear about it soon enough."

Lewis nodded. "Good thinking. If the test flops, Nord-quist can't hang it on us for distracting his team at a crucial moment," he said. They spoke low-voiced so Stannard wouldn't hear them.

Dr. Don Stannard was the youngest member and most recent addition to Perseus's inner circle. He hadn't been there long enough to get a parking space in the reserved area.

He was thirty, looked like a college undergrad, and held a doctorate in several advanced branches of applied physics. Jack had met Stannard and the other key members of the Perseus cadre during an introductory meeting in an office in the admin building a week earlier. He greeted him now.

"Uh, hi." Stannard blinked, his eyes owlish behind thick-lensed glasses. "I was supposed to meet you in the reception area . . ."

"We saved you a trip," Jack said. "How's the test going?"

"Fine. We're going to be firing soon, in about fifteen minutes."

"If you don't mind my asking, why'd they send you out to meet us? I'd think your presence in the control room is vital."

Stannard grinned self-consciously. "My work on the pre-ignition sequence is done, so Dr. Nordquist decided he could spare me. I won't be needed again until the firing. I'm glad of the opportunity to stretch my legs; I've been cooped up in there since early morning."

"We won't delay your return. Let's go."

Stannard reversed direction and the three men crossed to the blockhouse. "You've never seen a firing?"

"No."

"Me neither," Lewis said.

"It's something to see," Stannard said.

"I'm looking forward to it," Jack said.

"You picked a good time to come. Uh . . . but why are you here, if I may ask. If it's not a state secret, ha-ha."

"Just following up on a few routine matters for our files. You can help out if you like. You know Peter Rhee."

Stannard looked blank.

"From OCI," Jack prompted.

"Oh. Yes, I know him. Not personally but professionally. In the line of business. Your business, that is, not mine. Though I guess security is all our business. Sure, I've met him a couple of times. Nice guy. He came around after Freda's terrible accident and interviewed all of her coworkers. And then he came around again after Director Morrow was killed."

"Was he around this week?"

"If he was, I didn't see him. That means nothing in itself—the LRF is a big place. When I'm working on some calculations, somebody could be in the same room and I wouldn't notice them. I get tunnel vision when I'm concentrating. He certainly didn't talk to me. No, I haven't seen him since last month when he came in about the Morrow matter. Is that of any help to you?"

"Just routine, thanks."

They paused at the near end of the blockhouse, at an entrance in one of the short walls. A SECTRO Force guard stood on duty at the door.

"Hello, Bruno."

"Hi, Mr. Lewis," the guard said.

"This is Jack Bauer. He's with me."

Stannard was allowed to breeze through; Lewis flashed his badge and got the nod from the guard. Bruno examined Jack's badge and passed him through.

A short elevator ride took the trio up to the second floor. They went to the control room. All, including Stannard, swiped their badge cards through the scanner before entering.

The control room was decidedly unglamorous. It was a big oblong room whose long walls paralleled the blockhouse's short walls. Not so different from the bullpen where computer analysts labored back at CTU/L.A., Jack decided.

Rows of computer consoles were occupied by about twenty scientists, board operators, and technicians. Flat-screen panels on the walls imaged various views of the blockhouse interior beyond these walls.

Men and women hunched over monitor screens and keyboards, exuding an air of quiet concentration. The percussive rattle of fingers inputting data on keyboards was counterpointed by the well-modulated voices of operators giving their readouts. The ambience suggested the humming efficiency of a beehive.

Perseus Project Director Dr. Glen Nordquist stood off to the side in conclave with Dr. Carlson and Dr. Tennant. Nordquist, fifty-something, looked older. An oversized cranium and bulging forehead topped a long, angular face marked by sharp eyes, a beaklike nose, and sharp pointed chin.

Dr. Hugh Carlson, Assistant Director and second-in-command, was ten years or so younger than his chief. Big, bluff, and hearty, he had wavy brown hair, bushy eyebrows, moist brown eyes with heavy bags under them, and a firm jawline.

Dr. Cheryl Tennant was in her mid-thirties, short, stocky, with short straight dark hair framing a square-shaped face.

There could be no doubt that Nordquist was in charge; he was the one holding a clipboard.

Tennant broke away to confer with a technician. Nordquist made a beeline for the three new entrants. "Hmph! About time you got back, Stannard. Take your station in the viewing module."

"Yes, sir." Stannard crossed to the opposite side of the room, opened a door, and went through it, closing the door behind him.

Nordquist scowled at Jack and Lewis. "You two picked a fine time to go sightseeing."

"Nice to see you again, too, Doctor," Lewis said dryly.

"We won't take up much of your time, Doctor. Just a few minutes," Jack said.

"I don't have a minute to spare. The pre-ignition countdown sequence has resumed and we fire in ten minutes."

"We'll wait."

"The real work starts after the firing. We'll all be very busy."

"Just one or two quick questions, won't take more than a minute."

"Oh, all right. But not now."

Carlson stepped in to smooth things out. "I'll see to these gentlemen, Doctor."

"Make it fast, Carlson." Nordquist stalked off. "Bah!"

Carlson smiled tolerantly at the back of Nordquist's cramped form scuttling away across the control room. He turned toward the two operatives. "The firing's in a few minutes. Perhaps you'd like to watch?"

"Very much so, if that's possible. As long as we're not imposing," Jack said.

"Not at all. Believe me, it's something to see."

"We'd like that very much, Doctor."

"Glad to have you. Let me get you squared away in the viewing module and you can ask your questions later." Carlson led the way, Jack and Lewis falling in behind him. They crossed the room, going through the same door Stannard had taken earlier.

The viewing module was a kind of cube-shaped booth extending from the control room like a flying bridge on a ship. Its floor was a platform jutting out in mid-air. The interior was a modest-sized space, smaller, more intimate than the control room. It was low-lit, with indirect overhead lighting.

The wall opposite the door was solid from floor to waist-height; above it was a rectangular window whose long sides were parallel to the floor. There were a half-dozen computer workstations, smaller and less elaborate than the control room's big boards. All were switched on, their monitor screens alive, but only two were occupied, one by Stannard and the other by Dr. Ray Delgado.

Delgado was round-faced, chunky, with dark hair cropped close to the skull and a thick mustache. He glanced up briefly when the newcomers entered, then returned his gaze to the screen.

Stannard nodded, lifting a hand in greeting.

"Have a look at this," Carlson said, indicating the window and walking toward it.

Jack and Lewis followed. The glass pane was several inches thick and glittered as the result of some glazing treatment.

"Behold the Medusa—and the shield," Carlson said, a rich note of paternal pride shading his voice.

The window overlooked the interior of the blockhouse. From there it could be seen that the structure had a sunken floor that dropped ten feet below the ground floor. The Snake Pit, then, was an actual pit.

The hangarlike space was lit by strategically placed overhead floodlights and spotlights. They formed flowing cones and pillars of light in the dusky brown gloom of the space.

The basic principle was that of a firing range. The weapon was the laser cannon, Medusa. At the far end of the blockhouse lay the target, a shiny globe on a stand. It looked like a metallic lollipop.

The laser gun was closer to the control viewing module. The main body of the unit—the lasing chamber itself—was contained in a cylindrical housing as big as a school bus. It was bolted to the floor. Extending from its opposite end was a telescoping barrel mounted on a kind of ball-and-socket arrangement permitting it to go up, down, and sideways, allowing for a fair degree of mobility.

Bunches of power cables were bundled together and plugged into sockets in different parts of the housing. They looked like giant black anacondas looping and curving across the floor to batten headfirst on to the laser cannon. Snake Pit, indeed!

The target was a half globe six feet across, mounted on a vertically upright floor stand. The shiny metal hemisphere was hollow, concave. It faced and was aligned with the muzzle of the laser gun. An intricate motorized framework, remotely operated, allowed for large and small adjustments of movement in the target.

Midway between target and gun and placed to the left of both stood a cranelike construction the size of a steam shovel. Its squat boxy base was bolted to the floor.

Its jointed body terminated in a pair of pincerlike grippers; each claw was three feet long. Their inner faces were corrugated like the jaws of a giant pair of pliers. They held a massive slab of gray metal plate that could have been used to armor a battleship and held it aloft in mid-air.

Behind and to one side of the arm and slab was a steel-reinforced concrete block ten feet high, fifteen feet wide, and three feet thick. Block and slab were aligned on a tangent with the target stand.

"You understand the basic concept?" Carlson asked.

"I think so—although what you regard as basic is probably way over my head," Jack said. "You're trying to develop laser-resistant alloys, to harden satellites against being blinded or destroyed by enemy lasers—ground-based or space-based."

Carlson nodded approvingly. "That's pretty much it. Not so much laser-resistant alloys, though, as laser-reflective."

"What's the difference?"

"Resistance means durability. The metal absorbs the beam and resists heat. Reflectivity minimizes absorption and bounces the beam off it. So it doesn't have to undergo the grueling punishment of exposure to the heat.

"Laser beams are shaped and guided by mirrors. Perscus binds a mirrorlike finish to the alloy to make a proper shield. The hero Perseus slew Medusa because he was armed by the gods with the Shield of Athena, a shield that was polished to mirror brightness. By looking into the mirrored shield, he was able to avoid Medusa's destructive gaze and cut off her head.

"Our shield features a mirrorlike surfacing to the alloy to reflect the beam. That's the actual Perseus process. Once it's perfected, we'll finish the exteriors of our satellites so they're impervious to enemy lasers. The technique can also be adapted to the optics, the most sensitive and vulnerable part of a satellite.

"You'll see it in action during the test. The laser beam will strike the shield. The shield reflects the beam. For our test, we've positioned the shield so that it reflects the beam at an angle, toward that metal slab. The slab is untreated by the Perseus method and absorbs the reflected beam and—well, you'll see what happens.

"You'll want to wear protective goggles for the viewing. There's plenty of extra pairs in the room. An extra safety precaution. The window glass has been treated by the process to harden it against any stray bursts of laser light, but the goggles are an extra fail-safe. Strictly precautionary."

"There's no danger of the beam running wild and bouncing back at us?" Lewis asked, uneasy.

"Certainly not!" Carlson sounded slightly offended, as if someone had made an off-color remark. He went on, a bit stiffly. "The positioning of the beam is minutely calibrated and computer controlled. In the unlikely event of the beam going off-target—and the odds against such a freak happen-stance are astronomical—a fail-safe device instantly shuts down the laser."

"Oh. That's reassuring."

Carlson glanced at the nearest monitor screen to check on the countdown. "Now if you'll excuse me, I have some last minute details to go over. I'll be back directly to join you for the viewing."

Jack looked appropriately appreciative. "Thanks, Doctor. I appreciate your taking the time and trouble to explain the system to a layman like me. It helps me do my job better."

Carlson brightened, hearty once more. "Then I'm doing my job. Now I really must run." He exited into the control room. Jack and Orne Lewis stood at the window looking out into the Snake Pit.

"You laid it on a little bit thick at the end, Jack."

"Just soothing his feelings after your crack about the laser running wild."

They spoke low-voiced, so no one else could hear them.

"Those giant metal claws—that's the robot arm that did for Freda Romberg?" Jack asked.

Lewis nodded, solemn-faced.

A few minutes later, Nordquist, Carlson, and Tennant filed into the viewing module. Already there were Stannard and Delgado, completing the Perseus Project's key cadre.

Jack and Lewis stood off to one side at the window, away from the scientists. All in the room had donned protective goggles.

The firing was preprogrammed; the actual operation of the ignition was being handled by the technicians in the control room. Lewis nudged Jack in the side with his elbow. "Hey, we're the only ones in here without a doctorate," he said.

"Quiet for the countdown!" Nordquist snapped.

Firing time was at hand. Rhythmic pulsations vented

from the laser chamber as it neared the peak of its charging cycle, creating a powerful vibrating buzz. The buzz rose to a higher pitch. Jack thought he could feel it rattling the fillings in his teeth.

Stannard remained seated, hunched over a monitor. "Give us the final count, Don," Carlson said, voice booming to be heard over the power-up's shrilling.

"Here it comes: "Five—four—three—two—one—LASER ON!"

Electronic shrieking was instantly supplanted by a low bass drone. The overhead lights in the pit flickered, dimming, deepening the target range gloom.

A spidery beam of red light formed an acute angle between the laser gun, the shield, and the gray metal slab. One instant it did not exist; the next it did.

The beam was thin but a rich ruby-red color, like fine old wine. It painted a line from the cannon muzzle to the center of the hollow hemisphere, and another from the half globe to the slab.

A few beats later, and—

The back of the slab began to glow a dull red. A small spot, a blemish no bigger than a man's hand. Each successive eye blink found the red spot growing in size and brightening in color.

In less than sixty seconds the armor plate glowed red like the heart of a furnace. The slab sweated drops of molten metal. The center of the red zone grew yellow, then white-hot. Its heart began flaking off, sputtering incandescence.

Now a thin red line connected the plate's center to the concrete backing block. The reflected laser beam had burned through armor plate.

The red beam suddenly winked out. It was there—then it was gone.

A fist-sized hole smoked and sizzled in the center of the slab.

The Perseus-treated target half globe was intact, its scintillate sheen untarnished. The test firing was over.

"Results: good," Nordquist said.

3:53 P.M. MDT
Lobby, Administrative Building,
Ironwood National Laboratory

Jack Bauer and Orne Lewis stood strategizing off to one side near the admin's front entrance.

The demonstration had made a profound impression on Jack. "Looks like Nordquist and his team are on to something. The Perseus process could be a game changer in the next generation of advanced war weapons. It's a secret that many would kill for, not once but often. Now I understand the high price in human lives that's already been paid for it," he said.

Lewis nodded, thoughtful. "You get used to the fantastic after you've been at the laboratory for a while. But this—this is big."

Jack shook his head as if to clear it. "Let's not lose sight of the basics. Despite the space war trappings, it's the munitions makers' age-old quest: one builds an artillery-proof armor plate, while the next builds a shell that can destroy that plate. Only instead of shells and plates, it's laser beams and mirrored shields.

"Our business is the same way. Despite the total surveillance environment of Ironwood, we wind up asking questions and getting answers. Some of them may even be truthful. But which ones?"

Lewis was glum. "We made the rounds and it looks like a washout, Jack. Nordquist, Carlson, Tennant, Delgado, and

Stannard—none of them had any recent contact with Peter Rhee."

"So they say."

"You don't believe them?"

Jack thought it over. "I don't believe or disbelieve any of them—yet. I wanted to question each of them separately before Rhee's death was made public to get them on the record before they had a chance to think it over and get their stories straight. Catch them on the wing. Now they've made their denials. None had any recent contact with Rhee. That's their story and they're stuck with it.

"Next, we cross-check their statements against the badge scanners' records of their movements in the building and against Rhee's movements for the same time period. Against daily entries in his operational log and appointment books. McCoy's OCI people can do the legwork of putting that information together.

"If the Perseus cadre's statements hold up, we move on to something else, knowing that we've eliminated that possibility. If we find out that one or more of them lied, we question them more intensively and hammer at the soft parts of their story until they crack."

"You know, Jack, if anyone has vital information, they might have a good reason for withholding it."

"Such as?"

"Staying alive."

"There's that," Jack conceded. "Rhee might have contacted one or more of them away from the laboratory in the outside world. We'll want to get hold of his phone records and theirs."

Lewis stroked his chin with the ball of his thumb. "That'll take a certain amount of finesse. There's privacy issues and legal technicalities involved."

Jack was unmoved. "There always are. Six kills and the

high stakes we're playing for trump all legalities. You've been working here for years, Lewis. I'm sure you know what buttons to press to get these things done with a maximum of speed and a minimum of fuss."

"Your confidence in my abilities is touching."

Jack allowed himself a small smile. "Getting the same information on McCoy and Derr might be more of a challenge."

Lewis was wary. "How am I supposed to do that?"

"Ask McCoy for them."

"Just ask him."

"That's right. It's his duty to cooperate in every way with this investigation. In a matter as vital as this, there's no such thing as a right to privacy. He'll have to be an open book. Once he's kicked in his own info, he's sure to kick in on his deputy, Derr."

Lewis took a deep breath, exhaled slowly. "You suspect OCI?"

Jack wouldn't be pinned down. "I don't suspect them or not suspect them. It's a matter of ruling out possibilities and winnowing out suspects."

"Suppose McCoy doesn't want to give?"

"Any initial reluctance is understandable, given human nature. Snoops don't like to be snooped on. That's what we are, professional snoops."

"Agreed."

Jack went on. "At first there's sure to be some pushback. That's only natural. If you have to lay down the law to make him comply, do so. If he still insists on withholding, that would send up a red flag. Then we zero in on him. One way or another, we will get that information. We're not here to make friends."

"That part of your mission is sure to be an unqualified success," Lewis said. "You say 'we' but you mean me."

"That's a matter of professional courtesy. You know these people, I don't. I figure it'd go easier coming from you than from me. Make me the villain, hang it all on me, say I'm putting the pressure on and you have to go along. Because it's true. If you don't have the stomach for it, I do.

"Take a look at what's left of Peter Rhee and then tell me the niceties shouldn't go out the window."

"I'll do it . . . I suppose you'll be asking McCoy for the same information about me."

Jack said nothing.

"There's my answer," Lewis said.

"McCoy will spill on you. That should incentivize you to dig up the dirt on him."

A figure came hurrying out of the Science Section, angling across the lobby toward the entrance. Nordquist.

Jack drew Lewis's attention to the scientist with a slight nod. They were off to one side of the great hall. Nordquist took no notice of them as he forged ahead.

The guards at the front station saw he was a badge holder; that's where their interest ended. They went back to what they were doing. It wasn't their job to track exiting badge holders.

Jack noted the gap in the total surveillance program: the guards check you coming but not going.

The scientist exited the building. Jack watched him go. "Nordquist was really moving—I wonder why?"

"Maybe someone offered him a hot deal on a slightly used death ray," Lewis said.

They exchanged glances, then as one started off in Nordquist's wake and followed him outside. Nordquist crossed the porticoed pavilion and descended the stone stairway.

Jack and Lewis paused at the pavilion's edge at the top of the stairs. They stood beside a square-faced pillar, in the welcome shade.

A Cadillac Escalade stood idling at the foot of the stairs. A top-of-the-line model, it looked rich, expensive. It was a silver metallic job with a pearl finish and sparkling front grille and decorative trim. Inside it were two women.

The one in the front passenger seat was thirtyish. She had an auburn pageboy hairstyle and a clean, chiseled profile. She saw Nordquist approaching and raised a hand in friendly greeting. Nordquist nodded grimly at her and went around to the driver's side of the vehicle.

The driver opened the door and stepped down to the pavement. She and Nordquist stood facing each other.

She was a tall, leggy platinum blond with a sensational figure. She wore a red blouse, skintight white jeans with a red belt, and red leather ankle boots with pointy toes and spiked heels. A white leather handbag dangled by loops from a forearm.

Her coiffure was elaborate yet artfully disarranged, its silvery tones contrasting with her deeply tanned skin. A pair of oversized sunglasses gave her face an insectlike appearance. Mantislike orbs. High-heeled boots and masses of platinum hair piled high atop her head made her six inches taller than Nordquist.

"Fancy piece of machinery. An expensive toy," Lewis said appreciatively. "So's the car," he added offhandedly, after a pause.

"Who's the driver?" asked Jack.

"Sylvia Nordquist. The Mrs. Dr. Nordquist, that is." Lewis's gaze was intent, avid.

"Attractive woman," Jack said.

"Gee, you think?" Lewis said sarcastically.

"No point in getting overheated about it."

"You're not human, Jack."

"Who's the other woman in the car?"

"That's Carlson's wife, Carrie. Like goes to like. The

Assistant Director's wife chums around with the Director's wife. Nice lady, that Carrie Carlson. Good-looking, and is she built! As hot as Sylvia but a lot lower-maintenance." Lewis smacked his lips.

"You could use some of that Perseus process yourself," Jack said.

Lewis was only half listening. "How so?"

"You're starting to burn."

They were too far away to hear what the husband and wife were saying. Nordquist was doing most of the talking. Lecturing, it seemed like. Whatever his message, Sylvia seemed impervious to it. He might as well have been talking into the wind, except there was no wind. Her beautiful masklike face was impassive, except to make a remark or two when the other paused for breath.

"Spouses can access South Mesa?" Jack asked.

"If they have ID badges they can," Lewis said. "A lot of them do, especially when their mates are as highly placed as Nordquist and Carlson."

"That seems like a hole in the security net."

"Security is the art of the possible, Jack. Make conditions too onerous for the personnel here and they'll find jobs elsewhere, ones that pay better with less discomfort. Issuing visitors' badges to spouses is a courtesy. It makes life easier for employees and their families. If one of them needs the car to go shopping or pick up the kids, they can drop their spouses off and pick them up after work as needed.

"But I'll tell you this. Her husband may head Perseus, but I guarantee that not even Sylvia Nordquist could get past the guard station in the lobby. The badge gets them on Corona Drive and in the parking lots but not in the buildings." As he spoke, Lewis's gaze remained fastened on the woman, not looking away.

Nordquist soon wound down, running out of energy.

Going from agitated to resentful. He dug a wallet out of his pants pocket, thumbed through it, and fished out what looked like a credit card.

Sylvia Nordquist extended a red-nailed hand palm-up to receive it. With a deft movement, she made the card disappear inside her handbag. She leaned forward and bent down to peck a kiss on her husband's bulging forehead and got back in the car.

The Escalade drove past him and headed out of the parking lot, rolling past the gate guards to turn right on Corona and drive away. Nordquist stood watching the machine disappear.

When it was gone he turned and trudged up the stairs, thoughtful, self-absorbed.

He took a cigarette holder from an inside breast pocket, took out a cigarette, placed it in the corner of his mouth. He fished around in various pockets looking for a lighter or a match, coming up empty. He still hadn't found one when he reached the top of the stairs.

His path took him past the two others; he glanced up, noticing them. Lewis reached out, a lighter in hand. "Light?"

"Please," Nordquist said curtly.

Lewis wielded the lighter, igniting the other's cigarette while Nordquist puffed away. Lewis shook out a cigarette from a pack, stuck it between his lips. He offered one to Jack, who declined with a shake of the head. Lewis set fire to the tip of the cigarette, took a drag, vented smoke.

Nordquist smoked in compulsive, joyless fashion, taking no evident pleasure in it. He began to slow down, taking more time between puffs. He looked up, eyes glittering deep in shadowed sockets, looking first Jack and then Lewis in the face.

A cynical, bitter twist came to his lips, to the corner of his mouth that didn't have a cigarette in it. "Either of you married men?" he asked.

"Yes," Jack said, not knowing where this was going.

Lewis shook his head. "I'm between ex-wives."

"I know I'm married. That's what my bank statement keeps telling me," Nordquist said. "My wife spends. She burns through money like Medusa goes through metal plate. I'm called away from the important postfiring debriefing for an emergency.

"Why? Because Sylvia is on yet another shopping spree and she discovers she's maxed out on her cards and needs to borrow one of mine. *Borrow*, perhaps, being an artless term because it implies an eventual repayment."

"It could be worse," Lewis said. "You should see what I pay in alimony."

Nordquist glanced down, noticing that the cigarette had burned down to near the tips of his fingertips. "Having attended to the important business of the day, I may now return to my casual and insignificant chores as Project Director, as Sylvia has made clear she regards them. From the exalted perspective of the eighteen months of community college she managed to complete before dropping out. Good afternoon, gentlemen." Nordquist went inside the building.

Lewis shook his head, bemused. "Wow, that is one bitter guy."

"They say Einstein couldn't get along with his wife," Jack said.

Lewis looked interested. "Is that true?"

"That's what I read."

Lewis stubbed out the cigarette against the side of the pillar and flicked away the butt. "Back to work. I'll go collect that information we talked about from McCoy."

"Good," Jack said.

"While I'm busy doing that and making friends, where will you be?"

"I'm going to Rhee's apartment in town. Maybe I'll turn

up something useful. Sometime sooner or later I'll have to stop by the Trail's End Motel, too."

"Why?"

"To pack my bag and check out. I need a new place to stay. Let me know if Harvey Kling surfaces," Jack added. He got in his car and drove away.

· ·

THE FOLLOWING TAKES PLACE
BETWEEN THE HOURS OF
4 P.M. AND 5 P.M.
MOUNTAIN DAYLIGHT TIME

· ·

4:15 P.M. MDT
Arroyo Coyote, Los Alamos Canyon

They came to kill. There were five of them. Five shooters.
They had to hike in to get the drop on their target. A target
that could shoot back.

Los Alamos Canyon runs east-west between the Hill
and South Mesa. In its extreme northwest lies Arroyo
Coyote, one of countless twisty ravines, gulches, and bar-
rancas branching off the main trunk of the canyon. It is
hard, harsh, unforgiving country. Sun-seared and forsaken.
Wasteland has its uses, though, especially for those who fre-
quent places shunned by more sociable folk.

The mouth of the arroyo opens on the canyon's north
wall. It is hard enough to access for those coming by the
main route from the south. The shooters came in from the
north, from the arroyo's tail end.

The pickup truck bucked and jostled as deep into the arroyo as it could go, lumbering and inexorable. When it could go no farther it was parked under a rocky overhang and quit by its riders. The shooters shouldered arms and ammo and continued the rest of the way on foot, threading the winding, narrow course in single file.

Quinto took the point. He had a wide face and coppery skin; long arms, a long torso, and short, muscular legs. He went bareheaded under the high desert sun, and if the heat bothered him there was no evidence of it in his expression or his quick, surefooted movements. His footfalls were shadow-silent.

He went on ahead of the others, scouting the blind corners of the arroyo, making sure the way was clear before signaling the others to proceed. Then he moved on ahead to the next turning, scouting out what lay around the next bend, and so on.

The others trudged on after. It was a long, wearying slog through a tortuous inferno. That was why the attack had a good chance of success—the defenders would hardly expect anyone to approach from the rear by the near impassable northern route.

The shooters had begun their trek at noon, the worst time of day to set out on a hike, but vital to their plan. Varrin wanted to be sure they would reach their target in plenty of time to get set up and in position before striking.

Varrin was the planner, organizer, and paymaster. While Quinto scouted up ahead, Varrin took the point for the rest of the file, the remaining three trailing after him.

Varrin was wedge-faced, thick-featured, and popeyed, with a broad, thick-limbed body and oversized hands and feet. He was armed with an M–16. A drab canvas pouch slung over his shoulder by a strap held extra ammo clips; a semi-automatic pistol was stuffed into a hip pocket.

Next in line was Diablo Cruz, lithe, quick, and agile. He had matte-black hair and long, slanted green eyes.

Varrin would have preferred that Cruz bring up the rear; Cruz was impatient and energetic and would have sparked the file's forward momentum. Cruz wanted to be where the action was and would have considered a tail posting a slight. He was quick to take offense, and though Varrin had no fear of him, it was easier to let Cruz follow in third place. Cruz was already out of sorts because of the new man—no sense in getting him any further riled up.

Besides, he was a good shot, and if unexpected trouble broke Varrin wanted him up front where his firepower could make a difference. Two pistols were holstered under Cruz's arms and another pair was worn on his hips.

Trailing Cruz was the new man, Lassiter. A special-ist. A big man, light on his feet, he was powerfully built, broad shouldered, deep-chested. He had short dark hair and a craggy, square-shaped face. A rifle was slung over his shoulder and a gun holstered under his arm.

Porky was the tail man. He was big, heavyset, loose-jointed, and sloppy. His face was round and soft but his body was strong, hard. He had a big gut but it was hard, too. A pump shotgun was slung across his back; a .357 Magnum was holstered on his hip. The heat was especially hard on him. He had a tendency to fall back, to straggle.

Varrin didn't obsess over it, as long as Porky remained in view. You worked with what you had on a job like this. Most gunmen are lazy; this Varrin knew. They don't like hard work; they'd rather take the risk of a quick, violent shoot-out for a fast payday than apply themselves steadily to an arduous task.

Most gunmen of his acquaintance—and he knew plenty, from all over the Southwest and beyond—were lay-abouts, content to laze around day and night, drinking, drugging, whoring, and getting into trouble. Most gunmen were lazy? Most crooks, period.

No, it wasn't so easy to line up shooters for a job like this, where they had to expend some energy humping down a steeply slanted trail in a boulder-strewn, brush-choked, burning, breathless hell of an arroyo.

Varrin was glad to have the men he had; it was a pretty good bunch all told. They didn't come cheap but then neither did he. It wasn't his money, so what the hell? He was getting paid well, too, enough to make it worth his while to honcho the job.

And the fireworks were about to begin.

Up ahead a couple of hundred feet or so, Quinto had paused, crouching at the foot of a rocky knob. An M–4 carbine was slung by a strap over one shoulder.

The knob was on the west side of the arroyo, part of a towering rock wall that thrust out in a high, domed hill. There was a notch at the top of the place where it joined the cliff wall. Beyond it the arroyo took a sudden turning that put it out of sight behind the massive outcropping.

Quinto was giving Varrin the high sign, pointing up at the knob, then gesturing for the others to come ahead.

Varrin acknowledged with a wave. He paused, waiting for the rest of the file to catch up. Cruz was close behind, and Lassiter, but Porky was about twenty yards back. Once they were all together, they headed out, moving down the right-hand side of the arroyo to join Quinto.

They were all covered with dust. Porky was sweating hard and the dust had turned to a kind of paste in patches on his face and neck, giving him a mottled look. Where bare skin showed he was red-faced. He panted for breath.

A fall of soft dirt and loose stones skirted the base of the knob. It was yellow streaked with brown and gray, like the knob and the rest of the arroyo. A scattering of brown boulders studded the sandy fall; Quinto hunkered down with his back against the rock, facing his companions. "The shed's on the other side of the knob," he said.

"What about Torreon? He there?" Cruz asked, leaning forward, green eyes glittering. They spoke in low voices.

"I don't know. I couldn't get close enough to see. They got a spotter on the other side of the knob."

"He see you?" Varrin asked.

"Hell, no," Quinto said.

"Just the one?"

"As far as I could see. He was looking south, down toward the other end of the arroyo."

Varrin chuckled throatily. "That's how any sensible person would come by. Only a bunch of damned fools would have come in the way we did, sneaking through by the ass end. That's why it's gone work."

Cruz pushed forward, hot-eyed, intense. "What about Blanco's truck? Big-ass purple F4 with gold trim. You can see that mother from a mile off."

"All their vehicles must be parked in front of the shed. I couldn't take a look without showing myself to the spotter," Quinto said.

"I'll look—"

Varrin broke in. "The hell you will. You'll stick with the rest of us until I give the word to move out."

"You're the boss," Cruz said, after a pause.

"Damned right." Varrin's voice was a parched, dry croak. Not because of the heat and the dust. He always sounded that way. "I got a good tip Blanco is gonna be here. If he is, so much the better. If not, we still got a job to do, taking out the meth lab. Tell me more about that spotter, Quinto."

"He's on a cliff next to the knob. On a ledge about two-thirds of the way up."

"Alone?"

"I reckon."

"Damn it, is he alone or not?"

"Don't know for sure. When I saw him I ducked out of sight before he could see me. Maybe he's alone, maybe not."

"If you don't know a thing, say so. Don't dick around. See anyone else? Anyone patrolling the grounds?"

"No. But from where I was I could only see the back of the shed."

"Okay." Varrin turned to Lassiter. "That spotter is your bit."

Lassiter nodded. "I'll take the high ground. Climb up in back of him, take him out. That ledge he's on should make a good sniper's nest."

"Sounds good, if you can hack the climb."

"Can do."

That was what Varrin liked to hear. "It's your play. When the lookout is quashed, give us the sign and we'll move in. Stay up there and wait till we're in position. Once we cut loose on 'em, pick off any others we flush out."

"Soft job," Cruz said, sneering.

"Shut up," Varrin said without heat. "You know what Torreon Blanco looks like?" he asked Lassiter.

"I do from the photos you showed me. I guess I could pick him out from a crowd."

"Pick him off and you pick up a nice fat bonus. But wait until we open up first."

Cruz was restless, agitated. "You're gonna have to beat me to the target, hombre."

Lassiter cut a glance at him, his stony expression unchanged.

"That five-thousand-dollar bonus is gonna be mine," Cruz pressed.

"Pass me that canteen, Varrin," Lassiter said.

Varrin unslung a quart canteen worn in an olive drab carrier slung over his shoulder and handed it over. Lassiter unscrewed the top, pinching a fold of his shirt and using it to wipe the spout. He sipped some water, swirling it around in his mouth before swallowing it. He screwed the top back on and returned the canteen to Varrin.

"I'll get to it, then," he said, standing up. He adjusted the rifle strap so the weapon was slung across his back. He made sure his short-billed forager's cap was pulled down tightly on his head.

He picked his way between the boulders and climbed the fan of loose dirt skirting the knob. He had a light tread and didn't kick up much dust. At the top of the fan he planted a foot on solid rock and stepped up onto a shelf. The craggy knob afforded many footholds and walkways.

Lassiter switchbacked his way up the rock face. It was like climbing a giant pile of dusty building blocks. Several times he had to hook his hands over an edge and pull himself up to the next level.

Varrin, Cruz, and Quinto watched the ascent, heads tilting back as Lassiter scaled the knob. Porky stayed where he was, sitting on the ground with his back against a big rock and his legs spread wide. "Climbs like a freaking lizard," Quinto said.

"He's in a hurry to get out of the line of fire before the shooting starts," Cruz said. "Why bring a newbie on this job, Varrin?"

"He ain't no newbie. Lassiter's got a rep throughout the Southwest and into Mexico, too."

"I never heard of him."

"That makes it even-up. He never heard of you."

"He's gonna know me, if I take a notion to knocking him off his high horse."

"Save your fight for where it pays. You boys don't get a penny for shooting each other."

"He knows guns," Quinto said. "I watched him back at the ranch when he was sighting in that rifle and scope. Hit the target dead-center in the black, every shot."

"Shooting a live man's different from a paper target," Cruz scoffed. What does he think he's gonna do with that popgun? A little .22—that's a kid's toy!"

Quinto shook his head. "That's a target match model. High-velocity hollow point rounds and he knows how to place 'em."

"From where I sit that bonus on Blanco is still anyone's game."

"If Torreon's there he won't be alone. He never goes anywhere without his bodyguard, Stan Rull. Think you can take him?"

"Just watch me."

"Rull's a dead shot."

"They can carve that on his tombstone."

Porky's feet were turned toes-up. Varrin kicked the sole of one of Porky's shoes. "You're looking a mite peaked, boy."

"This is more walking than I've done all month. All year. Fighting ain't nothing, but the hike is killing me."

Cruz snickered. "Do you some good, Porky. Melt some of that lard off'n your fat ass."

"Gimme that canteen, Varrin," Porky said.

"Nope. You'll get all swole up and it'll slow you down."

"Come on—"

"Bad for you if you get gut shot."

Porky looked at him incredulously. "I get gut shot, a drink of water ain't gonna make a difference!"

"A small one, then." Varrin gave him the canteen. Porky uncapped it, took hold of it in both hands, raised the spout to his mouth, and started gulping. Varrin, hovering over him, was quick to take the canteen away. "That's enough."

"Lassiter's at the top," Quinto announced.

Lassiter stood on a shelf about ten feet below the knob's summit, using the knob for cover to avoid skylining. He was to the left of the notch where the knob joined the cliff wall, more or less level with the bottom of the notch. He unslung the rifle and held it level in one hand. He ducked through the notch and out of sight.

Time passed. Five, ten minutes.

"Nothing," Cruz said. "You bought a pig in a poke, Varrin."

"It ain't your money and none of your damned business, neither—"

Quinto pointed upward. "There he is!"

Lassiter showed himself in the notch, waved an arm above his head. Varrin waved back. Lassiter withdrew, disappearing somewhere on the far side of the notch. "Let's get to it," Varrin said.

Quinto and Cruz started checking their weapons. Porky hadn't moved from where he was sitting. "I didn't hear no shots," he said.

"You ain't supposed to. Lassiter's got a silencer," Varrin said. "Get it in gear, Porky. Time to start earning your pay."

Porky hoisted himself to his feet, groaning.

"I wish I had a silencer for your big fat mouth. Christ, why don't you just call 'em up at the shed and tell 'em we're coming," Varrin complained.

"Sorry."

"Dumb ass," Cruz said.

Varrin turned to Cruz. "Do your job and don't worry about his. You and Quinto circle around the right to the front of the shed. Me and Porky'll come in from the left."

4:37 P.M. MDT
Arroyo Coyote, Los Alamos Canyon

Beyond the knob the arroyo opened into a wide oval space, like the bulge an ostrich egg makes when swallowed whole by a python. At the south end of the oval the rock walls narrowed once more, becoming a twisty gorge.

The shed was long and narrow, a one-story wooden frame structure. It nestled at the base of a rocky cliff, its long-sided front facing south.

It had been built back in the 1960s by some idealistic squatters trying to found a back-to-nature commune. A single summer in the desert had been enough to send the communards back to the city. It was pieced together from found and stolen pieces of wood; planks, boards, and beams of different sizes and shapes were cobbled together into patchwork, crazy-quilt construction. Its flat roof was made of corrugated tin, now badly rusted.

It was currently under new management. Holes in the roof and sides were patched with squares of blue plastic painter's drop cloths. The fresh scents of sage, yucca, and aloe plants were replaced by a strong chemical reek. A pile of empty fifty-gallon drums lay heaped on the east side of the oval.

A handful of vehicles were parked in on the sandy flat in front of the shed. There was a dark green panel van, three motorcycles, and a dune buggy. A shiny new Ford F4 pickup truck stood by itself, apart from the others. It was purple with gold trim.

"Blanco's truck," Porky whispered, excited. He was motionless but breathing hard. He and Varrin were kneeling behind the pile of fifty-gallon drums, using them for cover. Keeping it between them and the shed.

The drums on the bottom level were full; the next layer or two stacked above them were empty. An industrial-strength miasma of chemical fumes hung over them, causing the eye to tear and irritating the insides of nose and throat. Varrin and Porky had worked their way down the arroyo to this place of concealment twenty-five yards from the shed's southeast corner.

The shed's front windows were bare of glass panes. Some were empty, open to the elements; others were covered by translucent plastic sheets. The door was missing; the door frame gaped open. The interior was alive with sound and motion. Shadowy forms crossed back and forth in front of the windows. Raucous bursts of talking, laughter, loud voices came from within.

Varrin gave Porky a hard look. "Hesh up. You're whoofin' and snortin' like a stuck pig."

"I can't breathe! What's in these drums?" Porky asked.

"Chemical waste from cooking up the meth, most likely."

"Gawd!" Porky rose on one knee, peering through a space in the stacked metal drums. He gave a sudden start, ducking down. "Uh-oh! Up on the cliff—I don't think he saw me—"

Varrin took a peek. A figure stood on a ledge on the rock wall seventy-five feet above the ground. "That's Lassiter, you damned fool," he told Porky.

"He didn't have no cowboy hat and this one does—"

"Must have took it off the spotter. He's showing hisself so the gang won't get suspicious if anybody looks up."

Porky scratched his head and ass, in that order. "How does Blanco get away with it, running a meth lab out in the open like this?"

Varrin had the easy disdain one in the know reserves for those in the dark. "He don't run it, Speedy Barnes does. He pays Blanco to stay in business. That's why Blanco's out here today. It's Saturday, time for the weekly rake-off.

"Nobody comes to Arroyo Coyote unless they got business here. Elsewise, they don't leave."

A loud shout sounded from inside the shed; a shot followed. More shouts, more shots. Handguns popped; machine guns stuttered.

Porky's eyes glittered. His mouth hung slackly open; he breathed through it. He shouldered his shotgun and pointed it at the shed. Varrin clamped a hand on the other's shoulder. "Not yet—wait."

"They must have seen Quinto and Cruz. Sounds like they're having a hot time of it—"

Someone screamed in agony.

"They're getting paid," Varrin said.

Two men ran out the front doorway. A burly man with long hair and a beard, holding a Thompson submachine gun. He was followed by a skull-faced bald man in dark glasses with gun in hand; a thin, skeletal figure.

Varrin released Porky's shoulder to bring his own weapon into play. "Now!"

The hairy man was first out the door but the skeleton put on a burst of speed and passed him, running into the first burst of autofire from Varrin's M–16. He folded, flopping to the ground. The hairy man tripped over him and fell, dropping the Thompson.

A third man ran out of a door on the east side of the shed. Porky cut loose, felling him with a shotgun blast.

The hairy man slithered across the ground, groping for the Thompson. Varrin squeezed off a burst, stitching him in the back.

A small explosion detonated in the shed. There was a crumpling sound. The walls swelled outward; the tin roof rippled.

This was only the precursor to a much larger blast. Yellow light flared inside the shed. Hissing white smoke clouds poured through the windows and door. There was a sharp cracking sound like the snap of a whip. Yellow glare turned red, filling the shed.

A man dove headfirst out a front window, rolling when he hit the ground. He got his feet under him, jumped up, and started running away from the building.

Torreon Blanco.

Varrin drew a bead on him; it was an easy shot. His finger curled to squeeze the trigger—

The shed blew. Rather, the volatile chemicals used for cooking up the meth blew.

The building's outer shell disintegrated. In its place: fire, noise, heat, and smoke. Black smoke and white smoke.

The ground shook. The shockwave knocked Varrin and Porky off their feet, sending a pile of fifty-gallon drums crashing down on them. The metal containers were mostly empty but still gave the two a tremendous walloping.

Varrin, stunned, was dimly aware of what sounded like a hailstorm, an ungodly racket. It was the debris of what had once been the shed, blown sky-high by the blast and now falling back to earth. He squirmed and wriggled, crawling out from under a pile of drums.

Fresh bursts of gunfire focused his attention. An engine thrummed, roaring into life. Varrin broke free of the drums. His hands were empty and he couldn't find his M–16. A gash across his forehead leaked blood into his eyes; he pawed at them to clear them.

A purple and gold F4 pickup truck zoomed past him heading south. Hunched over the wheel, scrunched up to present a minimal target, was Torreon Blanco. On the passenger side the door was open and Stan Rull hung half in, half out of the cab. Facing backward, he fired his gun in the direction where the shed had been and a hissing, sputtering, spewing ruin remained.

A figure emerged from the smoke, staggering after the truck, guns blazing in both hands, throwing lead at the pickup truck and not even coming close: Diablo Cruz.

Stan Rull returned fire; he missed, too.

Varrin remembered the pistol in his pocket. He hauled it out and started shooting at the fleeing pickup. It was already out of effective pistol range.

Its wheels churning up plumes of sand, the F4 slithered, slipped, and slid toward escape. The machine fishtailed, hit a bump that caused the wheels to lose contact with the ground for an instant, nearly shaking Stan Rull loose from his grip on the door frame. He held on.

Torreon Blanco got the pickup under control. It exited the oval, plunging south down a twisty gorge and away.

Cruz saw Varrin and pointed his guns at him. Varrin's gun was leveled on Cruz. "Shoot me and you won't get the rest of your money," he said.

Cruz wiped the back of his hand against his forehead. Some of the craziness went out of his eyes. He holstered his pistols butt-out under his arms. "I didn't know it was you at first, Varrin."

"You were looking a little kill-happy. Feel better now?"

"Yeah."

Varrin lowered his gun. Empty metal drums rattled, booming hollowly as they banged into one another. Porky crawled out from under them, one hand clutching the shotgun.

He was coughing, choking. He had taken a beating. His face was black and blue; one eye was almost swollen shut. His bare arms were covered with cuts and bruises. "You okay?" Varrin asked.

"No," Porky said through cracked split lips.

"Quit dogging it; you ain't hit and nothing's broken."

Porky loosed a string of obscenities. He hauled himself to his feet. He was wobbly, reeling.

"What happened?" Varrin asked Cruz.

"Quinto and me were sneaking around the back of the shed. When we rounded the corner, a guy stepped outside for a smoke. I burned him down. Barnes and his crew opened up. They had me pinned down behind some rocks."

"Quinto?"

"He ran into machine-gun fire."

"Dead?"

"Completely."

"Then what?"

"A hot round must have tagged the chemicals. There was a small explosion but they didn't all go up at once. The shed caught fire. Stan Rull laid down covering fire and he and Blanco got out of the building. The heat touched off the main store of chemicals and then there was a big blow."

"And Lassiter? What about him?"

"Over here," a voice called. They turned toward it. Lassiter stood between them and the smoking ruin where the shed had been. His forager's cap was turned right-side around on his head. The rifle was slung over a shoulder and his gun was held at his side. He looked clean, untouched. He crossed to them.

"Where the hell were you?" Cruz demanded.

"Climbing down from the ledge. You could break your neck on the goat path if you don't watch your step," Lassiter said. He was cold, unemotional, and phlegmatic.

Cruz spat. "Fat lot of good you did!"

"The biker-looking dude with the long red beard that was shooting a machine gun at you—his head didn't come apart because he sneezed."

Varrin was excited. "Biker with a long red beard—that's Speedy Barnes."

"I don't know him from Adam. But he wasn't Santa Claus."

"He was honcho of the meth lab. A sweet score!"

"If you believe it," Cruz said.

"He leaned too far out of the window trying to get a bead on you in the rocks so I potted him," Lassiter said.

"Prove it."

"I've got nothing to prove to you, sonny. But to keep the record straight, you can check if you've a mind to. He got blown out of the shack when it blew up. The body's pretty badly burned but most of the head is intact except where my round blew the top of his skull off. You won't find any bullet because the hollow points shatter on impact, but I guess you could find a few fragments in his cranium if you want to dig them out."

Cruz sniffed. "I got better things to do than go picking over corpses."

"We believe you, Lassiter," Varrin said.

"Speak for yourself."

"Shut up, Cruz. This is no time for bickering. We got to haul ass out of here."

"Now you're talking," Porky said, his voice quavering. "That smoke can be seen from a long way off. It's the dry season and the firewatchers will be looking for something like that."

The blast had spewed flaming debris far and wide. Some had fallen into the dry brush that choked the rocks bordering the shed. Dry brush and weeds, kindling ready to go up at the first touch of flame.

Varrin eyed the blaze. "The brush is burning like a bastard! We better vamoose before it spreads and cuts off our escape."

Lassiter turned, went to the vehicles parked in front of the shed. The blast had tumbled the motorcycles and overturned the dune buggy but the green panel van was upright and intact. The others followed to see what Lassiter was doing. They grouped around the van, facing the corpses littering the landscape and the smoldering crater that had been the meth lab.

Varrin nodded approvingly, grinning at the carnage. "Nice work, boys. We got everybody but Blanco and Stan Rull."

"What happened, hotshot? How come you missed Blanco?" Cruz demanded.

"I can't hit what I can't see. When that meth lab blew up

it laid down a smokescreen for him," Lassiter said. His attention was on the van. The cab was unlocked, its windows rolled down. He opened the driver's side door and peered inside.

"No keys. I haven't hot-wired since I was a kid," Cruz said.

Lassiter unslung his rifle, leaning it butt-down against the side of the van. He raised his gun, reached into the cab, and shot the ignition lock on the steering column. The unexpected move made the others jump. "Hot damn!" Porky cried out.

Lassiter holstered the gun and took a folding knife from his pocket, opening the blade. He slid in behind the wheel. The ignition lock was bent, twisted, hanging mostly off the column. He used the knife blade to pry it out of the way.

Removing the lock exposed the cavity in the column; inside was a bundle of wires with different colored insulation. Lassiter selected two different colored wires and stripped the insulation off their tips, exposing several inches of copper wire on each tip. He touched the exposed wires together, generating sparks. He worked the gas pedal at the same time.

The contact triggered the starter and the engine coughed, shuddered, turned over.

Lassiter tromped the pedal, giving it the gas. The engine roared into life. "All right!" Porky said.

Lassiter played the pedal to keep the engine idling high. "Why walk when you can ride? This beats humping it back on foot north up the arroyo."

"I don't know if I could make it again."

"You would if you had to, Porky."

"Yeah, Varrin, but now I don't have to."

"Varrin, get my rifle."

"Okay, Lassiter." Varrin picked up the .22. He held it in one hand and the M–16 in the other. He went around the front of the van and got in the passenger seat. He stood the rifles butt-down on the floor and held them by the barrels, out of the way.

"Where am I gonna ride?" Cruz said.

Lassiter laughed. "In the back, out of sight—where you belong."

Cruz colored, green eyes narrowing. "You and me are gonna tangle before too long, big man."

With one smooth, fluid motion Lassiter drew his gun and leveled it at Cruz's middle. "Why wait?" he asked. He said it easily, without rancor, as if he was just making conversation.

Porky edged away from Cruz. He moved with exacting slowness, not making any sudden moves while he was in the potential line of fire.

Cruz froze. His eyes bulged, gaze flicking from Lassiter's face to the gun bore and back again, fastening finally on the gun, unable to take his eyes off it.

"One more body out here won't make a good damn's worth of difference."

"Easy, Lassiter," Varrin said softly, guardedly.

Cruz tried to bluster it out. "Ain't you gonna give me a chance—for a fair draw?"

Lassiter said, "Be serious."

Varrin forced a laugh, weak and unconvincing. "Remember, you don't get paid for shooting one of our own."

"It's not always about money with me. Gun punks like this are a dime for ten dozen. He'll be easy to replace."

"I'd purely appreciate it if you wouldn't, Lassiter. Makes my job harder when our boys start killing each other off. It's bad for morale."

Lassiter thought it over. "As a personal favor," Varrin pressed.

"I should let it slide so Diablito can back-shoot me first chance he gets?" Lassiter asked.

"He won't. Look at him. He's tamed."

Cruz was bathed in cold sweat. Shivering. Varrin prompted, "You was just running your mouth as usual, Cruz. You didn't mean nothing by it."

"That's right—I was just funning. You know how I am. Just pulling the man's chain, nothing personal," Cruz forced out the words.

"Pull my chain and you're the one who'll get flushed."

"No, sir, I won't do that. I learned my lesson."

"The next time you get in my face I'll shoot yours off. Savvy?"

Cruz convulsively bobbed his head, nodding.

"Get in the back of the van, Cruz. You too, Porky."

"You don't have to tell me twice, Varrin. That fire is getting hot!" Porky said. He circled around behind Cruz's back, giving him a wide berth. He quick-timed it to the back of the van, threw open the rear door, and climbed inside.

Cruz remained in place, motionless. "Okay if I go?"

"Yeah," Lassiter said. "You've got four guns, Cruz. Reach for one and see what happens."

"I won't."

"If he does I'll shoot him myself," Varrin said.

"Go on, get," Lassiter said. Cruz walked stiff-legged to the back of the van and got in, closing the door behind him.

Varrin let out a long-held breath. "Obliged, Lassiter. I didn't fancy having to explain to my principal that I couldn't keep my team from killing each other.

"Of course, what you do on your own time is your business," he added.

A pall of smoke drifted across the van. It was largely wood smoke; the brush fire now ringed the rear of the oval with a wall of fast-growing flame. Heat wafted over them.

Lassiter threw the van in gear and drove south across the oval, plunging into the highballed narrow gorge that led out of the canyon.

"That's one meth lab that's out of business and won't be filling the Blanco till with payoff money," Varrin said. He had to shout to be heard over the bucking and jostling of the van as it threaded the dirt-floored track down its twisty course. "The gang will take a big hit to its credibility. After all, that's what those crank cookers were paying off for—protection—and Blanco and his bitch sister couldn't deliver."

"Sister?" Lassiter echoed.

"Marta Blanco. She and Torreon are partners. She does the bookkeeping—and most of the brain work, according to rumor."

"How much is she worth dead?"

"Forget it. Scratch Torreon and she's nothing. That five-thousand-dollar bounty on his head still stands, though. Probably go up after today. Interested?"

"Sure," Lassiter said.

· ·

THE FOLLOWING TAKES PLACE
BETWEEN THE HOURS OF
5 P.M. AND 6 P.M.
MOUNTAIN DAYLIGHT TIME

· ·

5:12 P.M. MDT
Highway 5, Los Alamos County

Jack Bauer drove north from South Mesa toward the Hill.
Destination: Peter Rhee's apartment.

A call came in on his cell phone. The cell was plugged
into the Expedition's digital media station. He took the call
on the speakerphone, leaving his hands free for driving.

"Bert Leeds here," the caller said. Leeds was SAC CTU/
ELP, head of the El Paso branch. "I've got a make on your
homicidal room maid. Hold on to your hat—it's a wild one."

"Fire away," Jack said.

"She's been positively identified as Helen Veitch." Leeds
pronounced Veitch so that it rhymed with *leech*.

"Doesn't ring a bell."

"I'm not surprised. She's from outside your usual

bailiwick—way out. A real rarity: one of the few documented female serial killers." Leeds sounded upbeat, en-
thusiastic; the enthusiasm of the hard-bitten, seen-it-all
professional who's surprised by something fresh and new.

"You getting this, Jack?" he said, after a pause.

"Just wrapping my head around it. Tell me more."

"Helen Veitch is—was—a classic Black Widow type. A
sadistic sociopath turned killer for hire. She used to be a
psychiatric nurse in a hospital for the criminally insane—
fitting, no? She started by killing for kicks, eliminating patients in the nursing homes and hospices where she worked.
She had to keep on the move—her patients kept dying on
her. Thirteen deaths have been definitely traced to her, with
suspicions in eight more, and the toll could be higher. A
nurse or doctor can get away with murder for a long time.

"By the time the authorities got on to her, it was too late.
She'd gone underground. Where she learned she could get
paid, and paid well, for doing what came naturally to her:
killing. Her specialty is sharp pointed instruments: hypo-
dermic needles, knives, scalpels, and whatnot."

"I know," Jack said tersely.

"I guess you would," Leeds said. "Helen was known in
the trade as the ideal private nurse or companion for that el-
derly rich relative who's left you everything in the will but is
too inconsiderate to drop dead. Not your usual international
terrorist or assassin, that's for sure."

"Which is why it almost worked."

"She's the type nobody notices while the body count
keeps climbing," Leeds agreed.

"That was fast work, Bert. Thanks. How'd you tag her?"
Jack asked.

"The first hit came up on an old Army Criminal Investigation Division file. Helen was fingerprinted years ago when
she went to work at a veterans' home for the aged in Cleve-

land, Ohio. The CID file was linked to a big fat dossier on the civilian law enforcement National Crime Identification System. The NCIS net had cases and sightings mostly in the Midwest and more recently in the Southwest. The complete file's available for downloading when you want it. Quite a story. Nice bedtime reading."

"Any international connections in her background?"

"None that I can see. It's not in her modus operandi. Helen was a real home girl. Never been outside the States, not even to Mexico or Canada, as far as we know. Nonpolitical, too. Not an ideological bone in her body. A purist: she was in it for the sport. The money, too, but the psychological profile says that was a secondary motivation. Almost an afterthought. Killing is how she got her kicks. Funny that she should turn up in your investigation, Jack."

"Hysterical. I almost died laughing."

"It's nice to know that with all the American jobs being shipped overseas these days, someone is still relying on good homegrown talent."

"Someone—who?"

"You tell me."

"I will, when I find out," Jack said. Leeds wished him luck, signed off, and broke the connection.

Jack stepped down harder on the accelerator, speeding the SUV north. A hazy gray curtain was rising out of the canyon between South Mesa and the Hill. Smoke, an inverted mountain of it, piling up into the heights. Helicopters and small propeller planes circled around the edges of it.

Must be a fire, Jack thought.

5:27 P.M. MDT
Ponderosa Pines Condos, Los Alamos County

Someone was in Peter Rhee's apartment.

Ponderosa Pines was on the Hill, one of many suburbs of the city of Los Alamos. Ponderosa Pines Condos was a self-contained housing development covering several acres.

The street scene was sunlit, sane, and normal. The buildings were two-story, two-unit dwellings; one tenant occupying the first floor, another the second. The structures were grouped along winding streets that looped back and forth throughout the tract. About eight feet of space separated each building from its neighbors.

Peter Rhee's apartment was in unit number 42. Numbered parking slots stood at right angles to the curb fronting the row of buildings. At one end of the street was a fenced-in tennis court; a visitor's parking area bordered it. Two other vehicles were parked there, a late model white SUV and a brown Toyota Camry that was ten years old if it was a day.

Jack pulled into a slot and got out of the Expedition, taking a sidewalk to the right of the court that ran the length of the block. The lowering sun had lost some of its brute force but was still breathlessly hot. It was filtered through a filmy haze of smoke rising from the southwest.

The surroundings seemed largely deserted. This was the dinner hour; most folks were inside their air-conditioned dwellings. A couple of kids were skateboarding at the opposite end of the street. The ground was level; there was no free downhill ride to be had. They had to put out a lot of energy for the minimal rides they were getting. Jack could relate.

He neared number 42, glancing up at Rhee's second-floor apartment.

He glimpsed a figure flitting past a side window.

Nothing in Jack's demeanor indicated he had taken any

notice of the sighting; he continued strolling at a leisurely pace. His course caused him to draw abreast with the building's facade. Curtains were drawn on the broad front window of Rhee's second-floor flat.

Jack moved on to unit number 40. He turned left, entering the space between 40 and the building to its right. The grass underfoot was stiff, dry, and yellow-brown. The passageway brought him to the rear of the row of buildings. A grassy strip twenty feet across separated this row from the back of another row of buildings on the other side of the street.

Each unit had two sets of outdoor decks, an upper and a lower, one for each tenant. The decks were mostly being unused at this hour. They came equipped with gas grills; a handful of tenants up and down the row were using them for barbecue but none took any special notice of Jack. The scent of grilled meat hung in the air, reminding Jack that he hadn't had anything to eat since breakfast, setting his stomach rumbling.

He walked out in the open, moving as if he belonged there and knew where he was going. He went to the rear of 42. Three stone steps led to a back door to the right of the lower deck.

Jack tried the knob; the door was unlocked. It opened onto a narrow entryway. Opposite the entrance was the rear door of the ground-floor apartment. No light from within shone under the bottom of the door. Jack put his ear to the door. He didn't hear anybody inside. No television, music, voices.

He reached under his vest, freeing the butt strap at the top of his holstered gun. A flight of stairs led to the second floor. Jack gripped the handrail and climbed the stairway, stepping on the far edges of the treads to minimize the noise of his ascent.

At the top of the stairs a landing fronted Rhee's back

door. The door stood slightly ajar; a starburst of splintered wood marked where the lock had been jimmied open. Jack eased open the door slowly, careful to avoid making any betraying noises.

From inside came sounds of movement. Jack entered, closing the door behind him. It wouldn't close all the way; the place where the lock had been broken prevented that.

He was in the kitchen. The air was close but bearable. The central air-conditioning must have been set to maintain a minimal level of comfort in the owner's absence, otherwise the place would have been a stifling hotbox.

At the opposite end of the kitchen a doorway opened into the rest of the apartment. Jack padded deeper into the space. To his left a hallway led to a bathroom and bedroom. Ahead lay the living room. Rhee had turned it into a home office. There was a desk, personal computer, fax machine, printer.

An intruder stood hunched over a filing cabinet in the corner, his back to Jack.

His gun was on top of the cabinet, where he'd placed it to free up both hands to go through the files. He had short dark hair, a broad-shouldered, square-shaped torso. Something familiar about him nagged at Jack's mind even as he closed in on the other.

At the last instant some sixth sense alerted the prowler he was not alone. He snatched up the gun and spun around. Jack dove, tackling him low. His shoulder connected with the prowler's legs below the knees, knocking him backward off his feet.

The prowler fired as he was going over. The gun boomed, drilling the ceiling.

The prowler fell heavily, crashing to the floor on his back. Jack was on top of him, grabbing the wrist of the other's gun hand and bending his arm back, pinning it to the floor. His opponent used his free hand to throw a wild punch at

Jack's head. Jack got his arm up in time, stifling the punch.

Grunting, gasping, working in close, the two struggled for an advantage. Jack clipped the other's chin and jaw with a sharp elbow strike, taking some of the fight out of him. Not enough—he pawed at Jack's face, trying to claw it.

Jack hammered an open-handed palm-heel strike to the prowler's solar plexus. A wicked blow to the central nerve nexus, it was debilitating, paralyzing. The prowler spasmed, bucking on the carpeted floor. His mouth gaped trying to draw a breath. His face turned gray. He was finished, no more fight left in him.

Jack pried the gun from the other's now feeble grip. It was a snub-nosed Smith & Wesson .38 Detective Special. Jack crouched over his incapacitated foe, giving him a quick frisk. A heavy bulge in the inside breast pocket of his jacket proved to be not a weapon but a half-pint bottle. The outside right-hand jacket pocket yielded a set of brass knuckles. Otherwise he came up clean.

Jack covered him with the .38. He stepped back, pulling a chair out from under the desk and turning it so it faced the figure on the floor. He sat down, leaning forward, resting his forearms on the tops of his thighs, pointing the gun at the intruder.

The prowler was on the far side of fifty, with stiff iron-gray hair cut in a crew chop, a pear-shaped face, bull neck, and barrel-shaped torso. He wore a dark gray sport jacket, white shirt, skinny black tie, gray slacks, and shiny black shoes.

Jack shook his head, his expression that of wry disbelief. One mystery at least had now been solved: the whereabouts of Harvey Kling. The wayward Ironwood OCI operative had at last surfaced.

Kling flopped around on the floor, hugging himself, arms cradling his belly. Glassy-eyed, he fought for labored, shallow breaths. Jack managed to restrain his sympathy—Kling had taken a shot at him. He looked up. A bullet hole cratered the ceiling where the slug had struck it.

He listened for the sound of someone raising an alarm; didn't hear it. He went to the front window, lifted the edge of the curtain, and looked outside. All quiet; no inquisitive bystanders looking around to see where the shot had come from. That was a break.

Jack sat back down in the chair, keeping the gun trained on Kling. Kling was recovering; some of the color had come back into his face and he was able to draw more normal breaths. He raised himself on his elbows, lifting himself to a sitting position, back against the wall.

"That's far enough. Stay where you are; you won't have so far to fall if I pull the trigger," Jack said.

"Bauer, don't!"

"Why'd you try to kill me, Kling?"

"I didn't know it was you, I swear!"

"Who'd you think it was?"

"One of the guys who killed Pete Rhee."

"So you know about that, eh? What else do you know? Talk!"

Kling's head sagged, chin resting on his chest. A sheen of sweat misted his face. He stared up at Jack through heavy-lidded, pain-dulled eyes. "You—you busted me up pretty good. Think I'm going to puke—"

"A bullet in the belly hurts worse." Jack wagged the gun barrel suggestively.

"Take it easy, Bauer."

"I don't have to—I've got the gun."

Kling raised a hand palm-out, holding his belly with his other arm. "I'll talk . . . Rhee and I were working together. On a special project."

Jack showed a cynical grin. "So special that nobody else ever heard of it."

"No—I mean, yes, you're right—it was confidential—confidential investigation."

"There's no mention of it in the OCI files, yours or Rhee's."

"There wouldn't be. It was—secret."

Jack scowled. Kling roused himself to protest. "It's true! Morrow—Rhodes Morrow—he put us on the case. He was afraid the INL computer system was compromised. Told us not to file anything there. He didn't, either. That's why there's no official record."

"No records? Convenient for you. Like the old saying: Three can keep a secret if two are dead. Morrow and Rhee are dead. Leaving only you."

Kling showed some animation, some fight. "Think I don't know that? That's why I went for my gun without looking when I heard you sneaking up on me. I figured they were coming for me. I panicked."

"Who's coming for you, Kling?"

"Killers!"

"Who are they?"

"I don't know. If I did I'd go after them instead of slinking around like a whipped cur. But I don't!"

"What do you know?"

"I know what they can do. I've seen their handiwork. Pete Rhee—what was left of him at Alkali Flats."

"You were there?"

"I was supposed to meet Pete there at noon. When I got there he was dead. I got scared and took off. Thought about taking it on the run, getting out while I still could. When I got my guts back, I came here."

"Why?"

"The same as you, probably. Looking for Pete's casebook, notepad, anything he might have left behind. A clue, a lead. Something, anything."

"And?"

"Nothing so far. I haven't been here long, I just got here a little while ago before you."

Kling reached inside his jacket. Jack motioned with the gun. "Careful—"

"Quit kidding, Bauer. You've got my gun and you patted me down. You know what I'm reaching for." Kling sneered—was the sneer for Jack or himself? He pulled out a half-pint bottle of vodka. An off-brand, two-thirds full. "Lucky it didn't get broken, huh?"

"Lucky," Jack echoed, expressionless. Kling's hands shook as he unscrewed the cap. He held the bottle in both hands to steady it. He raised it to his mouth and drank deep, his throat working. When he lowered it the bottle was one-third full. Some color had returned to his face; his eyes glittered. He carefully recapped the bottle and stowed it away in his breast pocket.

He looked up at Jack from the bottom of his eyes and smiled a sickly smile. "Pathetic, huh? You'd never know to look at me that I used to be a hotshot like you once. Not so very long ago, either. Four years."

"The Sayeed case," Jack said.

Kling nodded with perhaps too much vehemence. "The beginning of the end for me. Sure, I hit the bottle pretty hard before then, but I had a handle on it. It wasn't till afterward that it slid out of control and had a handle on me. Now I've got to have it all the time. Like medicine."

Jack was uncomfortable. "Look, Kling, this isn't an AA meeting. I'm not interested in your personal life, except how it impacts the investigation. Otherwise, keep it to yourself."

Kling smirked, looking wise. "That's what I would have said if our positions were reversed and I was in your shoes."

His gaze turned inward, as the memory flow began. "It all ties into Sayeed. Yesterday . . . and today. It figured to be an open-and-shut case. Classified data from the Argus Project turned up in Pakistan. Sayeed was a Pakistani. The time frame of his trip home to Islamabad fit the window for the secrets leak. His uncle is a big shot in ISI, the Inter-Service Intelligence directorate, the military-intelligence outfit that's the real power in that country.

"There was more. Sayeed's comings and goings at Ironwood and off-duty. Massive downloads of classified files from the lab's mainframe computers to his personal computer and laptop. Tracks that couldn't be wiped clean from the archives no matter how hard he tried—and the record shows that he tried plenty of times once the investigation began, on his own computer and on coworkers' computers that he logged onto. It added up to the fact that Dr. Rahman Sayeed was the spy who passed Argus data to ISI. It was all there and I proved it, by god, I proved it!"

"Why did the case go sour?" Jack asked.

Kling's face twisted like he'd smelled something rotten. "Lots of reasons, but they all boil down to one word: politics. There were bigger factors in place more important than nailing one atom spy.

"Washington was suffering one of its periodic fits of trying to make nice with Pakistan. Because they had nukes and Washington didn't want them spread to Islamabad's allies throughout the region. Because we needed their cooperation to fight the war in the tribal areas along the border with Afghanistan where the Taliban and al-Qaeda were hiding out. Because the pressure groups, ACLU, and all the usual suspects raised a big stink that Sayeed's rights were being violated because of where he was from and not because he'd been caught red-handed stealing secrets he had no right to. It got picked up overseas and turned into something big and the Administration and State Department couldn't take the heat.

"Sayeed hired himself one smart defense lawyer—Max Scourby—and that SOB turned the trial into a circus and me into the clown in the center ring. He painted it that we were the bad guys and Sayeed was some poor persecuted martyr. Scourby played the trial like a virtuoso, dealing the graymail card, threatening to subpoena all the big shots in Ironwood and have them spill their guts about all the secret projects they were working on in the lab. Divulging intelligence damaging to vital national security interests. That was enough to make the government fold right there.

"Then Scourby got me on the witness stand and tore me apart, made me look like fifty-seven different varieties of horse's ass. I helped him do it because, jerk that I was, I let him get under my skin. I knew he was trying to get me mad with his artful insinuations and snotty asides and smirks and winks to the jurors. I knew it but I blew my stack anyway and reamed him out good from the witness stand, and when I was done the case was sunk and my career along with it . . ."

Kling fell silent, brooding, and bitter. Jack prodded him to get him back on track. "But you came back to Ironwood all the same, you wound up working for OCI," he pointed out.

"Not until later, much later," Kling said. "That was Morrow's doing. He got Hotchkiss's job. Hotchkiss was his predecessor as OCI chief. Morrow was his number two man."

"I know about Hotchkiss," Jack said.

Kling fired back, "Then you know that he played his cards close to the vest and kept Morrow in the background as much as possible. Maybe he had an intuition that the Sayeed case could go sour and wanted to contain the damage. It finished Hotchkiss—hell, killed him—but Morrow was clean, none of that Sayeed dirt clinging to his skirts, so he got the top slot when Hotchkiss was forced into retirement.

"That's how I saw it then but I was wrong. Morrow was a lot savvier than I figured. Hell, he reached out and contacted me to offer me a job in OCI. It wasn't much but I jumped at it. I'd slid so far down the ladder that anything would have looked good. I was poison in the national security field. The jerk who'd torpedoed the biggest atom spy case since the Rosenbergs. Nobody in the private sector would touch me, either. The big corporations have no use for losers.

"Out of the blue came Rhodes Morrow with a job offer. I took it. It wasn't until later, months later, that I realized it was all part of a plan."

"A plan?" Jack prompted.

"Oh yeah. Morrow was better than me, better even than old Hotchkiss. Or maybe he just had more time to sift the facts and chew them over and dig deeper into them.

"He knew Sayeed was guilty but he took it one step further. By focusing on inconsistencies in the case, little odd details that didn't add up, he discovered that Ironwood was penetrated not by one but by two spies," Kling said.

He grinned wolfishly. "That's right—two spies. Sayeed was one but not the only one. There was another."

"Who?"

"I don't know. Nobody knows. But Morrow was getting close. Closer every day. Two spies planted in the heart of one of Uncle Sam's most advanced weapons research facilities. Two moles. Each buried deep, burrowing away. Each working separately, pursuing his own agenda. Maybe they were unaware of each other's existence, maybe not.

"Sayeed was working for Pakistan's ISI. They were too greedy for product and burned him, revealing his existence. He was the little mole. The other spy—call him Big Mole—was slicker. But not slick enough to stay hidden forever. Morrow figured out that Big Mole was a long-term penetration agent placed deep in the INL hierarchy. Someone with virtually unlimited access to all top secret classified data. He might be in research or security but he had to be one of the higher-ups. Someone who's been at Ironwood for a long time, longer than Sayeed.

"Sayeed joined six years ago. Big Mole's tracks go back

much farther than that. Before Argus, even; back to the days when the lab's top priority was overhauling the PAL codes."

"Explain," Jack demanded.

"I'll tell you but you won't like it. PAL: permissive action link. The digital codes that have to be input before a nuclear missile can be fired. An integral part of the fail-safe system to ensure no intercontinental ballistic missile is launched by mistake or design without proper authorization. The lab was assigned to overhaul the PAL codes and harden them against interference. Ironwood's last big project before Argus."

"My god," Jack said softly.

Kling looked pleased—he knew he was getting through. "Scary, huh? It scares me, too. Just like it scared Morrow. He thought the PAL codes were Big Mole's real target. That he was trying to crack them long before Sayeed was hired to work on Argus. That the Argus flap threw a scare into him and caused him to lay low for years. Now Big Mole feels safe enough to start up again where he left off."

"I don't buy it." Jack didn't want to believe it; the implications were too frightening. "Morrow tells you but not his bosses?"

Kling sat up a little straighter. "Sounds crazy. Morrow confide in a drunk like me? Sure, crazy like a fox. INL security is shot all to hell. Somehow Big Mole knew what was going on in OCI as soon as Morrow did. Morrow stopped inputting his notes on the mole hunt into his office computer for fear that the whole lab network had been compromised. He didn't have any hard evidence, only a pattern of omissions and disinformation. That and the instincts of a lifelong spy catcher that a rat was loose in the corncrib.

"The Sayeed affair worked to Big Mole's advantage by burning up the territory. INL's contracting authority had a bellyful of bad publicity and botched spy hunts. No way were they getting back on that horse. Morrow wasn't stupid.

He saw what happened to his mentor Hotchkiss—yeah, and to me, too. He knew that the only way he'd get any action was by delivering Big Mole tied up in a nice neat package."

"Who did he suspect? He must have had a few prime suspects in mind."

"The key is in the chronology, Bauer. The window of opportunity. Big Mole had to be working steadily at Ironwood for the last eight years or more. Morrow started out with a list of persons of interest. On the scientific side, Nordquist, Carlson, Fisk, and Romberg. In security: McCoy. They were all in place during the PAL overhaul eight years ago.

"Since then the list has gotten smaller. And you know why."

"The Ironwood kills," Jack said.

Kling pointed a finger at Jack and mimed pulling a trigger. "Bingo. The chain of deaths that brought you here. See how it all ties together.

"Yan was the first. Dr. John Yan. Not a suspect, didn't fit the chrono. He came in five years ago to work on Argus and then Perseus. But Morrow noticed some anomalies in Yan's download files. Classified data was being downloaded from the mainframe to Yan's computer at times when Yan was out of the lab. Someone else was using Yan's password to access the files. Before Morrow could get around to asking Yan who that someone might be, Yan was dead. Heart attack, they said.

"That was six months ago. Fisk was the next to die. He'd worked on the PAL overhaul, Argus, Perseus. The grand old man of Ironwood. He was in his early seventies—Nordquist had the contractor waive the mandatory retirement age so they could have the benefit of his mathematical expertise. Fisk fell in the bathtub, cracked his skull, and drowned. That was two months after Yan. Morrow must have guessed the truth even then. Although he didn't let me in on it until later.

"Freda Romberg was the third. That really blew the case wide open, at least as far as Morrow was concerned. She'd been at Ironwood the longest, close to twenty years. The deaths of Yan and Fisk must have got her thinking. She called to make an appointment to see Morrow. She wouldn't say what it was about over the phone, but anytime a top researcher contacts the head of OCI it's got to be important. In hindsight it looks like she'd gotten suspicious and discovered something she wanted to bring to Morrow. Morrow was away from his office at the time but his secretary took the call and made the appointment for later that day. Romberg was working alone in the LRF at lunchtime when the robot arm crushed her to death. Equipment malfunction, they said.

"That prodded Morrow into taking active measures. He had a two-part plan. Officially he started making noises that there was a possibility that the three deaths weren't accidental but deliberate. He didn't say it was murder, he only offered it up as a possibility for further study. He caught a lot of heat from management. The contractor didn't want to rip the scab off the wound by setting off a new round of investigations, bad publicity, and headlines. Morrow tried to make his point without making waves but there was a lot of pushback from the governing directors on the board. He took his suspicions to the local representatives of the CIA and FBI—Lewis and Sabito—but they weren't buying.

"Unofficially Morrow opened up a second front for direct action. He roped in me and Peter Rhee, brought us into the picture. I guess that's what he'd had in mind all along when he hired me, bringing me in as a sideman. He knew I was clean and Rhee, too. Rhee was a new hire, brought in after Sayeed. Morrow arranged for the three of us to get together after work in a bar in the Hill. He didn't even trust his own office to be spy-proof. Why not meet in the SCIF? Same reason! Everybody that uses it is logged in and out and he didn't want to tip that the three of us were in cahoots.

"At the meet he laid it out for us. Gave us the briefing about Big Mole. He deputized us as his special investigators in the mole hunt. It had to be a completely off-the-shelf operation. Conducted in secret outside office hours. Confined to the three of us. He gave us the assignments and Rhee and I carried them out. We were his legmen."

"He didn't bring anyone else in OCI in? McCoy, Derr, any of the others?" Jack asked.

Kling shrugged. "If he did, he didn't tell us. This spy hunt was no one-sided affair, though. Big Mole wasn't sitting still while we were looking for him. He's not alone. He has help on the outside. Killers on call. Yan, Fisk—and don't forget Ernie Battaglia. He was a retired ex-cop turned SECTRO Force security guard. I knew him to say hello to and pass the time of day with. Nice guy. He was the next to die, ten days after Romberg. Killed in a hit-and-run accident—run over while he was out walking his dog. The car—stolen car—was found abandoned downtown by the city cops. The driver was never found. The cops figured some punk kid boosted the car for a joyride, then got scared after tagging Ernie and dumped the car fast.

"Morrow figured different. Battaglia was one of the guards on duty outside the Pit when Romberg was killed. Could be he saw or heard something that could prove that it was no accident but murder. Maybe even point back to the killer."

"Why didn't he report it, Kling?"

"Maybe he didn't know the significance of what he'd seen. Maybe he hadn't seen anything at all but the killer thought he had. Another promising lead turned dead end. But Battaglia was the tipping point. I don't know about Lewis but Sabito was starting to come around. He wanted to get into it but his Bureau bosses wouldn't let him. They'd already gotten burned from Sayeed and didn't want to play with fire again.

"The kills had one positive effect. They narrowed the list of Big Mole suspects down to three. Nordquist, Carlson, and McCoy."

"The last ones left alive," Jack said.

"Then we got a break in the case. A new lead, a hot one. We didn't have to go looking for it, it came to us. A walk-in. Phone-in, actually. Pete Rhee took the initial complaint but he had an idea it might be something so he kept it out of official channels and took it straight to Morrow. Morrow had Pete and me handle the investigation unofficially," Kling said.

He went on. "That was about a month ago. Our new lead was starting to pan out. Then—disaster. Rhodes Morrow was killed. This time there was no attempt to frame it so it looked like anything but what it was: murder. You know the official story. Morrow was driving home late from work one night when he got a flat tire on a lonely stretch of road. Some crook or crooks came along and sized him up as an easy mark. Shot him dead and robbed him. His wallet and wristwatch were lifted to make it look good.

"Rhee and I knew better. Morrow's death cut the heart out of our investigation. It cut the guts out of me. What little I had left. The one person who could tie it all together was silenced. Only Morrow could have proved that we were working for him on an official investigation and not just freelancing.

"Hell, I was scared. We both were. If they could knock off the head of OCI, where did that leave me and Pete? Sitting ducks. We didn't know who to go to because we didn't know who to trust. Surfacing the mole hunt might mean signing our own death warrants.

"And they were on to us. Somebody broke into my place

and tore it apart. Looking for notes or files on the hunt. Waste of time. Morrow had them all. Where I don't know, but either Big Mole found them or Morrow hid them so good they haven't turned up yet.

"Pete thought he was being followed. I started seeing shadows everywhere I looked. I didn't know if I was actually being tailed or just seeing things. Spooking myself. And then I saw Pete Rhee with his head damned near blown off—"

Kling was working himself up. The fear was on him. Jack needed to keep him thinking straight. He'd left things untold—important things.

"Kling! The hot lead you were talking about, the one you and Rhee were following up—what is it?"

Kling opened his mouth to speak but before he could get the words out his face fell. His startled expression was the tip-off. He'd seen something behind Jack that jolted him.

Jack wasted no time in asking questions. He threw himself out of the chair sideways, diving to the floor. Gunfire boomed behind him. Bullets passed harmlessly over him, tearing into the curtained front window.

Jack rolled over toward the rear of the apartment. Two shooters stood there, handguns blazing. Filling the space with gun smoke.

One was a gray-haired, horse-faced man; the other was young with a rooster tail haircut and thin, wispy mustache. The young one looked barely out of his teens. Horse Face stood at the fore, the other was behind him and to the side.

Jack fired from the floor, placing two shots into Horse Face's middle. Horse Face crumpled up, backpedaling like he was bowing his way out of the room. He staggered into his partner's line of fire. A round from the young one's gun lanced into his back.

The young one shouted an obscenity.

Horse Face's back bowed, thrusting his shattered torso

forward. He stood with legs spread wide, swaying. Blocking Jack's shot at his partner.

The young one retreated into the kitchen, gun barking, not scoring. He ducked behind a kitchen counter in time to avoid Jack's shot; the round whizzed by so close that its passage ruffled his hair.

Horse Face was still on his feet. His gun hand fell to his side. He convulsively jerked the trigger, pumping a few rounds into the floor. He cried out, toppling.

The back door through which the gunmen had entered was wide open. The young one made a break for it, reaching behind him to throw more lead in Jack's direction. Gun smoke hung in mid-air.

The young one went out the door, clattering downstairs. Jack rose, starting after him. Horse Face lay on his back on the floor, not dead yet. He raised his gun, straining as if it weighed fifty pounds. Jack shot him in the head, finishing him.

He glanced back. Kling lay flat on the floor belly-down, hugging the carpet. "You hit?"

"I'm okay, Bauer! Give me my gun!"

Jack wasn't minded to have Harvey Kling at his back with a loaded gun. Kling was unharmed and would keep. Jack crossed to the rear of the flat. The stairwell was empty, the young one was already out the ground-floor door.

Jack went to the rear window, tore aside the red-and-white checked curtains. The young one was racing across the grassy strip between the two rows of buildings. Jack knocked out the glass pane with the gun barrel, reached outside, and fired at the fleeing form. Two shots, two misses. Though the second kicked up a tuft of grass and dirt at the young one's heel.

The hammer clicked on empty; all the rounds in the cylinder had been fired. The young one halted, turned, and pointed the gun at the window. Jack dodged to one side, sheltering behind the wall. A couple of rounds tore through the window, ripping into the ceiling. Shards of glass fell out of the window frame.

Jack placed Kling's empty .38 on the kitchen counter. He went out the door and down the stairs, taking them two at a time. He drew his gun and ran outside. The young one had reached the far side of the grassy strip. He darted between two buildings toward the street beyond.

Jack ran after him, rushing through the space between two buildings, breaking out into the open. The street was a duplicate of the one housing Rhee's apartment. Parked cars lined the curb. Jack halted, crouching, trying to look everywhere at once. The young one was nowhere to be seen.

A car engine roared into life; a sleek silver coupe catapulted out of a parking slot, the young one hunched over a wheel. Tires shrieked as he whipped the car into a hard right-hand turn, wheeling it around a corner.

Jack ran after it, squeezing off a few rounds at the fleeing car. Its rear window shattered but the car kept moving, swinging behind the cover of a building at the end of the block.

A yellow station wagon stood at the curb with its engine running. Its rear hatch was open. Behind it stood a suburban matron who'd been unloading groceries from it. She was deathly pale; only her eyes were alive.

Jack holstered his gun and flung open the driver's side door. The motor was running, the keys in the ignition. He gave the interior a quick onceover to make sure no kids were inside; no baby tucked in a safety seat in the rear. That would be all he needed, to pirate a car with an infant inside. The car was unoccupied.

Jack locked eyes with the car's owner. "Sorry, ma'am," he said.

He jumped into the driver's seat, adjusting it to get some leg room. He threw the car into gear and drove away, a sudden right turn throwing several bags of groceries out of the open rear hatch to the pavement. Spilling melons and apples on the pavement. A quart container of milk broke open and splattered onto the street.

Glancing in the rearview mirror he saw the woman still standing frozen in place, gaping openmouthed at her stolen car dwindling in the distance. It was a hell of a note when he had to carjack a housewife, but you did what you had to get the job done.

Jack followed the course the young one had taken; ahead he saw a flashing glint of silver as the coupe rounded another turn onto the main drive out of the condo complex. He took off after it.

· ·

**THE FOLLOWING TAKES PLACE
BETWEEN THE HOURS OF
6 P.M. AND 7 P.M.
MOUNTAIN DAYLIGHT TIME**

· ·

6:07 P.M. MDT
Skycrest Drive, Los Alamos County

The silver coupe exited Ponderosa Pines, heading west across the mesa. The coupe moved out fast, the yellow station wagon following in hot pursuit.

Jack Bauer was pleasantly surprised to find that the wagon was a pretty zippy model with good pickup and handling. It had a tall body mounted on a compact car platform, with automatic transmission and all-wheel drive.

The chase picked up speed when the silver car broke onto the open road, the long flat straightaways and banked curves of the highway. Jack finally had an instant's breathing room to fasten the safety harness seat belt. He sat leaning forward hunched over the wheel.

It was early Saturday night, before most revelers had

taken to the road in search of the evening's entertainment. Traffic was light and there wasn't a highway patrol car in sight. The silver car was leading him away from the suburbs, into the hills.

Ahead, west, the Jemez Mountains bulked against the horizon. An orange-red sun grazed the peaks. Long shadows fell across the land. The mountains' eastern slopes were purple. Blue-gray shadows pooled around the foothills, extending long fingers creeping east across the land. The sky was still blue; the spectral white half-moon floated in the west. Few cars had their lights on yet.

Jack was aware of the airstream rushing past over the car; it forced the rear hatch down, slamming it shut. The engine whine shrilled higher as the motor wound out more RPMs, tires thrumming along the road. He was conscious of the weight of the gun holstered under his arm. He longed to get it into play but was unable to close the distance between his vehicle and the silver car.

The coupe was the quicker machine. Jack had the station wagon crowding its upper limit. Over seventy miles per hour it started to shake. He regretted the absence of the Expedition. The SUV had muscle that would have allowed him to speedily overtake his quarry.

The silver coupe was in a hurry. When a car was in its way it crossed the yellow centerline and passed in the opposite lane, forcing oncoming cars to get out of its way. It left a track of near-misses and narrowly averted collisions in its wake.

Jack did no less; he was determined not to let the other get away. He changed up the routine by passing cars on the right, driving on the shoulder when he had to overtake them.

The highway now ran through empty land. The pall softened the sharp edges of mountain peaks, blurred the open vistas, and deepened the gloom of oncoming dusk.

A distinct smell of burning hung in the air: smoke from

the fire in the canyon south of the Hill. It had thickened since Jack had earlier driven to Ponderosa Pines.

The flat straightaway atop the mesa gave way to a series of foothills, the road curving and twisting between them. That was good. The station wagon couldn't beat the faster silver coupe on the long stretches but could regain some of its lost lead in the curves.

The jumbled hills and knobs featured many blind curves, causing Jack to frequently lose sight of the coupe. He always managed to catch up with it, though. The road forked; the silver car took the left-hand branch, the road curving hard to the southwest. The hills thinned and gave way on Jack's left, opening a view looking south across the mesa's edge to the canyon beyond.

Churning, roiling smoke clouds poured skyward as if the canyon was a vent to infernal regions below. Gray-black smoke poured out of it ceaselessly. It formed a curtain across the southern horizon, veiling South Mesa from view. Lurid red and yellow glare underlit it. The flames were invisible, hidden in the depths of the valley below, but their glow suffused the towering piles of smoke.

Sparks and embers rained upward, yellow-red-orange flakes of flame, a blizzard of them soaring up the thermals. Air flickered and rippled from heat waves.

The silver car slowed as it neared a crossroads. It flicked its headlights on and off several times as it went through. The station wagon flashed through the intersection.

A dark sedan sat waiting at the mouth of a thin dirt road coming down from the north. It was filled with men with guns. It powered out of its lurking place, churning up a plume of dirt and loose gravel. It slewed on to the paved road, tires yelping, biting as they gripped pavement.

The sedan arrowed after the station wagon, coming up fast, coming on strong.

Uh-oh, Jack said to himself. *The old squeeze play.*

He got the picture. While he was chasing the silver car, it had been leading him into an ambush. With its greater speed and maneuverability it could have shaken the wagon's pursuit. Instead it had lured him into a trap. The driver had played cat and mouse with him, staying out of reach but not losing Jack. He must have used his cell to call for help. Backup.

Here it was in the form of a sedan filled with hostiles. The newcomer was big, powerful; it ate up the distance between itself and the station wagon.

The silver car was slowing, looking to box Jack in. That was okay, there was plenty of highway for maneuvering. Red brake lights flashed on as the coupe suddenly braked hard, sliding sideways into a controlled drift, laying down curved rubber streaks on pavement.

It jerked to a halt, standing at right angles in the middle of the road. The driver scrambled over the seat and jumped out of the passenger side. The young one. He put the car between himself and the oncoming station wagon. He rested his gun on the roof of his car and pointed it at Jack, opening fire. The shots went wild except for one that went through the windshield. It passed through the car, punching an exit hole through the rear window. The windshield was ventilated by a half dollar–sized hole but otherwise remained intact.

Jack whipped the station wagon to the right onto the shoulder, around the rear of the silver car, and away. The young one kept firing; some slugs tore into the car's left rear fender.

The sedan followed, threading through the slot. The young one jumped into the coupe and took off after it.

Spear points of flame rimmed gun muzzles that jutted through the sedan's open windows. The station wagon's rear window totally disintegrated, spraying the back of Jack's head, neck, and shoulders with broken glass. Safety glass, fragmenting into cubes. They stung like being peppered with rock salt from a shotgun—but it beat being sliced to ribbons by jagged-edged shards.

Jack ducked down lower in his seat, working the wheel so the station wagon wove a bullet-dodging course on the roadway ahead. Slaloming back and forth across the center-line. Sharp curves in the road forced him to change tactics to stay on course.

The sedan crowded up from behind. Jack was in a tight spot. The smaller-engined station wagon's slim lead was fast melting.

A hundred yards ahead on the left loomed a dirt road. A farm road or ranch road. It was secured by a triple-barred gate. Jack worked the brake, feathering it, turning the wheel to put the wagon in a controlled slide. *Controlled* being a relative term.

He had a heart-in-mouth moment as the scenery rushed up sideways on the right side of the car. Tires squealed, laying rubber. If one of them burst it was all over. The sharklike sedan came at him on his left side.

With a bump and a jerk the wagon slid to a halt, pointing at the three-barred gate. Jack stomped the gas, charging the barrier. It was secured by a padlocked chain fastened to the gatepost and posted with a NO TRESPASSING sign.

The station wagon crashed the gate. There was an instant's gut-churning resistance. The wagon front's leading edge crumpled, headlights shattering, hood buckling.

The machine darted downhill along a rutted dirt path. The dirt track ran down a wooded hillside covered with pine trees. Trees on both sides of the road interlaced overhead, forming a canopy. Beneath them was premature dusk. Pine-scented gloom. The road ran through it like a tunnel.

The way was not straight but curved to follow the contours of the slope. It bent right, then left, then right again. Jack had to slow his descent due to the many blind corners.

A smashup against the trees and his run was over. Sometimes the grade was so steep that he all but stood on the brake pedal.

He was not alone. The sedan full of gunmen had also taken the plunge. The silver car followed behind.

The sedan's headlights flashed on, glaring high beams. Jack kept his lights dark. Despite the smoky murk there was enough daylight to see by.

The road wound into a series of S-curves. Sometimes its loops brought the station wagon in close proximity to the sedan, with only a belt of timber between them. That timber was his lifeline. The dense-packed trees screened him from the bullets sprayed at him by the sedan's occupants.

As he descended the gloom deepened. Banks of smoke rose through the trees, stinging his eyes, smelling of burning. Jack steered as much by intuition and instinct as by sight. He had to slow down to guard against crashing.

The station wagon was taking a beating on the rough road. Its all-wheel drive helped maintain traction, but the machine was not designed for too-rugged off-road motoring. The same applied to the sedan and the silver coupe, though. The wagon was slightly better suited to the terrain than its pursuers.

Stones thrown up by the wheels cracked against the undercarriage. The rutted road made the car feel like it was shaking itself apart. The steering wheel shuddered in his hands, fighting him, trying to break his grip.

Low-hanging branches beat against the wagon's roof and sides. Jack was tossed around by the rigors of the road. If not for the seat belt he would have been pitched headfirst through the windshield.

The road straightened out for its final descent down the slope. At the bottom lay a flat. The twisty course had worked to his advantage, allowing him to gain some lead on the pursuit. On the flat the powerful sedan would eat up his lead. Then its guns would eat him up.

The dirt trail went from the tilted vertical to the horizontal. The wagon was on the flat. The sedan swooped down on the level and tore off after him. The silver car was close on the sedan's tail.

Fifty yards of hurtling forward motion took Jack out of the woods. The wagon broke into bare, open country; a sprawling plain. The road ran straight across it due south through a landscape dotted with boulders and cacti. The flat lay in the immense trough of the valley between the Hill and South Mesa.

Fire from the demolished meth lab had earlier raced south down the arroyo, spreading into Coyote Canyon and beyond. The rugged terrain was choked with masses of dry brush that should have been regularly trimmed and cut back. Such preventive maintenance costs money. The last time the brush had been thinned was almost a decade ago in the disastrous Cerro Grande fires. Years had gone by with no follow-up. Years in which the economy had collapsed into recession and worse. No money could be found in the county budget for brush cutting and clearing, for building firebreaks and firewalls.

Now it was the peak of summer. Brush, grass, weeds, and carpeted pine needles all wrung dry of every drop of moisture had become ideal tinder. Kindling for an overdue conflagration. What man had failed to fix, nature was now remedying.

The blaze was part forest fire, part prairie fire, and all inferno. Of its origins Jack Bauer knew nothing. Its results were in full view as he raced south across the flat. A firestorm raged throughout the valley between the Hill and South Mesa. Its progress was not uniform but diverse, spreading by fits and starts across the terrain.

The valley was a patchwork of fire and unburnt land. Many square miles of the valley's wooded north slope were a raging hell. Sections were ablaze to the east and west of the flat where the station wagon was harried by its pursuers. Smoke blotted out the low-hanging sun into a ball of blood shrouded by swirling gray-black clouds.

The way south across the flat was open, smoky but free of fire. The ground might have been some rancher's grazing land, but if so it was bare of cattle now. The fire would have stampeded them elsewhere.

The sedan was closing the gap between it and the wagon. Ahead, the end of the dirt road was in sight. The flat rose in a low slope to a flat-topped ridge bordered by a wire fence strung on fence posts. The road terminated in a three-barred gate similar to the one Jack had crashed at its opposite end.

The station wagon plowed into the gate and smashed it open, batting it back on its hinges. It gave onto a two-lane blacktop road running east-west. Fire and smoke were thicker to the west. Jack made a snap decision and made a left-hand turn. The wagon slewed into a curve on the pavement.

Jack manhandled the wheel, whipping it around, feathering the brakes at the same time. The wagon skidded, the road's right bank rushing toward the passenger side of the car. The tires bit, digging in. The car straightened out, heading east.

The valley was thick with smoke. Not thick enough for him to hide in, to lose his pursuers. He couldn't shake them. He fishtailed back and forth over the centerline, abruptly weaving and switching lanes to avoid gunfire from the pursuing sedan.

The road ahead sloped gently upward. At the top of the ridge the ground was dotted with a number of low mounds and hills, the road winding through them. Beyond lay a fork in the road.

The right-hand branch drove a long, straight road through

level ground. The left wound into a cascade of stepped ridges. The left-hand branch offered a better chance of escape, slim though it was.

The station wagon punched through a low-hanging smoke cloud into the hills of the left fork. Fire had found a foothold here, thrusting an arm down from the valley's burning northern slope.

Jack coughed, choking, eyes tearing. He wiped his forearm across his eyes to clear them. The hillside on his left was on fire. He could feel the heat from it. Yellow sparks like hordes of fireflies spiraled up through churning smoke. Visibility was poor. Trees lining the left side of the road formed a row of torches. Trunks and branches were dark skeletons wreathed in yellow and red flames.

The road emerged from where two hills crowded it on both sides. Something loomed up ahead, too close. A burning tree had fallen lengthwise across the road, blocking it. The wagon was almost on it; there was next to no time to react.

Jack whipped the car to the right, trying to go around it. There was too much tree and too little road. The treetop crowded the shoulder. Branches crunched under wheels. For an instant Jack thought he might make it but no such luck.

He ran out of road. Beyond the shoulder's edge was empty space. No guardrail.

The station wagon went over the side. Its nose dipped, pointing downward. It plowed a furrow down the embankment of a shallow gully.

The gully's north wall sloped at about a thirty-degree angle. Its bank was peppered with bushes and barrel cactus. The station wagon mowed them under as it careened twenty-five feet down to the floor of the gully. The wheels on the driver's side left the ground. Jack feared the car was going to go into a roll. A heart-stopping instant and they touched down again.

The car came to a halt with a bone-jarring crash.

Jack took quick stock of himself. He'd taken a beating but nothing was broken. He unclipped the safety harness, grabbed the door handle, and put a shoulder to the door panel. Nothing. The fall had wedged it shut.

Jack threw his weight into it, slamming his shoulder against the door several times to no effect. He scrambled over to the passenger side, tried the door. It opened. He wriggled out, falling to the ground.

The gully was a dry watercourse, its floor lined with rocks. Ottoman-sized rocks, armchair-sized rocks, sofa-sized rocks. They lay on a bed of countless smooth, rounded, palm-sized stones, heaped in profusion. The gully ran roughly southeast, a meandering vein among the hills. The south side of the draw opposite the road was a steep incline fifty feet high. At the top were woods. They were on fire.

The light of the setting sun was muted by the smoke filling the sky. Deep twilight massed in the gully, except where it was dotted with hot embers that had fallen from the burning trees. They started little fires wherever they fell, speckling the cut with yellow tongues of flame.

The station wagon's rear was tilted up off the ground, thanks to a big rock beneath it. Fluids dripped and dribbled from the undercarriage. Oil—and gas. A fuel line was broken. Gasoline puddled in a rock-lined hollow.

Up on the road the sedan had rolled to a halt well short of the burning tree. Jack crouched down behind the passenger side of the car, using it for cover. A few beats later, the silver car pulled up behind the sedan.

The sedan's doors opened, disgorging its occupants, a half-dozen well-armed men. They had rifles, machine guns. The young one got out of the silver car and joined the others at the roadside overlooking the gully.

Jack needed a break, he'd be a sitting duck down here,

cover or no cover. They hadn't seen him yet. He low-crawled away from the wagon, blanking out the pain of rocks banging elbows and knees, their jagged edges scoring his forearms and belly. He wriggled behind a refrigerator-sized slab of a boulder.

Dark figures stood outlined along the roadside, backlit by fiery woods dimmed by a shifting pall of smoke. Silhouetted shapes, their faces hidden: a band of blankly anonymous killers.

"He's done," somebody said.

"Probably broke his neck in the crash," another said.

"I don't see him in the car," a third voice stated.

"Can't see nothing from up here," the first speaker said.

"Why don't you go down and take a look, Larry?"

Larry told the questioner what he could go do with himself. "Why don't you?" he added.

"Shut the hell up, all of you," a new voice said. The voice of command—the boss. The others fell silent. "Somebody go down and check on him," the leader said.

"I'll go, Pardee. I owe him. I was there when the bastard got Ralston and damned near got me."

"Okay, Nacio. Glad to see somebody in this outfit's got balls. We'll cover you."

The one called Nacio started down the slope, pistol in hand. Firelight fell on his face, revealing the young one who'd been one of the shooters at Rhee's apartment, the driver of the silver car.

Nacio climbed down sideways for better balance, walking on the edges of his shoes for traction, digging them into the side of the slope. He was craning, trying to see inside the car. "Hey, I smell gas—"

Jack fired twice, nailing Nacio with a pair of center shots. Nacio bent forward from the waist, plunging headfirst into the gully.

"Let him have it!" Pardee said. Jack fired a shot into

the pool of gas under the station wagon. The hot round ignited it.

Gunmen lined the edge of the roadside firing down into the gully. Pardee and his men opened up on the car, spraying it with lead. A tremendous fusillade, a hammering clamor. They hadn't seen where the shots came from, didn't know where Jack was except that he was somewhere near the car.

Rounds sieved the station wagon's crumpled roof and sides, blew out the windshield and rear windows, and wreaked havoc on the interior. Jack huddled in the lee of the big rock slab. Slugs thudded into the side of the gully, sending up sprays of dirt and dirt clouds. Rock chips flew; wicked ricochets whined and spanged.

A thin blue flame overspread the surface of the puddle of gas. The fuel ignited with a whoomping sound. Oil from the broken crankcase helped fuel the fast-growing fire. Yellow flames tickled the car's underside, touching the fuel in the broken fuel line, sending a line of fire back into the gas tank.

The gas tank blew, blowing the doors off and sending the trunk lid sky-high. The gully shook from the shock waves. The trunk lid came down like a flying guillotine not far from Jack.

One of the roadside gunmen leaned too far over the edge and fell into the gully, tumbling down the slope. He landed heavily in a thicket of brambles that had been set ablaze by flaming gasoline. His clothes caught on fire. He jumped up, frantically beating at himself in a futile attempt to put out the flames that swiftly turned him into a human torch. He rolled around on the ground, burning like a Yule log, trying to extinguish the hell that engulfed him.

The infernal brightness of the fireball dimmed dramatically after the initial glare. The car hulk burned steadily. Jack picked off another roadside gunman, tagging him in the side and knocking him down. The others dodged back from the edge, out of the line of fire.

Jack made his break. The cover was better going east, deeper into the gully. It did not run straight but twisted right, left, right again. Jack dodged behind the next boulder in line, got his feet under him, and dove for the shadowed safety of a nearby rock pile. Bullets tore up the terrain around him.

"There he goes!"

Jack scrambled in a low crouch, bent almost double. He dodged behind the blind corner of a rock outcropping. More slugs tore where he'd been.

The gully twisted and turned. Jack zigged and zagged from cover to cover, working his way eastward into the darkness away from the light. Shouts sounded from above, footfalls pounded pavement trying to keep track of him.

The gunmen were pacing him. They must have jumped the burning tree in the middle of the road to follow him on foot. Jack had to move forward, hoping that the terrain would cooperate and conceal him from the hunters long enough for him to break clear.

1 2 3 4 5 6 7 8 **9**
10 11 12 13 14 15 16 17
18 19 20 21 22 23 24

. . . .

THE FOLLOWING TAKES PLACE
BETWEEN THE HOURS OF
7 P.M. AND 8 P.M.
MOUNTAIN DAYLIGHT TIME

. . . .

7:05 P.M. MDT
Saddle Ridge, Los Alamos County

Firebombing the station wagon regained the initiative for Jack Bauer. It gave him a window of opportunity; a narrow one, but by putting the heat on his foes—literally—it took the heat off him, if only for a moment.

When the gas tank blew, the fireball was dazzling; Jack was careful to look away to prevent being temporarily blinded by the glare. A series of explosions brought the fire blast to its peak. It exhausted itself quickly, dwindling and dimming, but Jack was already on the move, taking advantage of the distraction.

Stones rattled and clinked beneath his tread. Noise from the burning car and the greater blaze beyond provided some masking for his footfalls.

Hot yellow-red firelight streaked the scene, fitfully illuminating it. The restless glare was in constant motion, flowing, shifting, and ever-changing. The effect was kaleidoscopic, disorienting. Objects cast multiple moving shadows.

Apart from the burning station wagon, the smoke from the big blaze was mostly higher up, streaming above the top of the gully walls. Leaving the gully floor relatively untouched.

That was a help. Smoke inhalation could be as dangerous as naked flame. Suffocation is no less lethal than incineration.

Jack's options were few. The sedan had contained six men. Nacio in the silver coupe brought the total to seven. Nacio was dead now; so was the gunman turned human torch. A third man shot on the roadside was either dead or disabled—either way, he was out of the fight.

That left four. Four hostiles armed with rifles and machine guns. Jack had a pistol and plenty of ammo: five spare clips in the pockets of his denim vest. The hunters had him outnumbered and outgunned. Their rifles were accurate from a long way off. Lethal well beyond the range of his pistol.

Their small machine guns made up in firepower what they lacked in accuracy. They could spray the general area he was in with a pretty good chance of hitting him. He needed to work in close for the pistol to be effective. Even then, one against four was bad odds.

This was one time where flight beat fight. Keep moving; force the pursuers to spread out. Isolating the enemy increased the chances of taking them out one at a time. If he could get hold of one of their rifles or machine guns, so much the better; he'd have something with which to hit back hard.

Or maybe he could lose the hunters, give them the slip. Live to fight another day at a time and place of his choosing.

This chain of reasoning came to him in a split second. He was a pro. Trouble was, the hunters were pros, too.

The gully turned southeast, bending away from the roadside. A racket sounded as one or more of the gunmen slid down into the gully behind Jack, blocking any retreat toward the west.

Two men—he could hear them calling back and forth to each other, though he couldn't make out what they were saying. They were working their way toward him. One had a flashlight, its beam lancing through the gully.

The many twists and turns prevented the light from falling directly on Jack, picking him out. But the beam was getting closer, its glare brightening behind blind corners as it neared.

Two in the gully meant two more on the roadside. Jack considered climbing the north bank and tackling the two up top. But the cover there was nonexistent, the firelight would outline him.

He kept moving east along the gully. About fifty yards ahead of him, a second flashlight beam speared down from the roadside. It was stationary, lighting up the floor of the cut beneath it. Anyone moving into the zone of light would be a nakedly exposed target.

Jack was bottled up between the light ahead and the hunters closing in behind him. He knew how he'd work it if situations were reversed and he was up top trying to flush out a quarry. He'd post a man on the road midway between the light wielder covering the gully on the east and the duo working their way from the west. The man in the middle would guard against any attempt by Jack to go over the top on the roadside.

No doubt Pardee would figure it that way, too, and act accordingly.

Now Jack's best chance was to lie low, letting the two

on the gully floor approach until they were within point-blank range to neutralize their superior firepower and then ambushing them. Risky, yes, but changing conditions were shaving his slim options still narrower.

He looked around for a place to hide, something, anything, to better his odds. A shift in the firelight revealed something that had gone unnoticed by him: a cleft opened in the gully's south wall. Until now that bank had been too steep to scale but the seam spelled opportunity. The seam was lined with loose rocks, most of them the size of a man's head.

Jack holstered his gun to leave both hands free. He started climbing. The rock pile was tricky. He had to place his feet carefully to keep from falling or dislodging any rocks that would give away his position.

He clambered up the cleft. It was deep, full of sheltering shadows. Twenty feet up the rock pile ended but not the cleft. A fallen tree lay wedged lengthwise in the seam, one end jammed against the top of the rock pile. It must have come uprooted at some time from the top of the bank and tumbled into the cleft.

It lay head-down; it was about twenty-five feet long, with a trunk three feet in diameter. Its branches were leafless, its bark was weathered, deeply grooved. Having fallen upside-down, its base was on top at the uppermost end. It mushroomed out into an umbrella shape made of gnarly roots.

Jack used the tree as a stairway, scaling it to the top of the root ring and ducking down the other side. Snaky roots extended all around in a sunburst corona about six feet in diameter, providing Jack with plenty of cover.

He was high enough on the south slope to look down on top of the gully's north bank and the roadside. A man lay prone on the edge of the bank, shining a flashlight into the gully. A rifle lay on the ground beside him on his right side. No one else was in sight on the road.

A hundred yards west lay the tree that had fallen across the road, blocking it. Parked on the far side of it stood the sedan, empty, its lights dark. Fire was closing in on it, burning through the brush on the north side of the road. The flames were less than a stone's throw from where the bushes crowded the roadside; gray smoke came wafting out of them.

Much of the valley between the Hill and South Mesa was ablaze. Wind blew north and east, whipping the fire in that direction.

Jack looked down into the gully. Its twists and turns hid the hunters working eastward along the floor toward him but the glow of their flashlight beam was visible and brightening.

The rifleman staked out at the east end of the gully was in an area as yet untouched by the blaze. Screens of smoke streamed across the open space.

Farther east, a pair of pale, ghostly white orbs floated into view out of the haze. They resolved themselves into the headlights of an approaching vehicle. It crept forward at a pace of a few miles per hour.

A figure rose out of a ditch on the north side of the road between the fallen tree and the rifleman watching the east end of the gully. Jack hadn't even seen the ditch, not to mention the lurker crouching inside it.

The lurker wore a wide-brimmed dark hat and wielded a small machine gun secured by a shoulder strap and held level in both hands. "Hey, Milt! Come on back here," he shouted.

"Okay, Pardee!" the rifleman replied. He held his rifle in one hand and the flashlight in the other. He trotted back to Pardee, Pardee strolling to meet him.

Jack itched to open fire on him. He was a dead shot with a pistol, but at this distance it would be a waste of bullets.

All it would do was betray his location and nullify his one advantage.

Pardee was still a faceless man, but the harsh twang of his voice was already indelibly imprinted on Jack's brain. No forgetting that voice. Jack promised himself that sometime he'd come face-to-face with its owner and look him in the eye right before silencing him forever. Sometime soon.

Assuming he got out of this fix with a whole skin. An assumption that was about to become even more of a long shot.

Pardee met up with Milt the rifleman. He took Milt's flashlight and set Milt to watch the stretch of road he, Pardee, had been covering. Pardee hustled over to Milt's previous vantage point. He went to one knee and shone the flashlight into the gully, systematically scanning it with a powerful beam that lit up the gully floor like a spotlight. Satisfied that his quarry was nowhere in sight, he stood up and stepped back well clear of the road's edge.

The vehicle from the east was still approaching, creeping along. Pardee stood in the middle of the road facing it, holding the flashlight at waist-height. Pointing it toward the vehicle, he switched the beam on and off in a pattern: three-one-two.

The vehicle responded with two toots of its horn. They rang with a jaunty tone. The vehicle blinked its high beams in a two-one-three pattern.

The machine eased forward, taking shape out of the smoke, materializing into a pickup truck. Its headlights caused Pardee and Milt to cast long, weird shadows across the road, shadows whose eeriness was increased by the palls of smoke rolling over them.

The pickup halted; four men piled out of the rear hopper. They, too, were armed with rifles and machine guns. The driver stayed behind the wheel.

Pardee started barking out orders to the newcomers. His words were drowned out by a mechanical drone, the sound of a low-flying plane. It came from out of the south, flying north over the valley.

It was a big aircraft, a propeller job the size of a cargo plane. It was coming in so low it might have been making a strafing run. Red and white lights flashed on its wings, body, and tail. Pardee and company stopped what they were doing to watch.

The plane's path took it over the eastern front of the firestorm eating up the north slope. It was a tanker plane. Its mission was to drop not bombs but water, tons of water.

It dumped its cargo along the leading edge of the blaze to retard its forward progress.

Mission accomplished, it banked east and then south, flying toward South Mesa. It vanished in the clouds, leaving behind a long droning tail of dwindling sound.

Jack Bauer didn't stick around to see the show. While the plane did its water dump, he was climbing. The cleft played out; it was steep going the rest of the way to the top. He had to climb on hands and knees.

His foot slipped, sending some rocks down the side of the bank. The rocks bounced off some other rocks and knocked them loose, too. They went clattering down the hillside.

The rock fall happened just as the two hunters who'd been working their way east along the gully rounded a turn and came below him. One of them shouted something. Gunfire opened up.

Jack tore at some exposed roots and bushes that were growing out of the side of the hill and used them to haul himself up over the edge. He threw himself flat on the ground.

Rounds ripped into the hillside and slanted overhead to clip the upper boughs of the trees on top of the south bank.

No point now in subterfuge; Jack might as well take advantage of the opportunity. He drew his gun and squirmed around on the ground, reversing position.

He peeked over the edge of the gully. The two shooters were directly below in a pocket where the gully widened at the foot of the cleft.

One of them was trying to climb up the cleft. He was in too much of a hurry; rocks flew out from under his flailing feet. He made no headway; he was in danger of falling. He stopped climbing and took up a stance, bracing himself, swinging his machine gun up and firing at the top of the slope where Jack was looking down at him.

His partner on the gully floor shouldered a rifle, angling for a shot around the machine gunner at Jack.

Jack opened fire. It was like shooting straight down into a well. He tagged the machine gunner with a couple of rounds.

The gunner fell backward on top of his partner. There was no room in the tight pocket below for the rifleman to get clear. The two fell sprawling in a tangle of limbs. The dead machine gunner pinned the rifleman to the ground. The live man struggled to get out from under the corpse.

When he got clear, he was drilled by three quick blasts from Jack's pistol. Then there were two corpses on the gully floor.

The rapid-fire exchange was over in a few heartbeats. It stung the rest of Pardee's crew into action. They spread out on the roadside, firing in Jack's direction.

He was already up and gone, zigzagging toward the burning woods. The gully's south bank crested on a wide level ridge top covered by a pine forest. An open space about twenty yards wide lay between the lip of the gully and the edge of the trees. Jack went in deep enough to take himself out of the line of fire of the triggermen below.

He paused, crouching, taking stock of the situation. The

shooting had stopped, only because Pardee's crew was coming for him. He ejected the spent clip from his gun, inserting a fresh one and jacking a round into the chamber.

The sun had set behind the mountains. Black night was offset by firelight, the lurid red glare waxing and waning according to which way the winds blew the smoke. To the west, the ridge and the valley below was a seething inferno.

He made his way east across the belt between the woods and the gully's edge. The terrain presented plenty of brush, dry weeds that came up to mid-calf level, clumps of prickly pear cactus that had to be skirted. Windborne embers set weedy patches of ground ablaze.

Jack suddenly ran out of ridge top. The land began to slope downward. He halted to survey the scene.

The sky was a panoramic backdrop of streaming smoke clouds rising to the heights, glowing with red-yellow-orange highlights from acres of blazing prairie and woodland. The ridgeline was not all of a uniform height. It took a sudden, dramatic dip, forming a saddle-shaped gap several hundred yards wide.

Jack now stood on the western rise of the saddle. He scanned the landscape laid out below him. The gully bent away from the ridge, winding northeast, its walls widening and dwindling to become a shallow crack snaking across a flat at the base of the slope of the saddle. The road roughly bordered it on the north. A long, gentle slope broken by boulders and stands of timber rose to the low-lying gap of the saddle ridge.

Pardee's crew was already starting up the north face of the slope. The wooded ridge on the west side of the gap was burning. If Jack stayed there, he'd burn, too.

Fire was creeping east down the hillside toward the saddle. Pardee and company were moving to occupy the high ground of the slope before Jack got there. That would put them in position to block him from escaping by descending the saddle's southern slope or crossing to the east side of the ridge and losing them in its as yet-unburned woods.

The manhunters mounted up along the hillside in a crescent shape like the horns of a bull. Some of them had flashlights. Smoke strands writhed across the beams as they danced over the slope, sweeping, probing.

Jack angled southeast down from the western end of the gap, trying to outrace the hunters at the nearer tip of the horn before they could outflank him. With a rifle he could have raised merry hell, picking off his foes as they were exposed out in the open of the long slope. The handgun was good only up close, and he'd prefer to keep his distance from the hunters.

With any luck, he'd reach the saddle gap before his pursuers, but not without breaking cover. Timber, boulders, and brush on the slope played out, forcing him to cross a stretch of open ground. Firelight from the woods above betrayed him, outlining his form, casting his long shadow over the slope.

Excited shouts greeted his appearance, like the baying of hounds when they sight the fox. Flashlight beams lanced across the ground trying to pin him. Shots popped, rattled; spear points of flame stabbing out from rifle muzzles.

He was in the gap; the ground fell away from his feet. He hit the ground rolling, absorbing the impact on his shoulders, clutching his gun as if his hand was welded to it.

He slammed into a rock with a bone-jarring thud, coming to a halt.

He groaned, sitting up on the ground. He was in a hollow, a shallow basin. Cover was minimal: small crabbed stunted mesquite trees, bushes, scattered boulders and rock outcroppings.

He crawled to the north edge of the hollow, looked out

and down at the slope tilting away from it. The nearest of his pursuers were about fifty yards away. The hunters were pressing him hard.

He turned around and started south, across the gap. Seconds were too precious to waste in doing anything else but flight. Halt too long and they would have him. That was the hell of being a fugitive. The hunters gave you no time to pause; to think, regroup, or plan. Or even catch your breath.

Jack Bauer was running on sheer nerves and adrenaline. He was in top condition but he didn't have much left in reserve to draw on. He hadn't eaten a real meal since breakfast. Thirst was worse. He was parched for a drink of water. His mouth was dry, his throat felt like it was closing up. Desert heat plus fire heat had leached the moisture out of him.

He was dirty, grimy, exhausted. The smell of burning clung to him, permeating his clothing. His lungs heaved, his limbs were leaden.

Behind him—too close—the hunters shouted back and forth to one another.

Jack plodded on, a slow, steady jog. He picked a path through some waist-high bushes. A twisted root he hadn't seen tripped him up and he fell forward, landing on his hands and knees.

He raised his head, glancing up—recoiling at the sight of a manlike figure looming over him. His gun was leveled on the apparition before Jack realized that he'd been about to blast a saguaro cactus. It was six and a half feet tall, and the limbs protruding from its trunk looked like arms bent at the elbows. Luckily he'd recognized it for what it was before pulling the trigger.

Yellow light flickered and pulsed ahead. The gap in the ridge opened onto a wooded plateau. The timber was about thirty yards away.

The ridge west of the gap was completely ablaze, its sides and summit blanketed with yellow flames. Black smoke poured out of it. Fire lines had thrust down the slope, establishing a beachhead on the west woods of the plateau. Pine trees became torches with astonishing swiftness. Jack would have to move fast before the swift-spreading fire cut him off and barred his way.

Footfalls, hard breathing sounded behind him, very near, almost on top of him. The hunters were closer than he suspected. He turned to face them, standing on one knee. He rested the elbow of his gun arm on top of his thigh to steady it.

Rustling sounded in the bushes. Voices:

"See anything, Croft?"

"Thought I saw something moving right around here, Steve."

Croft sounded closer of the two. He was on the other side of the brush. Steve was a half-dozen paces behind him. He was holding a flashlight. That's all Jack could see of him, the flashlight beam. It bobbed and wiggled, pointing off to the side toward a place where Jack wasn't.

"Bring that light up here, Steve," Croft said. He parted the bushes and stepped through them, coming face-to-face with Jack Bauer.

They could see each other by firelight. Croft had short dark hair, a low forehead, and a lantern jaw. He wore a dirty white T-shirt and jeans and carried a shotgun cradled under one arm with the barrel pointing down at the ground.

He and Jack saw each other at the same time. Jack fired first, squeezing two shots into the other's middle. They were fired in such rapid succession that they sounded in one crashing report. Muzzle flares from Jack's gun flashed like two strokes of heat lightning, underlighting the mask of agony that was Croft's face.

Croft jerked the trigger convulsively by dying reflex, discharging a shotgun blast into the ground. He dropped to his knees, pitched face-forward to the ground.

Jack wanted that shotgun, but before he could make a grab for it Steve popped into view. A straw planter's hat was wedged on top of his coconut-shaped head. Jack threw himself flat on the ground.

The flashlight fell from Steve's fingers as he took hold of his small machine gun with both hands and opened up. He panicked and cut loose on the saguaro cactus, chopping it in half.

Jack lay prone in the dirt firing upward. Steve fell backward out of sight behind the bushes. The flashlight lens cracked when it hit the ground but the beam kept shining, throwing a line of light at worm's-eye level.

Gunfire broke out along the crest of the slope. Brush screened the hollow so the shooters couldn't see what they were shooting at. Jack got out of there fast, putting a line of boulders between him and the fusillade.

"Spread out! We've got him now!" The command came in the harsh, metallic, unmistakable tones of Pardee.

But they didn't have Jack, not yet. Crouched almost double, he made a mad dash for the timberline. The hunters hadn't seen him, they were still focused on the hollow he'd just quit. Flashlight beams pinned it from several different directions. The site became a magnet for lead. Bullets tore up turf, pulped cactus, pinged off rocks with wicked whining ricochets.

The woods ahead were on fire in a dozen different hot spots. They hadn't consolidated into one big blaze yet but not for lack of trying. Jack put on an extra burst of speed, hating the glare that picked him out as a better target.

Pardee was rallying his crew, bawling at the top of his lungs. "Get him, you dirty sons of—"

They'd stopped wasting bullets on the empty hollow and were throwing lead at the distant figure at the edge of the woods. Jack slipped between the trees, angling through them for better cover. Bullets made woodpecker rappings against the timber.

Jack wove through the maze, seeking always the gaps in the flame, the arcades slanting southward toward the far end of the plateau. Hot embers and ash rained down on him.

The manhunters weren't so eager to follow Jack into the inferno. Pardee raged, cursed, kicked some butts, and swore he'd shoot any laggards. That got his crew moving. Pardee hung back, going in last behind the others. Now they had him at their backs with a gun—a powerful incentive not to retreat.

The hunters fanned out, trying to outflank their quarry on either side. Not so easily accomplished with the blaze raging all around.

A sharp cracking report burst overhead. For an instant Jack mistook it for gunfire. Instead it was the sound of a tree limb breaking off near the trunk where fire had gnawed it down so that it was no longer able to bear the weight.

Jack jumped back, dodging the flaming branch as it came crashing down, sending hordes of orange sparks skyward. The ground was hot underfoot. A tree trunk exploded nearby, spewing sizzling resin, spraying bark. Not fire but gunfire was the cause.

Jack spun, dropping into a crouch, pointing his gun. A rifleman swung his weapon in line with Jack. Jack pumped some lead into him. The impact spun the shooter around before knocking him down.

Shapes, outlines of men appeared nearby, their images rippling in the heat waves. Jack turned, ran down the winding trail, darting through the trees. He angled toward the southeast, arrowing toward the fast-narrowing avenue of woodland as yet untouched by the fire. It would be a close-run thing. Much of the woods beyond the saddle were ablaze.

Jack flattened his back against a tree trunk, bracing himself for—what?

Overhead, lights and swift rushing motion; titanic, irresistible. An airplane. Not just any airplane but a tanker plane, making another run. It flew so low that it was almost at treetop level.

It dumped its massive cargo of tons of water on the saddle to balk the advancing arm of the firestorm's southern front. Just as it or one like it had done earlier on the valley's northern slope.

The tanker plane's path overflew the fiery saddle between the ridges. Water cascaded earthward as though some giant knife had gutted a raincloud to unleash its contents all at once in a massive downpour of a tropical monsoon.

Jack was at the edge of the water drop but it struck with the impact of a high-pressure fire hose. It knocked him down, stunning him. He kept a death grip on his gun to avoid losing it.

Jack got his feet under him, forced himself to rise, leaning against a tree to keep from falling down. He looked around, unable to see much of anything except massive steam clouds that unfolded upward into the sky. He couldn't make out any sign of the hunters.

The air shimmered with glowing clouds that were great abstract masses of yellow, orange, and red, all shimmering and swirling. It was caused by firelight shining through banks of steam.

The tanker plane's water dump had literally been a drop in the bucket. It had blunted the firestorm's advancing front, nothing more. The firestorm itself continued to rage, turning the west into a sea of flame.

The ridge west of the gap was a blazing beacon. Jack used it to get his bearings. He went south through the unburned section of pine forest, crossing the plateau toward South Mesa and escape.

. . . .

**THE FOLLOWING TAKES PLACE
BETWEEN THE HOURS OF
8 P.M. AND 9 P.M.
MOUNTAIN DAYLIGHT TIME**

. . . .

8:43 P.M. MDT
Felderman's Station, Los Alamos County

A metal dragonfly that was a helicopter floated down from
a red and black sky toward a crossroads. The crossroads lay
south of the plateau where the tanker plane had made its
water dump.

Whatever effect the water drop might have had in slowing the firestorm's eastern advance had long since been nul-
lified. The plateau was a solid sheet of flame and the fire
had jumped the gap to begin eating its way across the next
ridge in line.

The fire had been balked by the sandy wastes of the flat
that lay at the base of the plateau's southern slope. It was
a broad expanse of reddish-brown soil too thin to promote
anything but some patches of brush and weed too sparsely
scattered for the fire to get a grip on.

A dirt trail that was an old logging road emerged from the south slope to stretch across the flat toward far-distant South Mesa. It intersected a gravel road running east-west. On the southwest quarter of the crossroads stood the moldering ruins of what had once been a stagecoach relay station and trading post: Felderman's Station.

All that remained were the crumbling stone walls of the structure's foundation. Jack Bauer lurked in the shadows of those walls, watching the copter descend. The stonework provided what little cover was to be found on the flat.

Jack was careful not to get too close to those jagged stone heaps. Such tumble-down rock piles were a rattlesnake's delight. On the other hand, he had no desire to show himself in the open in case any of Pardee's men was lurking in the area.

Earlier, the tanker plane's water dump had provided him with the diversion he needed to lose the manhunters. He'd plunged ahead into the drowned woods, a bleak vista of blackened skeletal trees, steaming ground covered with black ashes and embers extinguished by the deluge, and hissing white clouds of water vapor wafting through glades and trails.

He worked his way to the plateau's edge and then down its southern slope. The water drop hadn't held the fire back for long. The hillside was once more ablaze by the time he reached the flat.

At noontime the atmosphere had been dead calm. Now it was restless, rushing, as if the firestorm was inexhaustibly sucking up great masses of air to fuel its ever-mounting onslaught. Winds whipped into the sky a blizzard of fire flakes, glowing coals and embers, sending them hurtling northeastward. Where they fell they sowed new blazes.

Jack made his way across the sandy flat to the jumbled ruins at the crossroads. The sky was bright with firelight, the ground open. He hoped that Pardee had posted no snipers with night-scoped rifles on the heights of the ride east of the gap, where the fire was just starting to find a foothold.

He angled across the flat with his shoulders and upper back tensed in anticipation of being struck by a bullet. But it seemed that Pardee had given up the chase; there was no sign of enemy action.

Still, tension gripped him until he found himself sheltered by the cover of jumbled rock walls. He knew the blessed relief that comes from having evaded pursuit, to be able to draw a breath and recover his strength without being harried, hunted, and shot at.

He had the luxury of switching on his cell phone, something he'd been unable to do during the chase. For one thing the hunters had been pressing him too hard for him to take the time; for another, it would have been so much wasted effort because he'd have been long dead before any rescuers could arrive.

His cell had satellite phone capability, freeing him from worry about getting through if the fire had taken out some of the local cell phone towers. He contacted FBI SA Vince Sabito.

"Nice of you to check in from time to time, Bauer." Sabito's deceptive mildness was a threadbare cloak for heavy sarcasm.

"I've been busy, Vince," Jack said. He gave the other a quick summary of the events beginning with the shoot-out at Rhee's apartment, followed by his pursuit of Nacio in the silver coupe, Pardee's intervention with his gun crew, and the manhunt through the burning hills.

"Quite a story," Sabito said when Jack had finished. "Tell me: You didn't start the fire, too, did you?"

"Not guilty, Vince."

"That's something, anyhow. You can identify Pardee?"

"Only by voice. I heard him but I never got a good look at him. I won't forget that voice in a hurry, though."

"I'll put a pickup order on him. Not that it'll do any good; that bastard's got a million holes to hide in all over the county. He's a top Blanco gang hand. It'll give me a reason to roust Torreon, though," Sabito said, his voice expressing evident relish at the prospect.

"I could use some of that good interagency cooperation right about now," Jack said.

Sabito snorted. "That's rich, coming from you." He sighed. "Okay, what do you want?"

"A ride out of here, for starters."

"Where are you?"

"Out in the middle of nowhere."

"That's a big help, Bauer."

Jack didn't have to rely on any guesswork. His cell's built-in GPS pinpointed the exact coordinates of his position. He read them off to Sabito.

"Sit tight, your ride's on the way. You'll be going airborne—a chopper's coming to pick you up. Try to stay out of trouble in the meantime," Sabito said. He broke the connection.

Jack checked his voice messages. The only urgent one was from Harvey Kling: it had come in about an hour earlier. Jack played it back:

"Bauer? Kling here. I've got something for you. Something big. Remember that hot lead I mentioned before? I wasn't just talking through my hat. The proof of it is at number ninety-seven Meadow Lane in Shady Grove. Family name of Parkhurst lives there. They put me on to something that could break this case wide open. Ninety-seven Meadow Lane, Shady Grove. Meet me there as soon as you can. Come quietly so as not to tip your mitt. Come alone—I don't know who else to trust with this thing."

Jack called Kling's number; Kling didn't pick up. Jack left a message on his voice mail: "I'll be there as soon as possible."

Now the helicopter was in view, drifting down from the sky. The crossroads served as its mark. It dropped down right in the center of them. Rotor blade downdraft whipped up a ring of dust and sent it expanding outward like a ripple from a pebble dropped in a pool.

The helicopter touched down lightly, perching delicately on its rails. It was yellow with black trim, a sleek, hornet-looking aircraft. A hatch slid open on the forward starboard side of the cockpit. Framed in the hatchway was Hickman, cradling an M–4 carbine.

Jack jogged from the ruins to the copter. He moved in a crouch, keeping his head down. He approached the open hatchway where Hickman brandished the M–4. If Hickman was working for the other side, he'd never have a better chance to be rid of one Jack Bauer. Jack thought that Hickman was okay, but in this line of work there were no guarantees—

Hickman flashed his teeth in a knife-blade grin, moving aside so Jack could climb into the cockpit. He was still but toned down in the same suit he'd worn earlier that day. He hadn't even loosened the knot of his tie as a concession to the heat. He sat in a bucket seat up front in the passenger side of the compartment.

The pilot, about thirty, wore a set of earphones over a duckbilled khaki cap. He had wavy brown hair, dark brown eyes, jutting cheekbones, and an eyebrow mustache. He could have been a movie star playing a dashing World War I aviator—all that was missing was a silk scarf. He greeted Jack with a jaunty thumbs-up.

Hickman shouted to be heard over the noise of the engine

and rotors. "Looks like you got your tail feathers singed, Bauer!"

The helicopter lofted upward. The bottom of Jack's stomach felt like it was dropping between his knees. The ground fell away from the copter like a descending elevator car, turning the landscape into a tabletop miniature.

Jack leaned forward, shouting, "Let's take a look at the north side of the ridge—see if Pardee is still around!"

The pilot gave a quick glance at Hickman. Hickman nodded yes. The copter soared higher, wheeling above the plateau and the gap between the ridges. The sun had dropped below the western horizon, the sky was dark, smoke hid the moon and stars.

The helicopter zoomed over the north side of the ridges. The burning hills gave plenty of light by which to see the landscape. It was laid out below: the snaky gully, winding road, and blazing woods. A fallen tree blocked the road. West of it stood two burned-out hulks, the remains of the dark sedan and the silver coupe, engulfed and gutted by fire.

East, the road was empty; the pickup truck that had brought reinforcements was nowhere to be seen. "Gone!" Jack said. He'd expected as much. He leaned far forward and put his mouth near Hickman's ear so he wouldn't have to shout so loud. "Where's Shady Grove?"

"On the Hill. Why?" Hickman asked.

"That's where we've got to go."

"Why?"

"Because that's where we'll find Harvey Kling."

"So what?"

"Kling's playing a deeper game than you think. He knows things and he's ready to spill his guts."

Hickman was openly derisive. "He's an alcoholic. What's your excuse?"

"I got to Rhee too late today. Let's not make the same mistake twice," Jack said.

Hickman looked unconvinced.

Jack played his trump card. "What have you got to lose? If it pans out, you get the credit. If it doesn't, you can hang it on me while the Bureau comes out smelling like a rose. I'm sure Vince will like that."

Hickman allowed himself a wintry smile. He told the pilot to head for Shady Grove.

• •

THE FOLLOWING TAKES PLACE
BETWEEN THE HOURS OF
9 P.M. AND 10 P.M.
MOUNTAIN DAYLIGHT TIME

• •

9:05 P.M. MDT
Shady Grove Elementary School,
Los Alamos County

Shady Grove is a suburb of the city of Los Alamos, located
in the northern uplands of the Hill. It's an affluent, exclusive neighborhood; a pleasant place, well-wooded. It sits
on a height overlooking much of the city below. Handsome
houses are set on extensive grounds with plenty of room between neighbors. Streets meander in lazy, looping curves.

The fire was far away from Shady Grove and neighboring communities located farther down the hill. But smoke
haze was everywhere, blanketing the nightscape like acrid,
blue-gray fog. Los Alamos city lights were muted, blurred
behind a smoky scrim.

That same haze overspread the towns on the terraced
tabletop of the Hill.

The pilot set down the copter in the heart of Shady Grove, on the parking lot of the town's grade school. Kling had told Jack Bauer to come in quietly but Jack was in a hurry. Meadow Lane was some blocks distant from the school so it wasn't like the copter was dropping in right on top of it. Besides, with the firestorm raging, it wasn't necessarily so unusual for a helicopter to set down in the neighborhood—it could legitimately be ascribed to some kind of first responder plan.

The grade school was a sprawling one-story flat-roofed building shaped like the capital letter "I." It sat on a nice tract of well-tended lawns and fields. The building was dark but its exterior was well lit up. Ground-based floodlights lit up its face. Spotlights were mounted high on the building's corners. Tall lampposts illuminated the asphalt square of the teachers' parking lot.

The lot was a natural for a helicopter landing pad. It was empty except for a lone minivan parked near the side of the building. The pilot set the chopper down in the middle of the lot, killed the motor. He took off his earphones, setting them aside.

"He's good," Jack said, indicating the pilot.

"You're not telling him anything he doesn't know. Name's Ron Galvez—we use him when we've got Bureau business in the area. Operates out of a small private field on South Mesa. A civilian but discreet, he doesn't go telling tales out of school," Hickman said.

Galvez smiled, showing a mouthful of perfect teeth. "Neat and discreet, that's me. How long do I wait for you?" Galvez asked.

"Until we return or I call and tell you otherwise," Hickman said.

Jack and Hickman stepped down from the cockpit to the pavement. "Where's Vince? I thought he'd be here to meet us," Jack said.

"He took a squad out to the Blanco ranch—home base for Torreon and Marta Blanco and their gang," Hickman explained. "Your claim that Pardee was bossing the hit squad that was dogging you gives Vince a pretext for searching the ranch. He never passes up an opportunity to roust the gang, not that it does much good. But he likes to remind them he's around."

"Who are these Blancos anyway?"

"They're pretty much at the top of the garbage pile in the local pecking order. A big-time crime family that's been working both sides of the border for generations, trading in contraband: slaves, bootleg whiskey, hot cars, guns, drugs, people smuggling, you name it.

"Torreon and his sister Marta are the last surviving members of the clan; there's plenty of cousins and in-laws and whatnot, too, but they're all from collateral branches.

"Their father, the patriarch, and a half-dozen older siblings are all dead—killed by rival gangs or the law; only Torreon and Marta are left alive. He's the warlord, the enforcer; she's the actual brains and fixer of the outfit, when it comes to keeping the books and greasing the political protection and payoffs.

"The Blancos and others like them are the Bureau's meat and potatoes. Our priority here has traditionally been bank robbers, drug gangs, stolen car rings, and gun runners. Atom spies don't feature much in the all-important crime stats."

A car appeared on the road leading to the school; a police car. It came up the drive into the parking lot, halting a dozen yards from the helicopter. Its headlights shone on the aircraft and its occupants. "Here comes the welcoming committee," Hickman said.

Blazoned on the side of the car was the emblem of the County Sheriff's Department. The driver got out; he wore a Stetson-type hat, a uniform tunic with a star-shaped badge over the left breast, a sidearm, slacks, and cowboy boots.

"That's Ross, one of Sheriff Bender's deputies. Make no mistake—he's not dumb," Hickman said to Jack out of the side of his mouth.

"What's he doing here?" Jack asked.

"You planning on walking to Meadow Lane?"

"Where are your guys?"

"They're all out at the Blanco ranch. The Bureau is understaffed in these parts; we use the Sheriff's Department for backup a lot. Vince and Buck Bender are tight. Besides, we don't get along with the City Police Department worth a good damn," Hickman said.

Deputy Ross crossed to them, his boot heels clip-clopping on the pavement. He had gray hair at the temples, bushy eyebrows, and a tobacco-colored walrus mustache. He seemed stolid, phlegmatic. "Agent Hickman," he said.

"Deputy," Hickman said. They shook hands. Hickman indicated Jack, said, "Deputy Ross, this is Agent Bauer of CTU; he's working with us on special assignment."

"Glad to know you," Ross said.

"Likewise," said Jack. They shook hands. Jack's hand virtually disappeared inside Ross's pawlike grip.

"CTU, huh? We got terrorists up here in Shady Grove?" Ross asked. He was straight-faced, so Jack couldn't tell if he was kidding or not.

"That's what we'd like to find out," Jack said, seriously enough.

"Let's get to it, then."

Hickman reached into the cockpit and pulled out the M–4. "Bringing the heavy artillery," Ross observed.

"The Blancos have been acting up tonight," Hickman said.

"Them sum'bitches!" Real malice glittered in Ross's eyes.

Jack Bauer stuck his head in the cockpit. "Got a gun?"

"What for? I'm a flyer, not a fighter," Galvez said.

"Just in case somebody wants to hijack you for a quick ride out of here. It's shaping up as that kind of night."

Galvez reached under the instrument board, unclipping a first-aid kit the size and shape of a lunch box. He put it on his lap, unclipped the fasteners, and lifted the lid. Inside were a revolver and a box of ammunition. He broke the gun, checked that chambers of the cylinder were loaded, and closed it. He stuck the short-barreled gun into the right-hand pocket of his nylon Windbreaker.

"Nobody rides for free," he said, smiling.

Jack, Hickman, and Ross went to the deputy's car. Hickman was the local liaison; protocol dictated that he ride in the front passenger seat. Jack sat in the back, where the prisoners ride. A wire mesh grille separated the front seat from the backseat.

Ross hopped in behind the wheel, the front seat shuddering under his weight. He pulled out of the parking lot, following the driveway and making a right-hand turn into the street.

Shady Grove was an attractive piece of property, picturesque streets winding and looping around vacant lots where stands of pine trees grew. Streetlights were bright but few and far between. A number of houses had Georgian-style white columned fronts.

It was Saturday night but the neighborhood was quiet. A respectable district where all good law-abiding middle-aged homeowners were locked up and buttoned down for the night. Not necessarily so their teenage sons and daughters, but they went to points beyond Shady Grove in search of their good time.

The patrol car made a right turn into a winding street. "Meadow Lane, gents," Ross said.

There was money here. The proof was in the lawns. They were extensive and green, well-watered, unlike the parched vegetation and dry yellow-brown grass to be found in less exclusive precincts.

A pleasant place, where houses were set far back from the curbs. They were sprawling, expensive, but not in the mansion class. Some were split-level ranch houses, others were more traditional two-story jobs. Most homes had more than one new or late model vehicle parked in the driveway. Lights shone through curtained windows.

"We want number ninety-seven—Parkhurst," Jack said.

"Parkhurst? Don't believe I know the name . . . so they probably ain't been in trouble with the law," Ross said. "Shady Grove is outside city limits so the Sheriff's Department handles the complaints. And we get 'em, too: wife beating, breaking and entering, drunk and disorderly, peeping Toms, vandalism, you name it."

"Really? Seems like a nice neighborhood."

"It is, generally, but people being people, things happen."

The patrol car glided along the street. There were no sidewalks; the neighborhood was not particularly pedestrian-friendly. They passed a house numbered 92. "Almost there," Ross said.

Number 97 was on the opposite, left side of the street. A pair of curtained bay windows bracketed the front door; the second-story windows had blue shutters. Lights were on inside the house.

Parked in the street at curbside in front of the house was a battered Toyota Camry; Jack recognized it as having been parked in the visitors' area near Rhee's apartment at Ponderosa Pines. "Is that Harvey Kling's car?" he asked.

"It looks like the kind of heap he'd drive," Hickman said.

Ross pulled in at the curb in front of the Toyota. He radioed in to the dispatcher, reporting that he was going out of service to make a routine inquiry at 97 Meadow Lane.

He killed the engine and switched off the lights; he and Hickman got out of the car. Hickman held the M–4 in one hand along his right side, pointed downward. Jack knocked on the window to get his attention. This was a police car; the backseat being relegated to prisoners, the back doors couldn't be opened from the inside. Hickman had to open the door from the outside to let Jack out.

Ross reached into the front of the car, pulling out a riot gun, a police model twelve-gauge pump shotgun with a special chopped-down barrel and shortened stock. "Just in case the Blancos crash the party," he said.

"I been looking to clean up on that crowd for a long time," he added.

The driveway was on the right-hand side of the house. It led to a garage whose door was closed. "I'll cover the rear," Hickman said.

"Don't shoot Kling if he gets spooked and takes it on the run. Remember he's on our side," Jack said.

Hickman went up the driveway and around the right-hand corner of the garage, heading for the backyard.

A flagstone path curved across the front lawn to a brick stairway. The treads were made of rough-hewn slabs of gray stone and there was a black iron rail banister on the left. Jack and Ross climbed the stairs to a square-shaped stoop.

An electric fixture resembling an old-time black iron lantern was mounted over the top of the front door, shedding a cone of light. Small white moths fluttered around it. Jack rang the doorbell; chimes sounded inside the house.

Nothing happened. Nobody came to the door. He rang the bell two more times, to an equal lack of response. Jack opened the screen door and tried the front doorknob.

It turned easily under his hand.

He and Ross exchanged glances. "I'll go in first," Jack said. Ross nodded, stepping aside. He snaked his pistol out of the shoulder holster into his hand. His free hand pushed open the door.

Beyond it lay a front hall with a handsome wooden floor

covered by a woven Navajo-style rug. Opposite the door, on the far side of the hall, a carpeted staircase led to the second floor. To the left of the stairs, an archway opened into a living room. To the right of the stairs, a corridor led to the rear of the house.

A dead man lay sprawled on his back in the front hall. Jack came in sidestepping to the right. Ross came right behind him, riot gun leveled. Ross covered the living room, Jack covered the corridor.

The air smelled of gunpowder, blood, and death. It sounded like a television was playing somewhere in the direction of the living room.

The body in the front hall was that of a middle-aged man dressed in casual clothes: a sport shirt, slacks, and rubber-soled canvas shoes. He was a stranger to Jack. The unknown man was unarmed. He looked like an ordinary, respectable householder who'd been taking his ease on a quiet Saturday night at home—Parkhurst?

He was balding with short brown hair fringing the sides of his head. His eyes were wide open, staring. A bullet hole marked the center of a broad expanse of forehead. A single small-caliber slug had drilled him through the brain.

Ross moved off into the living room, stepping very quietly on large-sized, cowboy-booted feet.

Jack moved off to the right, down the corridor. He moved sideways, his back to the right-hand wall. The corridor was twenty feet long, opening on to a kitchen at its far end. A light was on in the kitchen. From where Jack stood he could see a round dinette table with several chairs grouped around it.

Midway in the corridor was a corpse. Another stranger, one cut from decidedly different cloth than the dead man in the front hall.

He sat on the floor with his back propped up against the left wall and his legs stretching out. He was in his late twenties. His scalp was shaved; he was thick-featured, with small round eyes closely set together. The eyes were circled with dark rings. The stubble of a three-day beard failed to hide the pallor of a lumpish, oval face. A diamond stud sparkled in his left earlobe and a swirling, near-abstract tattoo decorated his neck.

He'd caught two slugs in the left breast over the heart, the entry wounds spaced closely together. A nice bit of shooting, thought Jack.

The corpse's eyebrows were raised and his mouth gaped open as if he was surprised to be so completely and irrevocably dead. His arms extended out from his sides, right fist gripping a gun, a .22 Colt Woodsman pistol with a silencer attached to the barrel.

The weapon was one favored by professional killers. Jack figured it had been used to kill the man in the front hall. But who killed the killer?

A vertical blood track smeared the wall, mute testimony marking that the killer had been shot, fell back against the wall, and slid down it to the floor. He sat facing an open doorway on the opposite side of the corridor. Jack went to it, investigating—carefully.

The door on the right-hand side of the corridor connected to the attached garage. No cars were parked there, but it contained two more bodies.

Two short, narrow stairs descended to a gray cement floor. A man in his thirties lay near the stairs. Long coal-black hair was pulled straight back from his forehead and face and tied behind the back of his neck in a ponytail. His eyebrows were inverted "Vs," pointed in the centers of the arches. He wore a T-shirt with a fancy print pattern, jeans, and expensive sneakers.

A 9mm Beretta semi-automatic pistol lay on the floor where it had fallen from his dead hand. A bullet hole gaped where a round had tagged him in the middle of the face.

Across from him on the other side of the garage lay
Harvey Kling. Kling was turned away from the gunman,
sprawled in the opposite direction. He lay on his left side
with his left arm extended in front of him. The side of his
head rested on his left arm. His right side was uppermost.
His right arm lay along his right side, still clutching his
snub-nosed .38.

He had died hard. His middle had been shot to pieces;
it was a welter of gore that had soaked into his clothes and
pooled on the floor.

Jack went through the motions, crouching down beside
the body, fingertips probing Kling's neck for a faint throbbing pulse of life, knowing all the while it was an exercise
in futility. Kling had bled out a while ago. Jack straightened
up and took a step back, studying the scene, puzzling over
the layout of the bodies.

This was no ordinary suburban garage. It might have
started out that way, but sometime in the not too distant past
it had been converted into some kind of a sophisticated listening post.

Its centerpiece was a communications console, an array
of intricate electronic hardware housed in a heavy-duty
wooden cabinet. Its function was not immediately apparent.
Adjacent to it was a gray metal desk and swivel chair. A flat-
screen monitor and portable keyboard sat on the desktop.

Broad smeared blood tracks on the floor showed where
Kling had turned himself around, using the last reserves of
the life fading in him to position himself so that he faced
away from his assailants. His head was cradled on his arm,
that extended left arm.

The hand of which was pointing a finger at the electronics console.

Jack crossed to it for a closer look. The main piece of
equipment was built into the top of the bulky wooden
framework. It was a suitcase-sized piece of hardware inset

with its broad side face up. It featured mini-monitor screens, gauges, dials, and banks of switches.

Below it, installed on a lower shelf of the cabinet, was what looked like a customized, amped-up computer tower. Tower and suitcase were cable-interconnected. Other connecting cables ran from the back of the console to the desktop flat-screen monitor and keyboard.

A figure loomed in the doorway: Deputy Ross. He stuck his head in the garage and looked around.

He stepped down to the floor, circling the corpse of the ponytailed man to look him in the face.

"Like I figured—Chino Valdosta," he said, nodding solemnly. "I knew it was him when I saw Tommy Burke out in the hall. Had to be. Chino wouldn't have left Burke behind; he'd have carried away the body if he could. The same applied with Burke."

"Who were they?" Jack asked.

"Two bad 'uns. A couple of no-account, piece-of-trash killers for hire. They've been a burr under the saddle of law enforcement in these parts for a long time. Too long. They were a team. We used to call them the Ball Brothers—they hung together, get it?

"Did everything together: lived together, got drunk and raised hell together, ran whores together, killed together. Got killed together, too. And good riddance."

Ross indicated Kling. "That your man?"

"He was. That's Harvey Kling," Jack said.

"He done good. Chino and Burke were stone killers. Tough to take down," Ross said. "There's another deader in the den—a civilian. The missus, I reckon. She got it the same way as the fellow in the front hall. A bullet in the head from Burke's Colt. He always was the marksman of the two.

"I cleared the upstairs rooms. Empty—no more bodies, thank the Lord."

"Where's Hickman?" Jack asked.

"He must still be outside keeping watch. Talk about locking the barn door after the horse is stolen . . . I'll go get him."

Ross went back in the house, down the corridor, and into the kitchen. He unlocked and opened the back door and let Hickman in. Presently the two of them joined Jack in the garage.

Hickman surveyed the carnage without flinching. "This is what the tabloid TV shows call a House of Death."

"They will," Jack agreed.

"That closes the files on Burke and Valdosta."

"You know them, too?"

"Oh, everybody knows them. Two major league pains in the butt. Or at least they were," Hickman said. "This make any sense to you, Bauer?"

"I think so. The dead couple is probably Mr. and Mrs. Parkhurst. They were part of some operation Kling was running. Burke and Valdosta came here to clean house. Burke shot Parkhurst with the silenced pistol and then took care of Mrs. Parkhurst. Valdosta surprised Kling here in the garage and cut loose on him. Kling was mortally wounded but still managed to finish off Valdosta. Burke came to see what happened and Kling nailed him, too."

Ross pushed his hat back on his forehead. "That was some mighty sweet shooting."

"Kling was a top man in his field once. I guess he still had enough left when it counted," Jack said.

"Here's something that might help round out the picture," Hickman said. "Burke and Valdosta were freelancers, unaffiliated with any mob. But the word is that lately they've been doing jobs for the Blancos."

"One thing's for sure, the Blancos wanted Kling out of the picture. They tried for him at Rhee's apartment and when that didn't work they sent another hit team here," Jack said.

"Who were the Parkhursts and where did they fit in?" Ross asked. He gestured at the electronics console. "And what's all that junk, some kind of fancy bugging device?"

"Good question," Hickman said. He went to the console and examined it. "Looks like some kind of broadband scanner . . ."

"It meant something to Kling," Jack said. "Something so important that he had to point it out even though he was dying. You can see by the way the blood is smeared on the floor that he turned himself around to draw attention to the console. Why? It's not something an investigator who came after would overlook or ignore. It's the first thing you'd see after the bodies. So why go to the trouble of underlining it?"

"He was dying," Hickman said. "Dying men don't necessarily think straight. With the life running out of him, consciousness fading fast, it might have made some kind of crazy sense to him."

"Maybe. But suppose he knew what he was doing. In which case—what exactly was he pointing at?" Jack followed the direction of Kling's pointing finger, extending an imaginary straight line from the dead man's fingertip. The line ran across the floor to the bottom right-hand corner of the console cabinet.

Jack went down on one knee beside it. The cabinet had four short, squat feet and a heavy base. The top of the base served as the bottom shelf supporting the computer tower. The base itself was five inches tall. It did not fully extend to the floor; between base and floor was a gap of about four inches of empty space.

Jack rapped a knuckle against the base. It was well constructed but not necessarily solid all the way through. He reached underneath it, feeling around. On the underside, out of sight, was a row of dime-sized studs projecting from the framework. Jack began pressing them one at a time.

When he pressed the fifth stud, it moved under his finger,

sinking into a hole. There was a faint but unmistakable clicking sound from somewhere inside the base of the cabinet. Part of its vertical front face separated itself from the rest of the wooden block.

Hickman and Ross crowded around, craning for a better view. Hickman said, "What's that? A hidden compartment—?"

"A secret drawer," Jack said. The drawer's leading edge projected several inches beyond the base of the cabinet. Jack hooked his fingertips over the top edge and pulled it out, opening it. The drawer was mounted on well-oiled metal tracks that operated noiselessly.

Inside it was a black leather-bound book and a manila folder. The book was the size and shape of an appointment book. The manila folder held a sheaf of printed documents.

Jack opened the black book to the first page. It was filled with neat cursive script that he recognized as the handwriting of Peter Rhee. He began thumbing through the pages, noting that they contained a series of dated entries.

"What is it?" Hickman asked.

"It's the operational diary of an investigation done by Kling and Rhee for OCI Chief Morrow," Jack Bauer said. "I'll need some time with this."

· ·

THE FOLLOWING TAKES PLACE
BETWEEN THE HOURS OF
10 P.M. AND 11 P.M.
MOUNTAIN DAYLIGHT TIME

· ·

10:11 P.M. MDT
97 Meadow Lane, Shady Grove,
Los Alamos County

"Interference—that's what triggered this bloodbath," Jack
Bauer said.

He'd skimmed the notebook and the documents in the
folder. The information they contained allowed him to piece
together the backstory. He now ran it down to Hickman and
Ross. Not all of it, but as much as they needed to know. He
needed their help and goodwill. Hickman was Sabito's sav-
viest operative in Jack's estimation, and Ross was Sabito's
key contact in the County Sheriff's Department.

Jack went on. "It started with interference, electrical
interference, the kind that screws up the picture on your
TV. More specifically, Gene Parkhurst's TV. That's what
brought him to Ironwood's OCI. He came in about a month

ago. As far as OCI was concerned, he dropped in out of the blue. McCoy's people had never heard of him, had no professional interest in him. He was a walk-in.

"Walk-ins are the wild cards of the intelligence game. A citizen comes into the shop unsolicited. He might be there to pass along a hot tip, make a complaint, or make a deal. You don't know his motivation. Maybe he's what he seems, acting in good faith.

"Maybe he's got a hidden agenda. Maybe he's a crank, a nutcase. There's no way of telling until you hear out what he's got to say and evaluate it."

"It's pretty much the same in my business," Ross said.

"Of course an ordinary civilian can't just walk into OCI. Parkhurst phoned first, saying he wanted to report something suspicious. He wouldn't say what it was over the phone except that it was confidential. Maybe he had something worth telling; it wouldn't do any harm to hear him out. He was given an appointment to come in on a weekday morning. Kling drew the assignment to interview him. He pulled a lot of those kinds of chores. Routine security and background checks, mostly. Stuff that nobody else wanted to handle fell to the low man on the totem pole, and the lowest man on the OCI totem pole was Harvey Kling.

"Kling did a routine background check on Gene Parkhurst prior to the interview. Parkhurst was a retired master machinist who'd spent most of his professional life working in various capacities for LANL at South Mesa. He came up clean: a respected career professional in his line, solid security rating, ditto on the credit rating, no black marks on his record, good marriage. No suspicious contacts or associates, no substance abuse problems, no involvement with the law beyond a few parking tickets. He seemed like a normal, competent, levelheaded guy.

"But Parkhurst had a complaint: interference. For the last six weeks or so, he'd noticed a peculiar pattern of interference on his TV. Every now and then, for no particular rhyme or reason, the sound and picture on his set would get knocked out of whack and become a jumble of chaos and static. The disruptions lasted from one to two minutes, tops. They ended as suddenly as they began. They never came at the same time. They happened in the day and in the night. Sometimes several days would go by with no disruptions, other times there'd be a couple of them in one day or night."

"Kling must have been thrilled to have to interview what was basically a guy complaining about a bum TV set," Hickman said.

"He got more interested as Parkhurst told his tale," Jack said. "Parkhurst was a machinist by trade and a tinkerer by nature. The inexplicable interference irritated him, offended his problem-solving nature. The disruptions weren't reserved to a single TV set. They affected every TV in the house the same way. He ran diagnostic tests on the TVs— nothing wrong with them. He asked his neighbors if they'd been bothered by similar problems—none of them had.

"That introduced an interesting variable. Parkhurst subscribed to a satellite TV distribution network. A dish antenna on his roof received the signals. The neighborhood—this neighborhood and all the rest of Shady Grove—had recently been wired for fiber optic cable. Most of his neighbors had gone with the new system and got their TV off the wire. Parkhurst was one of the few to still have a satellite dish. Maybe that was the key to the problem.

"He had the satellite TV company repairmen come out to his house to inspect the setup. He asked if they'd had any problems like his. There weren't many sat-TV customers left in the neighborhood. One of the repairmen thought he remembered a couple of similar complaints from subscribers a couple of blocks away, but the interference was far less serious. Of course the disruptions weren't so obliging as to occur when the repairmen were there so they could see them in action. They found nothing out of order in Parkhurst's setup. Hardware and software checked out okay. 'Static,' the repairmen called it and let it go at that. These things happened some times, nobody knows why. Minor glitches somewhere in the system. They'd work themselves out sooner or later and go away.

"But they didn't. Parkhurst put his brain to work wondering what made his TVs go blooey. He had a thought: If the problem wasn't internal, maybe it was external. What causes interference? Competing wavelengths crosscutting each other. It could be that some powerful outside signal was causing the disruptions, a broadcast or transmission or some sort. A frequency that was close enough to that of the satellite TV's to override it and cancel it out.

"What was generating the signal? No other satellite TV companies were operating in the area. There hadn't been any over-the-air broadcast TV thereabouts for decades. He toyed with the thought that some facility at the lab was experimenting with some new kind of powerful transmitter whose frequency caused the disruptions. Then he realized that a signal powerful enough to reach out from South Mesa would have affected satellite TVs all over the Hill and caused a public uproar. That hadn't happened so he ruled LANL out as the source.

"Other satellite TV subscribers who lived several blocks away had experienced minor versions of the disruptions. That indicated that the source was a local phenomenon emanating from somewhere nearby. Amateur radio operators—hams—operated in a different part of the waveband too distant to interfere with the satellite signal, so it couldn't be one of them. Parkhurst concluded that someone was operating some kind of powerful new transceiver in the neighborhood.

"That's when Gene Parkhurst's gadgeteer hat came off and his patriot hat came on. He'd spent most of his life working in Los Alamos, steeped in the lab's national security culture. He was a true believer in security regulations and classified tradecraft.

"Who was most likely to have a sophisticated transceiver sending and receiving clandestine broadcasts? An enemy agent. A spy. 'If you see something suspicious, report it.' That's been the watchword of LANL's security-conscious culture since World War II, long before 9/11 imprinted the motto on the national consciousness. Retiree or not, Parkhurst knew where his duty lay. Patriotism for him was something from which you don't retire. He'd seen something suspicious and it was his duty to report it to the proper authorities.

"He'd worked at a lot of places on South Mesa but never Ironwood, so why did he choose to report his findings to OCI? He'd followed the Sayeed case closely from start to finish. He thought Sayeed was guilty as hell and the collapse of the case was a national disgrace. He'd been a big fan of OCI's then-head Seaton Hotchkiss during the trial, liked the way he'd fought for a conviction. That decided him on going to Ironwood. He didn't know that in the years since the trial Hotchkiss had gone into early retirement and died. He did recognize Kling from the trial, though, and was thrilled to be interviewed by him. It proved he was right in going to OCI.

"And he was right, though not for the reasons he thought. It was a fateful encounter, his meeting with Kling. Ultimately it resulted in the deaths of both of them and a lot more. Of all the people in the world, Kling was one of the few most likely to take Parkhurst's complaint seriously. The others were Peter Rhee and OCI Director Rhodes Morrow, for reasons I'll get to directly.

"Kling told Parkhurst that he'd come to the right place and that his tip would be looked into. He cautioned him to keep the information to himself and his wife and not to

discuss it or his visit to OCI with anyone else. He compli-
mented him on his good citizenship, and assured him he'd
be receiving a follow-up visit in the near future."

Here Jack paused for a moment. For security reasons he
now had to give his two allies the redacted version of the
rest of the truth. Hickman knew some of the background
of the Ironwood kills; Ross, virtually none. Ross's presence
made Jack more circumspect than he would have been had
he been reviewing the case with Hickman alone. Even then
he would not have told all.

"Most of what you've just heard comes from Kling's
initial reports, copies of which were in the folder files, and
from his and Rhee's handwritten entries in the operational
diary," Jack said. "What follows is directly involved with
an investigation I'm working on now. It's sensitive material,
classified top secret.

"I can tell you that OCI Director Rhodes Morrow had
Kling and fellow agent Peter Rhee investigating a possible
long-term security breach at Ironwood. The probe was
a closely held secret, so close that only the three of them
knew about it. It was insulated from the rest of the office
to keep it confidential. The probe had been operational for
about two months previous to Parkhurst's interview.

"Kling wrote up Parkhurst's story but didn't input it on
OCI's computer. He kept it off the office network, just as
everything connected with Morrow's secret probe was kept
off it. There were concerns about the integrity of the entire
INL computer system. Kling thought Parkhurst's complaint
might directly tie into the line of investigation they'd been
following. He reported on it directly to Morrow. Morrow
agreed. He wanted it looked into by Kling and Rhee as part
of their secret probe.

"Morrow didn't need human operators on the scene here
at the Parkhurst house to monitor the waveband for the mys-

tery transmissions that were causing the disruptions. He had something better: a machine. This machine."

Jack indicated the electronics console. "It's a signal frequency detector, a kind of wideband scanner designed to search the electromagnetic spectrum. It automatically samples up and down the EM band at ultrahigh speeds. When it finds what it's looking for it locks in on the signal.

"As OCI Chief, Morrow was able to requisition a detector with no questions asked. He probably did it outside normal channels to avoid leaving a trail. He arranged to have it installed in the Parkhurst house. Gene and Gladys Parkhurst were patriots and eager to cooperate. Kling and Rhee set up the detector in the garage, turning it into an automated listening post.

"The detector soon began picking up the mystery signal that was interfering with the house TVs. It logged in the time, date, and duration of the transmissions. A couple of times a week, Kling or Rhee would come out here to check on the equipment. The hard data was filed on disks which they routinely copied and collected. Where those disks are, I don't know. There are no copies of the disks here. No doubt Morrow kept them in his possession, but he hid them too well—they haven't turned up yet. Let's just hope they haven't fallen into the hands of the enemy. With any luck the data is buried somewhere on the detector's hard drive. If so, the experts should be able to retrieve it.

"Kling or Rhee—depending who was on duty—would make notes in the op diary during their visits. They kept it and a file folder on the case hidden in a secret drawer in the cabinet—most likely as a backup in case something happened to them. Which it did, just as it happened to Rhodes Morrow: murder."

Jack leafed through the pages of the op diary, glancing at entries. "The detector picked up several dozen transmissions this month. They peaked at mid-month, then dropped off, falling silent in the last week or so. All were of brief duration. The shortest was thirty seconds, the longest two minutes. Most fell somewhere in the middle.

"That indicates the source might be a burst transmitter—spy tech hardware designed for agents in hostile territory to communicate with distant handlers. Messages are digitized, encrypted, and compressed to contain maximum amounts of information in minimal broadcast time. They also randomly jump from frequency to frequency during a transmission to make it more difficult for scanners to get a fix on them."

Jack withheld the fact that NSA had intercepted Annihilax's encrypted burst transmission. That was his ultrasecret. He couldn't help but wonder, though, if Annihilax's coded message was part of the series of transmissions emanating from Shady Grove. NSA experts should be able to determine if they came from the same source, once they'd had a chance to get to work on the detector.

One thing was sure: Annihilax was no Ironwood weapons scientist. There was no way to make the profile fit. And none of the INL cadre's Big Mole suspects—Nordquist, Carlson, and McCoy—fit the Annihilax profile. So there were at least two key players in this game of espionage and murder: Annihilax and Big Mole. Were they working together? Maybe yes, maybe no. In any case, a sinister and lethal combination had set its mark on INL.

"Kling and Rhee—did they ever pinpoint the source of the transmissions?" Hickman asked.

"That's the first thing I checked, after skimming the reports to make sense out of what the assignment was all about," Jack said. "I looked at the last pages of the diary to see if they'd reached any conclusions. The answer is no, they hadn't. But they'd definitely determined that the transmissions were coming from this neighborhood. The detector narrowed the source down to a point somewhere within a circle whose radius is one-fifth of a mile, but no tighter than that.

"Which leads us to a very provocative fact." Jack opened the folder, glancing down at a document he'd put on top of the pile. "Two key members of the INL cadre happen to live in the neighborhood: Nordquist and Carlson. Carlson lives at one-oh-two Meadow Lane."

"Hell, that's right across the street," Ross said.

"And Nordquist lives at nineteen Colony Court."

"That's one block north of here!"

"Meaning that Nordquist or Carlson is a spy?" Hickman asked, his tone silky, sardonic.

"Not necessarily. But they are practically neighbors. A spy living around here could keep tabs on both of them. Pick up a lot of useful information about their comings and goings," Jack said.

Hickman's eyes narrowed, glinting. "At least it narrows the focus. I'd like to search both houses for the transmitter."

"Don't rush into things. According to the diary, the last transmission was about ten days ago. Since then, silence."

"Right about the time you showed up, Bauer."

Jack nodded. "And the investigation began to heat up. That's when Ironwood learned that CTU was on the case. Since then, the spy has had time to move his equipment. If it's a burst transmitter, it's not very large. It could be hand-carried out in a suitcase or backpack."

"I'd like to search both places anyway, just for the hell of it."

Ross pushed back his hat, wiping a sweaty forehead with the back of his hand. "Why don't you strap Carlson and Nordquist both up to a lie detector and grill 'em?"

Hickman laughed sourly. "Innocent soul! Since the Sayeed affair it's been virtually impossible to polygraph so much as a junior research assistant, even if you caught him stuffing secret documents down his pants. It'd take an

Act of Congress to lie-test those two mandarins. Especially without a smoking gun—which we don't have."

Ross stroked his chin. "Seems with all the homicides going on around here lately, whoever you're after ain't too particular about playing it safe. Better a few lie tests than a bullet in the head!"

"At least we got to the hardware in time," Jack said. "That's why Kling wanted to meet me here. He knew the other side was closing in on him. He and the Parkhursts were the last ones left alive who knew about the surveillance. Chino and Burke must have been hired to make a clean sweep of everybody in the house. And the machine, too."

Hickman started. "I just thought of something—Chino and Burke didn't walk here."

"No one walks here. Pedestrians, particularly if they're outsiders, ain't exactly encouraged in Shady Grove," Ross said.

"That's my point. The killers had to ride. But the only vehicles parked outside belong to the Parkhursts and Kling. Meaning Chino and Burke must have had a third man: a driver."

"Unless they parked their car a block away and walked."

"Pro killers want to do their job fast and get out. They don't want to have to go chasing after their ride after a kill. So there was a third man, a driver. He must've been spooked by the slaughter and fled."

"Can't say as I blame him, I'm a mite spooked myself."

"Whoever he was, he's long gone. Never mind about him. We've got bigger fish to fry."

"True," Ross agreed. "Like, where's Carlson and Nordquist now? Seems like a good time to check up on 'em, check their alibis."

"They're at Ironwood. They're running a series of tests that are scheduled to go on late into the night," Hickman said. He looked at his watch. "They should still be there; the tests won't be done for several hours."

"What about their families?" Jack asked. "With this onslaught, the violence could be moving into its final phase. The families might not be safe, either."

Hickman's face creased with lines of determination. "We can check up on that right now and in person. Their houses are nearby."

"Let's put these in a safe place for now," Jack said. He gathered up the manila file folder and op diary notebook and put them back into the secret cabinet drawer. He pushed it into place, the drawer closing with a click. It was so cunningly carpentered that once it was shut there was no telling it was there. Not so much as a hairline crack to betray its presence. "They'll keep while we look around the neighborhood," he said.

He, Hickman, and Ross went into the house, to the front hall. "The scene will have to be secured. The bodies aren't going anywhere but the detector and documents have to be protected," Jack said.

"I'll do it. That way I won't go stumbling into any more top secret information and you won't have to have me killed," Ross said good-humoredly.

"Thanks. Much appreciated."

Ross's gesture encompassed the whole scene. "Want me to phone this mess in? Not to the Sheriff," he added quickly. "To my specials. I got me a squad of hand-picked deputies that take orders only from me. Good tough boys who don't go telling tales out of school. Hicky here knows all about them."

"We'll need them later but maybe you'd better hold off for a while yet until we get the lay of the land," Hickman said.

"It's your call. Sing out when you want 'em and they'll come a-running."

"Will do," Hickman said. He set down his M–4, standing it butt-down in a corner. "I'll park this here for now. Might be controversial to go tramping around the neighborhood with it."

"I'll take good care of it," Ross promised.

"If you're a good boy maybe you'll get one of these for Christmas."

"I'll hold you to that, Hicky."

Jack Bauer opened the front door and stepped outside. The hot night sky was black with orange undertones. The neighborhood seemed quiet, peaceful.

"Looks like nobody's called in to complain about the gunplay," Jack said.

Hickman nodded, looked around. "Not so surprising. The houses are far apart and everybody's got their windows closed and their air conditioners running full blast."

"It's a break, anyway."

"The Parkhursts are number ninety-seven. The house on the left is ninety-nine. One-oh-two—Carlson's house—will be across the street."

Hickman pointed to a house across the street. A white wooden frame Cape Cod–style model with stone facing and a pair of bay windows flanking the front door.

We're a long way off from Cape Cod, Jack thought.

Lights were on on the first floor; it was all lit up. The front door was wide open, light streaming through the doorway on to the lawn.

"That can't be good," Jack said.

Hickman swore. He and Jack hustled across the street. The house looked normal, undisturbed, except for that gaping front door.

"The Carlsons live alone? I mean, no kids, if I remember the dossier."

"That's right, Bauer. He's got a couple of grown kids from his first marriage but they live out of state. This is her first marriage. No kids."

They went to the entrance, standing on a stone stoop. The front door hung wide open on its hinges; the screen door was closed. No one could be seen inside, the house was quiet, no TV or music sounds.

Jack and Hickman exchanged glances. "Now what?" Hickman asked.

"Ring the doorbell," Jack said. Hickman pressed the button, chimes ding-donging inside. No answer.

"Mrs. Carlson?" Jack called inside several times.

No reply.

Jack glanced back across the street. Ross stood outlined in the Parkhursts' doorway, watching them.

Jack tried the screen door. It was unlocked. He drew his gun and went inside.

Hickman filled his hand with a gun drawn from his shoulder holster and followed.

"If Mrs. Carlson is home she might shoot us," Hickman said, low-voiced.

"And she'd be within her legal rights to do so."

"That'd be a hell of a note, eh, Bauer? Well—after you."

"Thanks," Jack said sourly.

Just inside the front door in a narrow vestibule stood a shiny black plastic cylindrical container about three feet high and a foot in diameter. It was open at the top.

It looked like an umbrella stand, but in arid New Mexico there was little call for umbrellas. It held three wooden canes, all of the curved-handle variety.

Jack wondered who used the canes. Not Dr. Carlson. From what little he'd seen and all he'd heard about Carrie Carlson, she was a young, active woman. Something about the canes nagged at his mind but he couldn't recall what it was, couldn't summon the thought to consciousness. He put the thought from his mind and moved deeper into the house. "I'll check this floor," he said.

Hickman nodded. "I'll take the upstairs."

Jack prowled the ground floor, gun in hand, moving from room to room. Beyond the living room lay a room that Dr. Carlson used as his study. The walls were lined from floor to ceiling with bookshelves. There was a computer workstation.

Jack went through the dining room into the kitchen. A woman's handbag lay on top of the kitchen counter. Jack opened it and looked inside. A red wallet held various credit cards and a driver's license. The license was made out to Carrie Voss Carlson. Voss was her maiden name, he knew, and she'd kept it, adding it to her married name.

It had a postage stamp–sized photo of her in a corner. A full frontal facial view of the woman he'd seen earlier today riding in the passenger seat of Sylvia Nordquist's car.

The license gave her age as forty but she could have passed for ten years younger. She had wholesome, all-American good looks, expressive and full of character.

A heart-shaped face, hazel eyes, sculpted features, good bones, a wide, expressive mouth that was naturally turned up at the corners, a firm chin and strong jawline. A piquant expression, animated, alert.

Her hair was cut in bangs across her forehead and reached down to her shoulders, curling pageboy style. In the thumbnail-sized photo her hair looked brown and was described as such on the license; the photo had failed to capture the reddish-gold highlights that turned her hair auburn and that Jack had seen in person that afternoon in the INL parking lot.

The handbag held everything that one would have expected to find in a woman's pocketbook and nothing that seemed out of place. No weapons; no drugs, not even prescription pills.

In the rear of the kitchen a door opened onto a screened porch. It was empty, as was the backyard. The garage was not attached to the house. Jack went outside to search it.

He found a plain, ordinary garage. No observation post, no hidden spy equipment.

He eyed the parked car in the driveway. It was locked and he wasn't about to take the time to pick the lock to open it up so he could check the trunk to see if there was a body stashed inside. That could be done later. Besides, the scene just didn't have that kind of feel.

He went back into the house. Like many homes in the West and Southwest it had no basement, no cellar. A recreation room/den yielded nothing. He put his hand flat on top of the TV set. It was cool to the touch. His search of the first floor had turned up no bullet holes or bloodstains, no signs of forced entry, violence, or a struggle.

Hickman came downstairs, holstering his gun. "All clear upstairs."

Jack said that it was all clear where he had looked, inside and out.

Returning to the living room Jack took a closer look at the surroundings to see if they sent him a message. Furniture, decor, lighting, and design—all the elements were in proportion. Harmonious.

Well-appointed. A subtly understated showcase of moderate wealth and taste. The only drawback being that it was perhaps a bit sterile. A living room where not much living was done. A showcase.

One intriguing element was the selection and placement of various objects of art. Textile wall hangings and pieces of statuary, figures made of iron and bronze. Jack recognized them as pieces of African art. Originals, not copies. His casual acquaintance with the genre did not allow him to place what part of Africa they came from.

The fireplace sported a wide white mantel covered with framed photographs. The walls, similarly decorated, were hung with trophies and plaques, too. Most of the photos had been taken at formal dinners and events. They generally featured Carrie Carlson posing with various male and female dignitaries. Sometimes her husband was in the picture with her, sometimes not. The women were attired in formal gowns, men in dinner jackets or tuxedos.

The plaques and trophies had been awarded over the last few years by civic betterment associations, charity fund drives, and such to Carrie Voss Carlson to honor her charitable good deeds and philanthropic works. Literacy campaigns, free clinics for the disadvantaged, drug and alcohol abuse treatment centers, battered women's shelters, school lunch programs—all had benefitted from her generosity and hard work.

"A real humanitarian," Jack murmured.

"She's no idle housewife," Hickman agreed. "She devotes most of her time to doing good works. It's no whim but a lifelong pursuit. Before coming to Los Alamos she used to do full-time relief work in Africa, I'm told. Doctors Without Borders, that kind of thing." Hickman's tone indicated a certain guardedness about do-gooders and "that kind of thing."

"That explains the focus on African art."

"She's a founder and mainstay of the Good Neighbor Initiative, a central organizing committee that coordinates and raises funds for a dozen or more different local charities. That's how she met her husband, at one of the Initiative's fund-raising drives. He's an organizer of the yearly Community Appeal, raising contributions from lab personnel."

"A woman of parts," Jack murmured.

"Yes—let's hope they're all in the same place."

"You're a sour bastard, Hickman."

"I wasn't before today."

"Yes, you were."

Hickman's gesture said, *Let it go.* He looked worried. "God help us if anything's happened to her." There was real feeling in his voice.

"God help her," Jack said.

"The political heat and bad press the Bureau will catch will make that firestorm in the canyon look like a Cub Scout campfire."

Well, that explained the G-man's angst. Jack's mouth turned down at the corners.

"You—and Vince—might want to get your asbestos underwear ready. Carrie Carlson is gone. I doubt that she just got it into her head to go out for a stroll at ten-thirty on a Saturday night. Leaving the door wide open. Her pocketbook is on the kitchen counter. Ever know a woman to go out without her pocketbook?"

"Maybe she's with Sylvia Nordquist. They're friends," Hickman suggested without much enthusiasm.

"I know. I saw them together earlier today, when Mrs. Nordquist drove out to the lab to put the bite on her husband for a credit card that hadn't been maxed out."

"Maybe Carrie Carlson went over to Nordquists' for a visit. It's on the next block, she could have walked over. You know, the wives keeping each other company while their husbands are working late at the lab."

"It's a pretty story, even though I don't believe it. We better check the Nordquist place anyway, in case someone is making a clean sweep of the INL wives."

They crossed to the front door.

Jack indicated the umbrella holder with the three canes. One of ebony, one of mahogany, and one of Swedish blond wood. "Carlson gets around okay on both legs with no trouble, so it must be Carrie who uses a cane."

Hickman nodded. "She walks with a limp. Left leg. She broke it years ago in Africa and it was never set right."

"I didn't know. When I saw her, she was sitting in Sylvia Nordquist's car the whole time and didn't get out," Jack said. "Not very likely for her to go out for a stroll on a hot Saturday night, is it?"

"She gets around pretty good on that bum leg of hers. Better than most women—or men for that matter—do on two good legs. She's athletic, gutsy, and determined."

"Good—she may need it."

They went outside. Something nudged Jack Bauer again mentally, a sense of incompleteness as though he had forgotten something important. What it was he didn't know, but it had been prompted by the sight of the canes. He couldn't remember it, though.

He and Hickman crossed the street, angling toward number 97.

Ross sat outside on the front steps, fanning himself with his hat. He stood up when he saw the others coming. "Miz Carlson?" he asked.

Hickman shook his head. "Not home. We're going to check on the Nordquist place."

"Try phoning, it's quicker."

Jack shook his head. "You can't see what's happening at the other end of a phone. I prefer the personal touch."

"Colony Court's the next block over. You can get there quicker by cutting through the backyard," Ross said.

Jack Bauer and Hickman rounded the left front corner of the house. A strip of land lay between number 97 and 99. They followed it. Ross stood on the lawn with hands on hips, watching them go.

A line of trees marked the boundary of Parkhurst's backyard. The glow from the house lights blurred, fading into shadowed gloom. Smoke haze hid stars and moon.

The trees had been planted in recent years. They were young, tall, and slender; there was plenty of space between them.

Jack and Hickman went between two trees, entering the backyard of a Colony Court residence. A swimming pool took up much of the space. A waist-high chain-link fence bordered the long blue rectangle. The pool was not in use but was well lit to discourage trespassers. A humid haze hung over the water's surface. The smell of chlorine was heavy in the air, heavier than the smell of burning from the firestorm.

Beyond the pool stood a house. It was tall, bulky, with a mansard roof. "Nordquist's," Hickman said. "We'll go around to the front."

The house was not only tall but long, too. The houses on Colony Court were bigger and occupied larger pieces of property than those of Meadow Lane. Meadow Lane was a through street but this was not. It was a dead end but here they called it a cul-de-sac.

It was shaped like a lollipop, with a long broad drive terminating in a circular court. The Nordquist residence fronted the court.

Jack and Hickman neared the front corner of the house. There was the sound of a car motor running. Idling.

From inside the house a thin scream sounded.

. . . .

. . . .

11:05 P.M. MDT
19 Colony Court, Shady Grove

How had such an easy score suddenly turned so sour? Maxie Arnot didn't know and didn't care. All he knew was that the big house had turned into a shooting gallery and that he wanted out. His ticket out was fourteen-year-old Kendra Nordquist.

Arnot was of medium height, pudgy, with brown curly hair, a potato face, and a pug nose. The girl was barefoot, but even so she was several inches taller than he was.

She was slender, long-legged, and coltish, with long brown hair and a fine-featured face turned a stark mask of fear. She'd been sleeping in her bed only minutes ago. Now Arnot was using her as a human shield.

He stood on the ground floor of the grand hall with his

back to the front door, holding Kendra in front of him. Her back was to him. His left arm circled her waist, holding her pressed tight close against him. She was a skinny little thing and didn't provide much cover. His right hand held a gun to her head.

The job should have been a pushover: grab the woman and her daughter and take them to the hideout. Three of the gang had been tabbed by Pardee for the task: Arnot, Wade, and Cisco, violent professionals all. Arnot was a shooter, Wade a veteran housebreaker and burglar, and Cisco the wheelman for the getaway car.

A spotter had relayed inside information about the score, which Pardee passed along to the trio. It looked like a swell setup. The house had servants, a maid and a cook, but neither of them lived in and both had gone to their own homes hours ago. The mister was working late at the lab, his wife and daughter were home alone.

A Shady Grove locale meant burglar alarms but that was why Wade was along; breaking and entering was a specialty of his and he was skilled at neutralizing such home protection devices.

Shady Grove was outside Los Alamos city limits and fell under the jurisdiction of the Country Sheriff's Department. Sheriff Buck Bender made sure that the residents of this wealthy and influential suburb got plenty of police protection.

The firestorm had upset all that. The department's deputies were stretched thin trying to deal with the chaos of the big blaze. They already had their hands full coping with the wave of violence and murder that had erupted during this day and was still continuing well into the night.

That was a break for Arnot, Wade, and Cisco. The prowl cars that routinely patrolled the neighborhood had been pulled off to cover areas closer to the fire.

The house was on Colony Court. The would-be abduc-

tors didn't like that so well. The court was a dead end with
only one way in and out. The car was loaded with heavy
firepower, assault rifles and a machine gun. Arnot and
Wade were thugs with no compunctions about shooting it
out with police if it came to that. As wheelman, Cisco's primary responsibility was to drive the car and get them clear
no matter what, but he could shoot, too, if he had to.

The machine was a stolen car that had been worked over
by the gang's mechanics to make sure it was in fine working
order. It was a dark-colored job with a powerful motor. A
pair of stolen license plates had been slapped on it fore and
aft to further muddy the waters.

It rolled into Colony Court at the appointed hour. Smoke
haze from the fire deepened the welcome darkness between
the big, well-lit houses.

Cisco parked the car between two houses in a zone
of shadows, in a place where he had a clear sightline on
number 19's white-columned front. He killed the lights but
kept the motor running. The motor was always kept running
on a job; nobody wanted to risk their getaway on a car with
a balky engine that for some reason or another wouldn't
start. The mechanics had tuned up the car so it idled with a
low, thrumming purr.

Arnot and Wade got out. They left the heavy firepower in
the car. Handguns would be enough for this part of the job.

The smell of burning was in the air. The duo approached
the house from the side, crossing a patioed terrace to a set
of French doors. Wade took out his kit of burglar's tools and
went to work. Arnot served as lookout.

There was excitement in breaking into such a big, fine
house as this, an adrenaline rush that was a high. This must
be how a champion thoroughbred felt at the starting gate
waiting for the bell to go off and the race begin, Arnot told
himself. As he always did at the start of a job.

Wade had a neat little handheld electronic gizmo that he

patched into the burglar alarm's circuitry, which prevented its sensors from detecting an interruption in the current flow and triggering the alert. With the home protection system neutralized, it was child's play to pick the lock on the French doors. He could have just kicked them open but to do so would have offended the technician in Wade.

Then the doors were open and he and Arnot went inside. The interior was coolly air-conditioned.

The home invaders had a pretty good idea of the layout thanks to the information supplied by Pardee's tipster. They were in a kind of salon or drawing room, a wide, expansive space. The lights were off but an archway on the left let in plenty of light for them to see their way. A grand staircase made an elegant curve as it wound its way along a wall to the second floor. The steps were covered with rose-colored carpeting.

The invaders climbed the stairs, Wade leading. Arnot was close behind, quivering with excitement. They paused on the second-floor landing.

A long hallway stretched to the rear of the house. Rooms lay on either side of the hall. Whoever fingered the job had stated that the woman's bedroom was on the right front side of the hall and the girl's was farther back along the corridor on the left.

A doorway opened on the right-hand side of the hall a half-dozen paces from the landing. From it came television sounds.

Wade started toward it with a spring in his step. Arnot lingered behind, absently licking his lips.

Sylvia Nordquist and her husband had separate bedrooms. Hers was something of a suite, featuring lots of mirrors and a big bed. A smell of cigarette smoke mixed with a mélange of aromatic scents emanating from various bottles of perfumes, lotions, powders, and creams on the vanity table.

She was sitting up in bed. Plush pillows were heaped against the headboard, cushioning her as they propped up her back. Mounted on the wall opposite her was a big flat-screen TV. She wasn't really watching the program; she had it on for background. It was some bright, chatty home decorating show. She was avoiding all the local channels. They kept interrupting the regular shows with bulletins and updates about the firestorm.

The fire was a big bore. She was sick of it already. No matter how it raged, it would never reach Shady Grove, which was high on the Hill, so there was no worry on that score.

It had already proved inconvenient. She'd planned to visit with a few select friends this evening, to go out for dinner and then drinks afterward. Just because Glen was going to be working at the lab all night was no reason for her to be stuck in the house on a Saturday night. Quite the contrary, in fact.

But her friends had had to cancel due to the difficulty of traveling even in the areas far from the fire, because of all the detours, closed roads, and whatnot. So she'd stayed home instead.

She hoped that the fire wouldn't cause Ironwood to halt the tests and close down early. If there was anything more drearily boring than spending the evening at home, it was spending it with Glen.

She was leafing through a glossy fashion magazine, looking at the pictures. Several similar magazines and some high-line mail-order catalogs lay on the bed beside her. A glass of brandy and an ashtray crowded with the stubs of half-smoked cigarettes stood on a night table on her right.

The doorway to the hall was to the left of the wall-mounted flat-screen TV. Sylvia became aware of a figure looming in the doorway. Her heart sank. Glen already? She'd hoped to be fast asleep by the time he came home.

She looked up from her magazine, frowning as she glanced over the top of the page at the door.

Wade grinned at her.

Sylvia Nordquist screamed.

Wade stopped grinning.

He rushed into the room, crossing to the bed. He clapped a hand over Sylvia's mouth, silencing her. "Shut up," he said.

Her eyes were wide and staring. He waved the gun in front of her face to let her have a look at it. She didn't even see it. She was paralyzed with mind-numbing fright.

She had stopped screaming, though.

"That's better," Wade said. He was grinning again.

In the hallway, a light was switched on in a room on the left-hand side of the corridor. Kendra Nordquist came running out of the room to see what was the matter.

She cried out, "Mom—"

Arnot was waiting for her. She ran right into him. His gun was stuffed into the top of his pants, freeing both hands. He didn't need a gun for this kind of action. He hooked an arm around the girl's waist, halting her in mid-stride and lifting her off her feet.

She was just a kid, a skinny kid; she couldn't have weighed much more than a hundred pounds or so. He handled her like a sack of grain, scooping her up and throwing her facedown over his shoulder. He turned around and started carrying her toward the landing.

Wade stepped into the hall, holding Sylvia Nordquist by the wrist, yanking her after him. She staggered, stiff-legged. She saw Arnot carrying off her daughter. She cried, "Oh god no!"

Wade turned on her. "Do like you're told and you'll both stay alive," he said.

Arnot went down the winding staircase, toting the girl. He showed no sign of physical strain. The way he felt, he could have carried the girl to China. He was pumped up on an adrenaline high. He reached the bottom of the stairs.

Things started popping. Gunfire sounded on the upper landing. Wade was hit from behind by three slugs. They drilled him in the upper back between the shoulder blades. His body bowed forward in a convex curve. His eyebrows lifted in an expression of surprise.

He let go of his grip on Sylvia Nordquist's wrist and clasped both hands to his chest, one hand still holding his gun. Sylvia Nordquist fell backward and to the side on the landing.

Wade took a step forward. He couldn't find the next tread below and catapulted into empty space. There wasn't enough left of him to negotiate the descent of a staircase. Not in the usual manner, anyway.

Fumbling feet and legs got all tangled up and he pitched forward, taking a spectacular headfirst tumble down the stairs. His body thumping, bumping, and crashing all the way down.

Along the way he suffered a broken neck but that was strictly academic. He was already dead from the shots. He landed in a heap at the bottom of the stairs, slapping against the marble floor with a loud wet thud.

Arnot was temporarily stupefied. When he first heard the shots, he had thought that Wade had done something stupid, like maybe the woman had scratched his face or something, and in a fit of rage he'd pulled the trigger on her.

These things happened sometimes; they couldn't be helped. The girl was still alive and unharmed so the job wouldn't be a total loss, it would be a halfway success.

Wade's ass would be in a sling with Pardee—a bad place to be—but that was Wade's lookout. Arnot had done his job, he was in the clear.

Then he looked up and saw Wade come tumbling down

the stairs to land almost at his feet. Wade's head was pitched at a crazy angle and his open bulging eyes seemed to be staring Arnot in the face. Arnot said, "What the hell—?"

Upstairs, a man appeared on the landing, holding a smoking gun. It was Hickman. He'd climbed the back stairs and come racing down the hallway in time to shoot down Wade.

Arnot slung the girl off his shoulder and set her down on her feet, holding on to her with one arm while he hauled his gun out of the top of his pants.

Hickman stood at the edge of the landing, leaning over the top rail of the banister to point his gun down into the front hall. "FBI—freeze!"

Sylvia Nordquist lay sprawled nearby. One bare leg was folded underneath her, the other was extended straight out. Her palms were pressed flat into the deep-pile carpet, raising her upper body, holding it upright. She reached out one hand toward Hickman, crying, "My daughter!"

"Stay down, ma'am," he said, not looking at her. He ducked as Arnot pointed the gun at him and fired.

Arnot held the girl in front of him as a shield, backing away toward the front door while he blasted away at Hickman. Hickman went down on one knee, gun hand reaching between the banister rails. He didn't have a clear shot at Arnot; the girl was in the way.

Sylvia Nordquist whimpered, started crawling on her hands and knees toward Hickman.

Arnot held the gun to Kendra's head, muzzle pressed against her temple. "Back off!" he called up to Hickman.

"Put down your weapon and let the girl go," Hickman said.

Arnot barked a mirthless laugh, then told Hickman what he could do with himself.

"Throw down your gun or I'll kill her," Arnot shouted.

Sylvia Nordquist shrieked.

"Then I'll kill you sure," Hickman said.

Arnot believed him but was unimpressed. He had the whip hand. He had the girl.

"I'll be dead and she'll be dead and what'll that get you? You ain't gonna shoot. It's a standoff," he said. The hell of it was, he was right.

All this time he'd been moving backward, carrying the girl along with him. He bumped his back against the front door. "Let her go and I'll let you go," Hickman offered.

Arnot smirked. "Sure."

"You have my word on it."

Arnot told Hickman what he could do with his word. Sylvia Nordquist was behind Hickman, at his feet. She begged him to save her daughter, her pleas shrilling into hysteria. She grabbed hold of his leg, trying to pull herself up.

Arnot threw the bolts on the front door, unlocking it. "Stay where you are or she dies."

Now came the payoff. If the law was outside in force, he'd really be in a tight spot. He guessed they weren't. Otherwise they would have come crashing in by now.

He figured the guy on the landing was alone. There was one way to find out.

Arnot went through the doorway, stepping outside, taking the girl with him.

He would have liked to have fired a few more rounds at Hickman, but he might yet have need of every bullet in the clip.

He stepped to the side, removing himself from the firing line of Hickman's gun through the open doorway. He stood with his back to the wall, cowering behind the girl, trying to see everywhere at once.

No lawmen barred the way, no police cars massed in the court to seal it off. He'd guessed right!

The Fed was alone after all. He must have been following up a tip or something on his lonesome and gotten lucky.

A welcome sight met Arnot's eyes. The getaway car sat nearby at the top of the driveway, its front pointing at the street.

Arnot laughed out loud. His lucky streak was holding up. Say what you would about that lousy half-breed Cisco, he was a hell of a wheelman! He must have heard the shots and instead of taking off, he'd backed the car into the driveway where the others could reach it if they made a breakout.

The getaway car's horn tapped a couple of light beeps to get Arnot's attention but that was unnecessary, Arnot had seen it and was already in motion. He half carried, half dragged the girl across the lawn toward the car. The passenger side was facing him and its front door gaped open, ready and waiting for him.

Arnot glanced over his shoulder, looking to see if the Fed had made it downstairs and outside. No sign of him yet—

The car's headlights blazed but its interior was dark. The man behind the wheel gestured in a beckoning motion, as if urging Arnot to hurry. Arnot needed no encouragement. He and the girl crossed to the car.

He flung her inside, down into the well between the passenger seat and the dashboard. Kendra vented a wordless cry of fear and pain.

Arnot ducked his head beneath the door frame as he started to climb into the car. Then he saw what the dark interior dome light had prevented him from seeing up to now.

The driver was not Cisco. The driver pointed a gun at Arnot and fired twice.

Kendra's screams came a beat behind the gunfire.

Arnot fell backward. Lucky streak? His luck had run out. That realization expired in an instant along with Arnot himself.

Jack Bauer leaned out from behind the steering wheel and across the passenger seat to look outside the door.

Arnot lay faceup on the lawn. Jack's gun covered him but the precaution was unneeded. Arnot was dead.

Cisco was dead, too. His body lay on the ground at the curbside where the getaway car had been standing.

Earlier, when Jack and Hickman had heard the scream coming from inside 19 Colony Court, they'd split up, Hickman approaching the house from the rear while Jack went around to the front.

Jack spotted the dark car before Cisco could spot him. He sneaked up on it, catching a glimpse of assault rifles and a machine gun on the backseat. The driver's side window was rolled down. Cisco stuck his head out of it from time to time to peer at the house from a different angle.

Jack low crawled around to the driver's side, crouching there just out of sight. The next time Cisco stuck his head out the window, Jack popped up, hooking an arm around Cisco's neck. Cisco grabbed for his gun but by then it was too late. A sudden sharp, wrenching twist, and Cisco's neck snapped with a loud cracking noise, inflicting sudden death.

Jack hauled the body out of the car. He hooked his hands under Cisco's arms and dragged the corpse across the pavement, dumping it on the curbside ground.

He'd noticed when opening the door that the interior dome light had stayed dark.

A timeworn crook trick, to avoid revealing themselves in the light while doing dark deeds. It saved him the trouble of switching off the dome light himself. He got behind the wheel.

By that time, Hickman had broken into the house through a back door. He didn't know that Wade had gimmicked the alarm system, neutralizing it, but he had benefitted by it all the same since it allowed him to make a surreptitious entry. He went up the back stairs and surprised Wade on the landing.

Gunfire sounded inside the house, prompting Jack to put the car in drive, making a K-turn into 19's driveway and backing up to the head of it. Any of the gang exiting the house would make a beeline for the getaway car, running right into Jack's planned ambush.

When Arnot emerged with his female captive, the stakes had escalated dramatically. The kidnapper was dead and the girl was alive. Kendra lay huddled and trembling on the car floor, her long slender limbs pale in the dimness.

"It's okay, miss. You're safe now," Jack Bauer said.

. . . .

THE FOLLOWING TAKES PLACE
BETWEEN THE HOURS OF
12 A.M. AND 1 A.M.
MOUNTAIN DAYLIGHT TIME

. . . .

12:23 A.M. MDT
97 Meadow Lane, Shady Grove

Jack Bauer was at the Parkhurst residence. Vince Sabito was on-site, along with the FBI forensics team that had come down from Santa Fe. The crime scene lab crew had already had a busy day, and between the Parkhurst place and the Nordquist house they had their work cut out for them for this night. Plenty more could happen between now and dawn, too.

Jack and Sabito were outside the house, off to one side by themselves where they couldn't be overheard by others.

"I've got reinforcements coming from Albuquerque, including a Tac Squad," Vince Sabito said.

"Why not call out the National Guard, too, while you're at it?" Jack Bauer said.

He was joking—he knew only the governor of the state

could call out the National Guard. But there was an element of truth in his offhand remark and Sabito picked up on it.

"I would if I could. What with the fire and wholesale murder and all, it's like the lid blew off the county today. And it shows no sign of stopping. Instead, it's increasing," Sabito said.

He looked darkly at Jack. "And I keep finding you in the middle of most of it. Why is that?"

Jack shrugged. "Just lucky, I guess."

Sabito snorted. He gave the impression of a man doing a slow burn. "Don't give me that, Bauer. You're holding out on me. You've been playing it cute all day—from day one, the first time you got here last week."

Jack tried to look innocent, guileless. What Sabito said was true, of course. Jack had been holding out on him, keeping his knowledge of the Annihilax connection to himself. He would continue to do so for the time being. He didn't see where Sabito had any need to know about the international master assassin yet.

Jack held out his hands palms-up in a give-me-a-break gesture. "I shared the detector and Kling and Rhee's operational diary and file with you, didn't I?"

Sabito sneered. "You had to. Hickman knew about them, too."

"I could have declared them restricted data and kept them off-limits to you. My agency has priority over the Bureau on this assignment."

"I'm not so sure about that, Bauer."

"Call Washington and be sure before you get into a pissing contest, Vince. CIA has ultimate jurisdiction over all lab-related matters and CTU is CIA."

"Think again, hotshot. You didn't read the fine print. Central has jurisdiction over all lab-related matters involving nuclear weapons. Perseus isn't nuclear. There's no atom-smashing needed to fire a laser."

"Perseus isn't nuclear but Ironwood has done plenty of nuclear weapons research so that puts it right back under the CIA aegis," Jack countered.

He switched gears, coming at Sabito from a different tack: conciliatory. "I said I could have done it but I didn't. I'm not trying to throw my weight around here. I'm working with you. Hey, I'm sticking my neck out here. There's some higher-ups at CTU who won't be happy that I didn't insist on sole possession of the detector material."

Such as Regional Division Director Ryan Chappelle, Jack's immediate boss. Chappelle was a miser when it came to sharing intelligence with outside agencies. Not that Jack's attitude was so different, but he had a veteran field operative's flexibility on the subject. He'd made a judgment call about passing the detector and the Kling/Rhee documents to Sabito.

He was CTU's lone agent on the scene. He needed FBI cooperation to move his investigation forward, and there'd be no getting along with Sabito if he tried to freeze him out on this matter. Besides, the Bureau had the resources to secure and process the machine and documents.

"Gabe McCoy at OCI won't be thrilled that we didn't immediately turn the detector material over to him," Jack pointed out. He had inserted that *we* in there deliberately.

It was *we*, namely he and Sabito, who were tacitly denying the machine and the product it had generated to McCoy—the fruits of an OCI investigation that had been initiated by Rhodes Morrow, McCoy's predecessor, and that had been conducted by Kling and Rhee without McCoy's knowledge.

Sabito's eyes narrowed as he considered the possibilities of the situation.

"Considering the compromised position of OCI, maybe it's best that we keep knowledge of the discovery between you, me, and Hickman for now," Jack pressed.

Sabito gave a curt nod. "My thoughts exactly."

On the subject of withholding the intelligence from a third party, he and Jack Bauer could find common ground.

"So we're on the same page, Vince?"

"As far as that goes, yeah."

"And Ross?" Jack asked.

"He knows how to keep his mouth shut. He's my man in the Sheriff's Department. That's why he's in charge of taking the Nordquists to the clinic," Sabito said.

Sylvia and Kendra Nordquist had been scared to within an inch of their lives but had come through their ordeal pretty much physically unscathed. Both, however, were suffering from the effects of extreme shock. Ross had been delegated to deliver them to a small private clinic and had already departed with a well-armed escort of deputies on that errand.

Sabito went on. "The clinic's a modest-sized facility with plenty of privacy. It can be more easily secured and guarded than one of the bigger hospitals, in case somebody wants to make another try at snatching the Nordquist females."

"That's a concern," Jack agreed.

"Ross knows what to do. He's got a good head on his shoulders, unlike some of the jackasses working local law enforcement in this area. He'll make sure that mother and daughter both are guarded by special deputies so nobody gets to them. The specials are an elite unit directly under Ross's control. He'll see that everything's handled quietly— with discretion.

"God forbid that Sheriff Bender gets a whiff of what this is really all about! Buck's a good old boy but he never met a TV camera he didn't like. Luckily he's too busy giving interviews about how his department is handling the fire to get involved in this.

"The clinic's outside city limits so the Sheriff's Department has jurisdiction. That'll keep the Los Alamos Police

Department out of the loop. We sure as hell don't need them getting wind of this thing. The fewer people that know about it the better."

"What about Dr. Nordquist?" Jack asked.

"What about him?" Sabito demanded belligerently. "He's still at Ironwood, the last I heard. And that was pretty recently."

"Got a man inside there, too, Vince?"

"I have my sources."

"So Nordquist doesn't know about the kidnap attempt on his wife and daughter?"

"He didn't hear it from me. The first thing I did when I got here was to pull down the curtain on the whole mess. It's under a blackout—my people have been instructed not to divulge it. Ross slapped a hush on his specials so it won't leak out from them, either."

"What Nordquist doesn't know won't hurt him, eh?"

"The last thing we need right now is for him is to get frantic and go tearing out of Ironwood like a bat out of hell." Sabito smiled toothily. "Besides, he's given standing orders not to be disturbed while he's running a test."

"I suppose Carlson is unaware of his wife's disappearance, too?" Jack asked.

The toothy smile widened. "That would be a fair assumption, yes."

"McCoy and OCI are also in the dark?"

The smile turned into a snarl. "You got a problem with that, Bauer?"

"Frankly, no. It's best that Nordquist and Carlson be contained at INL until we get control over who has access to them."

"I'm glad that meets with your approval," Sabito said sarcastically. "But what's this *we* stuff?"

"You and me, Vince. The copter in the schoolyard could whisk us over to Ironwood."

Sabito shook his head. "No can do. I've got to stay here to meet the bunch from Albuquerque. Hickman will go in my place. By the way, when the public is finally told about how Sylvia Nordquist and her daughter were heroically saved from brutal kidnappers—and they will be, sooner or later—the Bureau should get a pretty big play, huh?"

"Tell it any way you like."

"You'd make some friends around here if the FBI gets the lion's share of the credit."

"I could use some friends."

"You sure could, with some of the stunts you've been pulling today, Bauer. Maybe we should leave CTU out of the media version altogether— when it finally gets told, I mean. To avoid confusing the public."

"The sooner I get to Ironwood the better," Jack said, through gritted teeth.

"I'll take that as a yes," Sabito said. "Here comes Hickman now. Ferney will drive you two to the schoolyard where the copter's waiting."

The toothy smile was back in place, beaming. It made Sabito look something like a well-fed crocodile basking in the contentment of a full belly.

12:47 A.M. MDT
Rancho Loco, Rio Grande Road,
Los Alamos County

Rancho Loco was a roadhouse located on the wide sprawling flat of the Rio Grande river valley east of the area's distinctive finger-shaped mesas. It sat far south enough of the Hill to be outside Los Alamos city limits. The County Sheriff's Department was more tolerant of dives like Rancho Loco than the city police.

"Folks have got to have a place to blow off steam some-where. Close up the honky-tonks and the joints and they'll just set up shop across the county line and some other county will be getting the benefit of the revenues they provide. Lord knows taxes are high enough already without having to raise them to make up the difference," Sheriff Buck Bender had frequently opined on the subject to reporters.

The folks kept reelecting him and the dives stayed open. The owners of said roadhouses, honky-tonks, and joints all contributed generously to Bender's campaign fund at election times and during the off-years, too.

Rancho Loco squatted on a lot east of a strip of two-lane blacktop running north-south out in the middle of nowhere. Respectable citizens knew it for a good place to get your throat cut and steered clear of it.

A big red barnlike structure sat on a patch of sun-baked ground that was as hard as rock. The parking area was covered with gravel to keep down the dust.

Behind the back of the building was a row of mobile home trailers, modest-sized jobs that could be hitched up to the back of a car or pickup truck and towed from place to place. They also served as handy cribs for the brisk prostitution trade that operated out of the roadhouse.

It was Saturday night—early Sunday morning, actually—and folks were letting off steam at Rancho Loco. The parking lot was filled with cars, pickup trucks, SUVs, and motorcycles.

The red barn was filled with noise, heat, smoke, and rowdy characters. Its wooden frame walls shook from the pounding beat of electronically amplified rock and country-western music.

Inside, pandemonium. A couple of hundred patrons were jammed into the space. Cowboy ranch hands, outlaw bikers, drug dealers, crooks, cutthroats, gunmen, whoremongers and thieves, drunks and dopers all contributed to the clamor.

The air was close, hot, and stifling, fogged with tobacco and reefer smoke. It stank of stale beer and raw whiskey fumes.

There was sawdust on the floor. There were a couple of bodies on the floor, too, drunks who'd passed out and gone horizontal. They stayed where they fell as long as they weren't blocking an aisle. When they finally came to, they'd be lucky if they still had their boots on. Everything else of value would have been plucked clean from them.

Customers were crowded three-deep at the bar. Tables and chairs were jam-packed with raucous fun seekers. Near-naked pole dancers did their thing on top of a wooden runway that ran along the center of the space. Thuggish hulking bouncers lurked nearby, ready to pounce on anybody who got too grabby with the dancers without first paying for the privilege.

Varrin's crowd was grouped around a couple of corner tables. Among them were about eight hard-core members and a dozen associates, hangers-on, and whores. The table-tops were crowded with bottles, beer cans, plastic cups, glasses, and ashtrays filled to overflowing with cigar and cigarette butts. A stream of circulating barmaids made sure none of the bunch went thirsty for too long; the gang drank faster than the empties could be carried away.

Varrin sat in the corner facing outward with his back to the wall. A smoldering cigar snipe was wedged between his teeth in one side of his tight-lipped mouth. From time to time he removed it to take a long pull from a tumbler glass of brown liquid. When the level dropped too low, he refreshed it from a whiskey bottle, filling it to the brim.

He smoked and drank methodically, his long, basset-hound face expressing no evident pleasure in these activities. His eyes were clear, level, and watchful.

The hard core of the gang, the shooters and killers, were clustered at his table. Other, smaller fry occupied the side table.

Two shapes loomed up on the other side of the table, opposite from Varrin. A man and a woman: Lassiter and a whore named Sherree.

Lassiter was sweating. His face and neck were slick-shiny; dark circles of wetness ringed his T-shirt.

Everybody was sweating. The air-conditioning in Rancho Loco was no good. All it did was listlessly stir the same smoky, choking, rebreathed air.

Sherree was one of the house girls, bosomy and long-legged. She was tall, almost as tall as Lassiter. She wore a cowgirl hat decorated with a peacock feather stuck in the hatband at the front of the crown.

A mane of platinum-blond hair framed a sharp-featured, vixenish face, hanging down to the small of her back. Over-sized breasts that were strictly from implants ballooned in the front of a tight halter top. A tight denim skirt reached down to the tops of her thighs. A pair of knee-high brown leather boots with pointed toes and three-inch heels completed her outfit.

She hung on to Lassiter like a vine clinging to a tree. Lassiter leaned forward over the table, resting big fists on its top as he lowered his head toward Varrin.

His eyes were half closed, glittering slits.

"You know where I'll be," he said, speaking loudly and carefully to be heard over the noise.

"Lassiter's going to the Sin Bin!" shouted Slim, one of the group's inner circle. He fancied himself a joker.

"Damned right! Damned right," Lassiter said, nodding heavily. He spoke to Varrin. "You know where to find me if you need me," he said.

"Do me favor, though—don't need me for an hour or so," he added.

Sherree ran her fingers through his hair. "I need you, honey. And you need Sherree, don't you?"

"We can get along fine without you both," Diablo Cruz

said. He sat at a side of the table that was the farthest away from where Lassiter had been sitting.

Sherree stuck out her tongue at Cruz; Lassiter ignored him. "Okay?" Lassiter asked Varrin.

"Have fun," Varrin said, seemingly not much caring one way or the other.

"Okay, then. Back in an hour or so," Lassiter said. Varrin acknowledged him with a quick two-finger salute.

Lassiter straightened up, slipping an arm around Sherree's slender waist, resting a hand on the curve of her hip. Not his gun hand.

Sherree, twenty, had a wide, red-lipped, smiling mouth and eyes that were as flat and dull as those of a dead fish. "Come on, sugar," she urged Lassiter. "Let's get it on!"

"Damned right," he muttered. They moved away from the table, weaving through the crowd toward a rear exit door.

Teed, another of the bunch, shook his head. "I'm surprised he can walk, the way he's been knocking back drinks tonight."

"That pig," Diablo Cruz said.

"Huh? You don't like Lassiter, Diablo?"

"No."

"How come?"

"Because he's a pig."

"Diablo don't like nobody," Slim said, snickering.

All the bouncers were big, hulking bruisers and the one working the rear exit door was no exception. He looked as big as a brown bear standing up on its hind legs. He stood to the left of the door, leaning against the wall, brawny arms folded across his chest. He wore a black leather vest over a bare, barrel-shaped torso.

To the right of the door, a woman sat on a folding chair behind a card table. She was in her late fifties, with an orange coiffure, bulldog face, and the body of a prison matron. A laptop computer lay open on the table. As did a twenty-ounce plastic cup filled with beer.

"Hey, Bev," Sherree greeted her.

The woman at the card table looked Lassiter up and down. "Looks like you got yourself a big one this time, Sherree," Bev said. Her rasping voice was harsh enough to file wood on. Her fingers worked over the keyboard, making a quick entry on the screen.

The bouncer at the door was watching the exchange. Bev looked up from the screen, nodding to him, giving him the okay.

Sherree steered Lassiter to the door. She opened it and they went outside, a coiled spring closing the door behind them.

Lassiter's black brows furrowed in a mighty frown. "What's with the old bat and the laptop?" he asked.

Sherree's laughter sounded like a bird's chirpings. "Don't let Bev hear you calling her no names or she'll give you a ass-whupping. She's ornery; she don't take no messing. She's management."

"So?"

"Us working girls got to pay the room rent on the trailers in the Sin Bin. Love for sale don't come cheap, big man. Bev keeps track of our, uh, comings and goings. Who goes out, how often, and for how long. That way the house knows its cut down to the last penny. And Lord help any gal who don't pay up."

"Kind of like traffic control," Lassiter said. His hand was on her rear, squeezing and kneading her buttocks through the tight denim skirt.

Sherree's chirping laughter sounded again. "You got it, sugar."

He rubbed her bare thigh. "Not yet but I'm gonna get it."

His frown returned. He was thinking. His strained expression indicated that for him thought was heavy labor. "I don't know as I like being clocked by the house."

"Honey, Bev don't know you from Adam and she don't care who you are. I'm the one on the clock, not you. So let's not waste any time, huh?"

"I'm paying for it," Lassiter said, glaring.

Sherree's brittle laughter was tentative, uncertain. "Whoo-whee, big man, you sure got a mean look on your face. Brrrr!"

"I don't like being rushed, that's all."

"That's fine with me—I like a man who takes his time." She squeezed his arm. It was like taking hold of a tree limb. "Lighten up, hombre. Don't be mean. You're like to scare the pants clear off of me."

"That'll save time," Lassiter said, baring his teeth in what might have been a grin.

Sherree led him away.

A half-dozen trailers stood in a row behind the building and at right angles to it. A strip of bare ground ran between them and the structure. A string of colored lights like the decorations on a Christmas tree connected each trailer to the big red barn, providing enough light to see by—but not too much.

Lassiter and Sherree walked it arm and arm. She walked out of step with him so her thigh kept rubbing against his.

Chassis frame springs squeaked from trailers that were rocking and shaking from the action inside. The trailers weren't air-conditioned. Small square curtained screen windows allowed the sounds from inside to be heard outside on the night air. One of the trailers sounded with high, thin falsetto shrieking.

"Is that a man or a woman?" Lassiter wondered.

Sherree giggled. "Who cares?"

Dim lights glowed behind the curtained windows of all

six trailers. "This way," Sherree said, taking Lassiter by the hand and guiding him past the end of the last trailer in line.

Ten feet beyond it stood a rectangular shape. Like a boxcar only smaller. It was not a trailer but a recreational vehicle, a big, bulky late model self-propelled mobile home on wheels, with a cab compartment at its head.

The RV stood parallel to the row of trailers, its rear facing the back of the building. The cab was dark but lights showed through curtained windows in its interior. No string of colored lights connected it to the barn.

A closed door stood in the middle of its passenger side. Three metal steps on a tube frame led to the bottom of the door. Open screen windows stood on either side of the door. They were rectangular with rounded edges, like the windows on a bus. Behind them were thick, dark curtains.

Sherree knocked on the door, not loudly. Behind it, movement sounded.

The curtain on the window to the left of the door was lifted at the corner. "What?" asked a voice from inside, hoarse and husky.

"It's me—Sherree," Lassiter's companion responded in a stage whisper.

The corner of the curtain dropped. The door was unlocked and opened from the inside. An oblong of yellow light slanted through the partly opened door to fall on the ground outside. "Okay, come on in," a man said.

"Slow and easy," he added.

Sherree climbed the stairs and stepped inside, Lassiter following. He closed the door behind him.

A center aisle ran along the middle of the RV's long axis. A wide, open center space was flanked on both ends, fore and aft, by dark-curtained doorways. The curtains covered the openings from floor to ceiling.

Two men stood inside, flanking the newcomers. They

were a study in contrasts, pairing a short, stocky middle-aged man and a rangy, raw-boned youngster twenty years his junior.

The senior man had a big, bouffant blond hairdo. He was dressed neatly in a button-down short-sleeved shirt, pressed khaki pants with leg creases, and dark green deck shoes. He held a .357 leveled on Lassiter.

His partner had a wavy sunburst corona of long brown hair and a brown beard that reached down to his chest. A goatish face peered out from behind all that hair. A gun was holstered under his left arm, the shoulder rig being worn strapped on over a red T-shirt with a psychedelic print design. A Bowie-type knife with a deer-horn plated hilt and a foot-long blade was worn in a belt sheath on his bony right hip.

The duo was all business. "Go up front and stay there," the senior man told Sherree. He was the owner of the hoarse voice. He stood to the side, where Sherree could move past him without putting herself between his gun and Lassiter.

Lassiter stood easy, hands held open and empty where the gunman could see them. Any traces of seeming intoxication he had displayed earlier were gone now. He looked cold sober.

Sherree parted the curtain to enter the forward passageway and closed it behind her, without as much as a backward glance.

"Lassiter," the senior man said.

"Who're you?" Lassiter asked.

"I'm Peck; my buddy here is Ted. You've got to be searched. That's the routine here. Nothing personal."

Lassiter shrugged, spreading his legs shoulder-width apart and holding his arms away from his sides. Ted moved in to frisk him, positioning himself so that Peck held a clear line of fire on Lassiter. "The gun's on my left hip," Lassiter said.

Ted lifted Lassiter's shirt, baring a flat semi-automatic pistol tucked into the top of Lassiter's waistband on his left side and relieving him of it. He put it away, out of reach, and resumed the frisk. "He's clean," he announced after a quick, thorough search.

Peck indicated the curtained doorway to the rear. "In there," he said. Lassiter crossed to the curtain, lifting it to step behind it.

A narrow passageway opened into a room at the rear of the RV. Amber light filled the space. A slab-shaped table was folded down to the horizontal from where it was hinged to the wall. Behind it, in a high-backed, black leather-cushioned executive-style chair, sat a woman.

She had long black hair, wide slanted green eyes, golden skin, and a generous red-lipped mouth. She wore a tan short-sleeved safari shirt with lots of flaps and pockets, black slacks, and low-heeled red leather ankle boots. She was smoking a thin chocolate-brown cigarillo; a strand of smoke rose from its tip in a thin straight line.

She was Marta Blanco, sister of Torreon Blanco, and a power in her own right.

Varrin would have paid a small fortune for information on her current whereabouts.

Her eyes were a vivid emerald green. They studied the newcomer for a moment.

"Lassiter," she said. "Let's talk."

1 2 3 4 5 6 7 8 9
10 11 12 13 14 **15** 16 17
18 19 20 21 22 23 24

. . . .

THE FOLLOWING TAKES PLACE
BETWEEN THE HOURS OF
1 A.M. AND 2 A.M.
MOUNTAIN DAYLIGHT TIME

. . . .

1:36 A.M. MDT
Ironwood National Laboratory,
South Mesa, Los Alamos County

The Snake Pit pulsed with rising power. "I thought the tests were over for tonight," Jack Bauer said.

"They are. The last firing was around midnight," Gabe McCoy said. He looked puzzled, frazzled, irritated.

"Something's happening," Hickman said.

They were in the INL Laser Research Facility, crossing the main floor toward the blockhouse.

The LRF had an otherworldly quality even in broad daylight at the height of a busy working day. At this late hour it was positively eerie, a mad scientist's surrealistic science fiction dream. Or nightmare.

Big as a blimp hangar, the huge space dwarfed the three humans hurrying toward the blockhouse. Floodlights and spotlights showed at various places on the structure. Windows were lit in the upper-floor control room area but their translucent nature hid what was occurring behind those squares of light.

An intense pulsating vibration now shivered through the surroundings. It oscillated, rhythmically rising and falling. Each time it reached the peak of a new cycle, the vibration grew stronger. Its source was the blockhouse.

Jack Bauer felt the hairs tingle at the back of his neck. A whiff of ozone touched his lungs, fresh, intoxicating.

"Look!" Hickman said, pointing to the blockhouse roof. A pale blue glow was coming into being at the top of the structure, forming an aura outlining the spiky array of conductors and antennae.

"That's a coronal phenomenon—a harmless by-product of the laser-energizing process," McCoy explained.

"Which means that the laser is charging up," Jack said.

"Well, yes—"

"And it shouldn't be happening now."

"No, it shouldn't." McCoy looked and sounded worried.

The trio angled across toward the blockhouse's front, double-timing it.

Earlier, pilot Ron Galvez had flown Jack and Hickman to INL, touching down on a helicopter landing pad at the site. OCI/SECTRO had been notified of their imminent arrival to avoid any unpleasant incidents resulting from an unauthorized aircraft entering the lab's airspace.

OCI Chief McCoy was instructed via secure scrambled communication not to allow Dr. Nordquist or Dr. Carlson to leave the building, and to monitor their whereabouts and any incoming or outgoing phone messages sent or received by either man. Otherwise, the scientists were to be left to their own devices, unmolested and unaware of the heightened scrutiny.

Jack Bauer gave these instructions to McCoy in the form of an order. He hadn't gone into details, merely informing the other that an emergency situation was in the process of developing. He'd had to pull rank on McCoy, invoking the authority to command that Washington had bestowed on him to be used as needed.

McCoy hadn't liked it at all, but he was a person of interest as far as Jack was concerned, and for now would be given only the information that Jack deemed necessary.

Jack then contacted Orne Lewis, CIA's permanent liaison with the lab, telling him to meet them at INL. "I'm on the way," Lewis said.

Galvez delivered Jack and Hickman to INL. He told them he had to return to his home airfield to refuel. Jack told him to remain at the airfield on call to be available as and if needed until notified otherwise. "In a fast-breaking situation like this, a helicopter ready at a moment's notice is a good thing to have," he said.

"That's fine with me as long as you're paying for it," Galvez said.

"Keep the meter running."

"You can be sure of that."

The helicopter lifted off.

SECTRO guards escorted Jack and Hickman to McCoy's office. McCoy was hopping mad. Veins stood out on his forehead and his neck was corded. He waited until his assistant Debra Derr exited his private office and he was alone with Jack and Hickman before demanding an explanation.

"You'll get it," Jack said coolly. "But first—Nordquist and Carlson are still on-site?"

"Yes, they're both in the LRF. The last firing was two hours ago and the rest of the staffers have gone home, but apparently those two stayed behind to review the data and correlate their findings. And before you ask, no, neither of them have made or received any phone calls.

"Now, considering that I'm only Director of Counterintelligence here, I presume it won't be asking too much for you to tell me just what the hell is going on?"

McCoy's voice rose and his face reddened as he was speaking, so that he was shouting and livid by the end of his remarks.

"Let's go to the LRF, I'll brief you along the way," Jack said.

"Damned decent of you," McCoy muttered, sarcastic.

"I think so."

The trio exited McCoy's inner office, entering the main working space of the OCI staff, now manned by a skeleton crew. Assistant Director Debra Derr's office was next to McCoy's. Her door was open. Her face expressed intelligent alertness and a keen interest in the mysterious goings-on, but she had the inbred discretion of her trade and asked no questions.

McCoy stuck his head in her office. "We'll be in the LRF," he told her.

"Has Lewis arrived?" Jack asked.

"Not yet," she said.

"When he gets here, please tell him to meet us in the control room."

Derr glanced at McCoy, who nodded affirmatively. "I'll tell him," she said.

"Thanks," Jack said.

"Lewis lives up on the Hill. It's a fair drive from his place to here," Hickman said.

"At least he won't have any traffic problems at this hour," Jack said.

Hickman grinned tightly. "A private helicopter is a handy thing to have at that."

Jack Bauer, Hickman, and McCoy went out of the OCI section into the lobby of the main building. The only others present were a pair of SECTRO guards posted inside the front entrance.

The trio began threading the maze of corridors leading to the LRF, each swiping their blue badge cards through the scanner readers accessing the secured portals along the way. They walked quickly, their footfalls echoing down the empty halls.

"Now—what's this all about?" McCoy demanded, peevish.

Jack thought it best to withhold the truth about Kling's death. The late Rhodes Morrow had used Kling and Peter Rhee to conduct a secret off-the-shelf investigation. He'd kept the rest of his OCI staff, including his then–Assistant Director Gabe McCoy, out of the loop. Maybe he simply hadn't trusted McCoy's discretion; maybe a more sinister suspicion had prompted him to withhold the information. Whatever the reason, Jack Bauer judged it prudent to maintain silence on the subject for now.

"Kling's dead," he began.

McCoy was surprised but not noticeably grief-stricken. "What? How—"

"He was killed trying to prevent a kidnapping attempt on Sylvia Nordquist and her daughter."

That news hit McCoy a lot harder than Kling's death. "Good Lord!"

"They're okay, except for a bad case of shock. They've been taken to a hospital for treatment and are under guard," Jack said.

McCoy's flushed face had gone pale. His eyes widened, pupils expanding into black dots. "When did this happen?" he asked.

"An hour or two ago at the Nordquist house," Jack replied.

"But—what was Kling doing there?"

"That was Harvey, always freelancing," Hickman interjected, taking up the thread of the cover story he and Jack had worked out earlier. "He was always going off on his own, snooping around for leads, digging for clues. This time he dug up a hot tip and was following it up. He died a hero, for what it's worth."

"There's more," Jack said.

McCoy groaned. "More?"

"Carlson's wife, Carrie, is missing. We don't know if she was abducted or went off on her own."

"Oh god!" McCoy became indignant. "I can tell you this: Mrs. Carlson is not the sort of woman to go wandering off on her own on Saturday night, or any other night for that matter!"

"No?"

"Certainly not!"

"You know her personally?"

"Socially—and I consider her a friend," McCoy said primly. "Carrie Carlson is a model of probity, a genuine humanitarian. Respected not only by our lab community but throughout the greater Los Alamos area, thanks to her charitable works."

"She wouldn't be the first respectable married woman to have a little something going on the side," Hickman suggested.

McCoy looked at him like he was something that had just crawled out of a sewer. "Preposterous! I know you keyhole-peeping G-men are inclined to believe the worst about everyone but this is going too far. It's a smear, a slander, on one of the finest human beings I've ever known."

"Kind of fond of her, eh?" Hickman said slyly.

McCoy openly sneered at him. "I admire and respect her, yes. But if you're trying to make anything more out of it than that with your nasty-minded insinuations, you can go to the devil—"

Hickman held up his hands palms out in an I-surrender gesture. "Don't get sore, McCoy. I'm only trying to get a fix on her, who she is and what her personality's like, that's all. The kind of thing I need to know to do my job."

"I can assure you that she didn't take it into her head to go out alley-catting on a night that her husband is working late."

Jack Bauer was grim-faced. "So much the worse for her. That means she was probably grabbed."

McCoy was agitated. He looked ready to tear his hair out, what was left of it. "This is monstrous! Ironwood is under attack!" He halted, grabbing Jack by the arm. "Is it terrorists, Bauer? Is it?"

Jack, silent, looked at McCoy's hand clutching his arm. McCoy got the message and released his grip. "The dead kidnappers were career criminals, associates of the Blanco gang," Jack said.

McCoy's eyes narrowed in recognition. "The Blancos? I've heard of them, seen them in the papers and on the local TV news. Drug gang crooks, aren't they?"

"And then some," Hickman said.

"What have they got to do with defense weapons research?"

"Plenty, apparently."

Jack said, "There's an extensive interface between the worlds of crime and terror and it's getting stronger every day. Organized crime routinely terrorizes its victims to promote underworld enterprises. Political terrorists use the tactic to promote ideological causes.

"Where does the political shade into the criminal and vice versa? The line between the two is blurred and crooks and terrorists jump the fence as they please. The Taliban uses the heroin trade as a major funding device. Mexican drug gangs kill prosecutors, police officials, politicians, and reporters to maintain their illicit empires. I could give you hundreds of similar examples from all over the world."

"Yes, but here in Los Alamos—it's unthinkable!" McCoy said.

"Maybe that's why it's working. It could be that some political intriguer or group has hired the Blancos to do their dirty work. How many files does your office keep on local drug gangs and gunmen? Not many, I'd say."

"That's outside the parameters of a counterintelligence office," McCoy said.

"Which is why it's proven so effective so far."

McCoy turned on Hickman. "It's the FBI's job to monitor violent criminals! Seems like you've been asleep at the switch."

"We're on the case, aren't we? That's more than you can say," Hickman fired back.

"What's being done about this Blanco gang?"

"Everything possible. The gang leaders are smart and tough—and lucky. A rival outfit blitzed a Blanco meth lab today. The firestorm that's eating up half the county is collateral damage from that strike. The attack put the Blancos on alert and they've abandoned their usual haunts and gone to cover. And there's a hell of a lot of cover with all the canyons and arroyos in this area. The fire hasn't made things any easier, either.

"The hell of it is that there's nothing to implicate Torreon Blanco or his sister Marta in any of the violence that's been turned against INL today. The shoot-out at Rhee's apartment, the attempts on Bauer's life, the botched kidnapping were all carried out by Blanco gang members.

"But there's no hard evidence tying Torreon or Marta to the assaults. Like other top crime bosses, they know how to legally insulate themselves from acts carried out by their underlings.

"Not that we plan to be too fussy about legal technicalities once we apprehend them. The attacks on Ironwood affect the national security and we can use the Patriot Act to hammer the Blancos once we apprehend them," Hickman said.

"It was negligent and worse of you not to share this information with OCI," McCoy accused.

"You can't share what you don't know. We just discovered the Blanco connection ourselves a little while ago. You're hearing it now. So what have you got to kick about? Hell, it's your office that's been maintaining all along that the Ironwood kills were purely coincidental and that there was no pattern behind them!"

"Let's save the finger-pointing for later and get down to the LRF now," Jack said.

He fit deed to word by moving forward, resuming the progress toward the Snake Pit that had been interrupted by the confrontation. The others fell into step alongside him and hurried through the halls. Crosstalk sniping and mutual suspicion continued along the way.

"I can see why you wanted Carlson's phone calls monitored, in case the kidnappers tried to contact him. But why Nordquist?" McCoy asked Jack.

"They might have tried to run a bluff on him that his family had been successfully abducted, spooking him into running so he could be more easily grabbed on the outside. The scientists are the object of the exercise; abducting their loved ones is just a means to an end to influence them," Jack Bauer said.

"But Nordquist and Carlson aren't the only members of the cadre. There's Stannard, Tennant, Delgado—"

"They'd already left the lab building by the time we got the big picture. Vince Sabito has arranged protection for them and their families. But they're the smaller fish. Nordquist and Carlson are the big brains of the project, Nordquist for the conceptual breakthroughs and Carlson for making them work," Jack said.

He neglected to mention the other reason for focusing on Nordquist and Carlson—and for that matter, McCoy. They were the only three—the only three still alive—whose ten-

ancy at INL predated the Sayeed affair, making them prime
suspects in Rhodes Morrow's hunt for Big Mole.

The final portal accessing the LRF opened up, allowing
the trio to enter the mezzanine overlooking the blockhouse.
Precipitating the discovery that the laser was in the process
of being energized.

Jack Bauer, Hickman, and McCoy now closed on the front
of the blockhouse. They approached it at an angle that allowed them to keep its front and long left side in view. From
where they stood, they could see that the area outside the
front entrance was unoccupied.

"Isn't there supposed to be a guard on duty outside?"
Jack asked.

"Yes—Harry Stempler's on duty now." McCoy was huff-
ing and puffing, winded from the long trot across the main
floor.

"He's not at his post," Hickman said.

"He must be inside," McCoy suggested. He swiped his
badge card through the scanner reader accessing the front
door. He started forward, stopping short to keep from
bumping into a closed door.

"What's the problem, McCoy?" Jack asked.

"The scanner didn't respond. I must have swiped it too
quickly. I'll do it again."

McCoy ran the blue badge edge-first through the slot.
Again, nothing. "What the—?"

McCoy slowly and deliberately inserted the badge and
repeated the process. Results: negative.

"What did they do, deactivate your badge?" Hickman
said.

"Don't be ridiculous," McCoy snapped. He made several
more attempts to activate the auto-door opener, all with an
equal lack of success. He held the badge card up to the light,
peering at the leading edge holding the data strip. He ran it

between thumb and forefinger to clean it. "Maybe there's some dirt or gunk fouling the strip so the scanner can't get a reading," he said.

He tried again.

Failure. "That's the damnedest thing! I don't understand it—

"Let's try my card. It's cleared for total access so it should work," Jack said.

He swiped his badge card through the reader slot several times, experiencing the same lack of success as had McCoy.

Hickman stepped forward to try his luck with his badge card, with the same results. He scratched his head. "Maybe they deactivated all of us," he said, only half joking.

"The badge cards worked fine all the way here," Jack pointed out.

"Maybe the scanner is broken."

"Not a chance," McCoy said. "The scanners have internal self-regulating software. In the rare event one goes out of commission—which almost never, ever happens— the reader sends a signal to SECTRO notifying them immediately."

"Could the reader have been shut down from inside the blockhouse?" Jack asked.

"Impossible! There's another reader indoors to monitor exits from the building. Even if it was defective, it wouldn't affect the reader controlling access—they're both on independent, self-contained circuits. All the scanners are."

"Maybe the locking mechanism is jammed," Hickman said.

McCoy shook his head. "Mechanical difficulties would trigger a red alert light on the reader. But the green on light is on. The scanner's simply not reading the cards when they're swiped."

"You better sound a general alert."

"Let's not lose our heads over what most certainly is a perfectly explainable minor snafu, Bauer."

"How do you explain it then?" Hickman asked.

McCoy ignored him. "There's any number of other entrances into the blockhouse. We'll try several of them first to assess the situation. Then we'll know what we're dealing with."

"The laser's charging for an unscheduled firing and suddenly we can't get into the building. I'd call those grounds for an alert," Jack said.

"Perhaps you would but you're not in charge here, Bauer. I am. I decide when to hit the panic button, and I'm a long way off from being convinced of the necessity for that drastic step."

"You'll have to take the responsibility for that choice. Or the blame," Jack said pointedly.

"I'm comfortable with that," McCoy said. He crossed to the left front of the building and rounded the corner, saying over his shoulder, "There's an access door to the blockhouse tank not far from here—"

A glimmer of light suddenly appeared near the far left corner of the blockhouse. It widened, becoming first an acute and then an oblique angle spilling through an oblong open doorway and slanting across the floor.

"What's this?" Hickman said.

"There, I thought other doors would be working," McCoy said, smug.

A figure exited through the door into the open. At this distance it was a black man-shaped silhouette, identity undistinguishable. "Who's that?" Jack said, pointing.

"Stempler, I suppose," McCoy said. Cupping a hand to his mouth, he shouted, "Hello, there!"

The figure started, then ran back through the doorway into the blockhouse.

"Uh-oh," Hickman said.

McCoy frowned. "I don't like the looks of this."

Jack Bauer was already in motion. "Cover the front and make sure no one gets out that way," he told Hickman and took off running.

"Hey, wait!" McCoy said, starting after Jack. Jack's pace did not slacken, he did not look back to see if McCoy was following. He made for the oblong of yellow-brown light that was the far doorway. It was a long run.

Jack Bauer slowed as he neared his goal. He knew better than to go charging in without looking. He stood to the right of the doorway, covered by the wall, out of any line of fire.

The light shining out through the portal was not a static thing. It was restless, stirring, pulsing. The color cycled, dark bronze ripening to a rich honeyed amber, then darkening back to bronze, all within the space of a few beats.

The door was mounted on oversized mechanized hinges, like a vault door. It was about a foot thick. It was motorized to move all that weight. It was now open, motionless.

Inside, a torrent of noise sounded like a power plant pumping itself up. Percussive machine sounds underlined a deep booming drone. The sound was as much felt as heard. Jack felt it in his bones; it rattled the fillings in his teeth.

The hum rose and fell, synchronized with the light. As the hum grew louder, the light dimmed. As it fell, the light brightened.

McCoy, exhausted and out of breath, finally caught up with Jack. He started toward the doorway but Jack stuck out an arm, holding him back. Jack ducked his head down and peeked inside.

The portal opened on the rear of the Snake Pit. The ground floor was a narrow border surrounding the sunken floor holding the machinery and testing apparatus. Grouped around the floor at the near end of the tank were armatures of various sizes and intricacies, each mounting various sheets, squares, and slabs of mirrored metal. In the middle ground stood the laser gun and its energizing apparatus. At the far end, a metal scaffolding staircase accessed the control room. The window on the viewing module was a horizontal bar of dimly glowing light.

There were lots of places where a lurker could hide. Jack drew his gun. That prompted McCoy to draw his gun, too, a small, snouty, big-bore semi-automatic pistol he wore under his jacket in a clip-on belt holster.

"Cover me," Jack mouthed to McCoy. McCoy nodded. It was the standard Alpha/Bravo pattern: one man advances while his partner covers his advance, then covers for his partner as the other advances.

Jack went in first, rushing through the doorway in a crouch and angling toward a nearby piece of equipment on the walkway hemming in the tank. The hardware was a podium-shaped and -sized console at the near corner of the sunken floor. Jack ducked down behind it, gun in hand.

He scanned the scene. Overhead lights flickered as the energies of the charging apparatus waxed and waned, providing an unwanted distraction. Shadows moved, restless, shifting.

The ceaseless motion fooled the eye into thinking it saw lurkers where none existed. Or did they?

The walkway was a strip of rubber-coated flooring about ten feet wide. Spaced on it around the tank were various odds and ends of equipment: a wheeled portable ladder, handcarts, crates, worktables, and the like.

Jack surveyed the immediate area for signs of the intruder, came up blank. He glanced back and saw McCoy edging around the outside of the door frame. Jack motioned to him, signaling him to advance while he covered him. McCoy made his move, darting through the doorway with leveled gun. He ducked down behind a waist-high metal tool bin.

At the opposite end of the blockhouse, a shape detached itself from the shadows in a corner and ran along the long walkway toward the front of the building.

Jack darted out from behind the console and started across the short walkway. Short only by comparison to those bordering the long walls. It seemed lengthy enough as he rushed across it.

One thing he knew for sure—he wasn't going down into the Pit, not while the laser was charging up. He wasn't entirely comfortable with an armed McCoy at his back, either. If McCoy should be Big Mole—

The intruder stopped running, turned, and fired at Jack Bauer. He was a long way off for effective handgun accuracy but some of his blasts were too close for comfort.

Slugs cratered the wall a few yards ahead of Jack. He stopped short to avoid running into the other's line of fire.

Shadows were thick along the long wall; between them and the flickering lights the intruder was a faceless, man-shaped blur whose gun spat streaks of orange light.

The intruder's sex was indeterminate, it could have been male or female. Impossible to discern if it was a man or woman.

When the gunfire stopped, Jack started forward again. The intruder still hadn't had his fill of fight. He stuck to his ground, covering behind a vertical support beam and snapping shots at Jack. Something struck the left side of Jack's face with a sharp sting. It was a rock chip gouged out of the rear wall by a too-close shot.

Jack dove, rolling across several yards of rubber-matted walkway. He came up out of the roll, crouching behind a handcart laden with stacked sections of pipe.

McCoy opened fire at the intruder. Jack was not far from the foot of the long walkway. McCoy, behind him, was halfway across the short walkway.

Motion at the opposite end of the blockhouse caught

Jack's eye. The motorized vault-type door was closing, sealing the doorway through which he and McCoy had entered.

The energizer droning in the Pit reached a new height in volume. There was motion down there, too—

The laser gun was rising, its snout lifting. Without warning a ruby red beam spat from its muzzle. Instantly a scarlet line extended from the tip of the laser gun to the rear wall of the blockhouse. It angled up out of the Pit, above the top of the tank, to lance into the wall about four feet above the walkway.

The power drain dimmed the overhead lights, filling the interior space with a murky yellow-brown glow. In the gloom the beam stood out with prismatic, jewellike brightness and intensity. A ruddy aura shimmered along its length.

The concrete wall melted where the beam touched it, molten stone running like water. It made a hissing, spitting sound. Smoke, dust, and vapors streamed up from the melting.

The beam was between Jack Bauer and McCoy. Jack was not far from the corner of the blockhouse. McCoy was near the midpoint of the short walkway. When the beam surged into being he recoiled, throwing up his arms and staggering backward. The beam swung left, following him. A horizontal line burned into the wall marked its path.

The beam sliced through McCoy above the waist, cutting him in half. The two halves of his body, upper and lower, fell to the walkway.

The beam switched off. Not the energizer, just the beam. The energizer continued to drone, buzz, and roar at full-throated power.

The laser gun traversed toward its right. Toward Jack Bauer. It moved damned quick, too.

So did Jack. He jumped up and ran toward the corner. The ruby-red beam sparkled into being, highlighted against a rich golden-brown gloom as the overhead lights again dimmed from the power surge. It touched the handcart behind which Jack had been sheltering only instants before.

The cart and its cargo of pipes were showered with blood-light. It made a dark outline at the heart of a ruby glow. The darkness dimmed as the cart and its contents took on a brick-red glow.

The glow brightened, incandescent. Now it was sizzling scarlet. The cart began to lose its shape, its metal tube framework softening, sagging like melted taffy.

Jack crouched in the corner, huddled down, shielding his eyes from the mounting glare. The beam radiated blast-furnace heat.

A door was nearby, twin of and opposite to the one through which he and McCoy had entered the blockhouse. Jack rushed to it, hammering his palm heel against the wall-mounted metal plate that opened and closed the door from inside.

No response. The vaultlike door remained closed.

The beam switched off. The overheads shaded into brightness. The cart and its contents were a still-glowing, seething mass of half-melted slag sizzling away in a puddle of molten metal.

The laser gun swung right, hard right. Jack had intended to run along the long walkway and outrace the limits of the cannon's angle of traverse, putting him safely beyond the reach of the beam. He now saw that the gun's free-swinging swiftness would block his ploy.

He checked and abruptly reversed course, running in the opposite direction back toward the corner. At the same time the red beam licked out, stabbing the long wall several yards farther up the walkway.

The beam operator—who?—had calculated Jack's gambit and struck to overturn it. Had Jack continued on his original path, he would have run straight into the beam and suffered McCoy's fate. Instead, his sudden reversal took him away from the beam.

For how long? There was no safety on the walkway, not at this end of the blockhouse. As if to underline that fact, the beam went dark and then thrust out again, trying to pin Jack in the corner.

Jack had guessed the unseen beam operator's intention. Instead of retreating, he moved forward at a tangent toward the edge of the Pit. The tank floor was about ten feet below. Jack lay flat, hooked his hands over the edge, and lowered himself down the sidewall. Hanging by his hands with arms extended, he had a short drop to the sunken floor.

Lights flared brighter as the beam went dark. He could hear the sound of the mechanisms that controlled the laser gun's movements. Its barrel tilted downward, aligning its snout with the walls of the Pit.

The walkway above was open and spacious; what cover there was could not long withstand the hellish fury of the beam. But the tank floor at this end of the laser target range was an obstacle course of different-sized armatures and mounts for the mirrored metal plates.

The plates were of all shapes and sizes. Some were thin flat squares, others were disks, and still others were half globes, concave and convex. They were mounted at varying heights and tilted at different angles. Interspersed between them were slabs and pillars of sensor-laded machinery for measuring the specifics of each tested blast beam. Together they formed a maze.

Jack moved inward toward the heart of the array. He zigzagged, doing broken-field running, advancing, checking, doubling back, and then darting off at a tangent. The laser gun fired a series of short blasts, trying to pin him. A number of beam shots were completely off, missing him by a wide distance. Jack guessed that the beam operator had more trouble seeing him in the Pit than he had on the walkway.

It was a good feeling, a morale booster. No time to get complacent, though. A sudden stab of the beam seared the air a few feet away from him. Jack jumped back, covering behind a vertical instrument board. Not pausing, he dove headfirst across an open space and came up in a roll.

A crash sounded as the top of the instrument board was sliced clean off and fell to the floor.

Jack's seemingly random movements concealed a hidden purpose. By fits and starts, he was working his way toward the center of the maze where a massive armature held a vertical slab of mirrored metal the size of a plate-glass window.

He jumped up from behind a cabinet and stepped into the open, showing himself for a few beats. He leaped forward, hurtling toward the upright slab of mirrored metal.

The beam lanced through the space he'd occupied a split second before. It swung after him in a sizzling sweeping arc—and then he was behind the square of mirrored metal, hunkered down behind it. He breathed a silent prayer that the alloy's designers knew what they were doing when they wrought their miracle metal.

The blood-red beam swung toward him. He tensed himself for a heart-stopping second—

The beam struck the plate of mirrored metal, the alloy specifically designed to be laser-resistant. Like a mirror reflecting a ray of light, the mirrored metal reflected the laser beam.

A red lance speared the mirror shield and bounced off.

Mirror metal threw the dart back at its source.

The beam thrust deep into the guts of the machinery that generated it, stabbing a sunfire stiletto into the energizer's complex array of coils, pipes, conduits, circuitry and hydraulics. It was like stirring up a man's guts with a red-hot poker—to similar effect.

The energizer housing shuddered like some intricate clockwork mechanism throwing a gear and tearing itself apart from within.

The laser's complex array of fail-safe devices switched on. Power leads went dead. Internal baffles and shielding screens dropped into place. Valves closed.

The beam winked out.

Jack Bauer feared that the energizer would terminate itself with a massive cataclysmic blast. Instead—it just stopped. Dead.

Medusa turned to stone by the power of her own ruby-red gaze.

....

THE FOLLOWING TAKES PLACE
BETWEEN THE HOURS OF
2 A.M. AND 3 A.M.
MOUNTAIN DAYLIGHT TIME

....

2:35 A.M. MDT
Laser Research Facility,
Ironwood National Laboratory

Medusa was dead.

So was FBI SA Hickman. His body lay outside the front entrance of the LRF blockhouse. He had been shot through the heart at point-blank range—so close that his jacket and shirt were scorched where the bullet had penetrated.

SECTRO Force guard Harry Stempler's body was discovered on the first-floor landing of the fire stairs at the front of the building. Like Hickman, he'd been shot at close range.

Dr. Hugh Carlson was missing.

Dr. Glen Nordquist was alive but in critical condition.

OCI Assistant Director Debra Derr and a SECTRO Force squad had had trouble getting into the LRF and the blockhouse. The scanner badge readers accessing the locales were inert, unresponsive. They had been deactivated. The massive system failure was the result of sabotage. Each scanner had to be manually overridden to free up entrance to the portals.

Jack Bauer's problem was the opposite. He'd been locked inside the blockhouse, in the Snake Pit, unable to get out. The intruder who'd lured him and McCoy into the testing range had made his escape sometime while Jack had been playing his deadly game of laser tag with Medusa.

Jack had had to shoot out a window of the viewing module and climb through it. In the control room he'd found Nordquist lying in a pool of his own blood, battered, strangled, but still alive. Of Carlson there was no sign. Jack had administered what first aid he could to Nordquist while waiting for help to arrive.

The security contingent's forced entry into the blockhouse was soon followed by the arrival of an ambulance from City Hospital. Emergency medical treatment had been administered to Nordquist, who now lay on a stretcher in the control room, conscious and aware of his surroundings.

Grouped around him were Jack Bauer, CIA liaison Orne Lewis, OCI Assistant Director Debra Derr, SECTRO Force Commander Brock Whitcomb, and Dr. Frederick Brand.

McCoy's death had left Derr Acting Director of OCI. She'd been joined by Brock Whitcomb, Ironwood's highest-ranking SECTRO officer. He'd been summoned to INL to deal with the crisis. Like his troops, he wore a sky-blue uniform. His cap and tunic were blazoned with Commander's badges. He had jug ears, a spade-shaped face, small round eyes, and a brown mustache.

Dr. Brand was a young intern at City Hospital working the night shift with an EMT ambulance that had been the first to respond to the call for help from Ironwood. He had thin blond hair, tired eyes, and a pale, fine-boned face.

Much of that pallor came from the grueling work schedule that is part of every intern's apprenticeship. But some of it came from the carnage on display at the blockhouse. His eyes were narrowed and his jaw set. Red dots of color showed in his cheekbones.

Jack Bauer, Derr, Lewis, and Whitcomb stood together in a loose arc. Dr. Brand stood facing them. A couple of EMT paramedics stood nearby, waiting to take their cue from him. Between the two groups lay Nordquist on the stretcher.

"I've done all I can for him here," Dr. Brand said, indicating Nordquist. "He needs medical treatment that can be given only at City Hospital. Speed is vital. Any delay is dangerous."

Nordquist looked bad. He had been beaten on the head by a blunt instrument.

His oversized cranium looked bigger than ever, thanks to the bandages that had been applied to his torn, lacerated scalp. His body looked correspondingly shrunken where it was outlined beneath the white blanket that covered him where he lay on his back on the stretcher.

His glasses had been broken during the assault. Without them his gaze was soft-focused, diffuse. Dried blood from his head wounds streaked his face. Purple-black bruises mottled his long, scrawny neck, marking the strangler's grip that he'd somehow survived.

Brand turned to the paramedics hovering nearby, motioning them to the patient.

The duo took up positions on either side of the stretcher, gripping metal tube frame rails preparatory to wheeling him away. "No," Nordquist said, his voice a weak croak.

Dr. Brand leaned over Nordquist. He spoke clearly and distinctly, as though addressing one who is hard of hearing. "You've been seriously injured, sir. We're taking you to the hospital now."

"Not until you've heard me out. You've got to be warned," Nordquist said.

"You can tell us later after you've been treated." Brand's voice had the tone used by medics on difficult patients whose wishes are about to be ignored.

"Later is too late—for you, me, and untold thousands."

Jack Bauer caught Brand's eye. "Let him have his say."

Brand shook his head. "This man is in no position to make an informed judgment. He's suffered a serious head injury and other major—"

Bauer had heard enough and stepped up to the doctor, their faces only inches apart. "He'll speak and you'll stand back and shut your mouth!"

The madness had begun about an hour earlier, when Nordquist's computer insulted him.

The last test firing was long done. Scientists and technicians had left the blockhouse building, leaving Nordquist and Carlson alone in the control room.

Nordquist sat at his workstation, hunched over his computer. He was rapt in contemplation of the streams of fresh data cascading across his flat-screen monitor. Caught up in intense concentration, he was more or less oblivious to what went on around him. He had tunnel vision when concentrating on his facts and figures, his beloved equations. He lost track of time, space, and his surroundings.

The screen was filled with columns of fresh data ceaselessly scrolling past. He skimmed the numerical stream, his mind selecting the significant and weeding out the irrelevancies. He was all but mesmerized by the glittering digi-curtain unreeling before him.

Suddenly—a force reached in from outside and took control of his computer. The data cascade vanished, winking out.

Nordquist stifled a groan. What new glitch was this? Had his computer frozen?

Or worse, crashed?

It happens—even at Los Alamos. Sometimes especially at Los Alamos. That's why each facility's computer network had multiple backups, fail-safes, and protective devices.

This observation gave him no comfort. Nordquist demanded the same thing of his machines as he did of his staff: perfection. What he got inevitably fell short of that goal. But he refused to compromise his standards.

What happened next left him slack-jawed and gaping. The computer was not frozen. In the middle of the screen appeared two words:

HELLO, STUPID.

Nordquist was mentally caught off-balance—a rarity for him. His mind temporarily slipped gears, unable to process what it was seeing. Sense returned after a few beats, bringing some sort of comprehension.

Someone had managed to hack into his computer.

No one was more aware than Nordquist of the countless, relentless computer attacks launched every minute of every day against the national security infrastructure of the United States. Lone nuts, wise-guy kids, gifted amateurs, attention seekers, vandals, megalomaniacs, criminal conspiracies, and even and especially organized attacks by foreign powers—

It happened all the time. More than the public dared suspect. Or could be allowed to know. But this! It went beyond attack into insult.

HELLO, STUPID.

Just the kind of "exploit" some smart-assed young punk would find amusing, to disrupt vital scientific research just to insert a mocking taunt!

But how had it managed to penetrate to the heart of the INL computer net with all its safeguards and firewalls? It was like some penny-ante burglar cracking into the gold vault at Fort Knox. Nordquist was unaware that he was talking to himself, muttering under his breath. His self-absorbed funk was jarred by an unexpected interruption.

Laughter sounded nearby. He glanced up, starting. Dr. Carlson stood behind him, looming over him. He'd thought that Carlson was at his own workstation several desks away.

Nordquist's cheeks burned at the realization that Carlson had seen the demeaning message now showing on his screen. Humiliation was almost instantly superseded by icy rage. Carlson had forgotten his place in the pecking order. Having his face rubbed in the dirt would remind him of his inferior status.

Nordquist pushed his chair back from his desk, swiveling around to face Carlson. There Carlson stood, big, bluff, hale, and hearty; showing every sign of immense enjoyment. Nordquist fixed him with what should have been a withering glare.

Carlson seemed impervious to it, his bland pudding of a face radiating great good humor. "Get the message, Glen?" he asked.

Glen? Glen! Of all the effrontery! The offense of this uninvited familiarity was compounded by its being ventured here in the LRF, the heart of Nordquist's undisputed domain.

"I wish you could see the look on your face. It's priceless—worth every bit of the years, the long years, that I've waited to see it," Carlson said.

He had a chip on his shoulder and meant to unburden himself. He went on, "Years of playing second fiddle to the great Glen Nordquist. Years of yes, sir; no, sir; how high do you want me to jump, sir? Being passed over for promotion while you took the top slot that should rightfully have been mine. Doing the heavy lifting of the research work while you put your name on the papers and patents and hogged all the credit. Years of eating dirt, of having to sit and take it and keep smiling while you poured it on.

"Look who's smiling now. Me—Hugh Carlson. I'm calling the shots now. I have been for some time. Literally, in some cases." He laughed to himself at that one.

"You thought you were so damned smart!" Carlson spat. "All of you, including the Board of Directors, the Senate Appropriations Committee heads, the Pentagon generals, the high-level bureaucrats. You all knew better than Hugh Carlson. 'That Carlson—bright enough, but not Project Director material. Capable in his way, but unsuited for the top slot.'

"Such a damned smart bunch of horses' asses! All the while, right under your noses, I've been stealing you blind! If you call it stealing to take the fruit of one's own labors—"

Nordquist opened his mouth to ream Carlson out, to say something, anything to halt his obscene diatribe.

Carlson beat him to it. "Shut up, Glen. Don't say a word. Save your breath—you'll need it." He laughed at that, too.

"I had to bite the inside of my mouth until it bled to keep from screaming during the Sayeed affair. Screaming with laughter," he said. "You thought you'd discovered a spy in the lab. So much fuss! Why, Sayeed was a pygmy compared to me; an insect!

"All he did was steal some of the Argus parameters—as if any scientist worthy of the name couldn't have deduced the numbers by himself!

"He was a big help to me, though. His clumsy efforts—he did everything but advertise his presence with a neon sign—actually helped me by throwing the bloodhounds off the trail. Argus, Perseus? Mere toys. Baubles compared to the real crown jewels.

"Ten years ago when I first came to work for you, I set my plan in motion. I saw the way of it, the lay of the land. Scientists, we who can split or fuse the atom, create or destroy like the gods themselves—

"And yet we're relegated to the back of the bus. Hirelings for the big bosses, the number crunchers and bean counters, the bottom-feeding money boys who suck the oyster dry and leave the empty shell for the rest of us peasants to fight over. They rule the world and revel in its treasures while we worry about mortgages and budgets and nagging wives.

"Not me. Not Hugh Carlson. The workman is worthy of his hire. From the moment I set up shop here, I've had only one objective: control. I got my hooks into the computer network early. Suborning, subverting, invading. Taking it over. Control the computer controls and you control all.

"That message on your screen is a sample of my handiwork. Our security watchdogs are experiencing my power all over Ironwood right now—like you are—and they don't even know it. With a few keystrokes I can nullify the built-in surveillance programs and fail-safes. No vault is secure from me. Divert any surveillance. Subvert any scanner.

"OCI was doomed from the start. Their network is an open book to me. Their system intersects ours at innumerable points and each one of those points is a highway right into their sanctum sanctorum, their holy of holies, where they keep the records of their constant snooping on all of us scientists. It's easy to crack their vault—when you're smart. But such control is only a means to an end."

"And what would that be?" Nordquist asked, keeping his tone mild, noncommittal, the way he'd talk to a crazy person, humoring him. He figured that Carlson had cracked up, suffering a nervous breakdown. Unfortunate that it had to happen when the two of them were alone in the control room, with no one close by to call on for help.

Carlson's eyes glittered in a face shiny with sweat. "While you've been fooling around with your petty little mirrors and ray guns, what have I been doing? Stealing the crown jewels. The day long ago that the PAL codes came to us for an overhaul and revamping, I saw the light. And it was brighter than a thousand suns, as Oppenheimer put it when the first Trinity A-bomb test was a success. In my hands were the secret codes that unleash atomic destruction."

PAL—permissive action link. The complex digital codes required to launch nuclear missiles, they neutralize the fail-safe mechanisms designed to prevent unauthorized launches of missiles with atomic warheads. The cyber keys to unlock the seals of atomic Armageddon.

There was more. No land-based missile in America's atomic arsenal could be launched without the PAL codes. But there was always the danger of the codes falling into the wrong hands by disaster or design.

From the need to prevent such a nightmare eventuality, PALO was born. PALO—the PAL overrides. The PALO codes were an auxiliary backup system. Inserted into a computerized launching sequence, they could override the PAL codes and shut down the launch, preventing the firing. They were the ultimate safety fuse to forestall unauthorized personnel from deliberately or by mistake unleashing a nuclear holocaust and triggering World War III.

Such awesome power was reserved solely for the President in his role of Commander in Chief, and the Joint Chiefs of Staff.

But PALO had a sinister corollary. Just as it could be used to override and abort an authorized PAL-input launch, the reverse was true. The PALO codes could be reverse-engineered to trigger an unauthorized nuclear launch.

In the year 2000, Nordquist's cadre at INL had been given the assignment of tweaking the PALO codes, refining, hardening, and improving the product. This was done over the course of several years. The new, improved PALO codes were then submitted to the custodianship of the Joint Chiefs.

But the data—oceans of it; seas of zeroes and ones whose sum total added up to overlordship of America's atomic arsenal—remained on the INL computer system.

Buried and locked up tight, so the guardians believed.

Carlson knew better.

"The PALO codes! Here was a prize worthy of my talents," he said. "A star-high goal. A Promethean quest. For endless years I endured the petty, bureaucratic vultures gnawing at my innards, tearing at my guts. Why? Because I had a purpose.

"I copied them—the PALO codes. Computations so big they took years to steal. Swiping a few screens of data here, a few there. Encoding them so they looked like something else, seemingly innocuous files from a host of unrelated projects.

"I salted them throughout the network, parking them for future retrieval.

"Copying, encrypting and moving them was the easy part. The hard part was the downloads. They were more closely tracked by our departmental network with its surveillance programs and by OCI's watchdogs. I took out the data bit by bit, block by block, piecemeal. Then reassembled them with my home computers.

"At times it felt like trying to drain the sea by carrying away a bucket of water at a time. It took years, almost a decade to do it properly without tripping any alarms. A supreme exercise in self-control, Will. One piggish excess of too much data downloaded at once might have upset all my plans. But I persevered.

"Now, they're mine. What do you think the governments of the world will pay for them? To render America's nuclear deterrent worse than useless—dangerous? A double-edged sword about to rebound on its wielder.

"What do you think about that, Glen?"

Nordquist's reply was straightforward and instinctive. "Carlson, you're fired. You'll be reported to OCI and the appropriate steps taken. Now get out."

Carlson preened with self-importance and droll bemusement. "Glen, you're beautiful. Talk about running true to type! You're priceless, you really are. Blinkered, hidebound, pettifogging—

"You haven't been listening, Glen. You're not in control here. I am. You couldn't contact OCI now even if you wanted to. Through my computer I control all. I've blocked you from all outside contact. There'll be no interruptions to this final little chat of ours."

"I'm curious about one thing, Carlson. What's the point of this exercise? What do you hope to gain from this pathetic confession of yours, apart from a life sentence in a federal super-max prison? Or, more likely, confinement to an insane asylum?"

"A fair question. Mainly I did it just for the doing of it. To show it could be done and that I'm the one who could do it. Me, Hugh Carlson, the smartest of them all. And then of course there's the rewards, the glittering prizes, treasure houses plundered. World-shattering power at my fingertips—"

Carlson jabbed a pointing index finger at Nordquist's monitor screen. "My little joke, to give you a taste of what I can do. It should say, 'Hello, Stupid—and Goodbye.' That's what this is: goodbye.

"My only regret is that you won't be around to see the results of my wizardry. It'll be a real game changer. Argus, Perseus, everything you've worked all your life to achieve will be so much dust in the wind. Meaningless.

"Seventy years of Los Alamos product. Millions of man-hours of calculation and computation, trillions of defense dollars spent in building and refining our intercontinental ballistic missile fleet, the linchpin of America's nuclear deterrent.

"Overthrown by one man—me! Talk about a New World Order! Too bad you won't be around to see it. You can go to hell knowing you've seen true genius at work—"

Nordquist's computer was equipped with a portable keyboard for greater mobility at his workstation. Carlson grabbed the keyboard with both hands. He raised it high and brought it down hard, clubbing Nordquist on top of his head.

The impact drove Nordquist deeper into his seat. Pieces of plastic broke and went flying, as did numbered and lettered keys.

Carlson struck again, opening a wide gash in Nordquist's scalp. Blood flowed. Nordquist's glasses broke in half at the nosepiece and went flying off his face. Sinking, failing, he raised his hands in a weak and futile attempt to protect himself.

Carlson battered, grunting each time he brought the keyboard down. Nordquist slumped in his chair, dazed, semi-conscious.

Carlson tossed aside the remains of the keyboard and lunged at Nordquist with both hands. An expression of fiendish malignity stamped his face.

Big hands circled Nordquist's thin neck and squeezed. Fingers sinking deep into flesh. Throttling. Shaking the other while strangling him, like a terrier worrying a rat clenched between its jaws.

Nordquist's bloody face darkened, eyes bulging, tongue protruding. Carlson leaned forward, putting his weight into it. Nordquist felt the room spinning around him, consciousness dimming.

Nordquist looked up at the faces of his listeners: pale, strained ovals. The auditors were motionless, silent. All except Whitcomb. The SECTRO Force commander was breathing gustily through his mouth.

"I thought I was dying. But I didn't die. The next thing I knew, this young man was trying to bring me around," Nordquist said, indicating Jack Bauer.

"Carlson did all this? Hugh Carlson?" Whitcomb asked, incredulous.

"That's what I said," Nordquist snapped, with a touch of his characteristic asperity. Jack thought that was a good sign that Nordquist was rallying and was going to make it.

"Carlson has the PALO codes?" Orne Lewis asked.

"He said he did," Nordquist replied.

"Do you believe him?"

"He's not without a certain facility in computer technology," Nordquist said, almost grudgingly.

"Does he have the skills to steal the codes?"

"Yes. Do I believe he did it? Yes—not because of what he said but what he did," Nordquist said. "Carlson's a time server. He's always had his eyes on the main chance, the sure thing. He wouldn't have burned his bridges without being damned sure he had something better lined up."

Nordquist's head sank back into the cushioned headrest. Debra Derr leaned in.

"Is there anything else you can think of that might tell us what Carlson is going to do next? Anything he might have said?" she asked.

Nordquist weakly shook his head no. His heavy-lidded eyes fluttered. He fought to keep them open. "That's all I know. I'm afraid I'm a poor prophet when it comes to predicting Hugh Carlson's next move. I didn't see this coming. Never thought he had it in him, to tell the truth."

Dr. Brand pleaded, "We need to get this man to a hospital." The paramedics were wide-eyed, stiff-faced. They'd understood enough of Nordquist's narrative to realize that they'd brushed up against weighty matters indeed.

"Everything that you've seen and heard here tonight is classified. Divulging this information to any unauthorized

persons is a federal offense," Debra Derr said, speaking to
Brand and the paramedics.

"We're all aware, we've been called to the facility before," Brand said.

"We'll get you the confidentiality documents to sign later," Derr said.

Brand motioned the paramedics to get moving.

As he was being wheeled away on the stretcher, Nordquist
fired a parting shot at the security contingent. "You'll get
him," he said confidently. "Carlson always was a second-
rater. A bungler! Why, he couldn't even manage to kill me
properly—"

Nordquist was wheeled out of the control room and into
the hall, to take the elevator to the ground floor and the ambulance waiting outside.

"I'll let the boys know they're coming down," Whitcomb
said. He spoke into his cell phone. "Dr. Brand is coming
down with Nordquist to take him to City Hospital. Let them
through to the ambulance. Have one of our men accompany
them to the hospital. Send along a couple more men in a
separate car as an escort. They can guard Nordquist at the
hospital. Make sure the doctor and the two paramedics do
not say anything or contact anyone on the outside. We can't
take any risks. Call me from the hospital with a situation
report."

Whitcomb put away his cell. "A patient like Nordquist
is a security nightmare. The things he knows should stay
locked up in his head. Doctors, nurses, orderlies will all
have to be screened and debriefed."

"Just be glad that Nordquist is alive. We can't afford to
lose a mind like that—a man like that," Jack Bauer said.

"Lucky that Carlson botched killing Nordquist."

"No, and he didn't kill Hickman or Harry Stempler,
either. He had an accomplice working with him tonight to
handle the rough stuff. The one who lured McCoy and me

into the Snake Pit while Carlson locked us in and turned the laser on us."

"Can you identify him, Jack?" Orne Lewis asked.

Jack shook his head. "I never got a good look at him."

A thought occurred to him and he amended his statement. "If it is a him. It could have been a her for all I know. Whoever it was could shoot, though—pretty damned accurate with a handgun."

"He'd have to be good to take Hickman. Hickman was nobody's fool."

"That was a loss," Jack said, his expression sour. "The shooter was someone who knew his way around the LRF. That lets out the usual run of thugs and killers."

Whitcomb was restless, agitated. "What about Carlson? Where is he and how do we find him?"

"When you figure that out let me know," Orne Lewis said.

"Carlson had time to make his getaway," Jack said. "It took me a good twenty minutes to break out of the Snake Pit. His control of the security system let him laugh at locked doors and scanner readers. He got out of the building through a side door, got into his car, and exited the main gate in the usual manner."

"But Sabito contacted OCI with orders to hold Carlson and Nordquist."

Debra Derr cleared her throat. That got the others' attention. "Sabito told Director McCoy to make sure that neither of those scientists left the building.

"McCoy instructed the guards in the lobby at the front entrance to detain Carlson or Nordquist if they tried to leave. That's the normal way in and out of the building for staffers. There's plenty of fire exit doors in the main building and the LRF but none of them can be used without setting off an alarm. McCoy didn't bother to instruct the gate guards to detain Carlson or Nordquist. He didn't think they would get that far. No one knew that the security system had been compromised and that Carlson could neutralize the scanner readers to enter and exit as he pleased."

Jack nodded. "Carlson exited undetected by a side door, got into his car, and drove out the main gate."

"And his accomplice?" Debra Derr asked.

"Carlson might have taken him out in his car. The other could have hid under a blanket in the backseat or in the trunk. Cars aren't searched on their way out."

"Or he may still be inside the building," Whitcomb said excitedly.

"It's possible," Jack deadpanned.

That produced an awkward silence. Debra Derr was the first to break it. "Proceeding at the speed limit, Carlson could have reached the badge holders' road portal at the west end of Corona Drive within ten minutes—well before the alert was put out on him and his car. They don't stop badge holders at the exit. We have to assume that Carlson got clear of South Mesa and is somewhere at large outside the security perimeter."

"With the PALO codes," Orne Lewis said.

Whitcomb ground a fist into his palm. "Hugh Carlson's going to be the object of the largest manhunt in history. He'll be the most wanted man alive since Osama bin Laden."

"With better results, I hope," said Jack Bauer.

• •

THE FOLLOWING TAKES PLACE
BETWEEN THE HOURS OF
3 A.M. AND 4 A.M.
MOUNTAIN DAYLIGHT TIME

• •

3:44 A.M. MDT
Wind Farm, Los Alamos County

"Here's a hot one, Jack:

"One of our informants tipped us that Adam Zane entered the country illegally tonight. He flew in on a private plane from Mexico. A twin-prop job, make and model unknown. It landed on a highway out in the boondocks outside Laredo, where it was refueled and took off again. We had a confidential informant on the service crew handling the refueling job. Zane's destination is Los Alamos. He'll be landing at a private strip at the Wind Farm, that alternate energy site owned by T. J. Henshaw that went bust.

"Sorry we couldn't get this to you sooner but our man on the service crew wasn't able to get away and report until now. We'll keep you posted on any details as they come in. Hope this is of some use to you."

That was the message posted on Jack Bauer's voice mail by Bert Leeds, SAC of CTU'S El Paso office.

"Think it's a good tip, Jack?" Orne Lewis asked.

"One of CTU/ELP's primary missions is to watch the border for spies, saboteurs, and terrorists trying to sneak into the country from Mexico. That's always been the nightmare, that a suicide squad of jihadists or al-Qaeda red-hots would enter the U.S. via the southern corridor. Leeds runs a tight ship with a powerful network of informants on both sides of the border.

"The wisest course is for us to check it out first. Without making too big a fuss that would divert resources from the search for Carlson. If the tip pans out, we can call for backup as needed. If not, no harm done. Besides, the fewer people who know about it, the less chance of Adam Zane being tipped off deliberately or by accident and taking evasive measures.

"Right now only two people in Los Alamos know about it—you and me," Jack Bauer said.

Jack was glad of the chance to be in action again. It beat sitting around stewing at the OCI office at Ironwood wondering where Dr. Hugh Carlson was to be found. He also welcomed the opportunity of putting some distance between himself and Vince Sabito. The murder of Special Agent Hickman was sure to enrage Sabito and inflame his suspicions to fever pitch.

Jack had enough on his plate now without butting heads with Sabito. He didn't want the Zane lead trashed by the overzealous participation of the FBI, either.

The new lead sent Jack and Orne Lewis racing through the night to the Wind Farm. They took Lewis's car. Lewis drove.

The dashboard-mounted digital media station's two-way radio was set to the police band frequency. An all-points bulletin had been put out alerting all city, county, and state law enforcement agencies to be on the lookout for Dr. Hugh Carlson. His description and that of his vehicle along with its license plate numbers were circulated as part of the BOLO—be-on-the-lookout—alert.

The authorities were moving fast to cordon off the county, blocking all roads.

U.S. Army Military Police were in transit to assist in the blockade. The Posse Comitatus Act prohibits the military from participating in civilian law enforcement operations. But the pilfered PALO codes were a matter of the highest national security. Therefore the strictures of the act were suspended and the MPs were joining the search.

The ongoing firestorm was both hindrance and help in the manhunt. The blaze created chaos and disorder, stretching law enforcement ranks thin. On the other hand, the law in Los Alamos County had already been reinforced by police and deputies from neighboring counties volunteering to help out. The many roadblocks that had been established throughout the disaster area to bar civilians from the fire zone and assure swift passage for first responders would serve as so many checkpoints screening the roads and searching for Carlson.

Proceedings were in the works to have the air space over Los Alamos County and environs declared off-limits to any unauthorized aircraft. Once invoked, the ban would be enforced by nearby Kirtland Air Force Base, whose fighter pilots would be instructed to shoot down any aircraft that were in noncompliance and refused to obey orders to identify themselves and land at the nearest airfield for inspection.

Lewis exited Corona Drive through the west gate, leaving South Mesa behind. An access road put his vehicle on Highway 5 South.

"It can't be coincidence that Adam Zane arrives on the

scene just when Carlson makes his big break," Jack Bauer said.

Lewis looked away from the highway ahead for an instant to cut a glance at Jack. He was excited. "The legendary Adam Zane!—One of the world's leading traders in stolen secrets. I've heard about him for years. He's been sighted in London, Paris, Berlin, Moscow, Tokyo, and Beijing. Even Washington, D.C., on several occasions. But I never thought he'd turn up in the godforsaken New Mexico high desert of Los Alamos."

"Probably neither did he," Jack said. "That's good for us. Only something as big as the PALO codes could lure him out of his usual haunts, to risk his skin by coming here in person."

"I just hope it's not a bum tip."

"You and me both. Right now it's the best thing we've got. This is a big county with lots of places for Carlson to hide in."

Lewis shook his head, his expression one of grim certainty. "Not for long. Carlson's strictly a city boy. No outdoorsman he. He'd be as out of place in the backcountry as a Gila monster at the Santa Fe Civic Opera."

"Not if he hooks up with the Blancos. They've got plenty of hideouts where they could stash him safely for a long time."

"The gang may have bitten off more than they can chew, Jack. This isn't one of the usual thug crime capers they're used to. The big heat is going to come down on them. Between the carrot of big rewards and the stick of life in a federal max prison unit, all but the most committed hard core of the gang is going to have plenty of incentive to roll over on their comrades," Lewis said.

"On the other hand, some of that Blanco hard core is pretty hard," he added.

* * *

New Mexico, Land of Enchantment. Enchantment? The bleak, rocky lunar landscape through which Lewis's car now coursed seemed not so much enchanted as haunted. No other vehicles were in sight on the empty ribbon of road.

To the northeast, the firestorm could be seen as a black smoky sky veined by red and orange streaks and infused with a glow from the inferno below. Rocky scarps and ridges hid the burning hills from view of the car going south on Highway 5. The fire glow shone on the canopy of black smoke streaming overhead.

Smoke haze from the fire had diffused west of the blaze, blurring the scene on Highway 5 and filling the air with the smell of burning. The car windows were rolled up and the air-conditioning was turned on but they couldn't keep out the smell of burning.

The Wind Farm was located on a rise west of the road. It was the brainchild of T. J. Henshaw, a magnate who'd made big money in oil, aircraft, and electronics. He'd gotten into alternative energy production in a big way. He planned to use windmills to generate electricity to supply the power needs of outlying ranches and suburban residential districts in the county and ultimately the city of Los Alamos. Leaving the more expensive coal- and petroleum-fueled power plants to supply the voracious needs of the laboratory complex on South Mesa. Thereby combining profit and patriotism.

Henshaw had built several dozen titan wind turbines on a piece of property with a western exposure in an open and unblocked notch pass in the Jemez Mountains. The north by northeast winds funneling through the gap would create a Venturi effect that would give an added boost to the wind turbines.

The economic crash had put an end to Henshaw's dreams of a wind-powered windfall. The recession had trashed his extensive financial and real estate holdings and wiped out his fortune. The Wind Farm had gone bust. Now it was in fore-closure, owned by banks that didn't know what to do with it.

Repossession companies had carted away the generators and miles of copper cable and wiring. They couldn't carry away the wind turbines. It would have cost more to tear them down and truck them out than whatever the sale of the scrap metal would have brought. The wind turbines were left in place. In this arid climate, it would be a long time before they rusted away.

The car neared the Wind Farm. It lay on the right, an eerie sight. The property was set several hundred yards back from Highway 5. A paved two-lane road ran from the highway to the property.

Before he went bust, Henshaw had been a high flyer. Literally. He did a lot of traveling by private plane between his various properties in the Southwest. Like the others, the Wind Farm had its own landing strip.

It ran parallel to the highway and lay between it and the wind turbines. A wood frame building stood at the strip's northeast corner. Its windows were squares of light. A couple of vehicles were parked beside it.

Lewis slowed, making a right-hand turn on to the road leading to the strip. He didn't bother to use a turn signal. Jack Bauer pulled the pistol from his shoulder holster and held it in his lap.

The car cruised toward the runway. The building was a one-story white wooden frame structure, a shack. A flood-light was fixed in the middle of the eave of the roof, shedding a glowing cone of radiance in front of the door. A plane stood on the runway near the shack, a modest-sized job with twin propellers.

To the left of the shack stood a pair of gas pumps on a small, oval concrete island. A lamppost stood between the two pumps. It was about eight feet tall and had a pair of electric lights at the top, arranged so that each lamp shone on a pump.

None of the lights, on the shack or the pumps, was overly bright. They were dim, minimal, so as not to draw attention to themselves.

Beyond the landing strip, a hundred yards back and west of it, stood the wind turbines, a steel forest of them. There were about two dozen metal poles, each fifty feet high and fitted with four rotors each. Some of the rotors made X-shapes; others made crosses.

The car neared the shack. The windows were open, covered by shades on the inside. Two figures came out the front door. A third stood outlined in the open doorway.

The car rolled to a halt, its front pointed at the shack. Headlights shone on it, outlining the men. The passenger side, Jack's side, faced the two men standing in front of the shack.

One was an uncouth, hulking figure. He wore a baseball cap and a pair of blue denim bib overalls. He was carrying a shotgun, a wicked pump-action piece.

The other man was small, neat, compact. Jockey-sized. He was bareheaded, short-haired, and clean-shaven, with a thin, angular face. He wore a black bow tie, a thin black vest over a white short-sleeved shirt, and black pants. He looked like a waiter or a member of a catering service. Except for the gun he wore in a shoulder holster rig.

The third man was an indistinct figure, a black silhouette framed and backlit by the doorway.

The hulk in the farmer overalls held the shotgun under his arm, pointed down at the ground. Jack wasn't fooling around with any shotguns. He knew what they could do.

"Hit the high beams," he said.

Lewis switched on the beams, flooding the shack and the men with harsh glare. Jack Bauer got out of the car and pointed his gun at the man with the shotgun. Fast, all in one motion.

"Easy, fella," the man with the bow tie said.

"Drop that shotgun," Jack said.

"Like hell!" the man in the overalls said. He started to swing the shotgun up.

Jack shot him twice in the torso. The big man dropped without firing a shot.

Lewis got out of the car with drawn gun. The man in the doorway ducked back into the shack, out of sight.

The bow-tied man stood very still, motionless. Lewis ran to the left side of the shack, to the window. Jack sidestepped, putting the bow-tied man between him and the shack. The other raised his hands in an I-surrender gesture.

The man in the shack picked up a machine gun and went to the window on the left-hand side of the front door. He thrust its snout outside, into the open.

The bow-tied man glanced over his shoulder, saw what the other was doing. "Hoke, don't!" he shouted, panicked.

Lewis reached in through the side window and shot Hoke. Hoke staggered sideways. He turned, swinging the machine gun toward Lewis. He stumbled in front of the open doorway.

Jack shot him twice. Hoke fell backward, finger tightening on the trigger. He sprayed an arc of machine gun fire up a wall and into the roof as he fell back. He hit the floor, thrashing. Lewis fired again. Hoke stopped thrashing, stopped shooting, stopped living.

Jack stood hunched in a combat crouch, arms extended in front of him, elbows slightly bent, one hand pointing the gun at Hoke, the other steadying his gun hand.

"That's all of them," Lewis said. He rounded the corner of the shack, crossing in front of it. "The one inside's finished, but I'll check anyway," he said.

He went into the shack, hunkering down beside Hoke. He felt his neck for a pulse. "Stone dead," Lewis said.

Jack pointed the gun at the bow-tied man's head, went to

him. He shucked the other's gun out of its shoulder holster and tossed it away into the weeds. He gave him a quick frisk for concealed weapons, found none.

The bow-tied man had thin hair, a pointy nose, a thin slitted mouth, and a pointy chin. His eyes were wide, bulging. They stood out against his pale flesh. It would have been normal for anyone to be pale under the circumstances, but the bow-tied man had the slick, waxy whiteness of one who has gone for long months without seeing too much sun.

Jack figured him for a jailbird.

The other swallowed hard a couple of times, his Adam's apple bobbing. He still held his arms in the hands-up position. "You crazy? What'd you kill 'em for?" he asked, his voice thin, reedy.

"They were waving too many guns around," Jack said.

"You're in big trouble, friend."

"Not as big as you."

"You came to the wrong place. Nothing here worth stealing."

"What're you doing here?"

"Hired to keep away trespassers and vandals."

"With a machine gun?"

The bow-tied man shrugged. "Lots of ornery characters in the backcountry. Like you guys. Okay if I lower my arms?"

"No. Keep them up. What's your name?"

"Dennison."

"Where's Adam Zane?"

"Who? Never heard of him."

"The man who came in not long ago in that plane on the runway."

"You don't know what you're talking about. The plane's been there for a long time. We were guarding it for Mr. Henshaw."

"Try again. The bank took away all Henshaw's planes.

His yachts and polo ponies, too. He's so broke he couldn't afford a watchman."

Lewis came out of the shack. "Plenty of hardware—guns—but nothing else. Not even a radio," he said.

"Where did Zane go, Dennison?" Jack asked.

"I don't know nothing about no Zane."

"Or the Blancos?"

Dennison shuddered. After a pause, he said, "You from them?"

"I'll ask the questions."

"Make sense then. I can't tell you what I don't know."

"You don't know what you're mixed up in, Dennison. If you did, if you realized the seriousness of it, you'd spill your guts and quick, and be damned glad of the opportunity to do so. Because you will talk."

Dennison tried to look sincere. "I would if I could, but I can't because I don't know nothing. And that's the god's honest truth, mister."

"How long have you been outside, Dennison? Out of prison."

"You got me all wrong, chief—"

"You've got that waxy look that comes from doing a long stretch behind bars."

"Not me. I don't get out in the sun much. I work nights."

"Damn you for making me do this the hard way, Dennison," Jack said, sighing.

He went to work. He slapped Dennison around, roughing him up. Dennison clammed up. Jack escalated the inflictions. Twisting arms, applying wicked fingertip pressure to nerve centers, pressure points. Cutting off Dennison's air supply until he nearly blacked out, letting him recover, and doing it again.

"Where is Adam Zane?" he asked.

Dennison shook his head, choking back a sob. Jack Bauer resumed the treatment.

Dennison lay on the ground, curled up in a fetal position, moaning softly between labored breaths. Jack Bauer and Orne Lewis stood looking down at him.

"Tough little monkey," Lewis said, half admiringly.

"I don't have the time to fool around," Jack Bauer said. "What're you going to do?"

"You crazy?" Dennison said, sputtering. Breathing hard, panting.

The shack had yielded the needed oddments. Dennison was tied to the flagpole. He sat on the ground with his back against the pole and his legs extended in front of him. His legs were spread wide apart, ankles tied to the ends of a wooden pole. The pole was a broomstick with the broom part snapped off it. The spreader bar kept Dennison from closing his legs.

A pile of kindling was heaped on his crotch and between his legs. A little teepee of twigs and broken branches. At the base of it was a mound of sawdust and fistfuls of dry grass. Pieced on top of them was a heap of twigs and wooden rods and spokes from a broken chair.

Dennison squirmed, his eyes wide black dots floating in a ghostly white face. "What—what are you gonna do?"

"A time-honored New Mexico tradition," Jack said. "I picked this up in a book about the old-time Indian wars. The Apaches used it to torture their captives. Of course the poor devils getting the treatment didn't have a choice. They were booked for the full ride.

"You can stop it any time, Dennison. Just sing out where we can find Adam Zane and you're off the hook. Don't wait too long, though. These fires are hard to control."

"I don't know, I swear—"

"Let me borrow your lighter, Lewis," Jack said.

Jack stood on one knee beside Dennison. He flicked on the lighter. The yellow flame burned bright and strong, underlighting Jack's face. Hard glittering eyes, tight-lipped mouth flanked by vertical creases at the corners. He had a workmanlike air.

Dennison pleaded, "Wait, wait—"

Jack Bauer touched the flame to the tip of a piece of crumpled paper protruding from the bottom of the pile of the kindling heaped between Dennison's legs. The paper caught fire, the flames crawling inward along its length, crawling through a hole in the pile of dried twigs and broken spokes of wood.

He said, "Don't wait too long. No water to put out the fire and it could get out of control fast—"

The paper touched off some of the dry grass heaped in bunches at the bottom of the campfire. The weeds burned better than the paper. They turned to flame with a crackling sound.

From Jack Bauer came no quips, no smart remarks. This was serious business, and he went about it in deadly earnest. Thin lines of smoke rose from the pyramid of kindling heaped between Dennison's legs and on his crotch.

"Where is Adam Zane?"

Crackling, sputtering, smoking. Dennison started humping and bucking, but the way he was tied to the flagpole allowed him little freedom of movement. Not much wiggle room.

Jack stepped on Dennison's taut thigh to pin his legs to the ground. The smell of wood smoke was strong. He said, "This is the day for fires I guess . . ."

Tongues and tendrils of yellow flame began licking up out of the mound to wind themselves around twigs and kindling. Crumpled paper and those dry weeds at the heart of the mound were blazing nicely now, yellow firelight leaping up.

"Where's Adam Zane?"

"I'll talk! I'll talk!"

A moth-eaten old blanket taken from the shack earlier served as a flail to disperse the mound of burning kindling, sweeping it off Dennison's crotch and out from between his legs.

Jack Bauer said, "No real damage. Just in time. Now spill it, Dennison, and it better be good."

Dennison talked.

Lewis watched the prisoner while Jack Bauer went into the shack. Jack came out carrying a toolbox and a flashlight.

He went around to the back of the shack. A mobile platform stood against the rear wall. It was something like a seven-foot-tall metal stepladder mounted on roller wheels. At the top of the ladder was a square platform large enough for a man to stand on. It was enclosed by a waist-high guardrail on three sides.

Jack pushed the platform on to the runway, positioning it at the front of the plane. He set the levers that locked the wheels in place, immobilizing the stepladder. He climbed the ladder to the platform. The engine cowling worked like the hood of a car.

He unfastened it, swinging it out of the way so he could get at the motor.

He held the flashlight in one hand. His other hand wielded a screwdriver, pair of pliers, and a wrench, switching from one to the other.

Ten minutes later, he'd removed certain key components, without which the engine could not start. He threw them as far as he could into the tall weeds on the far side of the runway.

"Zane won't be going anywhere in this plane," Jack Bauer said. He and Orne Lewis stood off to one side, out of Dennison's hearing.

"Would you really have gone through with it, Bauer? All the way, I mean—if Dennison hadn't talked?"

"What do you think?"

1 2 3 4 5 6 7 8 9
10 11 12 13 14 15 16 17
18 19 20 21 22 23 24

. . . .

THE FOLLOWING TAKES PLACE
BETWEEN THE HOURS OF
4 A.M. AND 5 A.M.
MOUNTAIN DAYLIGHT TIME

. . . .

4:33 A.M. MDT
Highway 5, Los Alamos County

Dennison had named Bluecoat Bluff as Adam Zane's destination, and Jack Bauer, Orne Lewis, and Dennison were on their way. Lewis was driving, Jack was in the passenger seat, and Dennison was tied up and locked in the trunk.

The car rolled north on Highway 5. Black was leaching from the sky in the east, replaced by a touch of growing grayness. The sky was overcast, its vaulted ceiling lowered by the pall of smoke that continued rising from the firestorm.

In the west a ghostly half moon inched toward the horizon, glimmering dully through streaming gray-black curtains. A scattering of stars winked through rents in the smoky haze.

"Bluecoat Bluff is a local landmark," Lewis said. "A state

historical site. It got its name from a U.S. cavalry fort that was there during the days of the Old West. The cavalry soldiers used to wear blue coats as part of their uniforms. It's lonely, secluded—a good place for a meeting."

Dennison was part of Varrin's crew. Varrin had sent a car and some men to escort Zane and his bodyguard, Hank Ketch, to the bluff.

T. J. Henshaw had nothing to do with the operation, as far as Dennison knew. The Wind Farm, foreclosed by the bank, had a conveniently located landing strip. The site was abandoned, unguarded. Varrin had refilled the below-ground aviation fuel tanks and put the pumps back into working order in anticipation of Zane's arrival. So Zane could fly in, transact his business, and fly out.

"Who's this Varrin that Dennison claims he's working for, Lewis?" Jack asked.

"Some gunman and gang boss, apparently. I've heard the name before but that's all I know about him. That's outside my area of expertise. Sabito could quote you chapter and verse about the local hoodlums. Why don't you ask him?"

"Maybe later. I'd just as soon steer clear of Vince for the moment. This is a delicate situation and I don't need him charging around like a bull in a china shop."

"Dennison was almighty scared of the Blancos. Not as much as he was scared of you, though," Lewis said, chuckling. "Apparently Varrin's bunch and the Blancos are having some kind of war."

"Good. The Blancos arc a handful. If Varrin can monkey wrench them, so much the better."

Tires thrummed on the pavement, the motor raced. Messages crackled on the police band frequency from time to time. An exchange of messages sounded a note of urgency and suppressed excitement.

"What's that?" Lewis asked. Jack Bauer turned up the volume.

A Sheriff's Department patrol car manning a roadblock on Ridgefoot Drive reported that they had apprehended a person answering the description of Dr. Hugh Carlson. The subject's documents identified him as one Jason Endicott. His car was different from Carlson's vehicle. Different license number, different make and model of car. However, the subject's suspicious demeanor and inability to explain what he was all about had prompted the deputies to detain him pending verification of his bona fides, which were now being processed at Sheriff's Department headquarters.

"Ridgefoot Drive—that's right on the way to Bluecoat Bluff," Lewis said, excited. "The bluff's just several miles north of the intersection, over a rise."

"Maybe Carlson's been headed off at the pass after all," Jack said. "How far away is it?"

"A couple of miles."

"We're headed in that direction anyway. Let's find out if they have the right man or not," Jack said.

Lewis's foot put more weight on the accelerator.

4:45 A.M. MDT
Intersection of Highway 5 and Ridgefoot
Drive, Los Alamos County

"Am I under arrest?"

"No, sir."

"Then why are you holding me?"

"We're detaining you pending verification of your identity, sir. Headquarters is running a check on your record. Once that comes through and checks out okay, you'll be free to go."

It felt like an arrest, though. So thought Dr. Hugh Carlson, now occupying the backseat of a Los Alamos County Sheriff's patrol car at the crossroads.

Carlson fought to keep a poker face. Inwardly, he cursed his luck. To have the work of a decade threatened by a twist of fate now!

He was not handcuffed. But the rear seat of a police car is a form of detention itself. A grille separated the rear from the front seat. Windows that could not be rolled down from inside. Doors with no interior exit handles.

They had his attaché case, too. Inside it: the PALO codes. The lawmen were as yet unaware of the significance of the computer disks in the metal briefcase.

Carlson had been heading west on Ridgefoot Drive en route to the rendezvous at Bluecoat Bluff when he'd run into the police roadblock. The patrol car sat at the intersection where the drive met Highway 5. It stood in the middle of the crossroads, barring the way in all four directions.

Ridgefoot Drive ran along the base of the north side of a ridge running east-west.

Rocky spurs and limbs jutted out from the ridge, causing the road to twist and turn to avoid them. The rugged terrain had screened the crossroads, preventing Carlson from seeing the police car until it was too late.

Rounding a blind curve, he'd come upon the roadblock. The patrol car's headlights were on and its red and blue rooftop flashers blinked lazily. Fear seized Carlson. Panic. For an instant he thought of flight, turning the car around and retreating in the direction he'd come from.

Too late for that. They'd seen him. Flight would be sure evidence of guilt. He had no illusions about his ability to outrace police pursuit. The only thing to do was brazen it out.

He had a few things working for him. He was supplied with documents attesting an alternate identity. Photo driver's license, insurance card, bank, and credit cards in his wallet were all made out to his new identity of Jason Endicott.

He'd switched cars, too. The car was registered to Endicott. The documents were not forgeries. Nothing as crude as that. They were the real thing, bought from corrupt officials in the Department of Motor Vehicles and other licensing authorities. The information substantiating his background had been entered into the appropriate data banks. He'd been assured by his associates in this venture that the documents would withstand official scrutiny.

The roadblock was manned by two deputies wearing the Stetson hats and tan uniforms of the County Sheriff's Department. One wielded a baton flashlight. Carlson drove up to the police car at the crossroads and halted. He rolled down his window. The deputies approached him. The senior man was Alvarado; his younger partner was Merritt.

Alvarado was moon-faced, with graying temples and a salt-and-pepper walrus mustache. His paunch swelled over the top of a low-slung gun belt.

Merritt was thin, wiry, with a dark eyes and sharp features. Merritt came around to the driver's side of Carlson's car. "Good morning, sir."

"Something wrong, Officer?" Carlson asked. Noting with satisfaction that his voice was smooth, assured.

"Just a routine check, sir. May I see your license and registration, please?"

Carlson fished the wallet out of his pocket. He handed Merritt his license, registration, and car insurance card. Merritt examined the photo license in the flashlight's gleam.

A far from casual scrutiny. He shone the light in Carlson's face, eyeing it. Carlson squinted against the glare. Merritt looked at the photo ID, then back at Carlson.

"Hey, Ray," he called to his partner.

Alvarado came over to him. He and Merritt stood several

paces away from Carlson, discussing him, low-voiced, with much handling of and referring to the photo ID.

"Let me see," Alvarado said. He took the flashlight from Merritt and shone it on Carlson. "Fits the description," he said.

Alvarado stood by the driver's side of the car. He stuck his face in the open window frame. He showed leathery skin with a small crescent moon scar near the corner of his left eye. "What brings you out this way, Mr. Endicott?"

"I'm on a buying trip for my firm. Going out to some of the Native American reservations to purchase jewelry, trinkets, and handicrafts." Carlson even had business cards printed up for that nonexistent firm in a real office building in Santa Fe.

"Kind of early for that, isn't it?"

"I wanted to get an early start because of the fire. I didn't know but that it might affect driving and cause me to have to make some wide detours."

"It's raised hob with local traffic conditions, that's for sure," Alvarado said. "Pull over to the side of the road and turn off your car, please."

"Did I do something wrong? Am I in any kind of trouble?" Carlson asked.

"The fire's brought a lot of hassle with it. Looting, theft, and whatnot. We have to check on everybody who comes through. Just pull over on the shoulder there."

Carlson did as he was told. He had a crazy thought about gunning the car and making a break for it. He recognized it for what it was and stifled the impulse to flee. The way to get out of this was by not losing his head. He made a K-turn, pebbles crunching under the tires as he rolled into the spot indicated by Alvarado.

"Turn off the car."

Carlson turned the key in the ignition, switching off the engine.

"Please open the glove compartment, sir."

Carlson knew his rights. The cops couldn't search him and his car or hold him without probable cause. He also knew the futility of quoting the law to the cops. That would really harden their free-floating suspicions. They could hold him until headquarters sent out a man with a warrant to search him.

Carlson opened the glove compartment. No worry there. Contents innocuous. Merritt came around on the passenger's side and riffled through the glove compartment.

He ducked his head down into the well and shone his light under the car seats, peering under them.

"Get out of the car, sir. Thank you," Merritt said.

They didn't frisk Carlson. It hadn't reached that stage yet. Alvarado shone the flashlight beam up and down, sweeping Carlson from head to toe, practiced eye scanning for the suspicious bulge of concealed weapons. Finding none.

Carlson was very glad that he'd rejected the idea of arming himself. He was no gunman. A killer, yes, several times over, but no gunman.

A metal attaché case sat on the passenger seat beside Carlson. "What's in the case, sir?" Merritt asked.

The most valuable intelligence hoard in the Western world today, Carlson thought but didn't say. He'd wanted it close by, right next to him. Its reassuring presence, the nearness of it. That was why he hadn't locked it in the trunk. "Just some disks—computerized sales records and the like," Carlson said.

"Open it up, please."

Carlson stood facing the left front side of the car. He set the base of the metallic reinforced carrying case on top of the car hood. Alvarado and Merritt came up close behind him, flanking him. He unsnapped the fasteners and lifted the lid. Inside, in a black velour lining with slots, were two rows of computer disks, each in its own hard clear plastic protective carrying case.

"Thank you, you can close it now. Put it back in your car."

They had him open the car trunk next. Carlson pressed a button in the front of the instrument panel that unlocked and opened the trunk.

"Please come with me," Alvarado said. He and Carlson went to the rear of the car. The deputy lifted the trunk lid. Nothing in the boot but a spare tire. Down went the lid, relocking it.

"I'll get on the horn to headquarters," Alvarado said. Merritt stayed behind to keep an eye on Carlson/Endicott. A very close eye.

Alvarado got in the passenger side front seat of the patrol car. He left the door open, leaving the dome light on. He worked the hand mic of the dashboard mounted radio, calling into headquarters at the Sheriff's Department. He reported that he and Merritt were detaining a man who fit the description of Dr. Hugh Carlson but whose license and registration identified him as Jason Endicott. He read the pertinent information off the cards to the dispatcher. He reported the attaché case with the computer disks.

The dispatcher said he'd run a make on the ID ASAP. After that there was nothing for it but the waiting.

"Bring him over here, Jim," Alvarado said. He opened the right rear door of the patrol car. "Sit down and make yourself comfortable while we're waiting for your documents to be processed and verified, Mr. Endicott. It'll take a few minutes. Make yourself comfortable."

"Thanks." Carlson was unable to repress a tart sting of incipient sarcasm that he quickly smothered. "Am I under arrest?"

"Any reason why you should be?"

"No."

"There you are, Mr. Endicott. Just routine."

Carlson got into the back of the police car. Alvarado

closed the door. The sound of the door closing had an ominous note of finality. Like a cell door closing.

So there was Dr. Hugh Carlson, sitting in the back of a police car. *Where all your scheming and masterminding— and treason and murder—have brought you*, he told himself.

But he was still in the game. The documents were real, his assumed identity had been prepared by professionals. They would pass muster. Of that he had no doubt. They were good enough to survive the scrutiny of a notoriously corrupt law enforcement agency headed by a buffoon such as Sheriff Buck Bender.

They would have to release him. *Play it cool. Keep your nerve, maintain your front, and you'll get clear of this. They'll let you out with an apology, and you'll get back in your car and be on your way.*

Alvarado and Merritt stood off to one side out of earshot deep in earnest discussion. They kept looking up and casting side glances at him.

Carlson had time to think. Recalling the last few frantic hours, events whirled in montage through his head. He was not alone. He had friends on the outside. Associates, confederates.

Alone, single-handedly, he had accomplished the most spectacular espionage/atomic secrets theft in modern history. Since the Rosenbergs had stolen the secrets of the atomic bomb and passed it to the Soviets at the start of the Cold War. They'd been caught and executed in the electric chair.

Carlson had achieved the theft by himself. But he needed help on the getaway. And to eliminate threats along the way. He'd made alliances. Potent allies who could make things happen. His elaborate machinations, spread across the years, had stirred suspicions. Especially in the last year.

Perhaps because he was so near to his goal, he'd rushed

things, becoming careless in his haste and eagerness. Naturally the first to suspect had been those who worked most closely with him. His colleagues.

Dr. John Yan had been the first. He'd made the mistake of failing to dissemble those suspicions. Carlson had caught Yan checking up on him, snooping. Yan didn't know that Carlson knew. That signed his death warrant. Carlson alerted his allies that Yan was on his trail. They assured him they'd take care of it.

Enter Varrin. Carlson knew nothing of the man personally, had never met him.

He preferred it that way and that's how it had to be. For Carlson's associates, Varrin was the go-to guy for assassination. Soon after, Yan dropped dead on the tennis courts. It looked like a heart attack. He'd been poisoned with an untraceable drug that counterfeited the symptoms of a heart attack.

Yan had communicated enough of his suspicions about Carlson to his close friend, the INL's venerable savant Dr. Hamilton Fisk. Fisk's clumsy fumbling attempts to follow up on the late Yan's efforts stood out like a neon sign to Carlson. Carlson passed the word to his associates and Fisk was the next to die.

The inevitability of it was comforting, reassuring. Knowing he could depend on his allies to do their part in enabling his great work of stealing the PALO codes.

Several months passed before murder once more came into play. It was the result of Carlson's own clumsiness. In his eagerness to finalize his tasks, he'd cut corners, gotten sloppy. He'd downloaded a chunk of the encoded codes (disguised as Perseus test data) onto Freda Romberg's computer, parking it there for temporary safekeeping.

She'd discovered the anomaly but hadn't realized its significance. She'd made the mistake of bringing it to Carlson's attention—never suspecting that he was the culprit. She'd planned to report it to Rhodes Morrow. Carlson had to act fast.

His newfound mastery over the computerized scanner readers had proved invaluable, allowing him to stealthily enter the Snake Pit when she was alone in it and activate the robot arm that had swatted her like a mosquito.

Doctoring the scanner reader data erased all cyber traces that he'd been in the tank at the time of Romberg's death.

But SECTRO Force guard Ernie Battaglia had seen Carlson in the vicinity near the time of death. If he should put the facts together, the results could be uncomfortable indeed for Dr. Carlson. The associates had seen to Battaglia, removing him from the game board by a convenient fatal hit-and-run accident.

The death of Rhodes Morrow introduced a troubling new variable, however. Carlson had nothing to do with it. Neither had his associates, or so they claimed, and he had every reason to believe them. They were baffled, mystified, upset, and alarmed by a murder they hadn't arranged.

It meant only one thing: an unknown player had entered the game. It could only be assumed that the mysterious newcomer's goal was identical to that of Carlson and associates: to possess the priceless PALO codes. Prodding Carlson and company to accelerate their timetable and get clear before the opposition party's efforts should upset the apple cart and doom the master plan.

Only in this last day had the cryptic and homicidal opponent tipped his hand with Peter Rhee's murder, the botched poison needle assassination attempt on Jack Bauer, the killing of Harvey Kling and the Parkhursts, the failed kidnap attempt on Sylvia and Kendra Nordquist, and the vanishment of Carlson's wife, Carrie.

The associates had learned that the explosion of ultra-violence had been carried out by the Blanco gang. Carlson knew nothing of the Blancos, had never even heard of them.

But he knew trouble when he saw it. And so did the associates. The roof was coming down on all their heads, and they had to make their move before it was too late.

Tonight was the night. The firestorm was a help, a godsend, with its chaos and confusion to the authorities.

One of the associates had alerted Carlson that the net was fast closing around him. He made arrangements to put a previously laid escape plan into motion. The associate arranged to be on the scene to facilitate Carlson's getaway. That was needful. Carlson was a killer but no gunman. He needed help with the wet work.

Bauer and Hickman were getting too close. Their elimination would remove two deadly threats and enable the escape plan. Carlson set about turning the Snake Pit into a death trap. His control of the scanner reader system allowed him to arrange for his associate to enter the LRF building through a side door, unobserved and undetected by the OCI watchdogs.

Now that the final curtain was near, Carlson had the freedom to indulge a long-cherished dream: the degradation and destruction of Dr. Glen Nordquist. For over a decade he'd chafed under Nordquist's domination, silently enduring his supercilious attitude, his smugly superior contempt, his slights, sneers, and slurs.

Here was his opportunity to revenge himself on Nordquist and he'd taken it. He hacked into Nordquist's computer to crash it with the insulting HELLO, STUPID message.

Confronting his nominal superior, he'd told Nordquist the facts of life, boasting of his achievement in running rampant over the OCI snoopers and stealing the PALO codes.

He'd done his best to bash out Nordquist's brains with the portable keyboard as a blunt instrument, finishing the job by strangling him with his bare hands.

His associate entered the scene, surreptitiously admitted into the LRF by a side door manipulated by Carlson from a control room computer. The associate took care of SECTRO Force guard Harry Stempler, herding him at gunpoint into a stairwell and shooting him dead.

Carlson used the remotes to deactivate the blockhouse's scanner reader, sealing the front door. The associate showed himself at the structure's rear door, luring Jack Bauer and Gabe McCoy into the Snake Pit. Carlson operated from the cockpit of the control room, trapping Bauer and McCoy in the Pit and turning an energized Medusa against them. His associate exited the building by a side door.

McCoy died under the laser's sizzling ruby beam. Bauer had somehow gotten lucky, tricking Carlson into shooting it into a mirrored metal shield that turned the ray against its source, slaying Medusa.

Carlson took it on the run, snatching up the attaché case containing the PALO codes and exiting the blockhouse building. The associate had already been at work, shooting Hickman dead. Consequently no one stood on guard in the LRF to thwart Carlson's escape.

Carlson exited via a side door that he'd preset to allow him to flee through it without registering on the scanner reader. He went into the parking lot, got in his car, and drove out through the main gate.

A short but nerve-racking ride across Corona Drive delivered him to the west portal and the happy discovery that his crimes were as yet undiscovered, allowing him to exit the badge-holders-only road and South Mesa without incident.

He drove to a secluded spot on the Hill where a getaway car awaited. He got rid of everything that identified him as Dr. Hugh Carlson, all his documents and credit cards, even his cell phone, shedding them like a snake sloughing off a dry, dead skin.

He pocketed the credentials so carefully prepared by his associates, the paperwork and plastic cards that certified him in his newly assumed identity of Jason Endicott.

He got into the new car registered to Endicott, placing the attaché case with the PALO codes on the seat beside him. That priceless storehouse of secrets would remain within his sight and reach.

He drove off, pointing the car west toward the rendezvous site of Bluecoat Bluff. He couldn't get there directly, because of the fire. He had to follow a wide-ranging and circuitous course with many lengthy detours before he finally found himself heading westbound on Ridgefoot Drive, weaving and winding toward the intersection with Highway 5 that would take him to the meeting place.

Where he drove right into the roadblock manned by Deputies Alvarado and Merritt.

Carlson was confident his assumed identity would withstand the Sheriff's Department's scrutiny. In the spectral cyber world of paper profiles and bureaucratic databases, Jason Endicott was as real as any other of the numberless identities who existed in the system as a set of programmed vital statistics.

Carlson wrapped that thought around himself like a comforter and clung to it for sanity's sake.

A set of headlights appeared south of the crossroads, driving northbound on Highway 5. They belonged to a car that slowed to a halt at the roadblock at the intersection.

Jack Bauer and Orne Lewis got out and went to meet the deputies.

• •

THE FOLLOWING TAKES PLACE
BETWEEN THE HOURS OF
5 A.M. AND 6 A.M.
MOUNTAIN DAYLIGHT TIME

• •

5:02 A.M. MDT
Intersection of Highway 5 and
Ridgefoot Drive, Los Alamos County

Dawn was breaking, a gray dawn thanks to the smoke hazing the sky. The sun was an orange ball floating in dun-colored murk. Long, thin, black streamers of smoke stretched vertically across the eastern horizon.

The patrol car sat at an angle in the center of the crossroads. Carlson's car was parked on the east shoulder of Highway 5, north of Ridgefoot Drive. Lewis's car stood in the northbound lane of Highway 5 south of Ridgefoot Drive.

Jack Bauer and Orne Lewis and Deputies Alvarado and Merritt stood in a knot on the pavement between the patrol car and Lewis's car.

Dr. Hugh Carlson sat in the backseat of the patrol car,

slumping down so that the top of his bowed head barely showed above the top of the front seat.

Jack and Lewis were showing their credentials to the deputies. Alvarado examined the CTU and CIA ID cards and returned them to their owners. "The suspect fits Carlson's description," he said. "A general description that fits several thousand men in this area. He's driving a different car and his ID holds up. Headquarters said it checked out okay.

"Just between us, we may have overstepped our authority in holding him, especially if he is who he says he is. But what with the urgency of the BOLO, we figured it was better safe than sorry."

"You did the right thing," Orne Lewis said. "Better to err on the side of caution. If it is the wrong man, we'll go to bat for you with your bosses to make sure there's no comeback."

"Thanks, we appreciate it."

"What's this Carlson wanted for, anyway?" Merritt asked.

"A couple of murders out at the lab, for starters," Jack Bauer said. No point in elaborating on the details. "There's one way to find out for sure. Let's have a look at him."

The foursome crossed to the patrol car. The man in the backseat was sitting slumped low as if trying to shrink into himself. He turned his head away to the side.

Lewis rapped a knuckle smartly on the window. The detainee started, almost jumping out of his seat.

"Bingo," Lewis exclaimed triumphantly. "That's him, all right. That's Carlson."

Jack Bauer breathed a silent prayer of thankfulness that Carlson had been stopped in time. But what of the PALO codes? Had he managed to pass them along to an accomplice?

"Outstanding work, men," Lewis was saying to Alvarado and Merritt.

Carlson seemed to have partly recovered from his shock. He sat upright in his seat looking straight ahead. Staring into space.

Jack Bauer's cell phone rang. It was Debra Derr at OCI. She'd be glad to hear the news about Carlson's apprehension. Besides, he might need her to help keep Sabito off his neck. "Bauer speaking."

"Jack, this is Debra Derr. This is important. Is Orne Lewis with you?"

"Yes."

"Don't trust him, Jack. Something's wrong. The gate guards here reported that they logged in Lewis at a little after one A.M. He came in a short time after you did. But the guards in the main building front entrance didn't log him in until one-forty A.M. Where was he during that time? And what was he doing?"

Jack's face froze. He fought to assume a breezily conversational tone as he spoke into the cell: "That's right, Vince, we're here at Ridgefoot Drive and—"

Lewis had drawn his gun—a fast draw. He took a few steps back so he could cover Jack Bauer and the deputies.

The lawmen were taken aback by Lewis's action. "Hey! What's this!" Alvarado demanded.

"A double cross," Jack said disgustedly.

Lewis arched an interrogative eyebrow. "Who was that, OCI? I was wondering how long it would take for them to put together the missing time factor—"

Merritt reached for his gun. Lewis shot him twice. Merritt fell writhing to the pavement.

Alvarado made a try, and before his gun could clear the holster Lewis put a bullet in him. Alvarado hit the pavement not far from Merritt. A hole above his left eyebrow marked where Lewis's shot had tagged him.

When the shooting started, the cell phone dropped from Jack Bauer's hand, which plunged toward the gun in his shoulder holster. He couldn't beat a drawn gun and he knew it. Lewis swung the smoking pistol back to cover Jack. Jack froze.

"The picture's falling into place now," he said. He wondered how many shots he could take and still bring it to Lewis.

He thought he might be able to make it if he were shot in the torso and not in the head. He knew he was going to have to find out.

Merritt wasn't dead. He lay on his side writhing on the pavement. Lewis glanced down and put another bullet into Merritt.

Orne Lewis was one of Carlson's associates. Not the only one but a key one. They'd been working together for a long time.

"I'm the missing piece of the puzzle," Lewis said cheerfully.

Why didn't Lewis just burn down Jack Bauer and be done with it? Jack could guess the answer to that one: ego.

Most traitors have a kink inside them. Something psychological. They're not in it for the money, although that's a good way to keep score. The act of betrayal—betrayal of friends, coworkers, family, country—satisfies a deep-rooted psychological need within them. A rage to get even with an oblivious world that's failed to recognize their worth as superior human beings and insists on treating them as just one of the crowd.

Lewis would have to boast of his achievements in treachery. It was no fun unless someone else knew how smart he really was, no matter how short-lived the confidant.

Jack Bauer wanted to get Lewis talking. To buy some time, precious time. Maybe something would turn up.

He knew he was going to go for his gun. Knew he was going to take some slugs from Lewis's weapon. He could only hope that willpower would keep him alive long enough to see the job through. It could be done, he knew. Had been done. He'd seen men who were technically dead on their feet live long enough to put the blast on their killers.

"Why?" Jack Bauer asked.

"For the money," Lewis said. "I'll be fabulously rich. But that's not all of it, of course."

"No, it never is."

"America is over, Jack. It's not a country anymore, it's a corporation—a busted corporation. The empire is in retreat all over the world. I don't need to tell you that, you see the same reports I do. Time to sell out while somebody's still buying. Time to sell while the dollar is still worth more than something to wipe your ass with."

Lewis's gun was pointed at Jack's middle. It never wavered. Lewis used his free hand to open the back door of the police car. "Get out," he said to Carlson without looking at him. Never taking his eyes off Jack.

Carlson got out of the car. "Thanks for pulling me out of the hole—"

"You have the codes?" Lewis said.

"Yes, they're in the car."

"Get in it and get out of here. Drive up to the bluff. We've already lost too much time. Mustn't keep the almighty Adam Zane waiting."

"What about you?"

"I'll be up directly. I've just got a few loose ends to tie up here. Get moving, Carlson—go. Don't cross in front of me, you dolt, go behind me. Don't block my shot on Jackie boy."

Carlson went to his car. He walked unsteadily, stiff-legged, with exaggerated care, like a drunk. He made a wide detour around the bodies of the two deputies sprawling in the road.

He got in his car. He started the car, stepped hard on the gas. The wheels spun, kicking up dirt from the shoulder. Jack was watching for an opportunity but this wasn't it. Lewis never wavered while holding him under the gun. Carlson swung the car onto the pavement and drove away, red taillights dwindling as he went north.

Orne Lewis said, "I knew that time factor would trip me. The delay between the time I was logged in through the main gate at INL and the time I entered the building. It was a calculated risk. Necessary, and it paid off. Took them long enough to tumble to it.

"Carlson left the side door in the LRF open for me. I got there just in time. Time enough for me to get rid of Stempler the guard. I showed myself in the Snake Pit to lure you and McCoy inside. I'll give you your due, Jack. You beat the laser. I didn't stick around to witness your triumph."

"You killed Hickman, Lewis. That explains the contact wounds from being shot at point-blank range. Only someone he trusted could have gotten that close to him."

"Oh, now you think of that. You're a day late and a dollar short, Jack. Yes, I killed him. That opened the way for Carlson and me to exit through the side door. He got into his car and drove out the main gate, I went around to the front of the building and was logged through at the front entrance. As if I'd just shown up.

"I don't mind telling you I had some bad moments there worrying that the time factor would be noticed in time to unmask me. But I had confidence in the inefficiency of OCI. They didn't let me down.

"You getting that tip on Adam Zane was a mixed blessing. Naturally it would have been better for all concerned if it had never surfaced. I decided to stick to you. Closely. That way I could run interference if you arrived in time to intercept Zane. Luckily you didn't. Those hirelings at the field were low-level gunmen of no importance. They didn't know I was working for the same side as them."

"What side is that?" Jack Bauer asked.

"The winning side."

"T. J. Henshaw?"

Lewis laughed. "Hardly. Henshaw has nothing to do with it. He's just another billionaire gone bust—so many of them around these days, don't you know. But the Wind Farm is in foreclosure. Not even guarded. It made a convenient secret landing field for Zane. We refueled the gas tank with aviation fuel so he could refill and take off from the spot.

"You ruined that. I let you do it so as not to blow my cover. Good thing I did. It paid off by putting me in the position to free Carlson. Ah, well . . . There's more than one way out of the country."

Jack knew with a sudden flash of insight why Lewis didn't just kill him and be done with it. Lewis was enjoying this. He was a sadist. He reveled in the cat and mouse toying with the victim. Jack Bauer laughed.

"What's so funny? I'm glad you've kept your sense of humor, Jack. You can die laughing."

"I'm laughing because you outsmarted yourself. You freed Carlson and you let him get away with the codes. That leaves you holding the bag. An empty bag. A prize chump. What does he need you for? He can cut you out of the payday. You've done your part. You're expendable, too."

"Nice try, Jack, but it won't work. It's not set up that way. Carlson still has plenty to worry about. The Blancos, for example."

"Where do they fit in?"

Lewis frowned. "Damned if I know. There's some third party involved. Someone else after the codes. He—they— hired the gang. For a while they were more of a help than a hindrance. They killed Morrow, Rhee, and Kling. They kidnapped Carrie Carlson and tried to snatch Nordquist's wife and daughter.

"Why? For leverage. The Blancos—rather, the unknown principal behind them—was in the dark about who was stealing the PALO codes. He knew something but not enough. Snatching Carrie Carlson and the Nordquist ladies showed he was hedging his bets, was unsure whether Carlson or Nordquist was the one they wanted."

"Then the Blancos have Carrie Carlson?" Jack asked.

Lewis shrugged. "I suppose so."

"Where does that leave Carlson?"

"Where does that leave Mrs. Carlson, you should ask. In a most unenviable position, I'd say."

"He won't deal?"

"He can always get another wife, but there's only one set of PALO codes."

"If he'll burn his wife, he won't hesitate to do the same to you."

"He can't, Jack. I'm part of the package. Carlson can't just sell the codes to Zane and waltz away. Zane needs Carlson and the codes both. Adam Zane's not one to buy a pig in a poke. He wants a surety that he's buying the real thing. A little demonstration. Nothing major. Just an atomic incident in the States far enough away from here not to do any damage but too big to ignore. I'll be around for that demo and afterward, too. I've helped arrange it."

"Why are you telling me all this?"

"I can't resist the urge to show off a little. I'm only human."

"That's a matter for debate."

"We all like to be appreciated for our cleverness. Who better to brag to than you? You won't live to tell about it—"

Jack Bauer laughed again. Not that he saw anything funny in the situation. But because he wanted to attract Lewis's attention to himself. Because of something he'd seen. Merritt wasn't dead. He'd moved. Not just reflex-action twitching, but with purpose and stealth.

"Goodbye, Jack—"

Merritt had fallen with gun in hand. He lay on his side, legs curled. He couldn't raise himself up but he had enough left to raise his gun hand off the pavement and shoot at Lewis.

Lewis jumped like he'd been goosed. Slugs tore the air around him, missing him.

Jack took advantage of the distraction to throw himself to the side, taking cover behind Lewis's car and drawing his gun at the same time.

Lewis shot Merritt. He dashed behind the patrol car just before Jack reached up from behind Lewis's car to throw a few shots at him. They exchanged gunfire.

Lights appeared in the north, coming southbound down Highway 5. Moving fast. Carlson returning? Police? Or some innocent civilian riding unknowing into the shootout?

Jack ducked down, peering under the car to see if perhaps he could take a shot at Lewis's feet and legs. If he could shoot the other's feet out from under him, he could finish him off when he hit the pavement—

But Lewis was too smart for that. He was crouching behind the patrol car where a rear tire shielded his lower body.

"You talk too much, Lewis," Jack said. "You were so busy enjoying your little game of cat and mouse that you talked yourself into the deathhouse. Give it up. Cut your deal now and you can save yourself from being executed for high treason and murder."

The vehicle was closing fast. Its high beams flicked on. It was a big black van.

It came on strong and quick and had to hit the brakes hard. It skidded, slid, tires squealing, laying down rubber. It bounced to a halt.

The back door flung open and armed men began pouring out of the back of the vehicle.

Lewis was caught between two fires. He circled around the rear of the patrol car. Crouching low to put the car between himself and the newcomers. There must have been a half-dozen gunmen, not counting the driver and the passenger in the cab.

Lewis crouched on the driver's side of the patrol car. He snapped a few shots at the SUV. One drilled the windshield high on the driver's side. Not hitting the driver.

The gunmen fanned out. One ran to Lewis's right. Lewis shot him and he fell down. Lewis shot him again.

While the shooters were occupied with Lewis, Jack crawled backward away from the car. He rolled across the east shoulder of Highway 5 and dropped into a ditch.

Lewis tried to make a break for it in the patrol car. He tore open the driver's side door. Tripping the interior dome light, which shone on him in the gloomy dawn light.

Bullets stitched the side of the patrol car. The shooter aimed high—the rounds blew out the side windows. On both sides.

"Careful, you idiots! You'll shoot Carlson!"—a familiar voice.

The shooting stopped.

"Sorry, Pardee," one of the shooters said.

"Shoot out the tires so he can't get away," Pardee said.

More than one gunman responded. Shooting crackled as the tires were targeted. Shredding them. The tires flattened, causing the car to settle lower.

Lewis jumped out, running toward his car. Gunfire stitched him, shooting his legs out from under him.

"Got him!"

"You better hope he ain't dead, asshole!"—Pardee again.

A gunman with an assault rifle hustled forward toward Lewis, who lay flat on his back on the pavement moaning and groaning. He shot the rifleman.

The rifleman dropped to his knees with a grunt, weapon falling from his hands to clatter to the pavement. Lewis pulled the trigger again. The gun clicked, hammer falling on an empty chamber. He was out of bullets. The man he'd shot stood on his knees, hugging himself, shrinking into himself, his middle leaking.

"He's empty," Pardee said. Other gunmen moved in, circling Lewis, guns pointed at him. Huddled low in the ditch, Jack still couldn't see Pardee's face. The gunmen checked out the scene.

"Hey look, two dead cops!"

"We didn't kill them."

"Who did?"

"They were dead before we got here."

"This joker must've offed 'em. Thanks, pal. You saved us the trouble," Pardee said.

"No Carlson here, boss. He's gone."

"Probably in that car we passed along the way." Pardee indicated Lewis. "He's a hijacker. Must be one of Varrin's crowd." He stepped on Lewis's wounded leg and put his weight on it.

Lewis shrieked. One of the gunmen giggled.

Pardee said, "The dispatcher on the police band said they might have grabbed Carlson. I guess this guy had the same idea."

"Let me live and I'll tell you," Lewis gritted out through clenched teeth.

"I don't need you. I know where Carlson went. To the big meeting up on that bluff. The big secret meeting. So-called. No secret to me. I guess you know where that leaves you, huh?"

"No!—"

Pardee shot Lewis, opening up his chest.

"Trash the cars. Light 'em up. It'll keep the cops guessing," Pardee said.

A man with a machine gun went around behind Lewis's car. Jack Bauer flattened himself even further, hugging the bottom of the ditch. The gunner opened up, spraying the rear of the car with lead.

Tough break for Dennison, who was tied up and locked in the trunk, Jack thought.

The gas tank was bullet-sieved; gas ran streaming to the pavement. Hot rounds touched off the gas; it caught fire. The gas tank blew.

Another shooter did the same to the patrol car. Lewis, still alive, barely, was sprayed with burning gasoline and set afire.

The gang got back in the Suburban and drove north on Highway 5.

· ·

THE FOLLOWING TAKES PLACE
BETWEEN THE HOURS OF
6 A.M. AND 7 A.M.
MOUNTAIN DAYLIGHT TIME

· ·

6:27 A.M. MDT
Intersection of Highway 5 and
Ridgefoot Drive, Los Alamos County

A gray sedan halted near the crossroads.

Lewis's car and the patrol car were smoldering, burned-out hulks. They'd sprayed flaming gasoline off-road, but the fiery patches had failed to get a purchase on the barren, hard-packed red dirt and played out.

Jack Bauer climbed out of the ditch where he'd been hiding while he checked out the newcomers. He recognized the gray sedan as an FBI car. Out of it came Vince Sabito, his assistant Ferney, and George Coates.

Smoke haze filtered the low sun's rays, causing the figures to cast long, ghostly shadows across the landscape. Jack went to them. They greeted his appearance with a uniform lack of warmth. Stony faces, unfriendly eyes.

"Well, well. Wandering Boy has come home again," Coates said.

Sabito drew his pistol and pointed it at Jack.

"What gives?" Jack asked. "We're supposed to be on the same side, remember?"

"That's your story," Sabito said.

"Meaning what?"

"You're a bright boy, you figure it out," Coates said.

"Shut up, Coates. I'll do the talking," Sabito said. He kept his eyes on Jack and his gun pointed steadily at him. "Where's Carlson, Bauer?"

"Gone. Lewis shot the deputies and set him free."

Sabito's expression was one of outright disbelief. "Where were you when all this was supposed to be happening?"

"Trying to keep from having my tail shot off," Jack said.

Sabito scanned Jack up and down. "Looks like you did a pretty good job of it. Not a mark on you that I can see."

"Next time I'll catch a bullet or two to keep you happy."

"There won't be any next time."

"You might get shot sooner than you expect," Coates chimed in.

"I told you to shut up."

"Sorry, Vince."

"Where's Lewis?" Sabito asked.

"There." Jack indicated a charred corpse lying next to the wreck of the patrol car. The body was in that drawn-up crouching position characteristic of incineration. It was blackened, smoking, unrecognizable.

"That could be the man in the moon for all I know," Sabito said.

"Some Blanco guns came along while Lewis and I were shooting it out. They were looking for Carlson, too. A couple of the bodies lying around are theirs. They shot up the cars and blew them up," Jack said.

"And you came out of it without so much as a scratch. I'm

not buying it. I've been doing some thinking, Bauer. Putting all the facts together until they fit. Here's how it comes out.

"This whole dirty business went into overdrive from the moment you showed up. All along you've been Johnny-on-the-spot. You gave Hickman and Coates the slip so you could meet Peter Rhee unobserved. He was killed while waiting to meet you—with no other living witnesses present. You were the first on the scene of his death.

"You go to Rhee's apartment—Kling is there—and somebody tries to kill him. Kling arranges to meet you at the Parkhurst place. When you get there he's dead and so are they. You go to Nordquist's house just in time to foil a kidnapping.

"Against my better judgment I let you go to INL on condition that Hickman goes along. He's there as much to keep an eye on you as anything else. What happens? McCoy is carved by a laser beam. You sabotage Medusa, the linchpin of the multibillion-dollar Perseus Project. Hickman is shot dead, allowing Carlson to escape.

"Instead of sticking around, you take off with Lewis. A couple of sheriff's deputies report that they're holding a suspect who looks like Carlson. You and Lewis are first on the scene. Now the deputies are dead and Carlson is missing. You say Lewis is dead. You show me a body that could be him or anybody else."

"You're thinking too hard, Vince," Jack Bauer said. "You've been in contact with OCI so you know Lewis was dirty. The rest follows from that."

Sabito shook his head, looking up at Jack from the bottoms of his eyes. "Lewis is the card that's showing faceup. You're the one that's facedown. I'm turning that card over and here's what I see:

"Lewis was CIA. You're CIA. CIA, CTU, it's all one and the same to me, and I say to hell with the whole lousy outfit. You were in it with Lewis. Thick as thieves, the two of you.

Lewis got wind of Rhodes Morrow's secret investigation—he passed it along to you. Peter Rhee might have been leery of Lewis but you were a fresh face, an outsider.

"He made the mistake of thinking he could trust you. He and Kling both had to go. You set Rhee up for a kill, setting up a meeting in the middle of nowhere. Maybe you did the deed yourself and passed the weapon to an accomplice—Lewis, most likely. Maybe you just put the finger on Rhee and let somebody else do the dirty work. And who better than Lewis to pull the trigger?

"Kling was next in line for the chop. All I have is your word for what happened at Rhee's apartment. You could have fingered Kling for a kill only he got lucky and shot his way out of it. As for your story about being ambushed by Blanco guns and escaping in the firestorm, all we have to go by is your say-so. No hard proof, no concrete evidence. The whole thing could have been an elaborate setup engineered by you and Lewis to shore up your cover story.

"You're the only one who knew Kling would be at the Parkhursts'. Kling trusted you and bought your story like Rhee did and wound up the same way. You passed the word and Blanco shooters came in to clean house. That's where foiling that kidnapping played into your hands. It was a gambit, a false flag to misdirect the rest of us. Carlson was the traitor, not Nordquist. So why snatch Nordquist's wife and kid? Any chess player could figure that out. It was a sacrifice move. The three kidnappers were pawns. They were there to be taken to establish your bona fides and make you look good.

"And it worked, at least for a while. That's why I let you fly to Ironwood.

"The Ironwood debacle was the worst. I was suspicious of you. All my instincts had you pegged as a wrongo. But instead of following my gut I let you persuade me to give you a free hand. I figured with Hickman along he'd smell out anything that wasn't kosher. The net was closing and you and Lewis had to get Carlson out. Carlson and the PALO codes. He's invaluable to making them work. He knows them inside and out.

"The codes by themselves are priceless but with Carlson along they're even better because he can show scientists of a hostile foreign power how to get them up and working fast, save all the time it would take for them to figure it out themselves. Lewis had to be sacrificed, too. It was the only way to get Carlson out of INL. In the process you got rid of McCoy and sabotaged Medusa, too.

"You still had one last card to play. Carlson wasn't home free yet. The dragnet was out for him. He was alone and he made a rookie blunder, driving right into a police roadblock. You knew where he was going, that's how you happened to be first on the scene. With some Blanco gunmen for backup. You slaughtered the deputies and freed Carlson to run. Maybe you killed Lewis because his cover was blown and he was of no use to you anymore; maybe not. We'll know better once the forensics crew examines the body you claim is Lewis.

"Meantime you stayed behind to maintain your cover and mislead the pursuit once again. A walking, talking, two-legged red herring. But it won't work. This is the end of the line for you, Bauer."

"You're adding up two and two and getting five, Vince."

"Go on, deny it. Prove me wrong. But you can't—because it's true."

Ferney was excited, his eyes shining, face glowing. "You busted this case wide open, Vince," he said admiringly.

Jack Bauer spoke directly to Sabito. "Hell, I could do the same to you. You're the one who's been here on the scene all along, not me. Going back to the Sayeed case and before. You and your people were denying there was a pattern to the Ironwood kills even as the bodies were piling up. What you're doing right now is what an enemy agent would do if he wanted to make sure that Carlson gets away."

Sabito's toothy grin failed to reach his hard, dark eyes. "The old reverse play, eh Bauer? Accuse the accuser. Too bad it won't work. I've got the goods on you. I've got the drop on you, too.

"Get his gun, Coates. No tricks, Bauer. I'm itching to put a slug in you; don't give me an excuse."

Coates moved in from the side, so as not to block Sabito's line of fire. He pulled Jack's pistol from the shoulder holster. "Chet Hickman was my partner—and my friend," Coates said. "You dirty son of a bitch!"

Coates slammed the flat of Jack's pistol against the side of his jaw. Jack saw it coming and rolled with it, turning his head away from the blow, falling backward. It hit with stunning force anyway, numbing him, making him see stars.

Coates had to come in close to deliver the blow. That was the break Jack had been waiting for. He grabbed the wrist of Coates's gun hand and twisted it away from himself and toward Coates.

Coates was between Sabito and Jack. Sabito couldn't get a clear shot at Jack. Jack used Coates's forward motion against him, falling back and to the side and pulling Coates along with him. Coates lurched forward, off-balance.

Sabito lunged forward, gun in hand, angling for a clear shot. Jack used a circular aikido move on Coates's wrist and arm, turning it in a direction nature hadn't intended it to go. Coates's yelp was cut off in a gasp as blinding pain shot through his wrist and shoulder joint, numbing his hand. Blood drained from his florid face.

Jack plucked the gun from the other's nerveless fingers even as he was spinning Coates around. He rushed forward, sweeping Coates off his feet and slamming him into Sabito. Sabito couldn't shoot without hitting Coates. He and Coates were tangled up in a mass of flailing limbs.

Jack reached around Coates, slamming his pistol down, knocking the gun from Sabito's hand. The gun hit hard pavement and went off, loosing a wild shot that hit nobody.

Jack stepped back as Sabito and Coates fell down in a tangle of limbs. He kicked Sabito's gun out of reach. The encounter had played itself out in a few breathless seconds.

Ferney stood there frozen, his only reaction a blink. Coates rolled over on his back, making grunting noises. He clawed for the gun holstered under his arm, hampered by the fact that his hand and wrist weren't working too well after the manhandling Jack had applied to the pressure points of the nerves.

Jack placed a short, tight, front snap kick to the point of Coates's chin. Coates fell back, unconscious.

Ferney remembered he had a gun, glanced at it. Jack pointed his gun at Ferney and shook his head. "Uh-uh," he said. Ferney remained motionless. Cursing and groaning, Sabito wriggled out from under Coates.

The side of Jack's face was red and swollen where Coates had clipped it with the gun. It felt numb, except for a throbbing that was like a second heart pounding away there.

Coates was still out. Jack leaned over and pulled Coates's gun from its holster. To remove temptation so Sabito wouldn't do something stupid. "Stay down or I'll put you down, Vince," he said.

Sabito was furious, so mad he looked like he could spit nails. Jack put Coates's gun into one of his vest pockets. He crossed to Ferney and relieved him of his gun. "Sit down," he said. Ferney sat down hard on the pavement.

Jack put Ferney's gun in another vest pocket. He was getting top-heavy with hardware. He circled around to where Sabito's gun lay. Jack was running out of pockets. He picked up the gun and took a few steps back.

"You can sit up, Vince. But don't get up," he said. He holstered his gun. "My draw can beat your heroics, Vince, so stay put."

Sabito had a revolver. Jack broke it, spilling the rounds from the cylinder to the pavement. He threw the gun far away into a roadside field. He released the clip from Coates's pistol, jacked a round out of the chamber, and heaved the weapon way out in the weeds. He defanged Ferney's weapon and tossed it, too.

He went to Ferney. Jack had dropped his own cell in the road earlier when Lewis had made his play. It had been run over by Carlson's car or Pardee's Suburban or both; it was squashed flat. "Give me your cell phone," he said.

Ferney obeyed, handing it over. Jack switched it off so it couldn't be used to track him, then pocketed it. He went to Sabito, standing too close. "I wish I had a picture of this. It would make a great CTU Christmas card," he said.

Sabito muttered a string of obscenities under his breath.

"What's that, Vince? I didn't quite get that last—I get the idea, though," Jack said. "If I was what you think I am, I could have burned down all three of you with your own guns and framed it so I'd be in the clear. Not a breath of suspicion would attach to me. Think about that while you're waiting for a ride," he added.

Jack Bauer crossed to the driver's side of the gray sedan. The keys were in the ignition. He slid in under the steering wheel and started the car.

He drove through the crossroads, circling the car wrecks, corpses, and G-men. He pointed the truck north on Highway 5 and drove away. He beeped the horn jauntily in a farewell salute to Sabito and company.

6:49 A.M. MDT
Bluecoat Bluff, Los Alamos County

Bluecoat Bluff was a few miles past the crossroads, north on Highway 5 over the top of the hill. So Orne Lewis had said, and in this, at least, he wasn't lying. The bluff was a low, flat-topped sugarloaf-shaped hill made of reddish brown stone a mile from the highway.

The bluff commanded a view of the surrounding countryside, an expanse of flatland strewn with jagged landforms. Standing rocks had been eroded into odd angular, twisted shapes that evoked wraiths, flames, battlements, spires, and steeples.

Jack Bauer drove past the unmanned entrance prominently marked with a CLOSED sign and kept on going. The car's springs, chassis, and undercarriage took a beating. Jack piloted it into the lee of a massive tilted land formation that blocked the view of the bluff from the highway and parked behind some dry, scraggly brush that provided some cover, partly screening the gray sedan from the road and any spotters around the bluff.

He got out and opened the trunk to see what he could find. He was pleasantly surprised to find a couple of Kevlar vests, but no guns. Stripping to the waist, he donned the bulletproof vest, putting it on over his bare flesh. He put his T-shirt back on and pulled on his shoulder holster, adjusting the straps to improve the fit. He put the utility vest on over the gun rig.

An indirect route to the bluff was a must. This was a state park recreational area, and a maze of trails surrounded the bluff. He set off on a hiking trail on the western approach that was layered with shadows from the various rock formations and plant life.

Jack went deeper into the park, pausing behind a screen

of brush to survey the scene. The bluff was about fifty feet high; it was wide, squat, and sprawling.

Hiding in the bushes, he scanned the south face of the bluff and its surroundings. A dirt road wound up the side to its summit. At base of the main approach stood a group of gunmen in the shade of the trees, loafing, smoking, and talking with their backs to the main entrance. They were experienced thieves and killers, but Bauer was thankful for the casual nature of their lookout skills. He'd exploited amateur mistakes before, and their setting up without a clear view of the highway certainly qualified.

There was a parking lot at the foot of the bluff and some picnic tables under a grove of trees. Near the parking lot was a rustic-looking cabin with restroom facilities for males and females on either side. The center area was an information center. No tourists or park rangers were in the park today, Varrin's crew and unrelenting heat had seen to that.

So this was the Varrin gang, Jack thought. They looked virtually identical to the Blanco outfit. From the look of things the real action was taking place on top of the bluff. There was movement there, figures, vehicles. Jack had to get there.

He hugged the base of the mound and worked his way around to the north side, where ledges and rock overhangs shielded him from the casual gaze of observers on top. He saw no lookouts posted on this side of the mound. Another mistake. The landform was worn and weathered, slumping and shot through with cracks, crevices, chimneys, ledges, and goat trails. Jack Bauer surveyed it for a moment, sizing it up, selecting the likeliest angle of ascent. It was an easy climb, honeycombed with a skein of hiking paths and goat trails.

He started up, careful to make no noise. No snapped twigs, uprooted branches, or rustling rock falls that might call attention to his presence.

He reached the top, hauling himself over the edge and onto the flat of the summit. Cracked boulders, tilted slabs, and stone needles provided welcome cover. Jack crept through the maze of rocks toward the center of the summit.

A fair amount of the tabletop flat was occupied by a gravel parking lot. The lot was now occupied by a pickup truck, a Range Rover, a Land Cruiser, a Denali, and Carlson's car.

The broad, flat expanse of the summit featured a number of fenced-in scenic lookout points scattered around the edge of the table land. Not far from the gravel lot was the cavalry post that once stood there in the days of the Old West, consisting of a standing chimney and roofless remnants of dry stone walls.

The gang's all here, Jack Bauer said to himself.

About a dozen men stood grouped together, and what a gang it was.

Prominent among them was Adam Zane. Jack Bauer had never met him personally but recognized him from his pictures, film footage and photographs that had passed his desk at CTU/L.A.

Zane would have stood out in any crowd.

Six and a half feet tall, distinguished-looking in a weathered way, he suggested the stereotypical image of the Great White Hunter of colonial yore. He wore a tan safari suit and brown hiking boots. Neat salt-and-pepper hair topped a long, strong-boned, clean-shaven face with jutting cheekbones, hollow cheeks, and a firm chin.

Zane was one of the shadow world's prime purveyors of stolen secrets. His trade was treachery and business was good.

Shadowing him was Hank Ketch, Zane's bodyguard. A stocky man with a thatch of sun-bleached palomino-colored hair and pale blond eyebrows so colorless they were almost invisible, he wore a gun holstered under each arm. Zane himself habitually went unarmed, trusting in his cunning, tirelessly scheming brain. Yes, it would have taken a pearl of ultimate price, a supreme prize, to tempt Zane from his home grounds.

Dr. Hugh Carlson had that prize. The PALO codes. Carlson stood milling around, holding the silvery metal attaché case containing the priceless PALO computer disks.

He was in the orbit of another local celebrity, one whom Jack Bauer had never met but whose presence explained much: Max Scourby.

Scourby, the celebrated Santa Fe defense attorney; high-powered, high-profile, high-priced. The legal wizard who had masterminded the destruction of the United States Attorneys' prosecution of the atomic spy case against INL's own Dr. Rahman Sayeed.

He cut a flamboyant figure with his leonine head topped by a mop of curly silver hair; wide, square-shaped face, scimitar nose, wide jack-o'-lantern mouth. He was built like a top, broad-shouldered, deep-chested, his massive torso tapering to a slim waist, narrow hips, thin legs, and small, elegantly shod feet. He wore a lightweight, light-colored linen suit with a yellow shirt and multicolored tie.

Scourby's presence explained much, as did his proprietary, possessive attitude and physical proximity to Carlson.

The others there were gunmen: Varrin, the lanky, desiccated desert rat and gang leader in Scourby's pay; and an honor guard of some of his best men and finest killers. Among them were Diablo Cruz, Reed Teed, Arnold Matti, Pablo Obregon, and Norvil Nolles.

Scourby, Zane, and Carlson had their heads together in deep conclave. They were talking about something important from the looks of it.

Jack Bauer edged forward, padding through brush and rocks, moving closer to the open area where the gang was assembled so he could eavesdrop on them. He eased into a clearing—and came face-to-face with Lassiter and Slim. Slim's gun was pointing at him.

"I told you I saw someone sneaking around back here," Slim said.

"You've got eyes like a hawk. I didn't see nothing," Lassiter said.

All pro, Lassiter moved forward and held his gun to Jack's head. "Blink and you're dead, stranger." He reached under Jack's vest, lifting his gun from the shoulder holster and sticking it in the top of his waistband. His free hand roamed up and down Jack's body, searching for weapons, finding none. He circled around behind Jack, out of reach of any hand or foot techniques that a desperate captive might try to get out from under a gun.

"March," Lassiter said.

The others on the bluff were surprised to see Lassiter emerge from the brush leading a stranger out at gunpoint. Slim followed a few paces behind in Lassiter's wake.

Jack Bauer's expression was grim, glum, resigned. He marched with his hands held up.

"Look what Slim found," Lassiter said.

"Bauer!" Carlson gasped, shaken.

"He belongs to you?" Lassiter asked.

"He's CTU! He almost got me at the lab! And at the police checkpoint! What are you doing here, Bauer? Where's Lewis?"

"Lewis sends his regrets. He's unavoidably detained by a slight case of death," Jack Bauer said.

"One of the deputies he shot lived long enough to shoot him but not before Lewis mentioned the meeting on the bluff," Jack lied. Why tip his captors to the fact that the Blancos were hot on their trail? He might be able to exploit that information for some kind of advantage, no matter how minor.

"He's alone—I checked," Lassiter said.

Jack Bauer turned to Max Scourby. "I see you're in the middle of this, Counselor. Looks like you traded in your observer status for a more active role."

Scourby couldn't resist the opportunity to show off. He loved the limelight. "What could I do?" he asked. "The good Dr. Carlson was so impressed with my defense of Rahman Sayeed that he sought me out. He had the secrets and I have the connections."

"You're wasting time palavering," said the ever-sour, hard-bitten Varrin. He spat on the ground not far from Scourby's elegant footwear. "Lewis is dead. No more reason for us to be sitting around here waiting for him. Kill this one and be done with it. Let's move out."

"Allow me," Lassiter offered.

Jack Bauer spun, breaking clear and dashing up a rise toward the edge of the bluff.

Lassiter's 9mm was already drawn and leveled. He fired, shooting Jack in the back. Jack lurched under the impact, stumbling forward a few staggering steps.

Lassiter fired again. Jack spasmed as another slug tagged him in the center of his back. He pitched forward, falling facedown on the edge of the rise.

Lassiter strode up to him slowly and deliberately. He stood over him looking down. "And one in the head to finish it," he said.

He pointed the pistol downward and fired.

He put a foot on Jack's shoulder and push-kicked the body. Jack Bauer tumbled over the edge of the rise, rolling downhill and falling into a ditch out of sight. Lassiter turned, smiling thinly, cradling the smoking pistol in his hands.

"That's cold, Lassiter," Teed said. He meant it as a compliment, and that's how Lassiter took it.

"I hate cops," Lassiter said. "Feds I hate even more."

- -

THE FOLLOWING TAKES PLACE
BETWEEN THE HOURS OF
7 A.M. AND 8 A.M.
MOUNTAIN DAYLIGHT TIME

- -

7:36 A.M. MDT
Bluecoat Bluff, Los Alamos County

An interruption of shouts from the men watching the approach sounded from below. The bunch on the bluff trooped to the southern edge to investigate the cause of the clamor.

A van stood at the base of the hill near the bottom of the road where it leveled out on the ground. A man in a black cowboy hat sat behind the wheel holding a white flag out the window. The flag of truce consisted of a white blouse tied to a broomstick.

Varrin's gunmen on the ground ringed the van, pointing guns at the newcomer.

Varrin leaned over the edge, cupped a hand beside his mouth. "What the hell's all the noise?"

One of the men from below shouted back, "It's Pardee. He wants to talk."

The announcement produced no small consternation among those massed on top of the bluff.

"You've got to be shitting me," Varrin said, speaking to himself.

Adam Zane turned to Max Scourby. "Who's Pardee?"

"Foreman for the Blancos. He's Torreon's top hatchet man," Scourby said.

Varrin drew his gun. "I'll talk to him with this."

Scourby considered the matter. "Maybe we should see what he wants. What harm could it do?"

"Plenty," Varrin said. "He's a slippery bastard, like his boss."

"So much more reason for us to find out what he's all about."

Lassiter stepped forward. "I'll get my rifle, I can pot him from here."

"He's got a white flag, Lassiter," Pablo Obregon said.

Lassiter shrugged. "So what?"

"You're a mad dog, Lassiter. You don't care who you bite," Diablo Cruz said.

Lassiter eyed him coolly. "Not particularly, no."

Scourby was thinking out loud. "If Pardee wants to talk he must have a pretty good reason. What can we lose by hearing him out? We can always kill him later. My curiosity's piqued," Scourby said. He reached a decision. "Send him up."

"You're the boss," Varrin said, his flat, curt tone implying his disagreement. He called downhill: "Is he armed?"

"We checked him for weapons and the van is empty!"

"Tell him to come up."

"What?"

"Tell him to come up, you deaf bastard!"

"Okay!"

The van drove up the incline, trailing a thin cloud of dust.

It crested the rise and leveled on top of the bluff. Pardee halted the van, switched off the motor.

He was in his fifties, with broad sloping shoulders, a thick middle, and spindly legs. He wore a high-crowned black cowboy hat and a belt with an ornate oversized engraved fancy buckle.

The black hat was tilted far forward; the brim just missed obscuring his eyes. His eyebrows were pointed in the middle. He had curly black sideburns and an eyebrow mustache. He wore a string tie with a silver bolo.

The white flag of truce was propped up on the seat beside him. It consisted of an off-white, long-sleeved satiny blouse. The sleeves were knotted to the broomstick.

Pardee looked over the assemblage, a wall of hostile faces. "Quite a coalition. You folks holding Sunday morning services?"

"Say your say, Pardee," Varrin said.

Pardee turned his face to the lawyer. "Morning, Mr. Scourby. You've sure been keeping us hopping lately."

"That's what comes of tying into things outside your usual line of work," Scourby said.

"Like that meth lab of ours you blew up yesterday?"

"A reminder to keep out where you don't belong. But you didn't come up here to talk about that, Pardee."

"No, sir, I didn't, and that's a fact. As you can see I come up here bearing a white flag of truce."

"Torreon suing for peace? You want an armistice, is that it?"

"Not hardly," Pardee said, chuckling. "You better look at this here flag of truce. Especially you, Dr. Carlson."

"I speak for Carlson," Scourby said. "What's so all-fired important about it?"

Pardee handed him the white flag. "Here, see for yourself. It's a blouse. Belongs to Miz Carlson. She was wearing it last night."

Carlson stepped forward, his expression unreadable. "That's true—it is Carrie's blouse, the one she was wearing today . . . There's blood on it. What have you done with her?"

Pardee made a placating gesture. "Don't get yourself in an uproar, Doc. It's nothing, just a couple of scratches. She's a feisty lady—full of spirit."

"Why show it to us?" Scourby demanded.

"Proof that we got her. She's okay. In a safe place. But she ain't gonna be safe for long if you don't start cooperating."

"Say what you mean, man!"

"Smart lawyer like you, I don't got to draw you a picture. We know what you're up to with the doc and Mr. Zane here. We want half."

Varrin laughed, spat. "Half? Is that all?" Scourby asked.

"Torreon ain't greedy," Pardee said.

"The hell he's not," Varrin fired back.

Pardee's tolerant expression indicated that reasonable men could disagree. "Half is fine."

Scourby put his fists on his hips. "Or else what?"

"Or else we send you back half of Miz Carlson . . . and I do mean half. After we've had our fun with her. She's a pretty lady. Why not keep her that way?"

"You've got Mrs. Carlson, and in return for her safe return you want half of whatever deal we cut with Mr. Zane."

"That's the situation in a nut," Pardee agreed.

"Well, well, well," Scourby said. "She's your wife, Carlson. It's up to you. What do you say?"

Like any good trial lawyer, Scourby knew never to ask a question that he didn't already know the answer to.

Carlson covered his face with his hands. His shoulders heaved.

Pardee tsk-tsked. "I hate to see a grown man cry . . ."

Carlson lowered his hands, baring his face. His eyes were dry. His expression a mask of mirth. "If I'm crying it's from tears of laughter," he said. "You can cut Carrie up into a thousand pieces as far as I'm concerned. The bitch means nothing to me. I'm sick of her and I'll be glad to be rid of her."

Scourby's face lit up in a big grin. "He's not bluffing, Pardee. I'm afraid the good doctor doesn't have an uxorious bone in his body."

"Now say it in English."

"Meaning he doesn't love his wife."

Carlson chimed in. "I don't even like her. Chop her up and sprinkle her on your lawn for all I care."

Pardee stroked his chin. "I do believe you're serious. Hoo boy, that's one on me."

Varrin stepped forward. "Doesn't make your flag of truce worth a good damn, does it? Your ace in the hole is running down your leg, Pardee. How much will Torreon pay to keep you all in one piece?"

Pardee took off his hat and placed it in his lap. "I'd hate to find out," he admitted. "Looks like you've got me," he said, sighing.

With rattlesnake quickness he reached inside the crown, pulled out a little .32, and shot Varrin right between the eyes. A red dot appeared there as Varrin fell back.

A fusillade erupted from the ruins of the old fort north of the gravel parking lot, as a handful of Blanco gunmen popped up from where they'd been hiding and opened fire on Varrin's men. It was a firing squad, a mass execution.

Lassiter fired his gun into Ketch's head. The back of Ketch's skull exploded, spraying those nearby with fragments of blood, bone, and brain.

Diablo Cruz spun around, gun in hand. Lassiter had been waiting for that and cut him down. A bullet in the belly folded Cruz up. Lassiter's next shot blew off the top of his head above the eyebrows.

Lassiter was careful to stand apart from the mass of

Varrin's men, physically separating himself from them and staying out of the firing line of Blanco executioners. Pardee's shooters had been tipped that Lassiter was working with them as an inside man.

More shooting sounded down below, where a quartet of Blanco gunners opened fire from the brush where they'd been hiding to rake the defenders on the ground beneath the bluff with machine gun and assault rifle fire. Catching them in the open and chopping them down.

Presently the shooting stopped, above and below. Up top on the bluff, only Carlson, Zane, Scourby—and Lassiter— were left standing.

A waist-high cloud of gun smoke hung in mid-air over the bluff. From behind the stone walls emerged Torreon Blanco, his inseparable bodyguard Stan Rull, and Brazos, one of his top shooters. Pardee climbed out, raising a hand in greeting to the others.

On the ground lay Varrin, Teed, Slim, Diablo Cruz, Obregon, and Ketch—dead.

Carlson and Scourby were quaking. Adam Zane scowled, wrathful, but otherwise uncowed.

Torreon Blanco faced Max Scourby. "Looks like the court finds you out of order, Counselor," Torreon said. He eyed Adam Zane. "So you're Zane. I've heard a lot about you; I've been looking forward to meeting you. Relax. You're safe. Nobody wants to harm a hair on your head."

"You killed my bodyguard," Zane accused.

Lassiter stepped forward. "I did that. He was too dangerous to live. In the excitement he might have shot Pardee," he said.

Adam Zane gave him a dirty look.

"One of you give Dr. Carlson a hand, he looks a little unsteady on his feet," Torreon Blanco said.

Brazos, big with curly black hair and a black beard, took Carlson by the arm. "Sit down in the van here, Doc."

Torreon eyed the metal attaché case whose handle was still tightly gripped by Carlson's fist. "Are those the codes? I'll just relieve you of the burden."

Carlson was reluctant to surrender his prize. Brazos pinned him with his dark eyes. "Now Doc, be sensible."

Carlson released his grip and Torreon took possession of the attaché case. "Many thanks. Don't worry, I'll take good care of it," Torreon said.

He turned to Zane. "Think of this as a new deal. You're still buying Dr. Carlson and his magical codes; he's just under new management—mine. You pay me instead of Scourby, that's all."

"It's a little more complicated than that, my homicidal friend," Adam Zane said.

"I know all about your planned demo. My people already control Mission Hill," Torreon said. "We'll go there now."

Adam Zane shrugged. "I'm flexible. I don't really care who I deal with as long as the deal gets done. A straight deal, mind you. But what about Scourby?"

Torreon shot Max Scourby in the belly. Scourby lay on the ground, writhing in the dust.

"Dr. Carlson will cooperate, won't you, Doctor?" Torreon said.

"Yuh—yuh—yes—"

Torreon Blanco beamed. "Brazos, you and Lassiter stay behind to clean up the scene. Rig it so it looks like Varrin's gang had a falling-out and shot each other. Stash Scourby out of sight. I don't want him identified for a day or two."

"Sure," Brazos said, smiling.

"When you're done, take one of their cars and meet us at Mission Hill," Torreon said. He put a bullet in Max Scourby's head.

He, Zane, Carlson, Pardee, and the rest of his shooters got in the van. Pardee drove, Zane sat in the passenger seat next to him.

Pardee started the van, turned it around, and drove down the road to the bottom of the bluff. He paused, the gunmen down there piled into the back, and they drove out of the park.

Up on the bluff, Brazos turned to Lassiter. "Let's get to work," Brazos said.

They finished the shallow grave, dumped Scourby in, and as Lassiter began shoveling the dirt back in, Brazos picked up a machine gun, leveling it at Lassiter.

"Now wait a minute," Lassiter began.

"You're part of the clean-up, too," Brazos said. "Torreon figures if you'd double cross Scourby you'd double cross him—"

A head shot exploded Brazos's cranium.

Fired by Jack Bauer.

1 2 3 4 5 6 7 8 9
10 11 12 13 14 15 16 17
18 19 20 21 **22** 23 24

. . . .

THE FOLLOWING TAKES PLACE
BETWEEN THE HOURS OF
8 A.M. AND 9 A.M.
MOUNTAIN DAYLIGHT TIME

. . . .

8:05 A.M. MDT
Bluecoat Bluff, Los Alamos County

Jack Bauer and Lassiter stood face-to-face. "My gun," Jack said, holding out his hand palm-up. Lassiter hauled the pistol out of a hip pocket and put it in Jack's hand.

"Thanks," Jack said, holstering the weapon. "Looks like it's time for Lassiter to retire."

Lassiter nodded. "That's what Torreon had in mind. A forcible retirement." He indicated Brazos's corpse. "Thanks, Jack."

"One good turn deserves another."

"Hope those two shots I fired into you didn't hurt too much."

"Not much. With the vest on it only feels like I got hit with a sledgehammer. Twice."

"Oh—were you wearing a vest?"

"Very funny," Jack said. "Now Lassiter goes back on the shelf and Tony Almeida comes back online."

Lassiter was Tony Almeida, a CTU/L.A. agent working under Jack's command.

Jack Bauer had approached the problem of the Ironwood kills with a two-pronged attack: from the inside and the outside. Jack was the outside man, operating more or less in the open. It made him a target, but that was one way to get fast action. The enemy knew who he was and they could take their best shot at him. He made himself a lure to flush them out from their hiding places behind the black curtain of secrecy. It was a great technique as long as he didn't get killed.

That was only one-half his strategy. Tony Almeida was the other half. He had been working undercover, from the inside. "Lassiter" was an assumed identity, one that Tony Almeida had used to great effect in the past. Lassiter had a well-earned reputation in underworld circles as a professional gun, a killer for hire. A cover identity that had proved extremely useful in penetrating that shadowy interzone where the secret worlds of terrorism and organized crime met and mingled.

As Lassiter, Tony was able to circulate freely among gunrunners, drug gangs, underworld enforcers, mercenaries, and similar members of the phantom legions of the subterranean half world.

Jack Bauer knew that Annihilax preferred to recruit local talent from the area where he was operating: thugs, thieves, whores, safecrackers, hackers, killers, and so on.

Expendables all. Once the job was done, Annihilax eliminated the underlings, leaving a clean slate. No witnesses, no accomplices able to furnish incriminating evidence or testimony. Annihilax's true identity would be safe from exposure.

Lassiter was another kind of lure. The hired killer with a solid gold reputation was dangled in the overheated gangland milieu of the Southwest underworld to see which big fish would go for the bait. And wind up hooked and netted. With Varrin and the Blancos at war, a stone killer such as Lassiter would not be a free agent for long. Nor had he been.

Lassiter made the rounds, frequenting the dives and gangland haunts where such criminal enterprise was conducted. Making moves, making waves. It had not been long before Varrin had approached him to undertake some contract "work." From there things had taken their inexorably murderous, treacherous course.

Tony Almeida explained, "I was playing both ends against the middle. Varrin hired me. Once I learned that his enemy was the Blancos, I contacted them to make a deal to double cross Varrin and his masters. It wasn't until today that I learned that Varrin's boss was Max Scourby, the celebrated criminal lawyer."

"In his case, the term *criminal lawyer* couldn't have been more appropriate," Jack said. "Think Torreon got wise that Lassiter was more than just a hired gun?"

"I doubt it," Tony said. "He figured that if I'd sell out Varrin, I'd do the same to him. Besides, I'd served my purpose. Varrin and his gang were wiped out. This way, Torreon didn't have to pay me. He doesn't need Annihilax to tell him to be a vicious SOB."

"Too bad you didn't put a bullet in Carlson's brain during the shooting."

"Things were kind of frantic at the time. Besides, I know where they're taking Carlson and Zane: Mission Hill. It's a mansion Scourby set up. Filled with all kinds of computer hardware and transceivers where Carlson can do his thing.

"Adam Zane wants a demo before he buys. Scourby's dead, but that won't change a thing as far as Zane's concerned. He'll still want a demo. Marta Blanco and some of the gang went there earlier today to take it over. That's where we'll find Carlson and Zane."

"That's where we'll go, too," Jack said.

"We can take the car they left behind for Brazos."

"I've got a better idea." Jack Bauer took out the cell phone he'd taken from Ferney. "Why ride when you can fly?"

8:40 A.M. MDT
Mission Hill, Los Alamos County

Mission Hill was a modern-day mansion done in Spanish colonial style. It occupied a splendid sprawling estate in the western heights of the Hill. Its neighbors were also mansions and none too close. The grounds were bordered by a ten-foot-high whitewashed adobe wall. Landscaped grounds featured patios, pavilions, gardens, hedges, lawns, and flower beds, all honeycombed with flagged paths and walkways.

At the center of the estate was a mansion three stories tall. Its roof was covered with orange ceramic tiles. They were overlapping, creating the impression of the scales of a fish or reptile. The structure was made of thick whitewashed stone walls. The second-floor windows had balconies. Ground-floor windows were caged with elaborate black wrought-iron grillwork.

An anomalous note was the rooftop ridgeline. The rooftop bristled with an elaborate array of antennas. In the center of the roofline was an old-fashioned bell tower. It was flat-roofed and square-sided, with arches opening in all four sides. The bell tower's flat roof was crowned with a massive satellite dish aimed at a forty-five-degree angle to the sky.

What had been a drawing room on the ground floor had

been transformed into an electronic nerve nexus. It was equipped with massive computer consoles, instrument boards, oscilloscopes, beam shapers, modulators, wideband signal frequency generators, amplifiers, resonators, transmitters, and the like. A cockpit of sophisticated electronic hardware.

Consoles and equipment cabinets lined the walls. Heavy-duty electric cables had been laid down, connecting to trunk lines that extended outside the lab room. The hardware pulled so much power that it required a special generator all its own to meet the demand. The generator was located outside on the patio, housed in a special outbuilding.

Torreon Blanco, Stan Rull, and two pistoleros escorted their "guests" into the hardware room. The pistoleros exited. Dr. Hugh Carlson was a prisoner. A valuable catch but a captive all the same. He'd been relieved of the metal attaché case containing the all-important PALO codes. Torreon Blanco was now in possession of them.

Adam Zane's status was somewhat more equivocal. He was a man with a vast store of funds at his disposal and a powerful organization at his command. He preferred to travel light and fast, but that massive organization was behind him and could wreak tremendous havoc should any harm befall him.

Adam Zane radiated a distinct aura of displeasure. He carried himself stiffly. His thin lips were tightly pressed. Knots of muscle the size of walnuts stood at the hinges of his jaws.

He'd submitted earlier to the indignity of a personal search that yielded no weapons. He carried none, except for the most potent weapon of all, the mass of gray matter housed inside his skull.

Torreon Blanco said, "Allow me to introduce you to our hostess. Senor Adam Zane, this is my sister, Marta Blanco."

Marta Blanco wore a red blouse, black slacks, red boots,

and a gun. Her top was a short-sleeved, military-style tunic, scarlet, with epaulets and gold buttons. High-waisted matte-black slacks that were tight in the hips with wide-cut, flaring legs tapering at the ankles, where she wore high-heeled ankle boots the same shade of red as her blouse.

A holstered gun was belted around her waist. No small-caliber lady's gun, this sidearm, but a big-caliber, long-barreled revolver.

"How do you do, Senor Zane. A pleasure to make your acquaintance," she said.

Zane took one of her red-nailed hands and kissed it Continental style—an air kiss in the traditional manner, his lips not quite touching her flesh. "I wish I could say the same, Senorita—or is it Senora?"

"Why not Marta?"

"Marta it shall be. I must express my regrets regarding the nature of our meeting, which somewhat undercuts the pleasure of your company. I'm sure you understand. An employee of mine has been senselessly murdered, I have been hijacked . . ."

"Deeply regrettable to be sure. You have my apologies. But it was the only way to ensure our getting together for a meeting which is bound to be profitable to both of us."

"That remains to be seen."

"It will be. You are a man of the world, so you will understand that sometimes one's plans are subject to sudden and dramatic reversals. That's business.

"I welcome you to my house. Not my house, not really. It belonged to the late Max Scourby. As you can see, he spared no expense in arranging the equipment necessary for your—our—transaction. Nothing has changed, except that instead of doing business with Senors Scourby and Lewis, you will be dealing with myself and my brother."

Zane's smile was as meaningless as it was polite. "No offense, but Max Scourby and Orne Lewis had a certain credibility and track record in matters of this sort. A certain trust existed, if only on the basis of similar transactions successfully carried out by both parties. If they said they could deliver, they did so. Charming though you most certainly are, you and your brother are an unknown quantity as far as I'm concerned."

"I understand your misgivings," Marta said. "Trust is so hard to come by in this unhappy world. You would like some sort of a guarantee. A bond of security. I am prepared to offer that to you.

"You smile. Perhaps you doubt me? Quite all right. I am not offended. Your opinion will change when you are made aware of my principal sponsor in this undertaking. The partner of myself and my brother. I give you a name that will mean much to you:

"Annihilax."

Adam Zane's sky-blue eyes narrowed; his jaw muscles flexed involuntarily at the naming of the name.

A name that meant nothing to Dr. Hugh Carlson. He was scared, dazed, and confused by the recent violent reversal of fortune. He took a certain comfort in the fact that he'd been neither manhandled nor abused. He knew this:

He was better off in the hands of his murderous captors than he would have been several hours ago in the custody of the two Los Alamos Sheriff's Department deputies.

Or in the hands of CTU's Jack Bauer. The late Jack Bauer.

He was, he knew, still a valuable commodity. The question was: Did his captors know it? For now, by conscious choice and nervous temperament, his way was to walk soft and keep a low profile while events shook themselves out and manifested themselves to give him a clearer picture of where he stood.

Annihilax? No, the name meant nothing to him. But it certainly carried weight with Adam Zane, and that meant something to Carlson.

"Annihilax? Yes, that would change things. If true," Zane said. "I'll go so far as to admit that rumors have reached me that Annihilax is alive and operating in this theater—but you'll have to prove it to me."

Marta Blanco's green eyes glittered. Her red lips curved upward at the corners in a kind of secret half smile. "You have met Annihilax. That is not a question, but a fact known to me and you. You two have had dealings in the past. You are one of a very few who has seen the true face of Annihilax and lived."

"Seeing is believing," Marta Blanco said. She indicated a door at the opposite end of the room. It was arched and made of ironbound wooden planks. It opened, creaking on its hinges. Framed in the doorway stood a figure.

"Meet your true host. Annihilax welcomes you," Marta said.

The figure started forward, entering the room, moving out of the shadows into the light. Moving slowly, deliberately, though not without a certain dogged stiffness.

Seeing the newcomer, Hugh Carlson was literally rocked on his heels by the shock of revelation. He cried out:

"My god! Carrie!"

Carrie Carlson advanced into the room, walking with a slight but noticeable limp. Favoring her left leg. She walked stiffly, wielding a cane in her left hand.

She wore a lightweight blue blazer, white blouse, gray skirt, and low-heeled blue-black shoes. Her hazel eyes looked yellow in the light; they glowed. She seemed serene, self-possessed. Her rubber-tipped cane made soft thudding noises against the tiled floor as she advanced.

She crossed to the others, stood facing them. A tight smile curved her lips. Her gaze shifted from Zane to her husband and back again.

Zane stared at her, studying her with a furiously intent frown. "My dear Jane, can it really be you?"

"Have I changed so much, Adam?" Carrie Carlson asked.

"Frankly, yes."

"Perhaps these names will jog your memory: Chen Li Chang. Principessa Senta Loquasto. Einar Saknessum. Count Bozzo-Corona. General Auric Frobe. Sir Percival Pickering—"

"Enough! No need recite a litany of the roster of the dead."

"They were all alive before you contracted me to liquidate them, Adam."

He eyed her like a jeweler appraising a valuable gem of dubious provenance. "You've had face work."

"What woman my age hasn't?" Carrie Carlson countered.

"I suppose it's the context more than anything else that throws me—you're the last person I'd suspect of being incarnated as an American suburban matron."

"Which is why it works, no? Only here I'm not Jane—it's Carrie. Though not for long."

She turned her yellow-eyed gaze on Hugh Carlson. "I don't know which of us is more surprised, you or I. For three years I've moved heaven and earth trying to find the mole in INL, and all the time he was living under the same roof with me.

"Of course you don't understand. It just goes to show that there are no strangers more mysterious and unknown to each other than a husband and wife who share each other's bed. Not that we've been doing much of that lately. Thank god.

"You really had me guessing. I never suspected that you were the traitor. Never thought you had it in you. In a way I'm impressed. I fool others, I'm not easily fooled. Especially after the others in the cadre started dying off. Your doing—thanks to Lewis and Scourby. They were protecting their investment.

"In the end I thought it would be Nordquist. That's why

I tried to have his wife and daughter kidnapped, to use as a lever over him if we couldn't get our hands on him. I faked my own kidnapping to muddy the trail, and maybe squeeze some secrets out of you. Never dreaming you were the arch-traitor. I must say, my respect for you has gone up."

Annihilax was Carrie Voss Carlson. Real name Jane Miller. The sole daughter of a wealthy family in the American Midwest. Parents of good, solid stock, well-established old money. Her father was an international banker; her background, cosmopolitan.

Early in life Jane Miller discovered she was not like the others, children or adults.

She was completely lacking in empathy. There was a curious blankness at the heart of her being. A lack of emotion regarding the pain and suffering of others. A hangnail to her was more real, more painful, than somebody else being crushed to death in an auto wreck.

Her emotional life was rich, intense, and vividly alive where her own wants and desires were concerned. But as for the feelings of others, playfellows, siblings, relatives, suitors—nothing. Other people were no more real to her than a set of paper dolls. If they got in the way, you just cut them out of the picture.

Her mother and father were sane, normal, loving individuals. Young Jane suffered no physical, sexual, or mental abuse. Her childhood and adolescence couldn't have been more idyllic—for her. For those around her, should they stand between her and something she wanted—a toy, a trinket, a school prize, a boyfriend, an honor, office, or position—a chain of inevitable fatality soon overtook them.

People kept dying all around her: a schoolgirl who was the ringleader of a clique who snubbed her; a teacher who threatened to report her for cheating on a test; a camp counselor who'd caught Jane and a cabin mate sharing a too-intimate encounter; a dowager aunt who'd made Jane the beneficiary of a considerable fortune in her will but then had the bad grace to keep on living.

Jane Miller had the benefits of a fine education. Swiss boarding schools, a finishing school in France, university studies and travel in Madrid, Munich, Vienna, Paris.

Pleasure she took where she found it, from beautiful people of either sex. But no pleasure matched the thrill of a successful murder.

Brains, beauty, a gift for languages, and a relentless amorality sent her drifting in the half worlds of drug, vice, and crime. Her talent for killing proved to be not only pleasurable but extremely profitable.

Jane Miller could abide no master. She would answer to no one. To avoid falling under the thumb of any crime boss or spymaster she created an alter ego, an assumed identity.

Her studies had focused on European art history, particularly of the medieval period. In the millenarian and eschatological writings and esoterica of the Middle Ages she'd encountered the dread figure of Annihilax, the Exterminating Angel, who would snuff out the lives of kings and commoners in the End of Days preceding the Last Judgment.

Annihilax became her nom de guerre, her war name. As Annihilax she plied her professional assassin's trade around the world, earning a place among the top-ranked assassins of the killer elite.

It was in Africa that she met her Waterloo, in one of the fractious mini-states of the Congo region. A mineral-rich province where the status quo was threatened by an upstart rebel leader and his horde of hungry, well-armed troops. A West European industrial cartel that controlled the lucrative mining concessions from the complaisant and infinitely corrupt provincial government hired Annihilax to eliminate the rebel warlord.

Posing as a freelance journalist, Jane Miller established

herself in the provincial capital and began building her clandestine network of mercenaries and assassins. One of her contacts on the scene was Murad Ali, a Pakistani agent. He had lots of money and connections.

Jane Miller became his mistress. Murad Ali liked to talk, especially afterward in bed. She learned that he was a high-ranking officer in Pakistan's all-powerful Inter-Service Intelligence, the military intelligence organization that not so secretly ruled Pakistan behind the scenes. Possessing the atomic bomb and seeking to augment its own stockpiles, the ISI had assigned Murad Ali to this war-torn Congo province to acquire yellowcake, a product of the region's uranium mines that could be refined for use in atomic weapons.

Among his boasts, Murad Ali confided to Jane that he'd been one of the debriefing officers of Dr. Rahman Sayeed, late of Ironwood National Laboratory in Los Alamos. After being released from custody for time served while awaiting and during his abortive trial for espionage, Sayeed had returned home to Islamabad. He had indeed been guilty of atomic espionage against the United States, and told his eager auditors in the ISI all he had learned during his American sojourn.

Among the intelligence windfall was the intriguing revelation that he had not been the only atomic spy seeking to pry loose Ironwood's secrets. Sayeed's delvings into the computer files had detected the presence of a second, unknown master spy who'd been working for years subverting the system and downloading critically restricted data relating to the PALO codes, the digitized fail-safe overrides that could shut down via remote control the launch of any land-based nuclear-armed intercontinental ballistic missile.

The identity of this master spy was unknown to Sayeed, although he'd confided the other's existence to his lawyer Max Scourby. The idea being that if things went badly for

Sayeed in his case, he'd have something to deal with to prompt the prosecution to lighten his sentence in return for the PALO espionage revelations.

As it had worked out, the government's case had fallen apart under the weight of politics and a bad press, and Sayeed had not had to play the trump card regarding the PALO codes as a get-out-of-jail card. In due course he'd passed the information to his ISI debriefers. It was a tantalizing nugget but they were in no position to capitalize on the lead, and so it had lain fallow all this time.

Finally reaching the ears of Jane Miller during a bout of postcoital pillow talk as she lay curled up beside Murad Ali in his bed. He had no idea that she was Annihilax. He believed her cover story, that she was a freelance Western journalist covering the Congolese provincial turmoil. And a shameless slut, like all American women, which suited him just fine.

For once in her career Jane Miller had bitten off more than she could chew. Annihilax could not deliver on the contract to kill the rebel warlord. The warlord struck against the capital in a boldly unsuspected move, taking it and unleashing an orgy of looting, rape, and murder.

Thousands of refugees fled the city, racing for the safety of the border. Murad Ali had been slain by a rebel machine gunner, dying in the streets while Jane Miller watched. Like any other ordinary fugitive, she had to run for her life.

A river marked the border between the revolt-torn province and the relative safety of its nearest neighbor. It was there, in a hamlet on the wrong side of the river, that Jane Miller crossed paths with Carrie Voss.

Carrie Voss was an American relief worker for an international philanthropic organization helping feed the starving Congolese masses. She was an only child whose parents were both dead and who'd long ago lost contact with her few aging, distant relatives. She'd been caught up in the rebel onslaught and had to flee for her life. She was roughly the same age and physical type as Jane Miller.

Annihilax saw her opportunity and took it. She cut Carrie Voss's throat and stole her identity papers. While making the river crossing, she was wounded by shrapnel from a mortar round. She woke up in a field hospital where she was being treated for her injuries. Passing for Carrie Voss, she was airlifted to safety and repatriated to the United States under her stolen identity.

A lengthy recuperation followed, including facial surgery to repair her damaged face and therapy for her wounded left leg. The left leg never healed properly and left her with a permanent limp, necessitating the use of a cane.

The world's intelligence services believed that the assassin code named Annihilax—gender unknown—had died in the Congo. Jane Miller was reborn as Carrie Voss.

She had a purpose.

The thought of the PALO codes obsessed her every waking hour. They were the Holy Grail of atomic secrets; their possessor could alter the balance of world power. A goal worth pursuing.

She relocated to Santa Fe, using that city as a base of operations from which to make her forays into Los Alamos. As Annihilax she'd established a number of secret Swiss and offshore banking accounts that now supplied her with funds for her quest.

Intelligence was the key to all successful field operations. She learned everything she could about Ironwood and its key scientific cadre. Fortune had smiled on her with the advent of Dr. Hugh Carlson. Carlson, a much-married man, was currently between wives. Jane Miller had contrived to make his acquaintance at a fund-raising dinner for the Santa Fe Opera, of which he was a devotee. She was at-

tractive, intelligent, and a master of sexpertise. Carlson fell
hard and they were soon wed. He already had several grown
children, and between them and the alimony payments he
forked out to his ex-wives, he had no interest in starting a
family, which suited Jane Miller's purposes just fine.

She immersed herself in charitable work, especially the
philanthropic Good Neighbor Initiative. This served several
purposes. It allowed her freedom of movement, the ability
to come and go at all hours of the day and night, under the
pretext of having to attend to various good deeds and related chores.

Two, it was an invaluable intelligence-gathering activity.
In the hospital charity wards, the battered women's shelters,
the substance abuse clinics, the halfway houses for proba-
tionary convicts, and so on, she received firsthand information about the criminal half worlds of vice and corruption
throughout the county.

She learned names and addresses of likely recruits for a
new network she was building, a criminal support system to
empower her quest for the INL mole and the PALO codes.
Just as she had done elsewhere to stage her Annihilax operations, she now constructed a new crime cartel. It was
in this manner that she had come across Helen Veitch, the
homicidal ex-nurse she had ultimately sent on a mission of
murder against Jack Bauer. But that came later.

The most important step in creating her new network
was contacting Marta and Torreon Blanco. She targeted
Marta first. They had a commonality of interest, both in
crime and in uninhibited same-sex partners. They formed
their first alliance in bed. Jane Miller had the advantage.
Marta Blanco was all passion and fire, grand gestures and
romance. Jane Miller was ice-cold, an artist at counterfeit-
ing the lineaments of desire and gratification.

To one of her fine-tuned instincts, the Ironwood kills signaled that the lab mole was not alone, that he had partners on the outside, and that his secret-stealing plan was nearing fruition. The death of scientists in the inner cadre eliminated them as possible suspects for the mole.

Her underworld contacts tipped her that the hidden hand behind the violence was Varrin, the gang leader. Who was behind Varrin she did not know but was determined to learn. The Ironwood situation took a deadly turn when Rhodes Morrow put Peter Rhee and Harvey Kling to work on his secret investigation. Part of that was her fault.

She'd been using a burst transmitter to send coded messages to some of her old contacts in Europe, feeling out the ground to see who was still around and could afford to broker a deal for the PALO codes. She didn't have them yet but it was only a matter of time, especially once she tracked Varrin's overlord, identifying him as Max Scourby.

That made sense.

Scourby had been Sayeed's lawyer and was in a position to know plenty. Either he had contacted the Ironwood mole or the mole had come to him. As a top criminal attorney, Scourby had the connections to create and control a goon squad to protect the mole, which he had done by working through Varrin.

But the burst transmissions had put Morrow on the track of Jane Miller. Not yet, not directly; but the fact that he knew the transmissions had come from her Shady Grove neighborhood and that he'd set up a detector in the Parkhurst house meant that he was getting dangerously close.

Through Marta she'd had Torreon Blanco liquidate Rhodes Morrow. Kling and Rhee had pursued the investigation even after their boss's death, marking them for demolition. Jack Bauer's advent on the scene had added urgency to the agenda. The past never really dies. He'd been a dangerous antagonist in Brussels years ago; she would not underestimate him. Helen Veitch had drawn the assignment to kill Bauer but he'd been too quick and clever for her. Rhee had died—she'd seen to that. Blanco guns had purged Kling and the Parkhursts, but Bauer had survived the Blancos' best attempts to cross him off the board.

Certain that Nordquist was the mole, Jane Miller had directed the Blancos to kidnap his wife and daughter, hostages to give her the whip hand over him. She knew the intimate details of the Nordquist house and had fingered the inside information about its disposition to Torreon, who'd passed it on to Pardee, and through him to the kidnap team. Bauer had foiled that plan.

At the same time, she'd faked her own kidnapping. It removed her from the scene and the surveillance that ensued, buying her freedom of movement. She had some idea in the back of her mind that she'd be able to parlay the "threat" to her safety into a lever with which to pry some atomic secrets from her husband.

Her master plan had come apart due to one fatal flaw: not Nordquist but her husband, Hugh Carlson, was the mole. She'd never seen that coming in a million years. It could have resulted in total disaster except for her ace in the hole: Lassiter.

She didn't know him except by reputation and had never met him. Marta Blanco was Lassiter's handler. At virtually the last minute this morning Lassiter had learned about the meeting between Scourby, Carlson, and Adam Zane and passed the information along to Marta. There'd been time to engineer a double cross, allowing the Blanco gang to massacre the Scourby/Varrin coalition and secure Carlson and Zane.

For icing on the cake, Jack Bauer had been killed at the scene. Of course, Lassiter had to die, too. He'd served his purpose, and besides, he knew too much.

So here she was, in possession of the field.

Adam Zane would deal, the PALO codes were priceless; he'd jump at the chance to acquire them. The leopard doesn't change its spots; he was the same as always and would react according to the predictable tropes of greed and power.

She was the same, too—Annihilax lives again.

And the mole, the master spy of this century, the atomic secret stealer supreme, was the one man she'd never suspected:

Her husband, Hugh Carlson.

THE FOLLOWING TAKES PLACE
BETWEEN THE HOURS OF
9 A.M. AND 10 A.M.
MOUNTAIN DAYLIGHT TIME

9:23 A.M. MDT
Mission Hill, Los Alamos County

"This family reunion is all very touching, but what about the demo?" Adam Zane asked.

He was right, of course. The purveyor of stolen secrets had seen clear to the heart of the matter as far as he was concerned; he had to be sure that he had secrets to purvey.

Dr. Hugh Carlson had gotten some of his guts back. "Without me you've got no demonstration. You've got the PALO codes, sure. What of it? Eventually you can peddle them to some foreign power. But it'll take a platoon of their best brains hundreds of man-hours to make them work properly. The data is there. The words but not the music. They're the building blocks, the bricks. But my brain's the mortar, the cement binding them all together.

"I know all the tricks and shortcuts and shades of interpretation. I can make them work now and later. Another thing, Zane—I know exactly what they're worth, what they can do. Invaluable for you in a negotiation. I can make sure you're getting full value and that the other side isn't trying to drag down the price with double talk."

"Prove it," Adam Zane said.

"I will—for the right payday."

"You're in no position to make demands," Jane Miller said.

"No? What are you going to do, kill me? Torture me?"

"Two very attractive options, husband dear."

"Bull. You're not going to throw money away. I'm worth it—big money. With or without the codes. Get rough with me, and I might get so nervous as to miss a vital keystroke and glitch out the process.

"That's not counting what I know about Perseus and Argus, too. A treasure trove of classified secrets. Use your heads. Stop thinking of me as a prisoner and start thinking of me as a partner. Then let's get the show on the road."

"There may be something to what you say, Carlson," Zane said thoughtfully.

"There is. And don't try any of the old soft soap. Take a good look around you at each other. I'm the only nonexpendable person here. I'm the creator. You others are just hijackers, brokers, and middlemen. I'm the one person you have to keep alive."

"What's your pitch?" Jane Miller asked.

"Equal shares," Carlson said. "I'm not greedy—unlike the rest of you. Equal shares all around. Of course, that number may dwindle if you decide to thin your ranks to up your shares, but that's your business."

Zane's jaws firmed. "Don't press your luck, Carlson. Live goods are a headache. They're a lot more difficult to transport than a case full of codes, so—don't overplay your hand."

Carlson was almost cheerful, or perhaps hysterical. "I won't ask you to give your word. Word of honor? What good's the word of a bunch of thieves and killers? No, I'm appealing to something a lot more solid. Good common sense. You know what I say is true. That's my insurance policy and it's better than all the solemn vows in Creation."

"It is if you can do what you say you can do. Otherwise . . . Well, get to it."

"Done. We're powered up so let's start inputting the codes."

The electronic arena was alive. Outside, in its protective housing, the generator was humming. Inside, green on lights glimmered on the faces of instrument boards and panels. Electronic machinery clicked, buzzed, droned.

Dr. Hugh Carlson sat at the main computer console like a virtuoso instrumentalist getting set at the keyboard of a concert piano. He selected a coded desk from the metal box and fed it into a slot. The machine's plastic tongue retracted.

"Takes time to input the correct coded disks," he said. "Just the purely mechanical act of feeding them in one at a time. Luckily we've got the right hardware with the proper specs. Well, luck has nothing to do with it. I selected the machines myself and Scourby followed my orders to the letter."

He input another disk. "It's all a matter of proportion. With these codes I could launch an ICBM and hit Moscow or Beijing. Impressive, but we don't want that. We don't want to start World War III. No money in Armageddon. What we want is an incident. Something to show we can do what we say we can do, convincing all buyers of its potential worth.

"We want to sell these codes to the highest bidder. It's

possible that that might be Uncle Sam. Not entirely likely, considering the state of the dollar and the national debt, but possible. So we want deniability. In case Uncle wants to pay to hush up the whole mess.

"So—we want an incident. Something that's too big to ignore but not so big that it triggers a worldwide nuclear holocaust. What we do, we light up a candle someplace far away from here. A nuclear missile silo somewhere up north. I was thinking Montana first but I decided on North Dakota. It's a wasteland anyway and nobody's going to miss a few hundred square miles of it if they go boom. Of course they'll stay hot for the next several hundred years or so.

"What I'm going to do, I'll detonate the atomic warheads of a Minuteman missile in a silo in North Dakota. I'll touch it off so it blows in the silo. The blast will create an electromagnetic pulse that will screw up communications and everything else for that part of the country and Canada, too, but that won't be so bad. The confusion will aid our getaway. Just make sure we go south.

"There'll be several thousand people dead from the blast, tens of thousands more from the radiation, fallout, and related phenomenon. The whole north Midwestern tier will probably go dark from the EMP. No power, TV, cell phones, computers, nothing. Back to the Stone Age. Washington will claim it's a terrible accident. To save face. If they can pay, fine. If not, the codes—and my services—go to the highest bidder.

"Once the codes are loaded into the computer, they'll be uploaded through our satellite transceiver to an orbiting communications satellite. The comsat will download them into the preselected missile silo. The override will negate all their controls, rendering them useless. I'll be controlling them from here. I'll arm the warheads and detonate them on the ground in the silo. After that, it's all over but the getaway and the payday."

9:59 A.M. MDT
Minuteman Missile Silo, Moosejaw, North Dakota

Being a missile man is a study in futility. It takes on much of the aspects of being a night watchman. There's an inherent contradiction. The silo is loaded with one of the most potent and deadly weapons in the world, an instrument of awesome megadeath potential. The other side of the coin is that nothing ever happens.

For the United States Air Force missile technicians serving out their duty shift, there are things to do. Routine maintenance programs. Drills. Occasional exercises.

Above ground is the flat, steppelike appearance of barren North Dakota flats, a sprawling emptiness of vast grasslands stretching out to all corners of the globe.

Below ground, beneath a hinged sealed camouflaged hatch cover, lies the silo, a concrete-lined, steel-reinforced vertical pipe sunk deep in the ground. It's well-named, this silo. Like an aboveground grain silo, only inverted. A sheath for an atomic-warheaded dart.

The vehicle, a Minuteman missile topped with an MIRV warhead. Multiple (targeted) independent reentry vehicles. Based on the principle of "bigger bang for a buck." Containing not one but several atomic warheads, each programmed to strike a different target in the area.

Today, like all the other days, all the other duty shifts, the USAF missile techs—a two-man crew—face another dreary round of exquisite boredom. Atomic war? Not a chance, brother. The superpowers have grown up. They stay away from no-win nuclear showdowns. The real threat today comes from nuclear "suitcase" bombs and dirty bombs made by rogue states and disseminated into the hands of terrorists.

The missile techs on duty in Silo 14 go through the motions by routine turned near robotized.

Suddenly—

Things started happening. Red lights flashed. Buzzers sounded. Somnolent, lazy readouts were suddenly goosed into spitting out masses of digits. Machinery switched on.

After a moment's disbelieving paralysis of mind and body, the techs started throwing switches, pressing buttons, trying to regain control of the system. To arm an atomic weapon is a two-man operation. Both missile techs must simultaneously insert their keys and use the day's PAL codes to arm the warheads.

Now, while they have done nothing at all to initiate a launching sequence, a phantom force has reached in, punching past their fail-safes and switched on the system, arming the atomics.

The nuclear warheads are alive and counting down.

Ignition is only minutes away. There is nothing they can do to stop it.

- -

THE FOLLOWING TAKES PLACE
BETWEEN THE HOURS OF
10 A.M. AND 11 A.M.
MOUNTAIN DAYLIGHT TIME

- -

10:13 A.M. MDT
Mission Hill, Los Alamos County

Mission Hill was a fortress. Max Scourby made it so. Torreon and Marta Blanco, its new masters, have reinforced it. The boundary wall was already a foot thick, its ten-foot height hardened with rows of black iron spikes with spear blade points. The main gate, made of motorized wrought-iron grillwork, has been reinforced by the simple expedient of parking a rented delivery truck inside the gates, blocking them lengthwise.

The grounds are patrolled by a small army of Blanco gunmen armed with assault rifles, machine guns, and shotguns. A smaller but equally well-armed cadre guards the inside of the mansion on every floor.

There was a flaw in the hardened defense system, however, a failure to think in dimension. Jack Bauer launched his assault by air. A long, slim, needlelike yellow helicopter with black trim hovered over the roof of the Mission Hill mansion. Pilot Ron Galvez was at the controls. In the cockpit were Jack Bauer and Tony Almeida. They'd armed themselves with weapons from the top of Bluecoat Bluff. The heaviest firepower they could find.

Earlier, Jack Bauer had used the cell phone to contact Ron Galvez at his home base at Black Eagle Airfield. Galvez had been dozing off on a cot in the hangar, where he'd set up station the night before, standing ready to respond to Jack Bauer's summons.

The helicopter had been serviced and fueled, and stood ready to go.

When Jack's call came, Galvez rose from the cot, gulped a paper cup of cold coffee that had been standing for hours on a nearby desk, and hustled out to the helicopter. After a preflight check, he'd lofted the copter into the sky, arrowing toward Bluecoat Bluff.

Jack and Tony had descended to the ground at the base of the hill. The copter touched down in an open field. The CTU agents climbed aboard and the copter soared upward.

A short time later the aircraft was hovering over the Mission Hill mansion. The fenced-in grounds below were a scene of frantic action. Like an overturned anthill. Blanco guards were running this way and that along the paths. They didn't know what to do or where to go first. Their confusion was compounded by the fact that they were under siege, not just from above, but also on the ground.

Jack Bauer had also put in a call to Vince Sabito. A torrent of obscene abuse directed at Jack poured out of the phone. Vince Sabito vented until he paused for breath. Jack managed to get a few words in edgewise—enough to get Sabito listening.

"This is the showdown. The Blancos and Carlson are forted up at Mission Hill," Jack said.

"Mission Hill? That's Scourby's place," Sabito growled.

"Not anymore. Scourby's dead and so is the Varrin gang, massacred by the Blancos. Torreon and company—and Carlson—are at Mission Hill. If you move fast you can bag them all.

"Unless I get there first," Jack said. He broke the connection, cutting off Sabito in mid-squawk. He'd thrown in that last crack about getting there first just to irritate Sabito and goose him into moving out fast.

Jack had also contacted Deputy Wallace Ross. "This is the big one. Bring out the big guns. You've been waiting to clean up on the Blancos—now's the time."

The results were plain to see from way up in the middle of the air. FBI agents and sheriff's deputies were besieging Mission Hill. Their vehicles surrounded it on all sides.

Sabito had apparently gotten those reinforcements he'd requested from Albuquerque, including an entire FBI Tac Squad in an armored war wagon.

Mission Hill was the scene of a battle royal. From above, gun smoke clouds bobbed around inside and outside the walls like floating cotton balls.

Ron Galvez brought the helicopter close to the central bell tower whose flat roof was topped by the satellite dish aimed at a forty-five-degree angle at the sky. A couple of Blanco riflemen were in the bell tower shooting at the helicopter.

The passenger side door of the cockpit was open and Jack Bauer hung by a safety harness half out of the cockpit, wielding an M–16. Tony Almeida crouched behind him and to the side, working an M–4 carbine.

Jack snapped a succession of three-shot bursts through the open arches into the bell tower, spraying the riflemen with gunfire. They spun and whirled under the fusillade.

One dropped to the floor, inert. Another flopped sideways out of an open arch, falling off the tower to come crashing down on the orange ceramic-tiled scaled roof. He broke some tiles and sent them skittering down the side of the slanted roof. He rolled, following the same trajectory. He fell off the edge of the roof and dropped three stories to land flat on the ground-level patio.

"Take out that satellite dish," Jack shouted. He and Tony unloaded on the transceiver, sieving it. Here was where he could have used a grenade launcher, Jack thought.

Bullets raked the flat roof and sides of the bell tower, stitching them. Jack poured more slugs at the base where a bundle of black cables fed upward into a box at the hub of the rear of the dish. His clip emptied. He ejected and slapped in a new clip, locked and loaded, and resumed firing.

Tony Almeida was a sharpshooter. He squeezed off tight bursts into the base of the dish where neat little framework steel feet helped anchor the dish into place. The dish wobbled shakily.

A prolonged burst from Jack's weapons severed the bundle of cables loose from where they fed into the hub box. Tony shot off the foot he'd been working on. The dish swayed, off-balance. It leaned backward, teetering precariously for an instant.

Jack and Tony sprayed some more slugs into the dish, ventilating it, shoving it backward by main force.

That did it. The dish leaned farther backward and tipped over, falling downward. It broke free from its remaining stanchions and pitched off the side of the bell tower, plummeting to the ground.

In Moosejaw, North Dakota, Silo 14, the phantom force from outside that had taken control of the control panel suddenly loosed its iron grip of control and ceased to exist.

As soon as they realized that the big board was once again under their control, the two missile techs went to work disarming the bomb.

The red lights on the board turned green, alarms fell silent. The danger was ended.

The FBI Tac Squad commandeered a fire truck and charged the Mission Hill main gate, using it as a battering ram. The wrought-iron grille gates flew apart with little resistance. The front of the fire truck plowed into the delivery truck parked on the other side of the gate, hitting it broadside. The fire truck's progress slowed.

The driver stomped the gas pedal and the fire truck lunged forward, bulling the delivery truck backward, sliding it sideways across the lawn. The gate was forced and Tac Squad members poured through it, charging into the Mission Hill grounds.

Jack Bauer motioned to pilot Ron Galvez to drop closer to the roof of the mansion. Galvez shook his head no. Jack was insistent, motioning vehemently.

Galvez worked the controls, hovering six feet above the roofline to the left of the bell tower. He had trouble holding the machine steadily in place.

Jack Bauer slung the M-16 over his shoulder. He unfastened the safety strap and jumped out of the cockpit to the roof.

He hit hard and slipped on the ceramic tiles, knocking some of them loose. His feet worked, seeking purchase. Jack succeeded in draping himself over the rooftop ridgeline, lying facedown across it at right angles, his middle in the center.

Galvez lifted up the chopper. The downdraft battered at Jack. It eased as Galvez guided the helicopter off to the side and away.

Jack got his feet under him and rose up into a low crouch. Like a tightrope walker he crossed the roofline to the bell tower, stepping through an archway to the tower floor. The dead body of one of the riflemen lay sprawled on his back on the floor. A square open hatchway accessed a flight of stone stairs.

Jack unlimbered his M–16 and held it leveled at waist height, pointing the muzzle down toward the interior recesses of the shaft. He climbed down the stone stairs, descending toward the bottom of the bell tower.

Things were out of control in the electronic arena on the ground floor. Adam Zane decided he'd had enough. He broke and ran toward the front of the building, holding his hands in the air, shouting, "Don't shoot! I surrender—"

Torreon Blanco drew his gun and shot Zane in the back. Zane lurched, almost falling. He recovered his balance and moved ahead, advancing slowly, laboriously, as if he were wading through hip-deep water.

Torreon fired again. Zane pitched forward, falling on his face. "I hate yellow bellies," Torreon said.

"What's your plan?" Marta demanded.

Torreon brandished his gun, fist-pumping it in the air. "We'll go down shooting!"

Marta nodded. "That's my brother—you're some kind of hombre!"

Torreon grinned, showing lots of teeth. Behind him, Hugh Carlson eased out of his chair facing the instrument board and began sneaking toward the rear of the room and the sunny patio beyond.

When he got clear of the masses of electronic equipment and saw daylight he broke into a run. His footfalls slapped the tiles, catching Torreon's attention. He spun around, gun in hand, arm extended as he drew a bead on Carlson's retreating back. "Another deserter—"

A nearby window shattered and rounds from the gun battle outside raked his chest. Falling, he gasped Marta's name and landed motionless.

Hugh Carlson ran outside on to the rear patio. The back grounds were filled with Blanco men in retreat, running toward the rear wall. A few of them had reached it and were trying to scale it. It was smooth and ten feet tall and they were meeting with little success. Hugh Carlson ran across the patio to join them.

Ahead, a Blanco gunman had turned to fire at some FBI men who appeared rounding the corner of the house on his right. He glimpsed Carlson in the corner of his eye and saw a stranger charging toward him. He opened fire, cutting him down.

The helicopter zoomed low over the back grounds, Tony Almeida strafing Blanco gunmen with his M–4. Galvez pulled up, made a wide, swooping curve, and came in for another run. Tony looked like he was having a hell of a time.

Jack Bauer reached the bottom of the bell tower just in time to hear a dull booming blast like the sound made by a shotgun. He flattened against the wall beside the doorway opening into the drawing room turned electronics installation. He peeked out cautiously.

On the other side of the room he saw Carrie Carlson standing alone. He went to her. As he neared her, he saw the body of Torreon Blanco sprawled on the floor, shot twice in the back, dead.

Coming closer, he got a good look at Carrie Carlson. Her face was a wide-eyed, staring, openmouthed mask of fear. She stood leaning against a computer console for support. She leaned heavily on the cane that supported her bad left leg.

Nearby lay Marta Blanco, or what was left of her. She didn't have much of a face.

Most of it had been blown away. Jack Bauer was able to

recognize her mostly from her gorgeous mane of hair, now gore-streaked, flecked, and splattered.

Her face was a mess, a red bubbling wreck. Somehow the damage had managed to spare one long, slanted green eye. It glittered like an emerald sliver. The extent of the devastation reminded Jack of the death of Peter Rhee. He'd been slaughtered in similar fashion.

No gunshot wound that, which had destroyed Marta Blanco's face, not even from a big-caliber gun. A shotgun blast had done the damage. At close range. Only—where was the shotgun? Jack saw no shotgun nearby, not a conventional model or a sawed-off job. Not in Torreon's hand, or Marta's, either.

"Thank god you've come," Carrie Carlson said. "It's been a nightmare! They kidnapped me, swore they'd kill me—"

Jack Bauer looked her up and down. A thin line of smoke was rising from the bottom of her cane. Smoke?

He got it then. It all came together:

The way Peter Rhee had died—the pair of curious round holes that had been pocked in the sand beside the car where he'd been killed—the nagging feeling that had irked him at the Carlson house when he'd seen the umbrella holder with the three canes in it—

Most of all, that telltale line of smoke, thin, straight, rising from the base of the cane that Carrie Carlson was now leaning on.

He swung the M–16 to cover her. "I wondered how anyone could have gotten close enough to Peter Rhee to take him out with a shotgun blast. He was on his guard against assassins. But you, Dr. Carlson's wife, the well-respected humanitarian and do-gooder—you could have got close enough to him," Jack said.

"How did you set him up? Did you tell him in confidence that you'd discovered something shocking about your husband that threw his loyalty into question and that you had to meet him in private to tell him the awful truth? Rhee would have bought that. He expected danger and treachery from all sides, but not from you.

"The African artifacts in your house were a tip-off, too. Or they should have been, if I'd been paying attention at the time. I'm sure when the dates are checked they'll show that you were in Africa at the same time and place as Annihilax."

"I don't know what you're talking about," Carrie Carlson said.

"The fatal clue is the hardware itself, lady. Another minute or two and you would have been in the clear. But you blasted Marta right before I came in and that's what tripped you up.

"Gun smoke is coming out of the bottom of your cane, smoke from the shotgun blast you discharged into Marta's face, just like you did to Peter Rhee. It's a trick cane, a single-barreled shotgun disguised as a cane. I'm betting the trigger is concealed somewhere in the handle. It'll make a hell of an exhibit at your court case," Jack said.

"No court case—no court case for Annihilax," Carrie Carlson said.

She leaned back against the console, taking her weight off the cane so she could swing it freely, raising it up to level against Jack Bauer to deliver another killing shot.

He squeezed the trigger of the M–16 unleashing a quick short burst into her middle. She fought to raise the cane higher and he tilted the M–16 upward and shot her between the eyes.

She fell and lay there with her eyes open. Jack pried the cane from her hand and examined it. The base where the rubber tip had been was a black empty bore with traces and flecks of rubber around the edges that the shotgun blast hadn't entirely dislodged.

The curved handle had a decorative metal band where it

met the shaft. When he twisted it, the curved handle came off, revealing the breech where a fresh shotgun shell had been loaded and was waiting for use. The trigger and firing pin were built into the curved handle.

Somewhere in the distance, church bells started ringing, reminding Jack Bauer that it was Sunday morning, about time for services to be letting out.

The church bells tolled, sounding a requiem for she who had been Annihilax.

Annihilax, the Death Angel—dead.